THE MAFIA AND HIS ANGEL

PART 3

Tainted Hearts Series

By Lylah James

THE MAFIA AND HIS ANGEL PART 3

Limitless Publishing, LLC
Kailua, HI 96734
www.limitlesspublishing.com

Formatting: Limitless Publishing

ISBN-13: 978-1-64034-996-4

Dedication

To all the beautiful Angels out there who are struggling to find their peace. You are beautiful. You are strong. You matter. Your tears might fall now, but I hope those droplets turn into a true, beautiful smile one day.

Prologue

Ayla

I had him…and then I lost him. I lost everything.

My wings were ready to fly, but the Devil clipped them, feather by feather, until I had nothing left.

Then my savior came, waging a bloodbath to find me. He loves me. He wants his Angel to be free.

But how could I fly again when my wings were broken?

***

Alessio

I had her…and then I lost her. I lost my Angel, the reason for every breath I took.

If he thought he could break her and just disappear, he was wrong. I was going to find him and break him, like he broke her.

1

This war wasn't over.

I made a vow to my Angel.

I promised to let her fly…I promised to save her soul.

And my vows are never broken.

This was a battle for my Angel.

Chapter 1

Viktor

He broke.

I watched Alessio break right in front of my eyes.

I have known him for years—since we were babies—and very few times had I seen him at his weakest moment.

Since his mother's death, I had never seen him shed any tears. Of course not. He was the boss of four families. The *Pakhan* of the most ruthless *Bratva*. He was cruel and heartless.

Alessio Ivanshov didn't cry.

But right now, he was breaking.

He didn't care that his men were watching. All his focus was on Ayla.

I watched him cry. As he rocked Ayla back and forth, his arms tight around her, I watched my boss, the man whom I have known to be ruthless, cry for his woman.

I stood frozen, just a few feet away from them.

3

My eyes shifted to Ayla, and my chest tightened. It was a small change of emotion, but it was painful. Painful because I had never felt this way before.

Nikolay moved to stand beside me, and I quickly shook my head, trying to clear my mind.

"This is messed up," he muttered, a look of horror masking his face.

As I nodded, I saw Nina rushing past me. She knelt in front of Alessio and Ayla. Nina was still and I counted the seconds in my head.

One. Two. Three. Four. Five.

She turned around, her expression cold, but her eyes spoke volumes. She gave a slight shake of her head.

I understood what she meant. It was bad. Very bad.

Nina turned back around, and I saw her quickly removing her jacket.

"Alessio, we need to go," she said, placing the jacket over Ayla's almost bare body.

He didn't move. Alessio was so lost, he didn't even hear us.

"My jacket is too short. It barely covers her."

Nikolay moved forward, removing his jacket. I closed my eyes and took a deep breath. We were wasting time.

Fuck! We didn't have time to waste. For all we knew, we were about to be ambushed as we stepped out.

I waited for Nina to wrap Nikolay's jacket around Ayla's body as much as she could with Alessio in the way.

When she was done, I nodded at her to move

away. Taking her place in front of Alessio, I looked down at Ayla. Her face was pressed in Alessio's neck, and it was hidden by her greasy, matted hair.

I leaned forward, ignoring the sound of Alessio choking back his cries. I even ignored the way my stomach cramped at the sight of Ayla like this. Moving her hair to the side, so that her bruised face and neck were visible, I placed my finger on the side of her neck, right over the pulse.

It was faint. Slow, but at a steady rate. It was good. At least for now.

My eyes shifted to her chest, watching the slow rise and fall. It was too slow, almost as if she was fighting to take each breath.

My gaze followed a path down her body to the shackles around her. I touched the heavy chain and pulled at the small latch on her left ankle. It gave way. The shackles weren't locked around her wrists and ankles. One after another, I pulled them off until she was no longer chained.

Sighing, I looked up at Alessio. "We have to go."

When he didn't respond, I touched his shoulder. "Alessio, we need to get out of here. Now!"

No response. What was going on in his fucking mind right now? Was he too far gone?

Shaking my head, I pushed the thought away.

My hand tightened on his shoulder. There was only one way to snap him out of his daze.

"We need to get Ayla out. She is not safe here," I muttered quietly.

His head snapped up, his eyes meeting mine. My heart might have stopped for a second. The look in his eyes was heartbreaking.

I remembered the day of his mother's funeral. Or even the moment we found him after his mother's death. He didn't cry. No, he stood there emotionless, watching everything happening around him.

You would think a man like that wouldn't understand heartbreak.

But the look in his eyes right now showed so much pain that even I felt it.

The look was there for a brief moment. Alessio changed almost too quickly, masking his emotion.

His eyes flared dangerously and I knew my words had hit home. Good. He needed to snap out of it.

Alessio looked down at Ayla again. His expression softened the slightest bit. "She...I..." he choked, pulling Ayla into his chest more.

"I know. We'll take care of her back at the estate. Right now, our priority is to get her to safety," I reasoned.

Taking a deep breath, he nodded. Alessio caressed Ayla's cheek, his fingers barely touching her skin. He handled her with a gentleness that I didn't think he was capable of.

I stared at Ayla, my eyes moving to her neck. My fingers were still on her neck too, but now I was mindlessly caressing her pulse, my touch light on her skin.

Quickly snatching my hand away, I stood up. My hands fisted at my side, my jaw grinding in sudden frustration.

Alessio shifted Ayla in his arms and slowly

stood up. My eyes went to his legs when I saw him limp forward.

"Let's go," Nikolay called. I nodded and quickly walked away. Following Nina and Nikolay, we started to climb up the stairs.

They made it out first, but I stopped in the middle to see Alessio still on the first step. I ran down the steps, stopping in front of him.

"Give her to me," I said with my arms out.

Alessio shook his head, his arms tightening protectively around Ayla. "Alessio, you can't carry Ayla out like this. You can't keep her safe with an injured leg."

His eyes glinted with anger, and he growled. "I can protect her. Move out of my way, Viktor."

With a sigh, I stared into his eyes. "After everything we've been through, do you not trust me?"

"Viktor," he warned. "Move."

"Give her to me. Damn it! Stop being so fucking stubborn."

When Alessio didn't move to do so, I finally understood. Seeing Ayla like this, there was no bound for his protective instincts. Hell, there was no fucking way he would let another man near her.

"I'll carry her out, Alessio. Think about it. You can't keep her safe with your leg. I'm faster." I sighed, my eyes shifting yet again toward Ayla. "I will protect her as if she were my woman."

Alessio's eyes glowed dangerously. He moved forward, his face mere inches from mine. "She is not yours," he snapped. Even though the anger was there, I saw his resolve slipping away.

He looked down at Ayla again. "If something happens to her, I will kill you."

"I know," I replied with a nod.

Alessio finally shifted Ayla into my arms, and I quickly brought her to my chest. Ayla was light, barely weighing anything. She felt fragile in my arms, and my eyes moved to her rounded stomach.

I avoided looking at it before, but now that she was in my arms, there was no avoiding the round bump.

I couldn't even imagine the horrors Ayla had to go through with Alberto.

Alessio touched her cheek in a soft caress before nodding at me. I returned the nod and quickly walked up the stairs with Alessio right behind me.

We didn't stop until we were out of the house. After Alessio climbed in the backseat of the car, I placed Ayla on his lap. He immediately wrapped his arms around her.

"Get us home as quickly as you can," he ordered.

"Boss," Nikolay acknowledged his words before climbing into the driver's seat. Nina was beside Alessio while I moved to the front with Nikolay.

"She's going to be okay," Alessio said. I glanced at the rear-view mirror and saw Alessio's gaze fixated on Ayla. He placed a kiss on her nose. "Nothing is going to happen to her. I won't allow it."

I closed my eyes, leaning against the headrest.

I hoped he was right. There was no other option.

Ayla had to be okay. Not only for her sake, but for Alessio's sanity.

Chapter 2

Alessio

The drive home was fast, thank fuck for that. I thought I was slowly going insane. Nobody spoke a word during the drive.

My eyes were only on Ayla. I watched her, waiting for any indication that she was okay.

But she stayed unconscious. Unmoving.

I caressed her, touching her, waiting for her to wake up. But nothing. Not even a twitch. Nothing to give me a little peace.

When the car finally stopped, I opened the door and climbed out with Ayla still in my arms. Viktor came to take her, but I walked past him, carrying Ayla close to my chest.

There was no fucking way he was holding her again. It took everything in me to hand her over to him before.

But not now. I didn't care that it felt like my leg was about to fall off. No, I needed Ayla. I had to hold her myself.

I needed her close to me, knowing that she was finally safe in my arms.

My injured leg dragged behind me as I walked inside. Without stopping, I made my way upstairs to my room.

The door was already open. I walked inside to find Lena standing by the bed. She rushed toward me as soon as I stepped into the room.

"Nikolay already called. I have the tub filled," she muttered, stopping in front of me. Lena leaned forward. She sucked in a harsh breath at the sight of Ayla.

Tears filled her eyes. "My sweet child."

"You should clean Ayla up before I have a look at her," I heard Sam say behind me.

I walked past him and into the bathroom. Just as Lena said, the tub was already filled. I sat on the edge, settling Ayla on my lap.

Lena helped me pull off the jackets wrapped around her shoulders. Holding the shredded dress, I ripped off what was left of it from her body.

"Let me clean her up. You're bleeding all over the floor, Alessio. Sam can look at your leg while I take care of Ayla," Lena suggested.

"No," I snapped. There was no way someone else was going to take care of Ayla. Not even Lena.

I would bathe her. I would take care of her. She was mine.

Mine to take care of. Mine to love.

After almost four months, I finally had her in my arms. I wasn't letting her go anytime soon.

"Alessio," Lena sighed but didn't push.

Standing up, I gently placed Ayla into the warm

water. I winced when my leg made contact with the floor. It hurt like a bitch. Pinching my eyes closed, I ignored the burn for a second before focusing on Ayla again.

I held Ayla in a sitting position, letting the warm water envelop her body. She was still so cold, and I feared she would never warm up again.

Lena knelt behind Ayla's head and made quick work of shampooing and washing her hair. The water turned a dirty brown, the smell touching my nostrils, almost making me gag.

I'm sorry. So, so sorry, Angel.

She was in more pain than I had thought. And I had no idea how I was going to bring her back to me. I was scared that we were forever broken.

I ran my hand over her neck and arms. When my hand neared her stomach, I paused, suddenly finding it hard to breathe.

Of all the scenarios I had running in my head, this was not one of them. How did Ayla live in that hellhole in this state? How did she stay alive?

Taking a deep breath, I slowly rubbed my hand over the fullness of her stomach. It was rigid, and the skin felt tight. My throat burned and my heart ached as I quickly moved my hand away.

I didn't know how to feel about *this*—him...or her?

"Alessio."

I turned my head to see Lena staring at me expectantly. I ignored the look of sympathy on her face and turned my attention to Ayla again.

Squirting some soap in my hand, I quickly washed her legs and then her back. When I was done, I pulled Ayla out of the water.

Lena quickly drained the dirty water. I placed Ayla in the empty tub again, washing her again, making sure she was cleaned from all filth. I poured water over her and rinsed off the soap. When she was clean, Lena wrapped a towel around Ayla's still form.

Sucking in an agonized breath, I stood on my legs and pulled Ayla into my arms again. I limped into the bedroom to see Sam, Viktor, and Nikolay standing at the bed.

Viktor's eyes moved to my injured leg, and his face tightened in frustration. "Sam, you need to take a look at Alessio's leg. He's bleeding too much."

"I'm fine," I ground out, placing Ayla on the bed. I wrapped the towel tighter around her and pulled the comforter up.

"Boss, let me stitch you up first," Sam suggested as he came behind me.

The anger I was holding inside of me finally bubbled out. "We don't have time for this!" I bellowed.

"You're bleeding out! You are no good to Ayla like this!" Viktor yelled back, his eyes furious.

I turned to Sam. "Make sure she is okay. I want her to be okay. Fix her!"

"But, Boss—" he started.

I sprang forward and wrapped my fist around his collar, pulling his feet off the floor. "Did you fucking hear what I just said?"

He swallowed hard and nodded. I released him, and he fixed his shirt. How did they think I would let him stitch me up before taking care of Ayla first?

I glanced at Viktor, and he shook his head in exasperation. "Sam, do what he says. He'll never listen to any of us. Take care of Ayla first."

Viktor went to the bathroom, and I turned to face Ayla again. Sam leaned forward, placing a knee beside Ayla on the bed.

He took hold of the towel but didn't move it from her. He glanced at me, his expression pensive. "Boss, may I? With your permission, I need to see how bad it is."

My hands fisted to the side. I hated the thought of another man seeing her body, but what choice did I have?

Sam waited for my permission. I felt the urge to yell and carve his eyes out but instead stood frozen.

When I felt someone touch my arm, I swiveled around to see Viktor holding a towel. "Tie it around your wound. It'll stop the bleeding for now."

I bent down and quickly tied it around the bleeding area. After making sure it was in place and wouldn't spill blood everywhere, I walked to the other side of the bed.

From the corner of my eye, I saw Viktor and Nikolay quietly leaving the room, giving us privacy. Lena stood beside Sam, looking just as worried as before. Her tears were long gone, but her face showed her sorrow and fatigue.

There was Maddie. And then there was Ayla. How much more could she take?

I climbed in bed beside Ayla. Moving closer, I molded my body around hers. I held her to me for a second, breathing in her fresh scent.

I sent Sam a fierce stare and then nodded. Lena

settled at Ayla's feet, her hands knotted on her lap. Turning my attention back to Ayla, I saw Sam carefully pulling the comforter and then the towel away from Ayla's body.

I heard him suck in a breath and glanced up to see his frown as he took in the bruises that marred Ayla's pale skin.

I had avoided looking at the bruises too, fearing I would snap from seeing the evidence of what she had been through.

Deep, purple bruises covered her arms and legs. Some were faded, but others looked fairly new. Maybe a few days. Her knees and elbows were scraped. Probably from the hard ground. The skin looked ragged in some places.

As I continued to look at her body, my breath became erratic and my lungs tightened. The side of her left leg was nearly black, and one of her arms was starting to turn an ugly shade of green. This bruise was probably less than a week old.

There were other small cuts all over her body. Her face was slightly bruised but looked much better than the rest of her.

One thing that took me by surprise was her stomach. The skin from her chest to the fullness of her stomach was pale and clear of any bruises. Not even a single one. It appeared as though her front was left unaffected and untouched.

I had no idea how Ayla protected herself in this state—all I knew was that I found her alive. She was breathing, and I would do anything to keep it that way.

With my face buried in her neck, I closed my

eyes. I couldn't lose her now. I lost her once, and that was it. Never again.

"She is badly bruised, Boss," Sam finally muttered after inspecting Ayla's body.

I lifted my head up just enough to look at Sam. "I can see that," I snarled. "I want to know what you can do."

If he was useless to me, I would have to find someone else to look after Ayla. I wanted to know if she was okay or not. If she *would* be okay.

"I can treat her wounds, of course," Sam started. He paused, his eyes going to Ayla's stomach. "She is pregnant, and I don't know much about pregnancy."

I clenched my jaw tight, grinding my teeth together. The words I didn't want to acknowledge.

She is pregnant.

Fuck! I knew that, but hearing those words made it more real. It was real. This was real. My Angel was pregnant.

And I didn't even know if the baby was mine.

My eyes moved to her round stomach again. I stared at the roundness for a few seconds before my gaze snapped up at Sam's voice.

"During her captivity, we don't know the trauma her mind and body took. And how that could affect her pregnancy and the baby," he continued.

I hated being reminded of her captivity and how close I had been to losing her. I thought getting her out of that hellhole would be the end. As long as she was in my arms, everything would be okay.

But nothing looked okay.

Sam laid a hand on Ayla's chest. "Her breathing

15

isn't laboured. So that's a good sign. She's probably just in a deep sleep. A lot of time, people who go through trauma, they tend to shut down. Sleep is one way to do so. Ayla would likely sleep through the day and night. It is best she rests. But you will need to keep checking on her."

"I will. I won't leave her alone," I said, placing a kiss next to her ear. "I will be with her."

As long as she took to heal, I would not leave her side.

I continued to pepper Ayla's face and head with kisses as Sam cleaned her wounds. He disinfected them and wrapped bandages around the worst ones. He then applied salve on the bruises.

I whispered sweet words in her ears. My words were from the heart—the very same heart that was aching as she remained still. I told her how beautiful and brave she was. How she was my beautiful and perfect Angel.

She was my everything. Everything I could say, I whispered in her ears, hoping that even in her sleep, she could hear me.

I caressed her. My hands wandered over her soft skin, never once stopping while Sam finished up.

I touched her, held her, kissed her. And all the while, she stayed immobile. If it wasn't for the rise and fall of her chest, she would have appeared dead.

It scared the hell out of me, and I prayed—hoped that she would wake up fast. I needed her beautiful green eyes. Her sweet voice.

When Sam was done, he leaned back, and I quickly adjusted Ayla's towel again. After properly covering her up, I tugged her closer to me.

16

"Boss, I did what I could. But I am not specialized in pregnancy. You will need—"

"Already taken care of."

Sam was cut off by Nina's voice. I lifted my head up to see Nina and another woman walking into the room. "She'll take it from here," Nina said, nodding toward the stranger.

"Mr. Ivanshov," she said in greetings. "I am an obstetrician. With your permission…" She nodded toward Ayla.

"How qualified are you?" I growled when she started to approach the bed. My arms went around Ayla protectively, glaring at the woman in front of me.

"Alessio, she's good. I have known her for years. And she pretty much knows about *us*," Nina said with a sigh.

The woman smiled. "My father is one of your men. Erik Cooper. I'm Ivy Cooper."

The name definitely rang a bell. Her father took care of my clubs with Mark.

Finally nodding at her, she approached the bed and settled beside Ayla. Ivy pulled the towel apart. When she placed her hand over Ayla's round stomach, I closed my eyes and ignored her.

I pushed my face in Ayla's neck; her sweet scent helped calm me.

A few minutes later, my eyes opened at the sound of Ivy's voice. "There is a heartbeat."

I didn't realize that I was waiting for her reassurance. As soon as I heard her words, a sense of overwhelming relief filled me.

I shuddered and took a deep breath. Placing a

kiss on Ayla's neck, I whispered, "We are going to be okay."

"I used both a stethoscope and fetal Doppler. If I can hear a heartbeat, then she is definitely past twelve weeks. But unfortunately, I can't tell for sure how far along she is or how healthy both mother and baby are. I will need to do an ultrasound for that and some tests. She needs to wake up too, so I can ask some questions," Ivy continued.

My fingers tightened around Ayla's where our hands were intertwined between us. "The baby isn't moving, either. Her stomach is too rigid for my liking. As long as there is a heartbeat, it's good. But you will need to make sure the baby moves sometime soon. If it goes hours or even days with no movement, that's not a good sign."

"You're saying something is wrong with the…" I paused, finding it hard to say the word.

Baby. A fucking baby.

Ivy ignored my slip and continued. "I can't say anything for sure. I would suggest keeping vigil today and tomorrow. I will come back tomorrow to look for any changes. Sam said that I can use a part of his office for the ultrasound machines. This way you won't have to move Ayla around much or take her out of the estate for checkups."

She placed a hand over Ayla's stomach, caressing the firm bump softly. "Ayla is a small woman. From the size of her bump, I would say she is past four months. Even though she was in captivity, her bump looks of a pretty healthy size. I would have to do the ultrasound for more information."

"I will call you when she is awake," I muttered, staring at the hand currently caressing Ayla.

Why did I find it hard to touch her stomach? I couldn't even bring myself to stare at the bump for too long.

Feeling completely disgusted at my reaction, I blinked away and stared at Ayla's sleeping face. She looked so peaceful, her face pale and relaxed. My Angel looked like a sleeping beauty.

But her sleep was probably plagued with nightmares.

I would be there to keep them away. I would fight her demons for her. After all, I promised to give her back her wings.

My chest grew tight, and my eyes pricked with unshed tears. For the first time in my life, I felt...*weak.*

Tears. Stupid fucking tears. I was crying.

"I will wait for your call," Ivy mumbled before standing up. Lena quickly took her place and adjusted the towel around Ayla. She pulled the comforter over her and stepped away.

I saw Nina looking at Ayla, her face expressionless as always. After a few seconds, she left with Ivy without a word.

Sam came to my side. "Can I stitch you now?"

Without answering, I pushed my injured leg in his direction. My teeth ground together as he removed the bullet and stitched the wound. It was painful and burned like a goddamn bitch, but staring at Ayla's sleeping face eased the pain.

I was lost in her, ignoring the needle as Sam finished up. After inspecting his work, he pressed a fresh bandage over the wound and stood up.

Sam didn't say anything when he stepped out of the room. Lena fussed over Ayla, her forehead creased with worry lines.

"How is Maddie?" I asked mindlessly, pushing Ayla's hair out of her face.

"She's sleeping," Lena replied quietly.

I nodded silently. So much happened, and I wondered how we were going to get back from it.

I started to pull the comforter over myself when I saw Viktor come into the room. "Painkiller," he muttered, handing me the glass and pills he was carrying.

"What did Sam and Ivy say?"

I shrugged, quickly swallowing the pills. "As far as the bruises, she will heal. Ivy wants to do an ultrasound."

"Alessio, the baby—"

"Not now." I stopped him. "I don't want to think about it now. My priority is Ayla."

When I turned away from him, I heard him sigh. After waiting for a few seconds, he finally left the room and closed the door behind him.

Placing a kiss on Ayla's forehead, I wrapped an arm around her chest, pulling her back to my front. I ignored the throbbing pain in my leg and closed my eyes.

"I'm sorry, Angel. For failing you. Disappointing you. If only I had listened. I don't know how you will forgive me, but I promise that I will never fail you again," I mumbled in her ear.

"You are my everything, Ayla. I just need you to wake up. We will figure everything else out after that. I promise I won't leave your side," I whispered.

She didn't stir. Not even a twitch.

Her lack of movement felt like knives stabbing at my heart. I was hurting for her.

As the seconds, minutes, and hours ticked by, I slowly lost my resolve. My eyes drooped, and no matter how hard I tried to keep them open, it became almost impossible.

What the fuck.

When my vision blurred and I weakened with weariness, I swore.

My arms tightened around Ayla one more time. As my eyes closed and darkness clouded me, I finally understood.

The fucking asshole. He drugged me. Stupid sleeping pills.

Chapter 3

Sleepily, my eyes blinked open. My vision was blurred, and I tumbled over the edge of consciousness.

My eyes finally adjusted to the glaring sunlight a few seconds later. Ayla was still wrapped in my arms, her body anchored into mine.

My eyes widened when I found my hand over her round stomach. I stayed frozen for a second, too scared to move.

My throat felt suddenly dry, and I swallowed past the lump forming there. I pressed my hand more firmly into the roundness. The towel had fallen away, and I was now skin to skin with her belly.

Her stomach was stretched tight, but the skin was still surprisingly soft.

I stared at the contrast of my hand over her skin. My hand was big and rough, my palm taking about half of the fullness of her stomach. While even bruised, she radiated beauty.

I was still staring at Ayla's abdomen, and

instinctively, I started to rub small circles. When I realized what I was doing, I went to snatch my hand away but stopped dead.

My eyes widened, and my breath left my lungs in a loud whoosh.

What the hell.

There. It happened again.

The first time was so light that I barely felt it. But this time, it was harder.

My hand had moved when I felt it.

Was that…?

I leaned closer, my face only inches away from Ayla's stomach. I waited and counted the seconds in my head.

When I started to give up, it happened again. And then again. Harder this time. I flinched and pulled away quickly.

"Mommy, can I feel the baby?"
She took my hand and placed it on her round belly. As soon as my palm made contact with her stomach, I felt a hard kick.
"She kicks hard," I whispered.
"You used to kick harder."
"I was feeling Princess moving."

Swallowing hard against the unwelcomed memories, I placed my hand over Ayla's pregnant belly again.

I felt it again. A kick. Or was it a punch?

It—*the baby*—was moving, and I was feeling him.

Without thinking, I caressed the spot where the

baby just kicked. "You have finally decided to make your presence known," I whispered.

There was another slight movement, and I stared at Ayla's stomach in awe. Completely mesmerized.

I had come to a point where I didn't know how to feel—I didn't understand what I was feeling.

One moment I hated the idea of the baby, while the next I was mesmerised by his movement.

The way my chest tightened and my heart fluttered told me a different story. I didn't *hate* the idea of the baby. I hated the situation.

But the baby came with this situation.

I was snapped out of my thoughts when the baby moved again. Pulling my hand away, I shook my head and looked up.

My heart stuttered, and I swore it stopped for a second.

Beautiful green eyes stared back at me.

I stared back, trying to catch my breath.

For so long, I wanted to look into those eyes. And now I was.

My lips wobbled into a small smile, and I sat up, leaning forward into her. Her eyes were a glimmer color of emerald. They sparkled brighter in the light of the morning sun. Her black hair was splayed across the pillows as she blinked sleepily at me.

So beautiful. She looked like a Goddess. A real Angel.

My Ayla was back.

I couldn't help but smile as I reached to palm her cheek.

"Ayla," I croaked, rubbing my thumb over her velvety soft skin.

Her gaze softened the slightest bit, and a sweet smile whispered across her lips.

"Y…you…ha…ve his eyes."

My eyes widened at her soft croaking voice. Ayla was talking!

But then confusion clouded my mind. "Whose eyes, Angel?"

I waited, but she didn't speak again. My muscles started to lock in tension.

She stared and then finally whispered, so soft I barely heard her, "A…Al…Alessio."

What?

"Ayla…what are you talking about? It's me. Alessio. I *am* Alessio."

And then she closed her eyes.

"No. No. No." I panicked. "Angel, open your eyes. C'mon, show me those pretty green eyes."

It wasn't enough. I barely saw them. She had to stay awake. I had to hear her voice. I would beg for it if I had to.

I had no shame. Nothing else mattered.

"Angel," I said, shaking her shoulders. "Please, say something."

She didn't even stir.

How long was she awake? Did I miss it? Was I sleeping the whole time she was awake?

How could I have been so fucking irresponsible?

This time I wouldn't sleep. There was no way I would close my eyes again.

My heart raced like the wings of a caged bird. I did feel caged, and it was suffocating.

It felt like I was watching everything from the outside. Ayla was far away, and no matter how

25

much I reached for her, she always ended up fading in the darkness.

She always faded away, and I was left empty.

No!

I took her hand in mine and talked. I talked for hours.

I begged for her to wake up. I begged for forgiveness. I begged for her love.

I made promises to cherish and take care of her.

But no matter how much I cajoled, fussed, and pushed, Ayla never moved or stirred.

Chapter 4

It was already the next day. Lena came with food, but I didn't eat.

I stayed by Ayla's side, holding her to me, caressing her and hoping she would wake up soon.

My men came and went. Viktor tried to get me to shower, but I refused. Lena said she would take care of Ayla while I rested, but I pushed everyone away.

I talked until my throat was completely dry and hurting. I thought that maybe she would hear my voice and wake up.

Maybe…maybe…so many maybes and I was still hoping.

Even when everything looked so hopeless, I still hoped.

Even when it felt as if I was breaking and being slowly cut from the inside, I still hoped.

Because as long as I had Ayla in my arms, I could hope.

I was her savior once. I would be her savior again.

My chest burned, and I rubbed a hand over my heart in frustration. Feeling, emotions, the heart—they were such a weakness.

I chuckled dryly and leaned my head against the headboard. It was too late now. There was no going back.

I now understood what Lyov and Isaak meant.

Mindlessly, I rubbed a hand over Ayla's arm. Looking down at her sleeping form, I saw her slowly stirring. Her forehead creased, and her lips twitched.

I sat forward, my heart beating wildly. My hands started to shake, and sweat broke out on my forehead.

"Angel," I whispered as she roused from her long hours of sleep.

She blinked her eyes open. Sleepily at first, and then finally she was fully awake.

We stared at each other. And just like the very first time my eyes had met hers, my heart stuttered and my stomach tightened in knots.

I could have flipped in joy and screamed from the top of my lungs.

But I only smiled.

I leaned forward and kissed her forehead. "My Ayla. My beautiful Angel." I peppered her face with kisses.

When Ayla didn't move, my eyebrows furrowed tensely, and I pulled back.

I quickly lost my smile.

Realization finally dawned that she still hadn't responded to me. "Ayla?" I said, touching her cheek and running a finger along her dried lips.

There was no recognition in her green eyes.

I suddenly felt sick.

She still hadn't uttered a word. No, she just stared.

I knew she wasn't seeing me.

She just stared into space without saying anything. I wasn't even sure if she understood what was happening.

I spent a few minutes trying to bring her back. But it was no use.

"Ayla," I whispered. "It's me. Alessio."

Nothing.

And that was the moment my heart shattered.

She only stared blankly at me. Her face was completely devoid of emotion, her eyes lacking the light that had always been there. They were empty.

I was wrong.

I finally had Ayla in my arms; she was safe. She was with me—but she wasn't *here*.

My Angel was gone.

In her place was an empty shell.

Chapter 5

I stared at Ayla, completely frozen. For so long, I wanted her eyes on me, but not like this.

Not empty and lifeless.

She wasn't seeing me. As if I wasn't even there.

I touched her cheek gently, hoping it would bring her attention to me. But instead she moved her eyes away. I watched her look around the room. Her attention stayed on the wall far longer than I liked.

Then her gaze moved around again, taking in every piece. Even though she looked intently around the room, I knew she wasn't seeing anything.

She was lost in her mind.

Her eyes saw what was there, but her mind didn't acknowledge it.

I feared this would be an outcome from her captivity.

I knew she would be hurt…maybe even beyond help…but I thought that at least she would recognize *me*.

Those beautiful green orbs moved back to mine.

I remembered clearly the day I first saw those eyes. They were filled with fear back then. But slowly, I had watched them change to something else. There was wonder, amazement, happiness, and finally love.

But now all of that was gone. In its place was nothing…her eyes held nothing.

Looking in them, even I felt empty. I realized that I lived through Ayla. Her happiness had been mine. Her smile and laughter had brought me to life. The look in her eyes, the love in them had brought me compassion and love. They taught me to feel.

Now I was left feeling too much while she closed in herself.

Her gaze bored into mine.

Blue to green.

My heart stammered heavily in my chest as I watched for any change. Any trickle of life. When none of that happened, the realization settled around me like a heavy cloud. We had been thrown back into the pit of darkness.

I was just a stranger to my Angel.

I was suddenly afraid I would push too hard and maybe too fast.

Shaking my head in dread, I swallowed past the lump in my throat. I couldn't give up. Not now. Not ever. I would fight until I had nothing left to give, until I had made sure she was fully back to me.

I forced myself to smile.

It was a strain, but I smiled—for *her*.

My finger softly trailed up her cheek, and I moved Ayla's hair behind her ear. She didn't move.

31

Her gaze stayed fixated on mine.

If I didn't know better, I would have said she looked mesmerized by my eyes. Like they were the only thing she could stare at.

I shifted around so our faces were mere inches apart. My lips touched the tip of her nose before I slightly leaned back. "I know you'll probably not hear me. Or even if you do, you'll not understand. But I want you to hear my voice. I want you to know that I am here."

I moved my head to the side. "Angel," I whispered in her ears. Placing a kiss on her head, I leaned back. "You are so beautiful; you know that?"

When she didn't respond, I smiled and rubbed her cheeks. They used to be round, but she had lost weight. It wasn't healthy for her or the baby.

At the thought of the baby, my eyes moved to her stomach. Taking a deep breath, I placed my hand on the bump.

Deep inside, I wanted to feel him or her again. The urge to feel the baby move, to connect with it in some way, was strong.

As soon as I placed my hand on Ayla's stomach, the baby shifted around. I couldn't help but smile. I felt strangely giddy at the thought of the baby moving at my touch.

I rubbed the bump. "You sure are a dancer," I said to the bump when it moved again. "Or maybe a fighter?" A small laugh bubbled from my chest. It was playing target practice in there.

A hard kick pressed against my palm. "A fighter it is then."

Another kick. Leaning down until my face was

32

over the bump, I pressed my hand a little firmer. "You need to let Ay—your," I paused, my throat suddenly closing up, "your mommy rest. She is tired."

I waited for another kick. When it happened, I shook my head, my heart feeling a little fuller than before.

I looked up to see Ayla still staring at me. "Are you hungry?" I asked, sitting up. She didn't answer, not that I was expecting her to.

"You need to eat." I continued talking even when there was no response from her. "If I tell Lena to bring some food, will you eat?"

I was already reaching for my phone. Quickly calling Lena, I told her to bring a tray of food up for Ayla.

I faced Ayla again. "Lena made your favorite fried noodles. Remember how much you loved them?" I sat down beside her and caressed her hair. "You would fight anyone for the last plate."

I talked and talked, telling her about Maddie and the things they would do together. I told Ayla how Lena adored her.

I waited for any sign of life in her green eyes, but there was none. She stayed silent. Just observing me.

When Lena finally brought the tray up, I helped Ayla sit.

She stared at the food and then looked up at me again. I brought the fork to her lips, waiting for her to take a bite. But she didn't. Lena coddled and urged her to eat, but Ayla stayed unmoving.

With my hands shaking, I brought the fork down

and pushed the tray away. "She's not going to eat."

"But Alessio, she needs to eat. It's not healthy," Lena argued.

I felt Ayla shift beside me. She laid down and turned toward me. Ayla stared at me for one final time before closing her eyes.

Her breathing was evened out in a span of seconds, her body going limp as she fell asleep.

My Angel really was broken, her wings clipped cruelly.

"Alessio," Lena whispered, her voice croaky with tears. I shook my head, keeping my eyes on my sleeping Angel.

Lena took the tray, and I heard her leave, the door closing behind her.

With my heart heavy, I moved closer to Ayla and held her to me.

When she sighed sleepily in my chest, my arms tightened around her waist. Her bump was pressed against my stomach, and I felt the baby shift one last time before it settled down too.

A few minutes later, both mother and baby were sound asleep.

But I stayed awake, my mind refusing to let the sleepiness take place. It was impossible to close my eyes. Every time the darkness surrounded me, all I saw was Ayla trapped in the dungeon. Pregnant, hurt, and alone.

So I held Ayla and watched over her as she slept.

For the first time in my life, I was clueless. And weak. I didn't only fail Ayla, but I also failed the baby she was carrying.

It didn't matter if it was mine or Alberto's. The

baby was innocent. It was part of Ayla. My hand moved to her round stomach again. Holding the bump in my hand, a sudden surge of possessiveness filled me.

Instead of pushing it away, I welcomed it. And with it, I let my anger fuel. Alberto wasn't only going to pay for hurting Ayla. No, his pain would be twice as much now.

Ayla shifted in my arms, snapping me out of my thoughts. I looked at the clock to see some time had passed since she fell asleep. Ayla sleepily blinked her eyes open, and they made contact with mine.

We stared at each other, both our gazes unflinching. After some time, I felt her slightly moving in my arms. Releasing my tight hold on her, I watched her sit up.

She looked around the room, her eyes focusing on the wall in the corner. Without sparing me another glance, Ayla got up, and I quickly sat up in shock. My eyes followed her like a hawk, looking for any reaction.

But even when she slowly moved toward the wall, her expression held nothing.

I followed behind her, my stomach in knots as I waited for her next movement. If only she would talk. I was left trying to figure Ayla out. And with her silence, it was difficult to think like her.

I paused in my steps when I saw her stopping in front of the wall.

Confused, I took a step forward but froze when Ayla knelt down and sat against the wall. She finally brought her lifeless eyes to mine. My heart may have stopped beating then.

Or maybe I stopped breathing?

I was suffocating as I watched Ayla lay down against the wall, curling into herself. When realization finally dawn to me, I closed my eyes tightly, trying to shut the image in front of me. My fist curled at my side, my jaw grinding.

My body shook with vengeance. And pain. So much pain. Seeing my Ayla like this was slowly breaking me. When it came to Ayla, she was my weakness, but I was fighting for her.

Strength and weakness. Both battling together.

Opening my eyes again, I stared at Ayla as she laid in the same position as I found her in the dungeon. For months, she stayed like this. This position had been her constant.

My fingers tightened in fists. Taking a deep breath, I took a step forward.

Now, I was going to be her constant.

Stopping in front of Ayla, I knelt down beside her. Palming her cheek, I caressed her. Her eyes closed with a sigh, and they didn't open again.

I laid down beside her on the hard floor and pulled her into my arms. She laid half on top of me, and I held her.

"I'm not going to leave you, Angel. No matter how much you fight against me, I'm not going to leave. I'm not giving up. You might have forgotten me, but I will make you remember again. That's my promise, Angel."

Those words were mere whispers, but they were everything to me.

I placed a kiss on her forehead and closed my eyes.

That was how we fell asleep.

On the floor, against the wall but in each other's arms.

Chapter 6

I woke up with a start. My heart drummed wildly, my body drenched with sweat. The nightmares still haunted me, even awake. I didn't think they would ever go away. Those memories were etched in my mind.

But it wasn't just the nightmare that had pulled me from my troubled sleep.

No, it had been because I was alone.

The bed was empty beside me.

I frantically looked around the room, but Ayla was nowhere to be found. She never left the room. Hell, if it wasn't me carrying her, she never left the bed.

I was out of bed in a flash and went to look for her in the bathroom. Panic clawed its way into my body when I found that empty too. My chest felt heavy as I ran out of the room.

"Ayla?" I called out. My feet stopped in front of the piano room, and I glanced at the door. I didn't want to hope, but my heart accelerated as I moved closer.

With my eyes closed, my hand shook as I opened the door. I blinked my eyes open to meet darkness.

My Angel wasn't here.

Fear welled up inside of me, and I shook with dread. A swell of noise burst from my throat. "Ayla?" I screamed as I ran down the stairs.

My fingers dug into my scalp in frustration and alarm. Screaming on top of my lungs, I hoped that my voice reached her.

"AYLA!"

I saw Viktor and Nikolay running down the stairs. Lena and the maids came out of the kitchen. Some of my men came running through the doors, looks of panic on their faces.

"Alessio?" Viktor questioned, coming to stand beside me.

"Ayla is gone," I said shakily.

His eyes widened. "What? How?"

"I don't know!" Growling in frustration, I pinched the bridge of my nose and paced. "We were sleeping. She was with me. I don't know how she got up without me knowing."

I saw Nikolay nodding at the other men, and they all rushed around the house. The maids followed suit to look for Ayla.

"Did you check the piano room?" Lena asked.

"Yes," I snapped. "That was the first place I checked."

"Where would she go?" Viktor muttered.

That was what I was afraid of. Ayla wasn't in her right mind. It had been a week since we rescued her, but she was still as lost as the first day.

The only change was that she started eating

39

yesterday. That was only after days of trying. I finally got her to stop sleeping on the floor. They were small changes, but they meant nothing as long as she stayed lifeless.

I walked around the house, my throat dry, my body feeling heavy as I searched for Ayla. My muscles were locked tight as I paced the house.

"Ayla? Ayla!" I called out, running down the stairs again.

Viktor followed closely behind me. He swore in frustration. I held the back of my neck, my fingers pressing against the muscle to release the tension building there.

She was nowhere. Where would she go?

If she wasn't in our room or the piano room then—

My eyes widened in shock, and I almost stumbled back. *No.*

"Alessio?" I heard Viktor call out to me.

I didn't turn around. With only one destination in my mind, I ran out of the house.

Was it possible? Ayla's memories stayed stubbornly locked away, no matter how much I tried to bring them back.

Ayla was refusing to feel. Like she'd rather stay numb.

I blindly ran, sometimes slipping over the broken branches but quickly picking up the pace again. My wound was healing up, but running with such force was causing my leg to weaken under the pressure. A painful burning sensation traveled its way up my leg, and I stumbled forward.

I swore, holding onto the tree. My leg seized up,

and I struggled to move forward. Fucking useless leg.

Pushing the pain at the back of my mind, I thought of Ayla.

With my wounded leg dragging heavily behind me, I limped forward.

When the trees started to clear up, turning into the beautiful field, my heart thumped a little wildly with hope.

I heard the rushing water, my eyes prickling as I remembered the times Ayla and I spent there. I hadn't been there since she was taken away from me.

When the field finally came into view, I stopped and leaned against the tree. I fought to catch my breath as my gaze finally found Ayla. Her back was to me as she looked at the rushing water. She sat silently on the rock, her long black hair hanging loose on her back.

Walking forward, I stopped beside her. She stared straight ahead, completely ignoring my presence. I looked down at her face, hoping to see a smile or maybe even a little light in her eyes.

When I found none, my heart sank, and my stomach tightened in knots.

She only stared at the creek, her face devoid of emotion. Ayla wasn't affected by the beauty in front of her, not like the first time she had been here.

I knew the creek was something buried deep in her mind. Could it be that she was slowly remembering? Or maybe she was looking for peace—like before.

The piano room and the creek were the places

41

she absolutely loved, the places that brought her peace.

And now she was blindly reaching for it again. Without even realizing it.

I knelt down in front of Ayla, wincing as my muscles protested against the pain in my leg. She kept her eyes on the creek behind me.

I smiled, being accustomed to this reaction. She wasn't ignoring me. She knew I was there. My Angel just didn't want to let herself feel.

Even thought I had realized that, it didn't stop the pain in my heart. It didn't stop the heartbreak I felt every time she stared at me with those empty green eyes.

The pain worsened every day. The loneliness clawed at me, the agony too much to bear sometimes. But I kept going. For Ayla, I stayed strong. I lived for her.

Palming her cheeks, I rubbed her soft skin. "You can't leave like this. Do you know how worried I was, Angel? Everyone is looking for you. Waking up and not finding you beside me was the worst. You can't do that again."

No response.

I didn't expect one. It was another thing I was accustomed to: talking to Ayla while I only got silence. Deep inside, she knew my voice. And stupidly, I believed that she heard me.

"You need to let me know where you go next time," I admonished gently. "Lena almost had a heart attack. Let's give the poor woman a break.

"Angel," I said, kissing her nose. "Will you talk to me? Anything. Just say something. I can't bear your silence anymore."

Her eyes finally moved to mine. I almost jumped with joy. Such a small thing, but it meant so much.

"Please," I finally begged. "Please, say something, Angel. I want to hear your voice. I need to hear your voice. Say something. Just one word..." my voice broke. Taking a deep breath, I continued. "...to let me know that you're hearing me, that you know I'm here."

When she stayed utterly silent, I looked down, trying so fucking hard to hold my stupid tears. What I saw made me suck in a painful breath.

This time...my soul cried.

Ayla was barefooted, and her feet were bruised and bloodied. She had walked from the house to the creek barefooted.

"Angel," I whimpered. I could hear the way my voice broke. The tears slid down my cheeks. Just a few drops but it was so fucking hard.

I buried my face in Ayla's lap and cried. "I am begging you. Say my name. I want to hear my name from your lips. I want to hear your voice."

Holding her knees, I pressed my face in her thighs. "Just my name. That's all I am asking. Please, Ayla. Please."

Without any care of the world, I sobbed and begged. My heart broke a thousand times then.

With my face still buried in her lap, I waited. I felt Ayla shift. I almost felt her hand on my arm but then nothing. My Angel didn't touch me. She didn't hold me. She didn't speak.

I waited some more. I waited for I didn't know how long.

But I only got silence.

When my tears had finally dried, I leaned back and wiped my wet cheeks. Ayla stared at me blankly, and her eyes moved toward the water again.

"You were always stubborn, you know," I whispered, touching her cheek softly. "I'm not giving up, Angel. You might not remember, but I once told you that I wasn't giving up on you, and I had told you not to give up on us."

I leaned forward, placing a feather-light kiss on her lips. "I am telling you this again. I am not giving up on you, so don't give up on us."

My lip tilted up in a small smile. "I am more stubborn than you. What I want, I get. And I want you."

Her eyes stayed fixated on the creek, and I sat down on the ground. I waited, giving her some time to admire the view. I palmed her stomach, feeling the baby move at my touch.

The little one always moved whenever I touched Ayla's stomach. It didn't matter if it was in the middle of the night, the baby always responded to my touch.

Sometimes I felt like maybe we bonded. There was no stopping the way my heart clenched whenever I felt the baby move.

After some time, I got up and swept Ayla in my arms. Holding her to my chest, I walked back to the house.

When I finally got inside, I saw Lena's eyes widen, and she rushed upstairs. Viktor came forward to help me but I walked past him. Making my way to my room, I walked into the bathroom instantly. Lena was close behind me.

"It's okay. I'll clean her up. Can you bring a tray up? She needs to eat," I said, settling Ayla on the edge of the tub.

Lena nodded mutely and shuffled out of the bathroom. I turned Ayla around so her feet were in the tub.

"This is going to hurt a little," I muttered. I cleaned her feet, rinsing away all the dirt and blood. All this time, Ayla didn't make a sound or even shift. It was *me* wincing in pain for *her*.

When her feet were cleaned, I saw that the dirt and little blood had made it appear worse than it was. I sighed in relief and dried her feet before helping her out of the tub.

"Feeling better?" I asked, holding her in my embrace. She sighed in my chest, and I smiled, rubbing her back. With her baby bump in the way, I couldn't hug her properly. But I held her as close as I could.

When my leg started to ache unbearably, I carried Ayla to bed and pulled the covers around her.

The tray was already on the nightstand. Sitting down in front of her, I picked up the spoon.

"Do you need anything else?" Lena asked.

I shook my head and held a spoonful of rice to Ayla's lips. She took the first bite silently, and my heart soared. After so many days of trying and begging, she started eating yesterday.

For a week, Sam had her hooked up with an IV. It was the only way to get something in her body.

I fed Ayla another bite, and she ate, chewing and swallowing slowly.

Lena moved away from the bed. "How is Maddie?" I asked before she left the room.

She didn't answer for some time, and I knew what her answer would be. "There is no change."

The door closed, and I sighed, my heart heavy for Maddie. She had refused to leave her room. Or eat. She was a living ghost. I thought when Maddie heard Ayla was back, she would come to see her, but she stayed away.

Maddie had yet to see Ayla. In some ways, it was better this way. I didn't think she had the strength to see Ayla in this state.

I continued to feed Ayla, taking a few bites as I watched her eat. Her gaze stayed fixated on me, as always. It was almost like a routine.

So I fed her and talked. She ate in silence and...maybe listened to me.

I talked about everything, sometimes mentioning Isaak and Lyov.

My father had been taking care of business all this time. He didn't complain. No, he fell right back into the position of the Boss. Even though I refused to admit it, I was thankful he and Isaak were taking care of things.

They visited Ayla once. No words were spoken. It was quick, but I saw the look in their eyes. I knew they were seeing their women in Ayla. When Lyov had seen the baby bump, he had paled and walked out in a daze. Since then, he hadn't come back.

When the tray was finally empty, I got up and stretched. Ayla's gaze followed my movement, and

I winked. "Do you want to go to the piano room?"

Silence.

I chuckled and lifted her off the bed. Placing a kiss on her head, I carried her to the piano room. I brought her there every day, hoping it would bring back memories.

I placed Ayla on the bench. She stared at me, and I gave her a small smile, even when the pain intensified.

This used to be our moment. And now, even that was gone.

"Do you remember playing?" I asked, kneeling beside her bench. Ayla looked at the piano keys but didn't respond.

"You used to play for me every night. It was our favorite time of the day. Just us together. You playing the piano while I watched you," I continued. "Do you remember, Angel?"

When she didn't answer, I let out a sigh. "It's okay. I know you will remember. Maybe not now. But one day you will. Do you know why?"

I leaned forward. "Because I am a stubborn asshole, and I am not giving up on you," I whispered in her ear. "One day soon, those beautiful green eyes of yours will look at me with the same amount of wonder and love as before." Placing a kiss next to her ear, I finished, "Be prepared, kitten."

I stood up and walked toward the couch. "I don't play fair when it comes to things I want."

I sat down, facing her. She looked at me for a second before turning her eyes to the piano again. We sat like this for hours maybe.

Until she played.

Just one key. One note.

My head snapped up, my eyes widening. I sat forward, hoping to hear more.

But that was it.

I smiled. So hard that my cheeks were hurting.

I wanted to be disappointed that there wasn't more, but how could I when my Angel finally made a move?

Ayla looked up at me, and there it was—it was so small. Barely there. Or maybe I was just imagining it?

But then it was gone so fast that I would have missed it if I wasn't staring so intently.

A very small glimpse of emotion in those lifeless green eyes. Ayla stared at me, her eyes empty again.

But my chest somehow felt a little lighter than before.

I stood up and walked to her, her gaze following me. I stopped beside her and saw that her fingers were still on the keys. Even though she played only one key, it felt like she had played a whole song.

"Do you know how beautiful you look? You are breathtaking, Angel," I whispered, sweeping her in my arms again. "Especially when you play the piano."

I carried her back to our bedroom, and I felt surprisingly light.

Ayla laid on the bed, and I pulled the covers over her. "You want to sleep?"

She only closed her eyes. I smiled. I got my answer.

I joined her in bed and held her close. The baby

danced around, and I rubbed the bump. "Settle down now. Your mommy needs her sleep."

He moved again. Another kick. So fucking stubborn.

Shaking my head, I closed my eyes. After some time, the baby finally settled, and Ayla fell asleep. Just when sleep started to cloud my mind, I heard a knock on the door.

I slowly moved away from Ayla. After making sure she was still asleep, I made my way to the door and softly opened it.

My eyes widened in shock at the sight in front of me.

"Maddie?"

Maddie stared at me, tears in her eyes. "Can I see her, please?"

Her voice sounded so small and fragile. I blinked a couple of times, trying to understand what was going on.

Maddie looked down, tears streaming down her face. "I should have come before but couldn't find the courage. I'm sorry, Alessio. For leaving this on you. It's…I…God, I can't believe I left her alone when she needed me the most."

I saw her face twisting in frustration as she wiped her tears away angrily. "But can I see her now? Please."

I only nodded, stepping out of the way. Maddie quickly walked inside. I closed the door and watched her stop next to the bed. She cried softly.

When she joined Ayla in the bed, my heart soared. Finally! This was what they both needed. They needed each other.

I walked forward and saw Maddie wrap her arms around Ayla. Her eyes opened, and she stared blankly at Maddie.

She whispered something in Ayla's ear and sobbed. Ayla closed her eyes again, and I knew she was asleep within seconds.

Maddie closed her eyes too. She continued crying softly, trying not to wake Ayla up. I moved the sofa chair next to the bed, beside Ayla, and sat down.

Leaning back, I watched Maddie cry herself to sleep. After some time, I heard the door open and saw Phoenix come in. His eyes instantly went to the bed, and when he saw Maddie there, I saw his shoulders sagging in relief.

He nodded at me and pulled a chair to Maddie's side. We watched both our women sleep.

I didn't miss the way Ayla slightly burrowed deeper in Maddie's embrace.

My lips tilted up in a ghost smile.

A silver lining. Small and barely there. But definitely there.

There was hope.

Chapter 7

1 week later

"We'll be there in ten minutes, Boss," Nikolay said from the driver's seat.

"Hmm…"

"What if it's a trap?"

"I don't think it is. Not after I tortured their president and we killed half of their men in a span of minutes. They're too scared," I muttered, looking out of the window.

I hated being away from Ayla. But when the Black Club called and told me they had an idea of Alberto's whereabouts, I had no choice.

Two weeks and he went into hiding again. A fucking coward he was. He had left the country the same day we found Ayla.

Shaking my head in disgust, I fought the urge to break something. He was a threat I had to get rid of as quickly as possible. As long as he was alive, Ayla was in danger. The baby was in danger.

I looked down at my phone, debating if I should

call Maddie or Viktor. It was the first time I had been away from Ayla since we rescued her.

Ayla was still the same. Little to no improvement.

She hadn't touched the piano again. No matter how much I urged her.

She still hadn't spoken a word. It felt like it had been years since I heard her voice.

If I didn't feed her, she wouldn't eat. And we had quickly come to realize that she would only eat if *I* fed her. Maddie had once tried, and Ayla refused to eat even a bite.

I looked down at my watch. Twenty minutes since I'd left the estate. Ayla was asleep when I left her, and I hoped she stayed asleep until I got home.

Five more minutes. I would walk in, get the fucking information, walk out, and then I would be on my way back to Ayla.

Five fucking minu—

My phone rang, snapping me out of my thoughts. Glancing at the screen, I saw Viktor calling. I quickly answered the call. "What is it? What happened?"

"Alessio," he started but never had a chance to finish.

I heard a scream in the background. *"No!"*

Panic coursed through me, and I sat up straight, my hands shaking. "What's going on?" I snapped, my voice heavy with fear. I saw Nikolay glancing at me in the rear-view mirror, his expression worried.

There were more screams, and then someone was sobbing.

Ayla!

"Alessio, it's Ayla," Viktor said quickly. "She woke up and didn't find you there. Fuck! She completely lost it. I don't know what to do." His voice sounded strange. My heart clenched. Was he crying?

"I tried to get her to calm down, but as soon as I came near her, she would start screaming. Even Maddie and Lena can't calm her down. She wouldn't let anyone near her, and we're worried she'll hurt herself," Viktor continued.

Something crashed in the background, and I sat, horrified, as I listened to Ayla screaming and crying.

"Alessio, she wants you. She won't respond to anyone else. We tried. We fucking tried, but as soon as you left, she woke up. Maddie was with her, and Ayla completely snapped when she didn't see you."

"Viktor, do something, please!" I heard Maddie cry through the phone. "She's going to hurt herself."

I heard Viktor swear, and my heart stammered painfully. I closed my eyes as a wave of pain went through me.

"Can you get close enough to give her the phone?" I demanded. "Make sure she doesn't hurt herself."

I heard screaming again. It was filled with so much pain, and I blinked away tears.

What have I done?

I should have never left her.

I opened my eyes to see Nikolay nodding at me. Without me saying anything, he was already changing the route and doing a U-turn.

53

Fuck the Black Club and Alberto. My Ayla needed me now.

I heard sobbing through the phone, and my heart lurched. "Angel," I said gently.

She only cried.

"I'm sorry, Angel. So, so sorry. I'm coming home, okay? I will be there quickly. I didn't leave you. I would never leave you. I just had something to take care of, and now I'm coming back home to you," I whispered, hoping my voice would bring her back.

"You are so strong; you know that? The strongest person I know, and I am so in awe of you. Don't cry, my sweet Angel. I am coming home and won't leave you again. I'm not going anywhere."

My voice broke over the words, and I closed my eyes as Ayla continued to quietly cry. Her cries were heartbreaking. It was agony to hear.

"Shhh…it's okay. It'll be okay. When I get back, I'll take you to the creek. We'll spend some time there. Just me and you, okay? What do you think? Would you like that?" I said, my fingers tightening around the phone.

"Will you play for me tonight?" I asked softly. "Or maybe do you want to dance? Remember how we danced before and you were smiling, laughing. You were so beautiful, my Angel. You took my breath away that day." I held the phone tighter, desperate to get my feelings across to her.

"I'm coming home. Just a few more minutes and I will be in your arms again." I kept talking even when I knew there would be no answer.

Her sobbing gradually dissolved to small

hiccups. When the car finally stopped in front of the house, I breathed out. "I'm home, Angel," I said before hanging up.

I opened the door and quickly got out. Running up the steps, I was almost at the door when a sharp pain shot through my wounded leg.

I limped inside the house. From the top of the stairs, I heard sobbing. Following it to my room, I pushed the door open.

My knees almost gave out at the sight in front of me. The room was completely trashed. Lena and Maddie were hugging each other next to the door, crying. Phoenix paced the room while Viktor stood in the middle, facing the corner next to the bed.

My hands curled into fists at my sides, and I moved forward slowly.

Ayla was on the floor, next to the nightstand. She sat against the wall, her knees pulled up to her chest, rocking back and forth as she cried. She was curled into herself, as if hiding from everything and everyone.

My heart stuttered at the sight. She looked so broken, so fragile.

I turned to Viktor. He looked in pain. Shaking his head, he walked out of the room.

My gaze moved back to Ayla. Her face was hidden behind her arms. I walked forward and knelt down in front of Ayla. "Angel," I whispered.

Her head snapped up, and she choked back a sob. Her eyes were red and filled with tears. Her cheeks flushed and wet. She looked at me with so much emotion that it was impossible for me to take.

So much pain. Sadness. Anger. Betrayal. Hurt.

I knew in that moment, she felt too much, too fast.

Ayla let out a loud cry, and in a flash, she was in my arms. We sank to the floor, and she climbed into my lap. With her face hidden in my chest, she burrowed deeper into my body like she wanted to hide in me.

I wrapped my arms around her and rocked her back and forth. "Shh…it's okay, Angel. I'm here now, and I am not leaving you."

Placing kisses on her head and face, I held her tighter. "I got you, Angel."

Her arms went around me, holding me. Her fingers dug into my side as she cried in my chest. She never uttered a word. I didn't urge her to.

I held her, and I knew it was enough for her. As long as she was in my arms, it was enough for me too.

The door closed behind us as everyone left. We stayed on the ground as Ayla continued to cry. I talked to her as I did before.

I carried her to bed. We laid under the covers, holding each other.

Her tears eventually stopped, and when silence fell upon us, I stopped talking too. I slightly pulled away and saw that her eyes were closed. I brushed her tears away and softly caressed her cheeks.

We stayed like this for some time, and finally, Ayla slowly blinked her eyes open. I tried to smile but found it hard to. My heart was in agony. It hurt so fucking much, it was almost impossible to breathe.

When Ayla stared at me, I sucked in a harsh

breath.

The emotions I had seen in them before were now gone.

"Angel," I whispered. "Let me see you...cry, be angry. Hit me. Scream at me. But I can't bear to look into those empty eyes anymore."

She continued to stare in silence and then closed her eyes.

That was it. I sighed and waited for her breathing to even out.

I slowly moved away and got off the bed. My leg continued to ache, the muscles contracting painfully as I limped.

After removing my coat and slacks, I examined the wound. It wasn't bleeding, but it hurt as if the stitches were being ripped away from my skin.

I was taking off my shirt when I froze.

"You...are...hurt."

My eyes widened, my mouth falling open.

That voice. That *beautiful* voice.

The words were so softly spoken, the voice slightly scratchy. But I heard it.

My throat was suddenly dry, and my heart drummed so loudly that I heard it in my own ears. My chest tightened. Swiveling around, I faced my Angel.

She was staring at my leg with her lifeless green eyes. But she fucking talked. To me.

I held my fist to my mouth, holding back my emotions before clearing my throat.

"I'm...okay," I replied, taking a step forward.

Her gaze stayed fixated on my wound for another minute before she looked at me.

We stared at each other. Blue to green.

No more words were spoken by her.

Eventually, she closed her eyes and burrowed deeper under the cover.

This time, I smiled.

I had promised to give Ayla back her wings.

And I would continue to fight until my Angel could fly again.

Chapter 8

Ayla

I hate him.

The man with those beautiful blue eyes, I hated him.

I hated that he made me feel. I hated that his touch made me feel.

I wanted to go back to being numb, but he was persistent, never leaving me alone.

Alessio.

That was his name. My savior. But he was no longer my savior. I didn't want him to be.

I wanted him to go away. I wanted to go back to not feeling anything.

I had fought it for so long. I fought *him* for so long. His voice, his touch, his gentle kisses, his soft blue eyes. I fought to stay numb.

But every day, it became harder.

I still wondered, though. *Is it all dream?*

Nothing made sense.

Everything was blurry. Everything hurt.

The Devil was no longer here. The Devil wasn't hurting me anymore.

Only *he* was there. Alessio.

Whether my eyes were open or closed, he was there. He just wouldn't leave me alone.

Sometimes, I didn't know how to feel.

I used to hope for my savior to come. But was he real? Or was this the Devil's trick?

Alessio's touch didn't hurt me. Not like the Devil's.

No, his touch soothed me. When everything hurt, he soothed me.

He would hold me tight and whisper in my ears. Like he was doing now.

I closed my eyes and refused to listen to him. I didn't want to hear his voice. His voice brought back memories.

Sometimes good. Sometimes painful. Everything was painful.

Even the good memories. But they didn't make sense. I was always happy. And in those memories, Alessio was always there.

I hated him. I hated him so much.

I didn't want him to touch me. I didn't want him to whisper in my ears.

I wanted to scream.

But I couldn't seem to find my voice. The Devil hated when I talked. So I stayed silent.

Even when Alessio talked endlessly and begged me to speak, I couldn't. I didn't. With my silence, I hoped he would go away.

"Angel, talk to me."

His voice was both soothing and painful.

I dreamed of you before you came into my life. When I was a little boy, I dreamed of you. Black hair and green eyes, with a beautiful smile. My Angel.

I closed my eyes tightly against the flash of memories. I felt my chest tighten. Every time he spoke, he brought back memories.

I didn't know if they were real. The piano, the flowers, or even that beautiful river.

He even called me *Angel*. Just like in my dreams.

My throat closed up, and I opened my eyes. I stared in his blue eyes. I always found myself lost in them.

He had those same blue eyes, just like I dreamed of. He really was my savior.

"Will you play for me, please?" He sounded like he was begging.

Do you want to play?

You can keep playing the piano if you want.

Have I done this before?

"I want to dance with you, Angel. I want to see you smile like before. I still remember that day. You were so happy, smiling and laughing. I can still hear your beautiful laughter as I twirl you around."

May I have this dance, Angel?

I heard his voice in my head, although I knew he didn't say them now.

There it was. Another memory that made it hard to breathe.

I felt his lips on my forehead. "I want to see you like that again."

I closed my eyes against his words. His arms tightened around my waist.

"Look at me, Angel. C'mon, give me those beautiful green eyes."

Ayla, look at me.

You know I'm not letting you go until you give me what I want.

Don't ever look away from me again.

My eyes snapped open, and I saw Alessio smile.

His voice was in my head again.

"There you are." He bent his head until our noses touched. "Don't ever look away from me again."

My heart stuttered. Those words—it was another memory. He hated when I looked away from him.

So many emotions crowding inside of me. I was going crazy. Nothing made sense. I was so lost.

But I didn't want to be lost anymore.

Alessio brought his hand up, his finger touching my cheek. His touch was gentle, the opposite of the Devil's.

"I'm going to change and then we'll sleep. Okay?"

He got up, and I closed my eyes again.

You are more beautiful with your hair down.

I opened my eyes again when I heard Alessio. Our eyes made contact. He had called me beautiful.

My skin felt warm, and I felt a strange sensation in my heart. My stomach tightened.

I saw him removing his shirt. He was only in grey pants.

I usually sleep naked, but I thought you wouldn't be comfortable with that. I can accommodate you with the sweatpants, but I hate sleeping in shirts.

His voice rang in my ears as he walked toward me. I saw him limping a little, his legs dragging

62

behind him.

I felt a sudden surge of emotion. Just like before, when I had seen him hurt.

When I had spoken.

You are hurt.

Seeing him hurt made it painful for me. It reminded me of when *I* was hurt.

It reminded me of when I wanted someone to comfort me. When I wanted someone to speak to me, to make me feel better.

So I spoke.

And then I realized my mistake.

I had let him win.

After fighting so long to not feel, I had let myself feel.

Feeling made everything hurt. It hurt so much.

I wish I was back there. With the Devil.

Because then, I was numb. That was much better. Nothing hurt. The memories weren't painful because I didn't have any memories.

I wanted it to stay that way.

I didn't want to hurt. Not anymore.

I turned away from Alessio. He only held me, his arm around my hips, his palm over my stomach.

He rubbed my belly gently. "Settle down now, little fighter."

Protect my baby. No matter what. I have to protect my baby.

I heard the words in my head. Closing my eyes, I breathed.

The voice in my head belonged to me. I didn't understand what the words meant; all I knew was that I had to protect someone.

Even when I was with the Devil, I protected the baby. Even when I didn't understand myself, I never let him touch my stomach. My actions were done unconsciously. Like it was drilled in my head.

"Sleep, Angel. I will watch over you."

Sleep, Angel. I will watch over you.

I hated him. I hated his voice. I hated the memories he brought.

But I also hated that I wanted those memories.

Even though I hated it all, deep inside, I lived for those tiny glimpses of my past.

Chapter 9

Alessio

I felt Ayla shift in my arms. She sighed almost sleepily and burrowed deeper into my embrace. Opening my eyes, with my vision still clouded with sleep, I stared down at her.

She was sleeping peacefully, a contradicting image after the nightmare she had just a few hours ago.

It had been a few days since she spoke, but nightmares had plagued her sleep every night since then.

She was *feeling* again. Her emotions were small, almost invisible, but definitely there. The nightmares were proof of that.

Ayla thought staying numb would be better, without realizing that she was slowly destroying herself by not feeling anything.

She had to let it out. I wasn't stopping until I broke every wall around her heart.

"Good morning, Angel," I whispered in her ear.

Placing a kiss there, I pushed myself on my elbows. She sighed again and blinked her eyes open.

Ayla stared at me blankly for a moment and then closed her eyes again, refusing to acknowledge me. Like every day.

Kitten. How innocent. She seemed to have forgotten that I was a stubborn fucker. She could fight me all she wanted, but I would win in the end.

I won before. I was going to win again.

"It's already late. You need to wake up and eat," I pushed, kissing her on the nose.

I noticed her wrinkling her nose, and she opened her eyes again.

Ayla moved out of my embrace and struggled to sit up. Placing an arm behind her back, I helped her in a sitting position.

I rested my palm over her firm abdomen. When I felt a kick, I smiled. It was impossible not to. "Good morning to you too."

Ayla tried to shift away from my hand, but I pressed it more firmly against her stomach, feeling the baby play target practice.

I moved my hand away, and Ayla placed hers over the bump, holding it protectively. At least she was acknowledging the baby.

I stared at Ayla until she looked away. Sometimes she would show subtle emotions, but they would quickly be gone.

She was fighting herself.

I guessed I had to fight her too.

I moved quickly then, surprising even myself. I was always patient. It looked like my patience was slowly running out.

Shifting myself over Ayla, with my thighs on either side of her hips, I moved my face closer to hers.

Her eyes widened in shock. There it was. Finally, an emotion. I saw her swallow hard, and her gaze moved slowly over my face.

I palmed her cheeks gently, our noses touching slightly. "Come back to me, Angel. I'm waiting for you. Let me help you. Give me a chance to make you whole again. Give *us* a chance. Fight for *us*."

She closed her eyes. Stubborn woman.

"Ayla, open your eyes."

Her eyes snapped open. "I told you before and I will tell you again: don't look away from me. I want your eyes on me. Looking at me. Seeing me. Only me, Ayla."

I didn't miss how her breath caught in her throat and how she stared at me with wide eyes.

Ayla licked her lips and tried to look away. I noticed her hands rubbing her stomach, almost angrily. They were shaking. When I looked at her face, I saw that she looked lost and scared.

Ayla seemed agitated.

Fuck! I pushed too hard.

"Angel," I murmured, kissing the corner of her mouth. "If you don't talk to me, I can't help you. And I want to help you."

Ayla blinked several times, and she turned her head toward me, a look of astonishment on her face. She cocked her head to the side as if waiting for me to continue.

I felt my own eyes widen. I had said those words to her before.

My heart clenched at the possibility of her remembering. My hands shook as I caressed her cheeks.

"You are worth more than you think," I whispered softly. So many months ago, I had said those exact words to her. And now I whispered them again, hoping it would make yet another difference.

I pressed our foreheads together, holding her to me. "You bring happiness to others. You bring light, my Angel. You changed me. You made me feel. I didn't realize I was letting the shadow control me all this time. Not until you came into my life. You bring *me* light. Just like a true Angel."

I was weak before. When she had cut herself and I had said those words to her, I kept my true feelings hidden. I had refused to tell her the truth I told her now.

But things had changed since then. I had changed.

And now I was going to rewrite our history.

With a sigh, I moved off her. She exhaled loudly, the comforter fisted tightly in her hands.

I placed my hand right next to hers. They were inches away. So close yet not touching.

"Can I touch you?"

Her gaze moved to our hands, but she didn't respond. I knew she wouldn't.

"Can I hold your hand?"

Ayla opened her mouth, and she gasped for breath. Her head snapped up, her startled eyes meeting mine.

It felt like my chest was being wrenched open

when I saw tears forming in her eyes. She looked down at our hands. So close. I wanted to touch her. I knew I could if I wanted.

But I didn't move. I waited for her.

Her tears didn't fall. She swallowed several times before moving her hand over her stomach, giving me my answer.

It was such a déjà vu moment.

I chuckled under my breath. "Okay. So this is how you're going to play."

I moved to my knees until our faces were almost touching. "I'll play your game then," I continued. "I won't touch you. Not until you ask me to."

I could almost see the memory flashing behind her eyes. The way her lips parted in surprise, it gave her away.

"I won't touch you. Not until you beg me for it," I finished, my voice low and deliberately seductive.

We were about to go back to the beginning.

Ayla flinched before she closed her eyes tightly. I was tempted to take her in my arms and hold her close. Take away all her pain. Keep her nightmares away.

But I had been doing this for weeks. It didn't make much of a difference.

So we were going to play it another way.

"Lena will bring our breakfast. After I feed you, I have to take care of some things. I won't be far, though," I explained.

This was almost a routine. After her panic attack, I explained to her what I was doing and where I was going. It was to keep her mind at ease. To let her know I was always there.

Walking away from the bed, I peeked at the full-length mirror, watching Ayla closely. She got out of bed and followed me into the bathroom.

Good. She was slowly doing things on her own.

I brushed my teeth, and she copied me. We washed our faces, and while I changed, she kept her dress on.

The breakfast tray was already waiting for us when we walked out of the bathroom. Ayla sat on her side of the bed, waiting.

Placing the tray between us, I fed her small bites while I ate too. I didn't speak. Ayla stared at me, confused, but never uttered a word.

When a knock sounded on the door, I got off the bed. "That must be Maddie," I muttered to Ayla.

"Come in," I called out, putting on my suit jacket. Maddie walked in and smiled at Ayla.

"Are you ready for the tour?" she asked, looking at Ayla expectantly. Not that Ayla ever replied.

"I can take you to the back garden today," Maddie continued, helping Ayla out of bed.

After Ayla's panic attack, Maddie thought it would be good to help Ayla become familiar with the estate again.

Ayla looked back at me, waiting for my reply. She always did that. As if asking for my permission. If I said yes, she would go. If I said no, she never said anything but would stay in the room.

Not anymore.

"Do you want to go with Maddie?" I asked.

I saw her eyebrows furrow in question, her hands trembling at her side.

C'mon, Angel. Don't be scared. I will be there to

catch you if you fall.

"Ayla, do you want to see the back garden with Maddie?" I pushed.

She stayed quiet, but I saw her breathing had accelerated. Maddie looked at me, worried, but I stayed focus on the beautiful Angel in front of me.

She stared at me. Ayla took a deep breath, her gaze never moving away from mine. It was like she was taking her courage from me.

Like I gave her strength.

I smiled encouragingly. Still staring into my eyes, she gave a small nod.

Fuck yeah!

I wanted to scream, throw my hands in the air and jump. She did it!

Holding my fist against my pressed lips, I cleared my throat, but the emotions were overflowing.

"I will be in my office. Enjoy your day with Maddie. She will take good care of you," I said.

She nodded again. This time, it was impossible to hold the smile.

Giving Maddie a nod, I walked out of the room. Taking my phone out of my pocket, I called the one person I knew would be able to help me.

"What is it?" the voice answered.

"Nina, I need you in my office in an hour."

"I'll be there," she replied. I hung up before she could say anything else.

Nikolay and Viktor were already waiting for me outside of my office. I nodded at them, and they followed me inside.

"What are Isaak and Lyov doing?" I asked.

"The businesses are running smoothly. Surprisingly. It looks like they haven't lost their touch yet," Viktor grumbled.

"That's good." I nodded. I knew they would keep everything in line.

"The women at the clubs?"

"With Alberto out of the country and his men hiding, we have full control over the clubs. Even the ones that belong to him. Under strict orders from Lyov, the women are being treated fairly," Nikolay replied.

"Those who have been abused intensively are under care," Viktor added. "If only we had Alberto in our hands. He's the only fucking problem now."

"Any news from him?" I questioned, sitting back against my chair.

They shook their heads mutely.

"I need answers!" I bellowed. "The information from the Black Club members led us to a dead end. It brought us nothing."

They said Alberto was hiding in Canada. By the time my men reached there, he was already gone.

Alberto was smart. He never stayed in one place. He moved every few days and left no tracks behind. It was almost impossible to track him down.

"We are doing everything we can, Alessio," Viktor muttered. He ran his hand over his face in frustration. "But don't forget. We might be powerful, but he is just as powerful. He has connections everywhere. When a Mafia man wants to go off grid, it is impossible to find him. You know that better than anyone. Lyov and Isaak pulled it off. You did it too once."

"I don't care who he is or what he's doing. All I know is that as long as he is alive, Ayla and the baby are not safe. I need him dead. I need his blood on my hands. Until then, I won't rest," I growled dangerously.

"We aren't stopping until we find him. Mark said he has some information too. I'm going there tomorrow. We'll see what he has and how it can help us," Nikolay added.

"Good," I muttered.

"What do you want to do with Artur and Enzo?" Viktor asked, crossing his arms over his chest.

At the mention of Artur, a sudden surge of fury coursed through me. I held the table tightly until my knuckled turned white.

"Keep them alive," I gritted out. "I need them alive until Alberto is found."

Viktor shook his head. "Are you sure? Artur is practically dead. So is Enzo."

"I don't care how you do it. I need them alive. When Alberto is found, I will finish them all together. Like a little family reunion. I'm sure they will like it," I growled.

Taking a deep breath, I released the table from my grasp. "After all, I'm not done with them yet. They haven't spilled enough blood. Their pain is not even half of what Ayla has had to go through."

I looked directly at Viktor. "By the time I'm done with them, they won't even be able to beg me to kill them. Not even if they wanted to."

I saw Viktor raise an eyebrow at me, and he smiled almost sadistically. "Now that's what I like to hear. I almost thought you were going soft.

Looks like I was mistaken. You are still a crazy fucker."

I shook my head at his stupid assumption. "I will always be one."

Before he could say anything else, I changed the topic. I didn't want to be reminded of who I was. Of what I had done.

I was a monster. I have killed without any remorse. I didn't care.

What always worried me was…what would Ayla think of me? When she found out what I had done to get to her?

"Is there anything else?" I asked quickly, trying to clear my thoughts.

Nikolay nodded and spoke of all the things I had missed while taking care of Ayla. Lyov and Isaak had been able to take care of things I had almost ruined.

Nikolay paused when there was a knock at the door.

"Come in," I called out, already knowing who it was.

The door opened, revealing Nina. She walked inside before kicking the door closed. "What did you need?"

"I need to speak with Nina alone," I said loudly. I saw Viktor raise an eyebrow, but he walked out without a word.

"Nikolay, I need you to stay outside at the door," I ordered. He nodded and walked out too, closing the door behind him.

I stared at Nina as she took a seat on the couch. "So what is it? Anyone I need to kill? You could have told me the name on the phone."

"Strip."

Her mouth fell open and then snapped shut again. "What?" she sputtered.

I crossed my arms. "You heard me."

"Look, I am no longer an undercover at the clubs. I'm not a stripper. And I'm not your fuck buddy anymore. So nope."

"I don't want to fuck you, either. That's not why you are here. I'm not interested in you," I replied drily.

"I don't know if I should be insulted or not," she shot back, sending me a fierce glare.

"It looks like I have to spell out everything for you," I said, sitting forward.

She rolled her eyes. "Oh please, enlighten me."

So I did.

And she laughed. "Do you really think it would work?"

I swallowed hard at the question and rubbed my forehead tiredly. "This could either go really bad or give us a good result."

"And if it goes bad?"

"Then we're back to square one. But I'm hoping for good results."

"Cool, I'll do it," she agreed. Nina removed her black jacket and shirt.

When she was only in her undergarments, she walked toward me. I pushed my chair back, giving her space to fit between my legs.

I blew out a loud breath and closed my eyes. I felt her kneel between my spread thighs. When her hands made contact with my legs, I froze.

I trembled with panic and fear. What if this went bad?

I grabbed Nina's hand. "Don't touch me," I growled, pulling her hands off.

"Got it," she muttered.

I counted the seconds in my head, and each second was overwhelming.

When I heard the door open and Maddie's voice, my fingers fisted around Nina's hair and brought her head closer to my crotch.

This better work.

I guided her head up and down, mimicking the movement of her sucking me off. I opened my eyes and saw Ayla staring at me.

I smirked and tilted my head back. My Angel stood frozen, her gaze going to Nina's head before moving back to my eyes.

There it was. The spark I was looking for.

There was a hint of anger in those beautiful green eyes. Her hands went to her stomach, and she rubbed her rounded belly, trying to soothe herself.

Her chest moved faster, her breathing becoming louder.

I groaned and fucking hated it.

Ayla shook her head, and I saw tears in her eyes. She looked hurt.

I should have been ashamed. I waited for the searing pain in my chest. It was there. It was definitely there at the sight of seeing Ayla hurt.

But I was also fucking ecstatic.

At least she wasn't numb to what she seeing.

When I groaned again and acted as if I came, I saw a tear slide down her cheek. It broke my fucking heart, and I instinctively pushed Nina away.

She stood up and walked around the desk, leaning her hips against it. "Hello there," she drawled huskily.

Ayla flinched and took a step back. It confirmed my suspicion.

Seeing Nikolay at the door again, Nina and I together, it definitely brought back some things from the past. A distant memory of us.

I just hoped this didn't push her further away from me.

I glanced at Maddie. She nodded and took Ayla's arm, pulling her out of the room.

As soon as the door closed, I stood up and faced the window, my muscles coiled with tension. "I hated doing this."

Punching the wall beside me, I closed my eyes.

"If I'm honest, it was pretty awkward. But did you find what you wanted?" Nina asked quietly.

"Yeah, I did. I just need to see the aftermath now," I muttered, my chest feeling heavy. My lungs were drawn up tight, and it was harder to breathe.

"I hope it works out," she said before leaving.

I stayed in the office for a few more minutes. Pacing the length of it, I couldn't shake the image of Ayla's tears.

Fear and worry were instilled inside of me, choking me. When I couldn't take it anymore, I walked out of the office. I knew Ayla would be waiting for me in our room. Maddie was strictly instructed to bring her back there.

I paused outside the door, feeling suddenly nervous.

Frustrated at the uncertainty, my fingers clenched into fists, and I took a deep breath.

I opened the door and walked inside to find Ayla sitting on the bed. Her head snapped up toward mine, her shoulder tensed. I saw fear in her eyes, but it was quickly gone when she saw it was me.

She stood up, her hand going to her throat. It was nervousness.

Ayla looked at me, her chest moving up and down, her breathing harsh. I took a step forward, and Ayla choked back a sob.

She walked back until she touched the wall. Ayla shook her head several times, and she rubbed at her throat furiously.

I saw her face crumble, and she cried quietly. When I tried to move forward again, she shook her head. Her eyes went wide, and she gasped for breath.

"I…I…breathe…can't…breathe…"

"Shit!" I swore, moving forward in a rush. Taking her in my arms, I carried Ayla to the bed.

I sat down on the edge, placing her on my lap. "Calm down. It's okay. Don't try to breathe too fast. Take it slow. Shh…I got you, Angel. Slow breath. In and out."

Ayla laid her head on my shoulders, but I heard her taking slow breaths, just like I told her.

When her breathing finally calmed, I heard her crying softly on my shoulder. I kept holding her in my embrace, never once letting go.

Ayla didn't try to move away, either. No, she had a death grip on my arms.

Her tears made my heart ache in the most painful

way.

It was a strange mixture of emotions building up inside of me. Agony and happiness. I didn't know which one to hold on to.

So instead, I just held my Angel. I let her be my anchor, while I was hers.

When her tears finally dried, I shifted her in my arms and laid her on the bed.

He eyes were closed, but her face was red and puffy from crying. This was the second time she cried since we rescued her. Both reasons had nothing to do with her captivity but everything to do with me.

In that moment, I realized that all my efforts were not going to waste. She knew me. Ayla felt me deep inside her heart.

I had to continue believing in us.

Giving her a final glance, I went to get up but felt something tighten around my wrist.

My eyes widened, and I looked down to see Ayla holding the edge of my sleeve, stopping me from stepping away.

My head snapped up, and I saw that her eyes were open. Our gaze made contact, and we stared. We breathed. A matching rhythm between us.

I saw Ayla swallow several times. She looked down at my hand before staring into my eyes again.

I waited...I didn't know for how long, but I waited.

Her lips finally parted, and her voice was melody to my ears.

"Can...you...please hold...me?"

The words were softly spoken. She stuttered

them but never took her eyes off mine.

My heart leaped and danced. My stomach tightened, and with my heart in my throat, I nodded.

"I'll hold you, Angel. I will hold you however long you want me to." Leaning forward until our noses were touching, I said, "And even when you don't want me to hold you anymore, I still won't let you go."

I saw her cheeks grow redder. Placing a kiss on the tip of her nose, I laid down beside Ayla.

Before I could move, she turned toward me and burrowed into my chest. I smiled then.

I wrapped my arms around her hips, pulling her closer. Her stomach was in the way, but I worked around it. When she was firmly held in my embrace, I kissed her cheek.

She sighed in my chest, her arms tightening around my waist. My heart soared.

We were both quiet.

I was almost asleep when she broke the silence.

Her words took me by surprise. Hell, her voice was a shock to me. I didn't expect her to speak again. But she did.

And I had never expected her to utter those words.

"You are my savior," she whispered so softly into my chest.

Her arms were a band of steel around my hips. I was her savior. Just like before.

My nose prickled with emotions. It was almost too much to bear, so I could only imagine what Ayla was going through.

"You are *my* savior," she whispered again. "Not

hers."

My eyes widened, finally understanding where she was going. The words were filled with innocence, her voice sounding so childlike, almost scared.

"You are not hers," she continued brokenly, stealing my breath away.

Bringing my hand up, I placed a finger under her chin and tilted her head up. She stared at me tearfully. Her green eyes were glassy. It reminded me of the first time we met.

"You...won't leave me?" she asked softly.

I shook my head and pressed our foreheads together. "No. No. No. Ayla, I won't leave you."

"She won't...take you...from me?" Her expression was so broken. She looked so hurt and scared.

I brought her body closer to mine. "No, Ayla. I'm never leaving you. I made a promise to you before. I said I won't ever leave you. I'm keeping that promise. She won't take me away from you."

Our lips joined together in a feather-light touch. "You are my Angel."

Ayla closed her eyes, and I felt the tension in her shoulders slowly slipping away.

"When I...was with...the Devil...you were my savior. You are not hers. You can't...be hers," Ayla continued, breaking my heart further.

"Shh...I'm not hers. I'm yours, Angel. Only yours. I was yours before. I am now. And I will always be yours. Just like you are mine," I whispered in her ears, hoping she would remember those words later.

"Just like I am your savior. You are my beautiful Angel."

She hummed against my chest. Her eyes were closed, and I knew she was quickly drifting off to sleep.

Smiling, I stared at the beauty in my arms.

I am going to wait for you, Angel. Forever. This is my fucking vow to you.

Chapter 10

1 week later

"Turn around," I ordered softly. Ayla did as she was told and gave me her back.

"Is the water too hot?" I asked, soaping up her spine.

"No," she replied quietly.

I smiled at her answer and continued to wash her. I rubbed down her legs and then turned her around. Squeezing some shampoo in my palm, I massaged her hair.

She closed her eyes and leaned toward me. I chuckled and quickly rinsed her off. "There you go. All done."

Ayla opened her eyes and stared at me, her eyes void of any emotion. "Thank you."

I kissed her lips and helped her out of the shower. After wrapping towels around us both, I dried her hair.

She sighed almost dreamily before leaning against my chest. "Does that feel good?"

"Yes." She nodded.

"Do you want me to brush your hair?"

She nodded again. "Please."

We walked into the bedroom, and she settled on the bed. I climbed behind her and started to comb her hair until it was smooth and shiny.

"All done," I muttered, kissing her shoulder. "You look beautiful, Angel."

I saw a small hint of a smile on her lips. It made me giddy, seeing our progress.

"The most beautiful." The corner of her lips tilted up in a ghost smile. "What about me?" I teased.

I got off the bed and stood in front of her. Ayla stared up at me, her mouth open. I knew I was pushing it. Ayla didn't speak more than a few words.

Yes. No. Okay. Please. Thank you.

Sometimes she would speak a sentence if it was something she really wanted to say. But that was rarely.

If she spoke, it was only to me.

It drove Maddie crazy that Ayla wouldn't speak to her.

Ayla was mostly quiet and observant.

If she showed any emotions, it was because I did something that reminded her of the past. She still hadn't played a song on the piano.

But I knew being in that room brought her peace. Just like the creek. She always wore a serene look on her face whenever she was there.

Her eyes would twinkle in the slightest way, showing the little bits of happiness she was feeling in those moments.

Ayla cleared her throat, snapping me out of my thoughts. She bit down on her lips nervously and looked down at her lap.

"It's okay," I quickly amended.

Holding her chin, I smiled. "You don't have to say anything you don't want to."

Giving her a kiss on the forehead, I pulled away. "I need to go change."

"You are beautiful."

My mouth fell open, and I quickly snapped it shut. I almost choked on my breath and had to swallow several times.

She had said it so quick, and now she was avoiding my eyes.

I smiled. She was so precious.

I couldn't help but smirk when I answered. "Thank you, Angel. Although I wouldn't have minded if you called me sinfully, deliciously sexy. It would have done great wonders for my already big ego."

She sucked in a surprised breath, her eyes widening. "You remember that too?" I muttered.

When she didn't answer, I kissed her lips and pulled away. "I need to take care of some things. You can nap, and we will go to the piano room when I get back."

Ayla nodded mutely, and I went into the closet. After dressing, I walked out to see Ayla already in bed.

Giving her a final glance, I walked out.

I met Viktor in the gym. "Ayla spoke for the first time when she saw me hurt," I started.

Viktor stared at me in surprise and then smirked before busting into laughter. "Oh, this is going to be fun."

"Fuck you," I growled, landing a punch on the punching bag. My knuckles were bare, and I knew they would be bleeding soon.

"Sorry, not interested. I love wet pussies better," Viktor laughed, rolling his sleeves up.

I landed more furious punches against the bag, my knuckles already raw and the skin bleeding.

"So how badly do you want me to fuck you up?" he asked, moving closer.

"I thought you said you were interested in pussies?"

"Can I use your spiral knife?"

"No," I snapped.

Viktor huffed. "Fine."

I didn't have time to block his punch. It landed painfully in my ribcage, and I groaned. I bellowed, "You have a death wish."

"You asked for it."

"Shit. She only needs to see me hurt a little! Just to trigger her memories."

"Oops, okay. You should have said that before." Viktor shrugged.

I glared at him and kicked at his knee. He went down. "You crazy fucker!"

It was my turn to shrug. "Lesson one. Always be on your guard."

We fought for hours. It turned out that it was more than just trying to make Ayla feel. We fought out our anger and self-loathing.

Our anger toward the men that had hurt Ayla was

taken out on each other. Phoenix and Nikolay soon joined us.

"I can't breathe. I think I broke something," Viktor wheezed.

"Pussy," Phoenix breathed through his pain.

"You went down before all of us," Nikolay reminded Phoenix.

I shook my head and limped out of the gym. I was time to get to my Angel.

I opened the door and saw Ayla sitting on the bed, staring blankly at the wall. Her eyes snapped toward mine. I stayed hidden in the shadows.

"I'll wait for you in the piano room."

Without a second glance, I left the room and went next door. Settling in my chair, I waited for her.

The door opened, and I heard a gasp. "Alessio," she breathed.

I closed my eyes at her voice. The sound of my name coming from her lips was heaven. For so long, I waited for this. For her to say my name.

Opening my eyes again, I saw Ayla coming toward me. She knelt down between my legs. "What...ha...ppened?"

Her voice was soft. But it was her eyes that got to me. She looked at me as if she was in pain.

"You are hurt," she whispered, looking down at my bloodied hands.

She was feeling *my* pain.

Ayla searched my face, and she winced when she saw the bruises there. "I was sparring. It's nothing."

"But you are hurt," Ayla said, taking my hands in hers. She bit on her lips nervously before looking around the room.

I knew what she was looking for.

"The first aid box is in our room. First drawer in the closet," I muttered. Ayla stared at me for a second. Recognition flashed in her eyes before she nodded.

She got up and left the room.

I closed my eyes with a sigh. I was so fucking proud of her.

When she came back, I opened my eyes and saw her kneeling between my legs again. Ayla went through the first aid box, and I helped her pick the antiseptic wipes and bandages.

She stared at my hands for a second, her eyebrows furrowed. Her gaze went up to mine before moving to my hands again.

And then Ayla slowly cleaned my knuckles. Gently and with care. She cleaned the blood off and blew softly over my ripped skin.

I couldn't take my eyes off her. Was she feeling this connection too? Did this moment mean something to her?

When she was done, she wrapped the bandages around my hands.

"Thank you, Angel."

She nodded mutely, still staring at my bandaged hands, confused.

"Does this seem familiar?" I finally asked.

Ayla gave me a sharp nod. "You've done this before. In this same room. And just like today, you were hurting for me."

Her fingers caressed my bandaged knuckles. "You might have forgotten me, but I still remember you. I still remember us. You used to play the piano for me every night. You would read while sitting on my lap. I would play with your hair while working. Sometimes we would go to the creek. You would play in the water. I was always scared that you would fall and get hurt," I explained, my voice rough with emotion.

She moved closer to me and laid her head on my thigh.

"Your favorite flower is the white peony. But you love the pink one too. You love reading. You don't know how to dance. I don't know either. But we danced together. I love your hair down, so you would always leave it down for me. Your favorite food is pasta. You like chocolate, especially white chocolate. You hate dark chocolate—it's too bitter for you. You would get mad if I didn't wake you up in the morning when I was leaving. I would get mad if you didn't kiss me good morning."

Ayla closed her eyes as I caressed her cheek. "You said I was your peace. Your anchor and your savior. You are my Angel. We are one. I just need you to remember."

Ayla stayed silent, but I could see the calm look on her face. After a few minutes of silence, I spoke.

"Play for me, Angel."

Ayla sat up and stared at me. Our eyes making contact. Green to blue.

She let out a resigned sigh. I knew it was harder for her to remember. "Give it a try."

She got up and went to the piano. When Ayla settled on the bench, I stood up and went to her. Standing behind her, I placed my hand over her round stomach.

When a hard kick pressed against my palm, I smiled. "The little fighter is feisty. He is cheering you on too."

Ayla placed her fingers on the keyboard, and I waited. She pressed a key. A note played. And then another key.

Two notes and she stopped. Her shoulder dropped in defeat.

When I couldn't bear the dejected look on her face any longer, I leaned forward. "It's okay, Angel. We have all the time. You can try when you are ready. I won't push you."

Ayla stayed quiet, and I kissed her cheek before moving my lips to her ear.

And then I whispered the one thing I had been desperate to say for a long time.

She stiffened, and I saw her hands shaking.

My lips turned up in a smile.

When I saw a single tear trail down her cheek, I kissed it away and whispered the words again.

"I love you, my Angel."

Chapter 11

The words slipped past my lips effortlessly. I said them without any remorse but full with adoration for the woman in front of me.

A year ago, I wouldn't have believed those words were possible. But now, it felt like I would suffocate if I didn't say them.

My chest felt lighter, and I finally could breathe. Ever since Ayla was taken from me, I regretted never saying those words to her.

Maybe it was because I never realized them before. I never thought of loving someone. Hell, I never thought I was capable of loving someone.

The moment Ayla was snatched from me, I realized my mistake.

She was everything and more. I would cherish her for the rest of our lives.

My hand lingered on Ayla's cheek. Another tear fell, and I trailed the drop with the tip of my finger. I saw her breathing change, and her cheeks flushed beautifully.

Ayla closed her eyes tightly, and she took a deep

breath. I waited for her reaction. I waited for her to say something—anything.

When she didn't respond, I kissed her cheek and leaned back, giving her space. I would wait for her, for however long needed.

Ayla opened her eyes again and stared at the piano. With her fingers resting on the keyboard, she caressed the piano keys gently. She appeared lost in her thoughts. Her eyebrows were furrowed in concentration.

A frustrated sound escaped past her lips, and I saw droplets of sweat start to form on her forehead and neck. When her hands tightened in fists, my heart sank.

Wrapping my arms around her waist, I lifted her up. After taking her place on the bench, I pulled Ayla on my lap. She froze for a moment. I saw her swallow hard before slowly settling against me. She burrowed in my chest and sighed almost dreamily.

"You want to remember, don't you?" I asked, holding her hands in mine. Ayla nodded, hiding her face in my chest.

I sighed, entwining our fingers together. "I want you to remember too."

She didn't say anything. Silence fell upon us, and for the first time, I didn't like the silence between us. I wanted her voice.

Ayla took her hands out of mine and placed them on the piano again. I sucked in a sharp breath as her fingers made contact with the piano keys.

My lungs felt like they were pressed together as I fought to breathe.

Ayla pressed down on the keys, and a few notes

filled the room. My heart stuttered when she closed her eyes, a pained look on her face.

My Angel hiccupped back a sob and pushed her face in my chest again. Her voice was a mere whisper. "I...can't..."

Tilting her head up, I kissed her softly. "Let me in, Angel. Just give me a chance to prove to you that there is a beautiful world out there. Let me love you the way you deserve," I begged against her full lips.

I sat frozen when Ayla brought her hands up. Her hands hovered over my cheeks for a second. I caught the flash of uncertainty on her face before she finally palmed my cheeks. Her eyes were closed, but her fingers moved over my rough stubble.

Ayla mindlessly caressed my cheek as she let out a pained sigh. "I don't remember. I try, but I can't."

She laid her head on my shoulder, her hand still touching me. "My head...hurts when I try."

Ayla brought her other hand to my chest. "And it hurts here too. I don't want to remember...because it hurts."

I didn't realize I was holding my breath until my chest began to burn. I forced myself to relax even though I was feeling anything but calm.

A mixture of grief, pain, regret, and love swamped me as I fought to catch my breath. So much grief. For everything we had lost. And love— for this woman.

I held her hand firmly against my chest, right over my wildly beating heart. "I'm in pain too, Angel," I said quietly. "Every time I see you in pain, it hurts."

Her hand paused over my cheek. "I...don't want you to...hurt. I don't like it."

I held her tighter, sadness so thick in my chest I could barely breathe. My heart ached at her words and the sorrow in her voice.

This woman. I shook my head. She was hurt and in pain, yet she was worried for me.

"Alessio," she murmured. My lungs squeezed at the sound of my name.

"Do you know how much I love hearing my name from your lips?" I said to her. I would never grow tired of hearing Ayla say my name.

She hummed against my neck. "I remember your name. And...your eyes."

My lips tilted in a small smile. She actually remembered me. "Say my name again," I begged softly.

"Alessio," she whispered. I felt her smile without even seeing it. My own smile widened, my chest finally feeling lighter. Placing a kiss on her forehead, I stood up with Ayla in my arms.

She wrapped her arms around my neck, holding on to me as I carried us back to our room. Just when I was about to place Ayla on the bed, I heard a knock on the door.

"Come in," I called out, already knowing who it was. Ayla settled on the bed and looked over my shoulder. A half-smile curved her lips, and her face softened.

"Ah, there is my girl," Lena said, stopping beside the bed. She pushed me away and sat down beside Ayla.

Lena placed a small bowl of warm coconut oil on the nightstand. "Are you ready for your massage?" she asked with a wink.

Ayla nodded enthusiastically. She looked up at me, a beautiful smile playing across her lips. Her cheeks were slightly flushed with giddy excitement. She looked…happy. A little shy, but at peace.

"Here," Lena said, adjusting the pillow and helping Ayla recline back. Ayla pulled her dress up until her rounded stomach was bare. Her hands went to the bump, and she caressed it softly.

I couldn't take my eyes off her. With her black hair spread across the pillow, her cheeks pink, and her green eyes twinkling, she looked like an Angel. She was glowing.

"I loved having my belly rubbed when I was pregnant with Maddie," Lena said, her voice snapping me out of my thoughts. She took some oil in her hand and brought it to Ayla's stomach.

Lena had been doing that for a few nights now. And it was something Ayla excitedly waited for. I could see it was how Lena and her bonded again.

I watched Ayla stare at her stomach as Lena rubbed the warm coconut oil over the roundness. I saw the bump move under Lena's touch.

"Ah, she is dancing in there," Lena laughed. "Such a happy baby."

Lena continued to gently massage Ayla's stomach. "You have a beautiful pregnant belly. But you see how your skin is stretched tight?"

Ayla nodded, waiting for Lena to continue. "The coconut oil will smooth out your tight belly. This way you won't feel too uncomfortable. And it soothes itching skin too."

Ayla nodded again. She bit on her lips, suddenly looking nervous. Her eyes went up to meet mine before quickly moving back to Lena's. "It feels good," she whispered.

Lena paused, her lips parting in surprise. It was the first time Ayla spoke to her. From where I was standing, I saw tears forming in her eyes, and she looked down at Ayla's stomach.

"I'm glad," Lena replied, her voice a little hoarse. I took a few steps back, giving them privacy. This was their moment.

Lena talked mindlessly. And Ayla, she listened attentively, taking every word in.

After massaging the baby bump and Ayla's back, Lena pulled the comforter over her.

Ayla was almost asleep. Her eyes were drooping, her breathing evening out. A small contented smile was still on her lips.

Lena came to stand in front of me. She patted my cheeks. "Keep doing what you're doing. She...spoke to me after so long. And I know, if it wasn't for you fighting to bring her back, she would have never taken that step. It's all you."

My chest grew tight at her words. My eyes moved to Ayla's sleeping form, and I could almost feel my heart stutter.

"She's been through hell. But you give her so much love, all the love you can give, so it'll erase her pain and suffering. Don't stop loving her," Lena whispered before leaving.

She closed the door, leaving me alone with her words ringing through my ears.

She has been through hell.

I pinched my eyes closed at the reminder.

My beautiful Angel.

I dug my hand into my hair. I was the cause of her pain and suffering. If I had protected her, this wouldn't have happened. I fucking failed her.

My eyes opened to see Ayla sound asleep. She was holding her bump, and my throat felt tight.

Ayla should have been loved, cherished, and pampered all through her pregnancy. She should have been waited on hand and foot, treated like a queen.

But instead, she had to live through hell. *He* broke her.

I took a step toward the bed, fighting the tears. If only I could rewrite the past.

Don't stop loving her.

Never. I could never stop loving her. It was impossible. She was under my skin, etched deep in my heart. Ayla had broken through my walls and was there to stay.

My father was right. I was incomplete without her.

Ayla was like a drug. The most addictive kind.

Stopping in front of the bed, I caressed Ayla's hair. She moaned sleepily and didn't wake up. Smiling, I climbed on the bed and pulled her into my arms.

Ayla settled in my embrace and wrapped her arm around my waist. She pushed her face in my chest and sighed sleepily.

Ayla once said that she was fire. I had to agree. She was fire. We were both burning, but it was too late. There was no stopping our love—it was indestructible.

Chapter 12

Ayla

Do you want to play?

I ran my fingers on the keys but never pressed down. Opening my eyes again, I looked directly at Alessio. He was staring at me intently, waiting.

With our gazes still connected, I let my fingers move. Softly. Gently. And a sweet melody came through. The music washed around us like a slow, gentle wave, and I smiled.

You can keep playing the piano if you want.

Play for me, Angel.

I want to hear you play.

I woke up with a start, my eyes snapping wide.

Do you want to play?

The words resonated in my ears.

Play for me, Angel.

I looked down at Alessio and saw him waking up too. He quickly sat up, staring at me in confusion.

"Angel?"

Play for me, Angel.

I rubbed at my chest, trying to get rid of the tightness there.

You can keep playing the piano if you want.

My eyes moved to the door, my breathing coming out faster than before.

"Ayla, what's wrong?" Alessio asked.

Play for me, Angel.

My fingers were itching. The urge was fierce and intense. My body was humming with the need to play. I didn't understand the feeling.

But it felt like I would suffocate if I didn't play.

Alessio's voice kept ringing through my ears.

All the memories were coming like flashes behind my eyes.

Play for me, Angel.

I gasped, trying to breathe as my lungs constricted. Without thinking, I got out of bed. I felt a sharp pain in my stomach but ignored it.

I heard Alessio calling my name...I ignored him too. I ran out of the bedroom, my feet taking me to the piano room. I opened the door and walked inside.

I turned on the lights, and the room was instantly illuminated. I felt Alessio behind me, and my tensed shoulders started to relax.

Taking a deep breath, I walked further inside and stopped in front of the piano.

"Angel," Alessio whispered. I could hear the surprise in his voice.

Do you want to play?

Yes. Yes. Yes. I wanted to play. There was a fiery desperation in my heart. I wanted to break down and cry from the feeling. It was too much. It felt too much.

Play for me, Angel.

I wanted to. I wanted to play for Alessio.

But I didn't know how.

I closed my eyes, feeling a slow ache in my temple.

Play for me, Angel.

I sat down on the bench, keeping my eyes closed.

The moment my fingers made contact with the piano, I was lost. Lost in this feeling that took over me.

I was no longer my own. My mind went back to so many days ago.

My fingers glided over the piano. I didn't think. I just let it happen.

Softly. Gently. I played.

Notes kept spilling from the piano, and a sweet melody came through. The music washed over me like a sweet, gentle wave.

I opened my eyes and made direct contact with Alessio's blue ones. He was sitting on the couch, his expression filled with astonishment.

I saw it change into something else. I didn't understand what it was, but his face softened, and a smile played across his lips.

He brought his fists to his lips. I noticed his hands shaking.

My lips moved…I was *smiling*.

With the melody playing around us, I stared at Alessio.

We stared at each other.

Blue to green.

It felt like I could finally breathe.

In that moment, I forgot everything. Every hurt. Every pain. Every bad memory.

Only this moment existed.

Me playing the piano. Alessio watching me.

I felt…peace.

I didn't realize the song had ended and I had stop playing until Alessio stood up. Snapping out of my daze, I watched him move beside me.

Alessio knelt down beside me and took my hands in his. "Do you remember, Angel?"

My heart sank at his question. Shaking my head, I closed my eyes in despair.

"I only remember playing…the piano. I don't even remember the song or how I played. It…just…happened," I said quietly.

"Open your eyes, Ayla."

My eyes snapped open at his demand. "It's okay. Take your time. I will wait for you," he soothed.

He palmed my cheeks. "Hearing you play, that was the most beautiful thing ever. I feel like I can finally breathe, Angel."

He was the same as me. I pinched my eyes closed when they stung. Alessio swept me up in his arms and carried me out of the room.

On the bed, I burrowed deeper into his chest. His lips touched my forehead softly.

This was how we fell asleep. In each other's arms.

And nothing hurt.

***

"You know, I'm feeling very jealous right now. You talk to Alessio and even spoke to Mom a few days ago. How is that fair?"

The woman with dark hair wrapped her arms with mine. Her name was Maddie. She was always with me if Alessio wasn't. She took me everywhere around the house. Maddie spoke a lot too.

"You still won't speak to me," she muttered.

My chest grew tight at her pained expression. "Why won't you talk to me? Are you angry with me?"

I shook my head quickly. Swallowing hard, I looked in her eyes. She seemed familiar, but I just couldn't remember her.

When I didn't say anything, she sighed and gave me a sad smile. I didn't like the sad smile on her face. She was nice and sweet. Just like Alessio and Lena.

Maddie started to walk again, but I didn't. She turned around and faced me. "What's wrong?"

I closed my eyes and took a deep breath. Opening my eyes again, I looked at her. "I...don't remember you."

Her mouth fell open. We stared at each other in silence before she started laughing.

I didn't understand why she was laughing. She wiped away tears from her eyes and pulled me into her arms.

"Ayla, you just made me the happiest woman," she said in my neck.

I hugged her back.

Her laughter died, and I heard sniffling. My heart stuttered when I felt wetness on my neck. Was she crying?

I went to pull away, but her arms tightened. "I'm sorry, Ayla. I'm so sorry. If only I knew," she cried.

What was she talking about?

Maddie continued to sob. "It hurts, Ayla. It hurts so much. Sometimes it feels like I can't breathe. I lost him. I...lost...him. I'll never hold him."

Confused, I just hugged her. I didn't understand what was happening. I didn't know how to help, so I just held her. Like Alessio held me when I was hurting.

I hoped it was enough for Maddie.

When Maddie finally calmed down, she pulled away. She gave me a sweet smile. "Thank you," she whispered. "I needed that."

Bringing my hand up, I wiped her tears. "Okay," I replied.

Maddie's lips wobbled, and she pinched her eyes closed. "Damn it, Ayla. Don't make me cry again."

"I don't...like...it when you cry."

"You really are an Angel." She laughed.

I nodded. "Alessio calls me Angel."

Maddie rolled her eyes. "Yeah, because he is such a romantic at heart."

She raised an eyebrow at me. "I will tell you a secret."

"Okay," I said as she pulled me closer.

"If it wasn't for me, that hard-ass Mafia man and his Angel would have never been one. Let's just say, I'm the captain of the ship."

Maddie winked and smiled. She was really pretty when she smiled.

"I don't understand," I finally said.

"You don't have to understand. Just know that this ship will never sink under my watch," Maddie replied.

We walked down the stairs, but my steps froze when I saw who was standing at the bottom. Maddie stopped beside me too.

"Ayla, how nice to see you again."

The woman with blonde hair smiled at me, but it didn't look nice. She was the same woman who was with Alessio before.

I felt a sudden surge of emotion inside of me.

I didn't like her.

"Nina," Maddie growled beside me.

The name sounded so familiar. I felt like I knew her before. But I couldn't remember.

"Fine, I won't say anything *this* time."

"Please don't. Nobody wants to hear your bullshit," Maddie snapped.

Nina rolled her eyes and walked up the stairs. She kept her eyes on me, and I almost shuddered at the cold look she gave me.

"I don't know why Alessio is still interested in you," she muttered, walking past me.

You are so...stiff

Do you really think you can keep Alessio interested for long?

I'm more like him. We have always been compatible.

My lips parted as the memory crashed through me.

"I remember you," I said, turning around. Nina

stopped and faced me.

"Oh really?" she asked, raising an eyebrow.

I didn't understand the memories, but they were there. She was there.

I rubbed my forehead, trying to get rid of the small ache.

"I don't like you," I whispered.

I saw Nina smile. But it was quickly gone.

"I know," she said before walking away.

Maddie huffed beside me and started to pull me down the stairs. "I swear I will kick her one day."

I was still lost in my thoughts, trying to understand what just happened, when Maddie halted in her steps.

I stopped and looked up to see Alessio coming through the door. At the sight of me, he quickly made his way to us.

Alessio pressed his lips on mine and then said, "Do you want to go the creek?"

I simply nodded, lost in his embrace and beautiful blue eyes.

I quickly forgot about Nina. I only saw Alessio.

He nodded at Maddie and pulled me away. I waved at Maddie and followed Alessio.

We walked away from the house and toward the trees. My hand was held firmly in his much bigger one while we made our way to the creek.

The trees started to clear up, and I could hear the sound of rushing water. My heart drummed faster, and I felt giddy.

We stopped in the middle of the clearing, surrounded by flowers.

Alessio knelt down in front of me and removed

my sandals. "You love to be barefooted here."

"Thank you," I murmured when he stood up.

He stepped back and walked toward the flowing water. I remembered this.

Closing my eyes, I let the memories take over my mind. My heart felt lighter, and I breathed in the fresh air.

My eyes opened when I got closer to the water. I looked back at Alessio. His arms were crossed over his chest as he stared at me.

My gaze moved back toward the water. I stepped forward, my feet making contact with the chilling, rushing water. I shivered as I walked ankle deep.

I felt the rushing water against my feet and closed my eyes, letting this new feeling wash over me.

I didn't hurt.

It felt nice...I felt content.

When I felt an arm around my waist, I leaned back against Alessio's chest.

"May I have this dance, Angel?"

My eyes snapped opened.

May I have this dance, Angel?

We had done this before. I turned in his arms, and Alessio pulled us out of the room. My feet dug into the grass as I stared into his eyes.

"I don't know how to dance," I muttered, completely lost in his gaze.

Alessio chuckled. "Neither do I."

He brought my hands to his shoulders and wrapped his around my waist.

And then we moved. We glided across the field, and with each step, my chest felt fuller.

My stomach rolled and twisted. My heart drummed just a little faster.

We never once broke eye contact.

We were lost in each other.

Alessio gathered me even closer to him, his arms tight around me.

In that moment, all I felt was peace. I felt protected. Safe.

He was my lifeline.

And I knew, as long as my savior was with me, I was safe.

Chapter 13

I was sitting on the bed waiting for my Alessio. My hand was on my round stomach, feeling the baby move.

The door opened, and Alessio walked out of the bathroom. His towel was around his shoulders as he dried his hair. His chest was bare; he wore only black sweatpants.

Alessio caught my eyes and smiled. "Why don't you go and wait for me in the piano room?"

I nodded and got up. Alessio placed a quick kiss on my lips as I walked out of the room. I stood in front of the piano room.

Taking a deep breath, I walked inside. The piano was the first thing I saw. Feeling excited, my body hummed in response.

Since I started playing some days ago, Alessio and I never missed a night.

Playing made me feel at peace, and I wanted to bask in the warmth of Alessio's stares.

Walking further into the room, I stopped beside Alessio's couch. A small sigh escaped my lips as I waited for Alessio.

As I was looking down, something else entirely caught my eyes.

My gaze shifted toward the couch beside Alessio's, and I took a step toward it. My breath froze in my throat.

I took another step, stopping right in front of the couch.

The scene, right here, felt so familiar.

Even through the shock, my eyes didn't lose focus on the sight in front of me.

A single white flower lay on the seat.

It looked so soft and delicate. Reaching out, I took the flower in my hand and brought it to my chest.

I was right. It was soft and delicate. The petals were open, and it looked absolutely beautiful.

Did Alessio leave this flower for me?

I couldn't help but smile. Of course he would.

He was so sweet.

I held the flower close to my racing heart and closed my eyes.

My stomach flipped, and it felt like my heart was dancing.

"I can safely assume that you love the peony."

My eyes widened at Alessio's voice, and I turned around, facing him. He was leaning against the door, regarding me with curious yet adoring eyes.

His head was cocked to the side, and the corner of his mouth was stretched up in a half smile.

My cheeks burned, and I looked down. "I love it," I replied softly. "It's really beautiful."

Alessio walked closer and stopped in front of

me. He tilted my chin up so our gazes met. His was filled with warmth. His eyes shifted to my lips, and I licked them nervously.

He moved even closer, until our chests brushed together. I sucked in a deep breath and waited for him move.

"I'm going to kiss you," he murmured, his gaze moving back to my lips.

"Okay," I whispered back.

As soon as the words were out of my mouth, a flash of pain went through my skull. I winced, my fingers tightening around the flower.

Memories after memories flashed behind my closed eyes.

I couldn't stop them. They kept coming without a pause. So much. Too much at the same time. My head felt like it was going to explode.

My heart raced as each memory made its way into my thoughts.

Another wave of pain crashed through me. It was crippling, and I dropped the flower, my hands going to my head.

I dug my fingers in my head, the world spinning around me.

No. No. No. No.

Stop!

It hurt. It hurt so much.

"Ayla!" I heard a voice calling out my name.

Alessio. He was calling for me.

I tried to respond, but my tongue felt heavy. My lips parted, but instead a wounded cry left my mouth.

My throat closed up, and I rubbed at my neck

furiously, trying to fight for my next breath.

My knees buckled, but an arm caught me. "Ayla! Fuck."

My head pounded as I sank into oblivion.

This. This was why I didn't want to remember.

The pain. It felt like my heart was being wrenched open. I was bleeding. From the inside, I was being cut open.

I would never forget the pain. I wanted to forget; I wanted to be numb.

But it was too late now.

I had remembered, and now I had to live with those memories.

Chapter 14

My head ached as my eyes slowly opened. I felt heavy. I blinked my eyes open, trying to understand what just happened.

I focused on the ceiling, my head a little fuzzy.

"Ayla?"

At the sound of my name, I turned my head toward the voice. My eyes made contact with blues one.

Alessio!

My heart stuttered, and I let out a choked cry. I remembered everything. Every moment. Every word he said. And everything after.

Alberto.

My eyes widened, and I sat up quickly. There was no escaping him.

"Shhh…I'm right here, Angel," Alessio soothed. He held my hands in his as he tried to smile. He looked worried, and I saw the fear in his eyes.

I couldn't stop the tears. Alessio found me. He was here. He was really here.

He saved me…

I was safe.

He took me away from hell.

My heart soared, and I quickly scrambled into his lap. "Alessio," I sobbed, wrapping my arms around him.

Burying my face in his neck, I cried. I had believed in Alessio. I had trusted him.

For once, I was happy that I never lost hope.

No matter what, I knew he would come for me.

My heart soared, and I held him tighter. I never wanted to let go.

I would never let go. He was mine as much as I was his. The day our eyes met, our fate had been decided.

"I got you, Angel."

Those words. His voice. It had the same effect on my heart just as before. His voice was exactly what I needed to hear.

And those words…I had been desperate for them.

I knew he got me. He always did.

Alessio held me against him, and he whispered sweet words in my ears, letting me know he was *here*.

He placed gentle kisses over my face, soothing away all the pain.

"Alessio," I whispered brokenly. "I remember, Alessio."

His arms tightened around my waist. His lips pressed against my temple. "You remember?" he asked hoarsely.

I could hear the emotion in his voice. His hands were shaking on my hips, and I held him tighter. I nodded against his neck. "I remember everything."

Alessio pulled away so he could stare at me. His eyes roamed over my face and then stared deep into my eyes. I saw the glassy look in his.

"You really remember?" he asked again, his soft voice caressing me.

When I nodded, Alessio crushed me to his chest. "Ayla. Fuck. I was worried. So scared. I thought...you would never..."

"You found me," I hiccupped back a sob.

"I found you. I will always find you, Angel," he agreed. I looked up, staring into his captivating blue eyes.

"Alessio, I'm not the traitor."

His hand pressed against my lips, stopping my flow of words. "No. You are not. I know you aren't. I never thought you were. I trusted you before, and I trust you now."

"You believe me? But...before...at the beach..."

Alessio flinched at the memory, and even I felt a sharp pain in my chest.

"I was hurt, Ayla. I just found out the woman I desperately love was an Abandonato. I was just angry, but never once did I think you were the spy. I just needed some time alone. When I had time to think, I understood why you didn't say anything," he explained.

I saw him swallow hard. He bent his head until our foreheads were touching. "I didn't turn away from you because you were an Abandonato. I turned away because I was hurt that you lied. When I finally came to terms with everything, I was too late. You were already gone. I ran after you, but I

115

was still too late. Ayla, that day...I had never felt such pain. It felt like I was being torn apart."

My throat closed up. "I fought, Alessio. I fought against him. I didn't go easily. I screamed for you. He said...he said that you didn't want to see me. He said you were giving me away."

Alessio's expression thundered with fury. "Who?" he growled. But I saw a hint of recognition in his eyes.

"Artur," I whispered. "He gave me to Alberto. He said you never wanted...to see me again."

When his face twisted in pain, I quickly added, "But I didn't believe him."

Alessio pressed his lips ever so gently on mine. The kiss was so soft, almost feather light. I could taste our tears as our lips made contact.

"I never said those words, Angel. You are my everything. I would never think of giving you away," he admitted, his voice filled with distress.

"I know. I believed in us, Alessio," I said, wrapping my arms around his head. I held him to me, our lips still touching.

"I believed in us, too. I never stopped believing."

At his words, my heart raced. My chest didn't feel like it would explode anything. I felt...lighter.

"You kept me from going crazy," I muttered, closing my eyes as he peppered my face with kisses.

Alessio wrapped his arms around me, and we held each other. I sighed and burrowed deeper into his safe embrace. I felt loved...cherished...adored and protected.

I felt his cheek in my palm, feeling his rough stubble. When was the last time he shaved? My hands roamed over his face, touching him, feeling him.

I ran my fingers over his lips, and he kissed my fingertips. I closed my eyes as a loving feeling washed over me.

I sat up straighter on his lap and kissed his lips. I never wanted to stop touching him.

But my thoughts halted when I felt a kick. Looking down, I stared at my round stomach. I felt Alessio follow my gaze.

My nose stung as I fought against the tears.

When I felt another kick, it was impossible. I cried, holding my stomach, feeling my baby move.

Alessio placed his hand over mine. We held the bump firmly, protectively.

"He hurt me, Alessio," I whispered. "He hurt me so much. He kept going. It didn't matter that I cried and begged him to stop. He just...kept going. He kept hurting me. Over and over again," I cried, my hands pressing firmly against my stomach.

The tears streamed down my cheeks as the baby moved again. Oh, baby.

I pressed my face into Alessio's neck. "He was so cruel. He never stopped, Alessio. I don't know how long it kept going. I just didn't have the strength...to fight anymore. I just...wanted it all...to go away. I just wanted...to be happy. I wanted to be...with you again."

"Angel," Alessio groaned in pain. He held me tighter as I felt the anger course through him.

When the baby rolled again, I closed my eyes. "He said he would kill...my baby."

Alessio froze underneath me. His muscles

117

tightened. I thought he stopped breathing for a second. "What?"

His tone was dangerous. Even I trembled at his voice.

My heart ached at the memory. Alberto was ruthless. He tried to break me every way he could. He took me until I had nothing else to give. Still, he kept taking. He kept breaking me.

As if his actions weren't enough, he tried to break me with his words.

"He said he would let me give birth but…deliver the dead baby to you," I choked out, my breathing coming out faster in panic.

Alessio's arm curved protectively around my stomach. "He's a dead man, Ayla. When I find him, he will regret ever hurting you. He will regret even thinking of hurting our baby."

My eyes snapped open, my breath leaving me in a loud whoosh.

He will regret even thinking of hurting our baby.
Our baby.

My heart clenched, and I looked up at his angry face. I saw the killer there. The Monster. But I wasn't scared. I knew the Monster would protect me.

He was *my* Monster.

I palmed his cheeks, looking into his blue eyes. "You said *our baby*."

Alessio's eyebrows furrowed at my words. His gaze shifted to my stomach and then back up. "Yes. Our baby."

I swallowed past the lump in my throat. "How do you know the baby is yours?"

118

Alessio brought his hand up and swiped my tears away. "Is it? Is the baby mine, Ayla?"

I winced at the question, a sense of despair falling over me. Closing my eyes, I leaned my forehead against his. "I don't know," I whispered. My voice broke as the baby moved again. "I don't know. I'm sorry. I'm so sorry, Alessio."

"Why are you apologizing, Angel?"

When I went to answer, he pressed his fingers against my lips, stopping my tide of words. "Not a word, Ayla. You have nothing to apologize for. At this point, I don't even care who the father is. The baby is mine. You are mine. He is ours. That's all that matters."

His hand went to my round belly. He caressed the bump gently. "I think I already love him, Angel."

My hand went over his. "I want him, Alessio."

A surge of protectiveness and possessiveness coursed through me.

I didn't know who the father of my baby was. I didn't want to know. I just wanted to love my baby.

I wanted to give my baby all the love I never had.

Alessio pressed his lips to mine again. He kissed me with so much care and love, like he treasured me. He held me gently, as if I were made of glass.

I felt cherished.

His touch was soft and gentle. His words were sweet.

He was everything I needed and wanted.

I love you.

The words were stuck in my throat. I didn't say

119

them. I wanted to, but something stopped me.

He told me he loved me, yet I couldn't say the words. I didn't know why.

I didn't think I needed to say them anyway. What we had was more powerful than those words. We just had to feel our love for each other.

Even without those words, our hearts were entwined together.

"Alessio," I said quietly. "You are my peace."

He smiled against my lips. "I know."

His answer brought a smile to my own lips. We kissed, our lips touching softly. It was slow, gentle, and soft. His tongue mated with mine, and I sighed into his kiss.

A knock on the door broke us apart. Before Alessio could answer, I saw Maddie running inside, followed by Lena.

She stopped in the middle of the room, her eyes on mine. "Sam told me Ayla fainted."

Her gaze roamed over me, fear in her eyes. Lena stopped beside her, her expression panicked too.

Alessio chuckled lightly. "She remembers," he announced.

Maddie's mouth fell open, and Lena gasped. Before I knew it, I was swept in their arms. They hugged me too tight. We cried together.

I missed them so much.

"I'm sorry for taking so long," I breathed through my tears.

"You have come back to us. That's all that matters," Lena admonished gently.

Maddie didn't let me go for the longest time. Lena had long left, but Maddie still held me. "I was so scared, Ayla. You have no idea. I'm so happy. I feel like every sacrifice I made was worth it."

My forehead pinched in confusion, and I stared at Alessio's blank eyes. Maddie paused and pulled away. She swiped her tears away and smiled, her eyes twinkling merrily.

"What are you talking about?" I asked, confused.

She shook her head. "Don't worry about it. You sure know how to stress someone out. By the way, I am still a little pissed that you talked to me last. Not fair that Alessio got your voice first."

I ducked my head shyly, feeling my heart warm with her words.

"Ayla needs to rest. You can talk to her tomorrow, Maddie," Alessio said, pulling me into his arms. My back was to his front as he held me.

Maddie nodded. "You're right."

She kissed me on the forehead before pulling away. "You need to rest and sleep a lot. I'm sure remembering everything has taken a toll on you."

"I do feel a little weak," I admitted, relaxing in Alessio's arms.

"That's it," he growled, sweeping me off my feet. "I should have known."

He placed me on the bed and pulled the comforter over me. "You need to rest," he ordered, leveling me with a hard look.

I heard the door close as Alessio gave me a pill. "Sam told me to give you this. It's for your headache."

I took the pill, and Alessio held the glass of water to my lips as I drank. When I was done, he pushed me on my back and turned off the light.

He climbed in bed behind me, pulling me to his chest, his arms wrapped around my waist, his hand over my baby bump. I placed mine next to his. The baby moved once before settling down.

"Sleep, Angel."

I closed my eyes.

Sleep, Angel. I'll watch over you.

I knew he would watch over me. Just like always.

As sleep started to take over my mind and body, my lips tilted up in a small smile.

He came for me, just like I knew he would.

"Thank you for loving me," I whispered into the dark.

"Never thank me for loving you, Angel," he muttered back.

Chapter 15

I pulled my pink dress on. It stretched over my round stomach, and I stared in the mirror.

The dress was a beautiful baby pink, and it came down to my mid-thighs. I was so thankful that Maddie bought these dresses.

They fit perfectly over my pregnant belly.

I turned from side to side, staring at my reflection. The day before, Maddie had cut my hair. It now lay in the middle of my back, the same length before I was taken away.

I purposely left it down, knowing Alessio loved it that way. My cheeks were rounder and flushed from my bath. My lips were pink from hours of kissing Alessio.

It had been four days since I got my memories back. Four days and every day felt like a fairy tale.

From the mirror, I saw Alessio walking out of the bathroom. He wore a black dress shirt, the top buttons left undone and black pants.

"Ready?" he asked, coming to stand behind me. I nodded at our reflection.

We were going to see Ivy. For an ultrasound. To see our baby for the first time.

I swallowed nervously and leaned against Alessio's chest. He rubbed the baby bump, and I saw him smile when the baby moved.

Placing a kiss on the side of my neck, he pulled me out of the room. "Let's go."

We walked downstairs toward Sam's office. The door was already open, so we walked inside. Ivy was sitting behind the desk.

She sent us a warm smile and stood up. "Good morning."

"Good morning," I replied. She gestured for me to get on the table. Alessio helped me recline back. The room was filled with machines I didn't recognize.

"How are you feeling this morning?" she asked. Ivy measured my bump and wrote something down on the notepad.

"I'm okay. Just a little nervous."

She chuckled. "Of course."

"Do you feel nauseous in the morning or when you eat?"

I shook my head. "Not really. I'm just really tired most of the time."

"Ah, you should be happy. It's an excuse to sleep all the time," she teased. "Can you pull your dress up? I need your stomach bare."

Before I could move, Alessio walked around the table and pulled my dress up over my stomach. It bunched across my breasts, hiding most of my view.

Ivy applied cool gel to my stomach, and I flinched at the coldness. "What are you doing?"

"Preparing you for the ultrasound. I'll do a quick sonogram for dates and measurement to make sure everything is okay."

I nodded, and Ivy began moving the wand over the roundness of my stomach. She typed something in her computer. "Everything looks good. The baby looks healthy. There's the little one," Ivy said, pointing at the screen. "That's the head."

Alessio crowded in, almost pushing his head into the screen. "Why is he so small?"

"The baby measures fine. You have nothing to worry about."

From my position and Alessio in front of the screen, I couldn't see anything. I craned my head up, and Alessio's eyes snapped toward me. He hastily moved to my side and helped me up in a half-sitting position. Alessio supported my neck so I could see the screen.

"These are the hands."

"They're so small," I murmured. His tiny little fingers. It was so cute.

Tears welled up in my eyes, and I sniffled as Ivy continued to show us our baby. "He's so beautiful," I whispered.

When Alessio didn't say anything, I turned my face toward his. I saw his eyes filled with tears. He was completely mesmerized. His gaze was transfixed on the screen as he stared at our baby.

I saw the love in his eyes. He already adored the little one. I also saw the possessiveness there. I knew he would protect our baby with his life.

"Is he okay?" Alessio asked huskily. Tears streamed down my face at the emotional tone in his voice.

"He is. There's nothing to worry," Ivy assured us.

She continued to move the wand over my stomach. Just then, the baby moved. I smiled, feeling content.

"You keep saying *he*. Do you want to know what you're having?" Ivy asked, looking at us expectantly.

Alessio and I stared at each other. I bit on my lips and nodded. Alessio turned back to Ivy. "Yeah."

Ivy moved the wand for a few seconds. "The baby is a shy one."

And then she smiled.

"It's a girl."

My lips parted, and a gasp escaped. Alessio froze beside me. I stared at the screen, watching my baby.

A girl. We were having a baby girl.

"A girl," I whispered.

Alessio was still silent, his eyes glue to the screen. He held a fist to his mouth and closed his eyes. My heart sank when he didn't say anything.

Did he want a son? I noticed that Alessio kept saying *he*. Even I had started to address the baby as a boy.

When Alessio opened his eyes again, he bent his head, kissing me softly on the lips.

"A princess."

His words were a mere whisper, but my heart soared.

"We're having a princess, Angel."

I heard the love in his voice. And I knew, he was

just as happy as me, if not more.

Ivy smiled at us and turned off the screen. She pulled a paper out and cut it in two pieces. She handed one to Alessio. "Here's a picture."

He stared at the picture far longer than he should have. But I didn't complain. I just watched him watch our daughter.

Daughter. A baby girl. A smile stretched across my lips.

"Ayla, do you know when your last period was? I know it's not easy to remember, but it would really help to know. This way I can get an exact due date," Ivy explained.

I looked at Alessio in panic, my chest feeling suddenly tight. He held my hand, giving me an encouraging look. "I don't really remember. But I know I had my last period before…"

My voice caught in my throat, but Ivy nodded, as if she understood. "From the measurement, I would say you are about twenty-four weeks pregnant. That's five and a half months. You are almost six months pregnant."

You are almost six months pregnant.

Alessio told me I was taken away eighteen weeks ago—almost four and a half months ago.

That meant…

My eyes met Alessio's. "She is yours."

He swallowed hard and nodded. His forehead touched mine, and he placed a kiss on the tip of my nose. "She is ours."

I smiled, my cheeks wet from my tears. Alessio swiped them away. "No more tears, Angel."

"They are happy tears."

Alessio smiled. "Okay, happy tears are acceptable."

Ivy cleared her throat, and we pulled away from each other. "The baby is healthy, and so are you. I will be checking back with you in five days. I am staying here for two more weeks, as a precaution in case you need me."

I nodded. Alessio took some paper towels and wiped off the gel from my stomach. He pulled my dress down and eased me into a sitting position.

"Now, because of your trauma, I need you to be careful. No stress. Bed rest is important too. Eat healthy. A happy mom is a happy baby," Ivy finished, patting me on the knee.

Alessio helped me stand up and pulled me close. "Thank you," I said softly.

We walked out of the room, my cheeks hurting from smiling too much. Maddie and the others were waiting for us in the living room.

"So?" she asked.

Alessio and I looked at each other. He smiled before turning to face everyone.

"A princess," he announced proudly.

Maddie squealed and pulled me into a hug.

Lena smiled sweetly and came to hug me too. "Congratulations, dear. Thank you for giving us a princess. It's been so many years since we have had a baby in this house."

She pulled away to give Alessio a hug too. Maddie took me in her arms again. "I'm so happy, babe."

When she pulled away, I noticed the men arguing. Phoenix smirked at Viktor. "Give me my money."

"Fuck you! It's a boy, I'm telling you," Viktor snapped. "Ayla, go back in there. Ivy is wrong. It's a boy."

"No, it's a girl," Maddie growled.

"It's a girl," Alessio agreed.

"Five thousand dollars, Viktor. Stop being such a pussy," Phoenix said.

They placed a bet?

I shook my head when Viktor glared at Phoenix. Nikolay stood silently, as always, but this time he wasn't as brooding. There was a half smile on his face.

From the corner of my eyes, I saw Isaak and Lyov come out of the gym. Lyov stopped dead in his tracks when he caught sight of me. His eyes moved to my stomach, and he moved his gaze aside.

Alessio wrapped an arm around my shoulder, pulling me into his chest. When Lyov and Isaak approached, Alessio cleared his throat.

"We are having a baby girl."

Lyov froze, and I saw him swallow hard. There was a flash of pain in his eyes, and his face twisted in sorrow. My heart ached for him.

His hands fisted at his side, and without a word, he walked away. Alessio sighed beside me. I pulled away from Alessio and went to follow Lyov.

I couldn't bear the thought of him being in pain. He was still hurting. His wife's and daughter's death still haunted him. If I could...I wanted to ease his pain.

Alessio grabbed my arm, pulling me back. "Let

him be, Angel."

"I need to do this, Alessio. Please," I begged, my eyes following Lyov as he walked upstairs.

I pulled my arm away and gave him a small smile. "I'll be okay."

Giving Alessio a kiss on the lips, I followed Lyov. My steps faltered when I reached his bedroom.

When my fist made contact with the door, I trembled slightly with nervousness.

He didn't answer. I waited and waited.

Finally, I opened the door and peeked inside. The room was dark except for a night lamp. It cast a soft glow around the room.

I walked further inside and closed the door behind me.

Lyov was sitting on the edge of the bed, a photo frame in his hand. Walking over to the bed, I sat down beside him.

There was only silence between us. Now that I was here, I wasn't sure what to say, how to soothe his pain.

Finally, he broke the silence.

"You remind me a lot of my Maria."

His voice was broken, and my stomach twisted. "She was just like you. Sweet, beautiful, and so gentle."

"I look at you, and all I see is my Angel," he whispered, his fingers lingering over the frame. I saw that it was a photo of a woman. I guessed it was Maria.

"I'm sorry," I muttered, looking at my lap.

"It's not your fault." Lyov opened the drawer

and removed another picture. He handed it to me. It looked like a sonogram.

"We were having a princess too," he said, pointing at the baby.

"I know," I said softly. My fingers traced the picture. My heart was in agony for his loss.

Lyov handed me the photo frame. "This is my wife."

This is my wife.

Not *was.* Even after so many years, Maria was *still* his wife.

Looking at the picture, I saw that Alessio had her eyes. "She is beautiful."

"The most beautiful," he agreed with a small chuckle.

"I'm sorry for your loss. Maria and your daughter didn't deserve that. *You* didn't deserve to go through that pain. My heart aches for your loss," I admitted truthfully. "But maybe they are in a better place right now. I'm sure they're watching over us."

"Are they?" he asked brokenly, staring at the picture.

"They are Angels."

A tear fell on the photo, and I quickly realized that Lyov was crying. "Your Maria loved you a lot. I don't think she would have wanted you to punish yourself like this. She would have wanted you to be happy. Honour her memories by living and remembering her with a smile. I'm sure she would have wanted that for you."

Silence fell upon us. I grew nervous and started to play with the hem of my dress. After some time, he finally spoke. "You sound so much like her."

When I didn't know how to reply to this, I stood up. Just then, the little princess moved. Maybe it was meant to be. Maybe it was fate, but in that moment, I knew what I had to do.

I bent down and took Lyov's hand. His head snapped up, and he stared at me in surprise.

Taking his hand, I placed it over my stomach just where the baby was dancing.

He sucked in a harsh breath, and his face crumpled up as tears streamed down his cheeks. The photo fell in his lap as he brought his other fist to his mouth.

It reminded me of Alessio. There were so many similarities between father and son. I was just seeing it for the first time.

Lyov was just another broken man.

Princess landed a hard kick at my side, and I winced. "She is strong," Lyov mumbled. There was a ghost smile on his lips.

"Just like her papa." I laughed.

"And her mother."

I never expected him to say that, but my heart flipped, and I smiled. "Thank you," I whispered as our princess continued to move.

"Lyov, I know you don't really like me, but this little princess here, she needs her grandfather," I started. "You never got a chance to meet your princess, but please, don't turn away from this one. She is just as precious."

She moved again, punching right into Lyov's palm. Looked like she agreed.

"You can be a part of her life if you want. I will

never stop you. Please, don't run away from this, from her," I added.

Lyov didn't answer, and after some time, the baby stopped moving. His hand fell away, and he stared at the pictures on his lap.

I waited for his reply. When he didn't, I closed my eyes as a wave of sadness washed over me. I stepped back and started to leave when his voice stopped me.

"I would like that."

My heart stuttered, and I pressed a hand against my stomach. *Did you hear that, Princess?*

"I never got a chance to hold my princess. But I want to hold this one."

His words were confirmation enough. "I think she would like that, too."

Chapter 16

I walked out of the room, leaving Lyov alone with his thoughts. He would be okay. This little princess just gave us all hope.

Alessio was leaning against the wall. As soon as I walked out of the room, he pulled me in his arms.

I sobbed in his chest. "He's going to be okay, Alessio."

Alessio didn't say anything. He just let me cry. When my tears finally dried, I placed a kiss in the middle of his chest, right over his beating heart.

"Can we go to the creek?" I asked, pulling away.

He smiled. "Let's go."

We walked down the stairs, and I waved at Maddie. She waved back and went into the kitchen.

Our walk to the creek was slow. We took our sweet time, our hands intertwined. No words were spoken. It wasn't needed. The silence was enough. It was comfortable. It was us.

When we arrived at the creek, I settled on a rock, my feet in the water. Alessio stood behind me, his hands on my shoulders.

"Are you happy?" I asked, rubbing small circles around my pregnant belly.

"I'm more than happy, Angel. I'm fucking ecstatic."

"You always addressed the baby as a boy. Are you happy that it's a girl?"

When he didn't answer right away, I grew nervous. Finally, I felt his lips next to my ear. He placed a kiss there before saying, "I'm happy."

I sighed in relief, and when he continued, my heart soared higher with contentment. "I think deep inside I always wanted a princess. After losing..." He paused, but I got what he meant. "I was just scared. I didn't want to hope. But when I heard it's a girl, I felt like my heart just flipped. I swear it stopped for a second. I'm the happiest I can be right now."

I leaned back against his chest and tilted my head backwards. Alessio looked back at me. "I'm happy too."

Alessio smiled and kissed my forehead, my nose, and finally my lips. He took my lips sweetly.

"Such a sweet moment. I almost feel bad for interrupting."

My eyes widened, and my heart stopped. I froze and slowly went numb.

No. No. No. Please no.

My mind screamed, my heart wept, and I was suddenly hurting everywhere.

That voice.

This couldn't be happening.

Not again. Not now.

I felt Alessio freeze behind me. From our

position, I saw his lips curl in a snarl. I tilted my head down, fear clouding my vision. I shook with terror.

In that moment, I just wanted to disappear into thin air. I didn't want to exist. I wanted to be far...very far away from the Devil.

Alessio stood straight, and I felt him turn around. I slowly got up and turned around too but stayed hidden behind Alessio.

I couldn't see Alberto from where I was. I was completely hidden, protected behind Alessio's back.

Alessio moved his hand to his waistband, where his gun was.

"Ah. Ah. Don't move or I will shoot. Trust me, this time I will," Alberto warned. "Step away from her."

Alessio didn't move. "Step away from her or I will shoot. What's the point of being a hero? After I shoot you, I can shoot her. So step the fuck away from her."

Alessio's hand stayed on his waistband, and he still didn't move. I heard Alberto laugh. My ears rang with it, and I pinched my eyes closed.

Without thinking, I stepped from behind Alessio's back and came to stand beside him.

Alberto's eyes roamed over me, and I saw his vile smirk. "There you are, love."

I shuddered at his voice but kept my eyes on him. He looked different. He had a beard, and his clothes were rumpled.

His eyes appeared red, tired, and...crazed. Their maniacal gleam pierced me until all I felt was absolute fear.

My head ran wild; my stomach cramped. My heart ached. It hurt so much.

"If only you hadn't run away," he tsked. "I would have kept you alive. But now you just pissed me off. I don't feel generous anymore."

Panic clawed at my throat, and I glanced at Alessio. He was staring at Alberto stoically. How did it come to this? Everything was perfect just moments ago.

Alberto took a step toward us, pointing the gun in my direction. His gaze moved to Alessio. "One move and I will shoot her brains out. You know it takes only seconds."

Alessio's hands fisted at his side. I wanted to fall down and beg for mercy.

My breathing accelerated, and my chest grew tight. Alberto continued to walk forward until he was only a few steps away.

He pointed the gun at Alessio and then at me. "Hmm…I wonder who I should shoot first."

Alberto pointed the gun at me. "The little Angel?"

He cocked his head to the side before pointing the gun at Alessio. "Her savior?"

My heart stuttered in pain, and I rubbed my stomach. I could barely breathe.

"You are such a coward, Alberto. Why don't you fight like a man?" Alessio growled.

Alberto tsked and pointed the gun at me again but this time toward my stomach. "Or the baby?"

NO! I wanted to scream. My heart was trying to pound its way out of my chest. My hands shook, but I cradled my pregnant belly protectively.

"Aww, how cute," he mocked. "The baby it is, then."

My eyes widened. Everything happened so fast. I saw Alessio lurch forward, and his leg kicked out. He got Alberto in the hand, and the gun flew away.

Alessio tackled Alberto to the ground, and I stood frozen, watching the two men roll on the ground, fighting.

I couldn't lose Alessio. I just couldn't.

I was blind with terror as I watched them fight. They were out for blood, and in that moment, I didn't know who would win.

With wide eyes, I looked for the gun. Where did the gun go?

When I finally noticed it next to a tree, I took a step forward but stopped when Alberto pushed Alessio off him.

He had another gun in his hand.

Oh please, no.

He laughed, a laugh filled with so much madness that made my skin crawl in dread and disgust.

Alberto didn't even appear out of breath. He looked like a man on a mission. There was something making him stronger, crazier.

Alessio slowly stepped toward me.

Alberto moved his dead eyes to mine, smiling grimly. "Did you really think you could escape? Ayla, you seem to forget. You are mine."

He really was the Devil. For a split second, I wondered how it was possible for someone to be this cruel.

But the thought was quickly gone when he pointed the gun right in the middle of my stomach.

"Say good-bye to lover boy."

I whimpered, holding my stomach as if I was trying to hide my princess from this horror.

But the Devil had found us, and this time there was no escape.

This was it. This was my end.

My heart hammered when I saw him pull the trigger. My eyes closed as two gunshots sounded. Terror washed through me as I waited for the pain.

Seconds ticked by, and I felt nothing.

My eyes snapped open.

I gasped and cried out when I saw Alessio standing in front of me, his face a mask of shock and pain.

"No!" I screamed, moving forward. I wrapped my arms around him, moving my hands over his body, looking for where he was injured.

No. Please. This was a nightmare. This wasn't happening. I couldn't lose Alessio. My face contorted as wave after wave of pain crashed through me.

"Alessio," I sobbed, running my hands over him. "No. Why, Alessio?"

Alessio grabbed my waist and pulled me to his chest. His hands went to my stomach, holding the bump. His other hand traveled the length of my body, like I was doing to his.

"Where are you hurt? Ayla, where are you hurt?" he asked urgently, his voice hoarse. "Please, say something!"

A crippling grief swept over me. I cried in his chest. "I'm not hurt. You…took…the bullet…"

"Ayla!" Alessio shook me, his face horrified.

"No. You got hit! I didn't. I was too late."

Agonized sobs tumbled from my mouth, my lungs constricting painfully as I shook my head. My stomach started to cramp from the severity of my sobs, and I palmed Alessio's cheeks. "You are not hurt?" I asked.

I saw confusion in his eyes, and he slightly pulled away, his eyes roaming over my body, inspecting me. I did the same for him.

"You are not hurt," he stated.

And he wasn't either.

My eyes widened as my blood rushed so fast through my body that I felt suddenly weak. I couldn't hear anything but the wildly beating pulse in my ears. What was happening?

"Then...who took the bullet?" I whispered. Alessio swallowed hard, and he held me to him.

We turned around, Alessio protecting me with his body.

The sight that beheld me took my breath my away. Agony shattered my heart, and I sank to my knees, too weak to stay upright, too weak to think.

I wailed in anguish.

"NO!"

Chapter 17

Alberto

She really thought she could escape.

How naïve of her. Stupid even. I thought she had learned her lesson from way before, and even now—but it looked like she still had so much to learn.

Too bad I had reached my limit. I was no longer patient. She tested me every day. Every time she escaped. Every time she uttered *his* name.

Ayla was mine. Even if she didn't want to be. It wasn't her choice. It was never her choice.

Only because she didn't have a choice.

How much do I have to break her until she finally understands?

I thought I had her bent to my will. She was mine. No other man would touch her.

But I had clearly assessed her wrong. That was my first mistake.

Since the first time I saw her, it was only Ayla and me. But then Alessio came and fucked everything up.

If it wasn't for him, Ayla would have still been mine.

From my place in the shadows, I watched them. I watched him hold her, his arms around my woman.

I watched her smile—laugh with him.

My fingers tightened around my gun. Fury rolled off me in heavy waves.

This was the end.

It was time for *their* end.

My eyes moved to Ayla's round stomach. *His* baby. Not mine. Every time I looked at her, it served as a reminder.

He *touched* her.

I should have gotten rid of it when I had a chance.

At the thought, my lips turned up in a small smile. It didn't matter anymore. I would get rid of it now.

I would take everything from her until she had nothing left. Until she would have no other choice but to fall back at my feet.

I watched them.

When he kissed her, I rubbed my finger over the trigger. I was itching to pull it. To end their lives.

That would be too easy.

I wanted to see the fear in their eyes. In Alessio's eyes. I wanted to see him helpless.

He had taken everything from me.

And I was going to return the same favor. *After all, payback is a bitch.*

With my fingers wrapped firmly around the gun, I walked out of the shadows.

"Such a sweet moment. I almost feel bad for interrupting."

I laughed when they swiveled around to face me. The surprise in Alessio's face was almost comical.

But he wasn't my target.

My target was the woman hiding behind his back.

When she came into view, I smiled. This was it, love.

Ayla didn't realize what I wanted, I got. It didn't matter if I had to take it by force; in the end, I always got what I wanted.

She wasn't any different.

Pointing the gun at Ayla, I stared at her. I saw the fear and panic. It didn't faze me.

I was going to drag her to hell with me.

She would be mine in the end.

Chapter 18

Ayla

My throat hurt from screaming. I had no tears left. I couldn't even find my voice. Shock coursed through me, and I froze at the sight in front of me.

This couldn't be happening.

Not after everything we had been through. After coming such a long way, this couldn't be the end.

My palms met the grass, my knees hurting as I looked at my lap. My baby was going crazy, moving around wildly. It was like she could feel my stress. She knew something bad happened.

Oh baby.

There was yelling. I could hear people fighting, but I chose to ignore everything.

When someone grabbed my shoulders, my eyes snapped up to meet Alessio's blue ones. I could see the panic and shock there too, but all his attention was on me.

"Are you okay?" he asked in panic.

I nodded and looked over his shoulders. "But

he…he…"

Alessio closed his eyes tightly. After taking a deep breath, he stared at me again. "Can you stand up?"

"I think," I muttered. Alessio helped me stand up, and he wrapped his arms around me.

"It's going to be okay," he whispered in my ears.

"No. It's not. Your father…" I trailed off, my words catching in my throat. "How…why…?"

Isaak knelt down beside Lyov. He coughed into the grass. When I saw blood, I pushed away from Alessio. "We have to help him! Oh my God, we have to help him. He's bleeding badly…and he's coughing blood."

My fingers tightened around Alessio's arm. I looked around wildly, looking for something to ground me. My skin itched with uneasiness and my head was pounding.

When my eyes made contact with the scene behind Lyov, my lungs constricted.

Alberto was on the ground with Nikolay on top of him. Viktor was standing beside them, his gun pointed at Alberto's head.

It would take only one bullet to end his life, but Viktor made no effort to do so.

I saw Nikolay landing furious punches in Alberto's face. He tried to cover his face, to evade the ruthless punches, but there was no escape.

The only thing I could hear was the sound of knuckles making contact with skin. It sounded harsh. Bringing my hands up, I covered my ears. I didn't want to hear it. I didn't want to see it. I didn't want to think of it.

My eyes moved back to where Lyov lay, unmoving. My breathing came out harder and harsher. "Alessio, we have to help him!"

"Ayla, calm down! You shouldn't be stressing out like this. It's not good for the baby," Alessio snapped, his hand molding over my stomach protectively.

My eyes widened, and I pushed his hands away. "Are you crazy? Your father has been shot! He took the bullet for us. How can you be worried about me and the baby right now?"

Without giving him a chance to answer, I ran to Lyov's side. I felt a hard kick and winced when I knelt down beside him. Lyov's eyes were closed, his breathing labored. I choked back a sob when I saw his bloodied stomach.

There was so much blood.

His face was pale, his eyes pinched closed. I saw the line of stress on his forehead. My palm pressed against his clammy skin, and I tried to soothe his aggravated movement.

"Please don't move. You will only hurt yourself more," I said softly.

I heard Isaak swear. Alessio came to stand beside me. "Let's move him," he muttered.

I stood up and moved out of the way. Isaak and Alessio helped Lyov stand up.

"Ayla, walk in front of us," Alessio ordered. His tone held no room to argue. His eyes begged me. I knew what he needed.

Alessio needed me in front of him. His eyes on me. He needed to make sure I was safe. Giving them a final glance, I turned around.

The others were already gone. I had tuned them out and didn't even realize they had taken Alberto away. I breathed out a sigh of relief, my shoulders sagging.

Alberto had finally been caught.

***

We made our way to Sam. Even Ivy was there. Maddie and Lena were standing in front of the door.

Isaak and Alessio dragged Lyov into the room and pushed him on the bed. Before I could go in, Maddie grabbed my arm. "I think we should wait here," she suggested in a gentle tone.

My eyes went to Alessio and saw him coming my way. He opened his arms for me, and I went into them gladly. Burying my head into his chest, I let out my worst fear. "Will he be okay?"

When I heard no answer from him, my arms tightened around his waist. That was when I noticed his arms trembling. It was a slight shake but enough to tell me what he was feeling.

I felt his lips on my temple, and my eyes stung with unshed tears. I placed a kiss over his beating heart, not wanting to let him go.

We stayed locked in an embrace. In that moment, I was his strength. "He's going to be okay, Alessio. He promised that he will hold Princess. Lyov needs to meet his granddaughter."

The words were hard to speak. My voice came out scratchy as I tried to keep the tears at bay. I couldn't cry. I couldn't be weak. Not now. I had to be strong.

Lyov saved us…he took the bullet for us.

I had to be strong for all of us.

Now that Alberto was captured, everything would be okay. We were safe.

Fear. Anger. Relief. Sadness. Disgust. Shock.

At the moment, my feelings were a dormant volcano. I buried everything inside and concentrated on Alessio and Lyov.

"Ayla."

My name brought me out of my thoughts, and I looked at Maddie. "Why don't you go rest? When Sam is done, we'll call you."

I shook my head and hugged Alessio tighter. "No. I'll stay here until I know he is perfectly fine."

"Ayla," Alessio warned.

Before he could say anything, I pulled away and stood on my toes. Bringing my lips to his, I kissed him softly. "I'm not going anywhere, Alessio. Please, let me stay here," I whispered against his lips.

He sighed, his eyes closing. "You are so stubborn."

"I know," I muttered back, hugging him again. "We will wait together, Alessio."

And that was exactly what we did.

The air around us was heavy with uncertainty, like a dark cloud settling over us.

With every minute that passed, I grew more scared. I felt chilled to my bones at the thought of Lyov not making it out alive.

"Ayla…Ayla…wake up."

I groggily blinked my eyes open and stared into Maddie's smiling face. Rubbing the sleepiness away, I went to stand up. "I'm sorry. I fell asleep."

"Sam was able to take the bullet out. Lyov is okay. He's resting now," Maddie said excitedly.

My mouth fell open, and my heart leaped at Maddie's words. When I felt a kick, my hand instinctively went to my stomach.

I rubbed soothing circles around my belly. Turning, I looked for Alessio. His tensed back was to me as he faced the wall. I walked over and placed a hand over his shoulder.

He instantly relaxed under my touch, and I heard him release a long, painful breath. "He's okay, Alessio."

He gave me a sharp nod. "I know."

"Do you want to see him?" I asked when silence fell upon us.

I moved in front of Alessio and palmed his cheeks. "What are you scared of?"

I sucked a harsh breath when I saw the pain in his eyes. "I thought he never cared, Ayla. He wasn't really a father. After I lost my mother, he never acted like a father. I was just a forgotten son most of the time."

Alessio bent his head, burying his face in my neck. "I don't know how to look him in the eyes and thank him for saving you. He took that bullet for you."

Wrapping my arms around his head, I rubbed my fingers on the back on his neck. "You're wrong. He saved *us*. If it wasn't for him, you would have gotten shot. In that moment, I don't think he cared who he was saving. Whether it was me, you, or Princess. He's a good man, Alessio. Just a little lost and broken, but a good man."

I felt Alessio's sigh against my skin before he pulled away. "Let's go."

I smiled, looking into his captivating blue eyes. Taking hold of my hand, he intertwined our fingers together before pulling me into the room.

Lyov was on the bed with Isaak beside him. When we approached, his gaze went to us. His face was a mask of pain, but he sent us a smile. "Glad...you...are...both okay."

I gave him a wobbly smile. "Thank you...thank you so much."

He chuckled but quickly gasped, his face turning pale. "Don't...thank me."

Isaak looked at us before standing up. "I'll leave you guys alone," he muttered before leaving the room.

I took his place on the chair beside the bed. Taking Lyov's hand in mind, I looked at his stomach.

He was covered with the bedsheet, but I grimaced, remembering the bloodied scene from before. "Does it hurt really bad?"

Lyov shook his head. "Not at all."

Alessio huffed. "No need to act all tough, old man."

Those were the first words he spoke since we came into the room. His voice sounded gruff, and I looked up to see him glaring at Lyov.

In fact, they were both glaring at each other.

A tense moment passed between both men before they lost their glare. I sighed when they both stayed silent. We had a long way to go.

Alessio walked around the bed, coming to stand beside me. "Ayla, let's go. You need to rest. I also need to…" Alessio trailed off, his expression turning furious.

I understood what he meant.

Alberto was captured, and Alessio was itching to have his revenge.

I saw his hands tightening into fists. Taking them in my hands, I placed a kiss on his knuckles. "You go. I will be here. When I get tired, I will go up and sleep."

He opened his mouth to argue, but I continued. "I'll be fine, Alessio. Really. Please go. Do what you have to do."

This was me letting him know that I was okay with anything he had planned for Alberto. I refused to think about the Devil, because that brought up all the memories I wanted to bury. My eyes met Alessio's. Blue to green. I smiled, taking strength from his furious stare.

After a long moment of silence between us, he wavered. Bending down, he kissed my lips. "I will come for you," Alessio declared before pulling away.

I smiled, knowing he would keep his word. He brought his hand up and brushed his thumb over my cheek. His touch was soft; his stare held the same gentleness.

Alessio pulled himself away. I stared at his retreating back when he suddenly paused.

I felt my eyebrows furrow when confusion bloomed inside of me. His shoulders tensed before he spoke. The words were softly spoken, but they were just as shocking to me as they were to Lyov.

"Thank you for saving us."

With that, Alessio walked away.

I couldn't help but smile. My brooding man. He was so stubborn.

I looked back at Lyov to see him staring at the closed door. "Am I dreaming?"

This time, I laughed. "No. You are not."

He closed his eyes with a sigh. "I never thought I would hear my son say that."

My throat closed up, and I looked down at my lap. It was such a beautiful moment. I wanted to capture it and hold it in my heart forever. I still remembered when father and son once hated each other.

"You should rest," I whispered, adjusting his bedsheet.

His eyes were already closed. A few minutes later, his breathing evened out. I knew he was asleep. It wasn't long before my eyes started to get heavy. The last thing I remembered was staring at Lyov's sleeping form, thinking how much father and son looked alike.

I woke with a jolt when I felt someone wrap their arms under my knees. My eyes widened when I was swept up in Alessio's arms. He cradled me to his chest, and I instinctively laid my head on his shoulder.

I hummed sleepily and closed my eyes again. "I told you to go to bed, Angel," he admonished. "You've been sitting in this chair for hours. You never listen. It's not good for you or the baby."

"I'm fine," I mumbled, holding on to his neck.

"I'm taking her upstairs," I heard Alessio say. Opening my eyes, I saw Lyov was awake. He nodded at Alessio and sent me a small smile.

Alessio didn't wait for me to say good-bye; he was already carrying me out of the room. "You are so stubborn. How many times do I have to tell you? You need to take better care of yourself. Did you even eat? Fuck, Ayla. Please tell me you ate something."

I winced at the reminder. He was going to be angry. "Ayla," he growled in warning. "Did you eat?"

I pressed my lips together, refusing to answer. He huffed in frustration but stayed silent. I peeked up at his face and saw his lips were thinned in an angry straight line.

I placed a kiss on the side of his neck. "Please don't be angry."

"I'm not."

I closed my eyes. He definitely was.

When he reached our bedroom, he didn't turn on the lights. Alessio placed me on the bed and pulled the comforter over me. He climbed in bed and pulled me into his embrace.

With my back to his front, he held me. His hand laid on my stomach, and I laid mine over his.

There was one question burning in my head.

He was gone for hours.

"Is he dead?"

The question was whispered in the dark, but my heart hammered painfully in my chest.

"No," he replied.

My breath left me with a loud whoosh. My hand

tightened around his, my chest feeling tighter.

"He is not going to have an easy death, Angel."

I bit on my lips, closing my eyes against his words.

I didn't know if it was relief I was feeling or something else.

"Go to sleep. I don't want you to think about it. We will not speak of him in our bed," Alessio said. His voice was soft in my ears, but I knew anger was fueling inside of him.

He was an angry man, driven by fury and vengeance. I didn't know what he was capable of, and in that moment, I didn't want to know.

So I did what I was told. I slept.

Held safely in Alessio's embrace, I fell asleep while the man who hurt me for years was held captive in the basement—being mercilessly tortured.

Chapter 19

The bowl was placed on the ground between us. He kicked it away a few feet.

"Eat."

He kept his eyes on me when the simple command was given. The tone of his voice held a hint of rage, but it also held no space for questions.

I sat up and stared at the bowl a few feet away from me. Without wasting another second, I got to my knees obediently. That was what he wanted.

When I reached the bowl and bent down to eat, he kicked it a few feet away again. I crawled again. He kicked the bowl again.

This process was repeated until I had used all the length of my shackles and I was straining against them to reach the bowl.

Still on my knees, I bent down and licked the soup.

It was tasteless, but I still ate. It was the only thing I could do.

The devil unzipped his pants, and I waited for what was to come.

I sat up with a start, my mind foggy with sleep and the nightmare.

No, it was my reality.

The memories flashed behind my closed lids in rapid images. Everything hurt...even my soul.

I didn't want to remember, but it was impossible. The memories always came back to haunt me.

I always heard the Devil's laughter in my ears. No matter how much I wanted to tune him out and forget, I just couldn't.

It always came back to this. Remembering. The painful memories. Reliving them over and over again.

When I felt a hand on my shoulder, I flinched. My mind went black.

The Devil had found me again.

My stomach rolled, and I tasted the bile on my tongue. My lungs constricted painfully, and I closed my eyes tightly.

"Ayla, it's me."

The soothing voice penetrated through the black fog. I opened my eyes to see Maddie sitting beside me. She gave me a gentle look and brought her hands up in surrender.

"I'm not going to hurt you. Alessio had to go, but he didn't want to leave you alone," she explained quietly.

I felt my muscles relax, my breathing returning to normal.

The Devil wasn't here.

He was captured, waiting for his fate. His death.

A sudden surge of energy went through me at the thought of Alberto.

156

"I want to see him," I announced.

I struggled out of bed, and Maddie followed me. "Alessio?" she questioned.

"No." I shook my head, making my way to the door. I didn't wait for her. My brain turned off...every thought was gone except one.

I wanted to see the Devil one last time.

I wanted to see his face...I wanted to see the fear in his eyes. The same fear he had instilled inside of me, I wanted to see the same reflecting in those soulless eyes.

I wanted to see my Savior rise above him.

My heart hammered as I walked down the stairs. Maddie was hot on my heels. She was talking, but I didn't hear her.

I concentrated only on my destination.

I wanted to feel safe...and the only way for me to feel that way was to see *him* captured.

When I reached the basement, I saw two men at the door. Their eyes widened at the sight of me, and they took a step forward.

"Miss Ayla. You shouldn't be here."

I looked past their shoulders, staring at the closed door. "I want to see him."

"Boss said nobody was allowed," one of them replied, giving me a strange look.

The air around us was colder. It was heavy with the essence of death. The atmosphere felt vile and suffocating.

A shiver went through me. I rubbed my arms, trying to get rid of the chills. "Please let me through. I want to see him."

"Miss—"

Maddie cut them off. "Let her. She needs to do this."

All four men looked at each other. An apprehensive look appeared on their faces, and I knew they were worried about Alessio's anger. If they disobeyed his orders, they would pay severely.

"I will tell Alessio that I forced you. He won't say anything," I tried to bargain.

The men parted to let me through. "Are you sure, Miss? This is not the place for you."

"I'm sure," I replied.

No, I wasn't sure. I was scared of what I was about to see, but I knew I had to do this.

The door opened, and my heart hammered. I thought it skipped a beat because of how hard it pounded against my ribcage.

My hands trembled, but I clenched them into fists. I walked inside to see Alessio swiveling around, facing me in shock.

I flinched at the sight in front of me.

The first thing I noticed was how bloodied his clothes were. His hands had blood on them too.

The second thing I saw was Viktor, Nikolay, and Phoenix staring at me with wide eyes. They had blood on them too.

And the last thing…was Alberto.

He was strapped to a chair, his arms tied behind his back. His head hung low, his chin almost touching his chest.

He looked dead.

But I knew he wasn't.

I could hear his labored breathing.

Blood was everywhere. The copper smell of

blood in the room made me nauseous, and my stomach rolled painfully.

"Ayla," Alessio breathed. He took a step toward me, and my lips wobbled, trying to keep the tears in.

"What...?" He shook his head, dropping his knife to the floor. My eyes followed it. There was blood on the blade too. Actually, the whole knife was covered in blood.

My eyes went to Alessio's hand. The same hand that held me gently and loved me.

I should have been scared, but I wasn't.

Because I knew these hands would keep me safe. They were bloodied for me.

I looked at Alberto again.

He moved slightly. The Devil raised his head with great difficulty.

And when his eyes met mine, my heart found its way to my throat. It felt like sharp knives were piercing me. His stare made me sick.

This man broke me. Humiliated me in the worst way possible. He was my nightmare for so many years. The Devil in my life.

I quaked as I kept my eyes on him. He represented every ugliness in my life.

I wanted to sink to the floor. I wanted to sink and sink into a pit of darkness. To shut out everything. Every pain. Every hurt the Devil caused me.

I wanted to fade away into nothingness.

I didn't want to feel. My legs felt numb, and my whole body felt heavy.

It hurt so much. Everything hurt.

In front of me, I saw the Devil. But I also saw

every painful memory.

Every rape. Every sinister laugh. All the torture I went through. I remembered being shackled to the wall, being fed, beaten, and then raped.

I remembered the years he let his men take me over and over again until I would fade in and out of blackness. Until I would feel nothing but pain.

I saw everything. I felt everything.

The agony made me dizzy.

All those emotions that were dormant inside of me, they all erupted.

Fury, disgust, sadness, pain. They coursed through me, fueling something deep inside of me. Something I didn't even realized I was capable of.

Without thinking, I lunged forward. Alessio reared back in shock when I grabbed his gun.

I held the gun in my hand and pointed it at Alberto.

I saw Viktor moving forward, but Alessio stopped him with a raise of his hand.

My hands trembled around the gun, but my grasp never slipped. I just had to pull the trigger.

I wanted him to hurt, just like he hurt me.

My eyes moved back to Alessio for a second. His gaze was already on me. He looked shocked but proud.

When I saw him smile, I relaxed.

It wasn't a sweet smile. No, it was a smile filled with promises of darkness. A sadistic smile.

"You want to shoot him?" Alessio asked, walking toward me. His steps were deliberately slow. He looked powerful and ruthless. Alessio Ivanshov looked like the King he truly was.

He appeared like the very monster he was described as. The monster everyone feared.

I nodded my head, keeping my eyes on Alberto.

Alessio stopped beside me. "You really want to do this?"

I nodded again.

I wanted to shoot him. But now that the gun was in my hand, I couldn't move.

I froze, my throat closing up, tears streaming down my cheeks.

"Viktor," Alessio growled. Viktor looked at Alessio before nodding. He untied Alberto and hoisted him off the chair.

Viktor held him by the nape and dragged him across the floor toward me. Wiping the tears away, I felt a sudden fear rake through me.

Viktor kicked Alberto's leg, making him kneel in front of me. I stiffened, taking a step back. My back hit a chest, and I knew it was Alessio.

When did he move behind me?

I sucked in a breath and held the gun tighter. My finger feathered against the trigger, but I couldn't do it.

"Angel, you don't have to do this," Alessio whispered in my ears.

I shook my head wildly.

"No," I replied brokenly. "I want...to..."

He swore under his breath. "I'm letting you do this *only* because you want to. Only one shot, Ayla. That's it."

My gut clenched as I stared at the Devil kneeling in front of me. I held the power, yet I couldn't do it.

"Alessio..." I begged.

161

He sighed and wrapped his hand around mine. We held the gun together. "I'll help you, Angel."

His voice was gruff in my ears, almost impatient but filled with so much pride.

The gun was pointed at Alberto's kneecap. "One bullet, Angel. But don't kill him. I'm not done with him yet."

When I didn't move, Alessio urged me. "Go ahead."

Our fingers latched onto the trigger.

Bang!

My ears rang, and I winced, closing my eyes.

Alberto screamed so loud it echoed around the chamber. My heart leaped, and my breathing came out harsher.

His scream of agony kept on going. When I opened my eyes, I saw him writhing on the floor. Blood was everywhere, even on my dress.

Before I knew what was happening, Alessio was in front of me. The gun was taken out of my hand, and I was being pushed back.

Alessio put his arms around me. I buried my face in his chest. Alberto was still screaming as Alessio half-carried me out of the basement.

The door closed with a bang, and I flinched. It sounded so much like the gunshot.

I shivered from cold and pain. So much pain.

I didn't think the pain would ever end.

I cried in Alessio's chest. He smelled of blood. He was covered with it.

But I was covered with it, too.

The thought made me gag, and I pushed away from Alessio.

I just shot another person.

How…?

My baby moved, and I felt a hard kick. *My princess.*

Alessio pulled me into his chest again. "Don't pull away from me, Angel."

"I hurt him," I whispered. "I hurt him, Alessio."

"I know. You were so brave in there. So beautiful. Like an avenging Angel," he whispered. "I'm in awe and so fucking proud of you."

I felt light-headed and sagged against Alessio, all energy deserting me.

"I never wanted you to see him like this. I know you want to kill him, Angel. But you won't be able to live with it," Alessio said, his voice low but filled with understanding.

"Killing someone is never easy. It will haunt you forever. Your hands will always be tainted with his blood. I know you. Even though he deserves it, you won't be able to live with the fact you took another's person life," he continued.

I hiccupped back a sob and held him tighter. He understood me. Of course he understood me. Alessio could read me like an open book.

Sometimes I felt like he knew me better than I knew myself.

"I don't want you to dirty your hands as long as I am alive. Let me do this." Alessio paused and palmed my cheeks. He tilted my head up, staring into my eyes.

"Let me be your monster. Let me kill for you, Angel."

I nodded silently. Bringing our lips together, we

kissed. Softly and gently. A contrast of what was happening around us.

Pulling away, I placed my hand over his beating heart. It matched the rhythm of my own. We breathed together, our eyes never leaving each other.

"Make him pay, Alessio. I want him to hurt...like he hurt me," I whispered. "Does that make me a bad person? For me to wish death upon someone else?"

Alessio shook his head. "Never. He deserves everything he got and will get. By the time I'm done with him, he won't even be able to beg for his death."

I wiped my tears away. "I just want to be safe from him. I want our princess to be safe from him."

"He will never hurt you again," Alessio promised. We kissed again, our tongues dancing together. Alessio deepened the kiss, and I held him tighter.

Princess landed a hard kick to my side, and Alessio pulled away, looking down at my stomach. "Damn, that was a hard kick. Is she practicing in there?"

"You felt that?"

He nodded, rubbing the bump. "Go upstairs and take a hot shower. I will come for you at night. Wait for me in the piano room," Alessio demanded, his eyes softening just the slightest bit.

His face wasn't soft or gentle. My sweet lover was gone. In his place was a man filled with vengeance and the need to kill.

I had learned to love this side of Alessio too.

And now I would patiently wait for my sweet lover to come back.

In the meantime, I would let him wreak havoc.

I placed another kiss on his lips. "Do your worst, Alessio."

Chapter 20

My back was aching as I walked up the stairs. Even the soles of my feet were aching. And I barely did anything today. Nobody would let me do anything. I wasn't allowed to leave the bed or the couch.

I sighed, my shoulders dropping. I was bored, and I missed Alessio.

Eighteen hours without him.

The last time I saw him was the night before, when I played the piano for him. After that, we went to sleep.

But I woke up without him, his side of the bed cold. Like he wasn't even there.

He must have left as soon as I fell asleep.

I didn't even catch a glimpse of him, and it was already night. His whole day was spent in the basement. I tried not to think about that.

I acted as if he was out, dealing with some other kind of business.

Just not *that* type of business. The one I knew he was dealing with right now.

I still shuddered when I thought about what I did

to Alberto. It might have been only one bullet, but his screams still resonated through my ears.

All the pain he was going through at the moment at the hands of Alessio was almost unthinkable.

The thought of it should have been revolting. Even if it scared me, I didn't feel bad. He deserved it. After everything he had done, Alberto deserved it.

His end was here.

When I reached the landing, I paused, taking a deep breath. Rubbing my aching back, I made my way to the piano room.

"Phoenix, it's okay. You can go now. Alessio will be here soon," I said when I reached the door.

"Boss said—" I cut him off with a shake of my head.

"I know what he said. But it's only for a few minutes. Please go and take some rest. You must be tired," I said, sending him a smile.

Phoenix shook his head. "I'm sorry, but you are not to be left alone. It's a strict order from Boss, and I have been assigned as your bodyguard for the moment."

A frustrated sound came from my throat. It had been like this since Alberto was captured and Alessio spent most of his time in the basement.

I was followed everywhere. If it wasn't Phoenix, then it was either Viktor or Nikolay.

They were always behind me, keeping an eye.

"Alessio will be here any moment now," I tried to reason with him. There was an uneasy feeling inside of me, having the men always following me around.

"I will leave when he gets here and you are in his protection." Phoenix placed his hands behind his back, his legs widening in a protective stance. His face was expressionless. In that moment, he reminded me of Nikolay.

They were related after all, and the resemblance was there. Especially when Phoenix was serious in a matter.

"Stubborn men," I muttered under my breath.

"His mind will be at ease if he knows you're safe and under our watch. Grant him this wish, Ayla."

My shoulders dropping in defeat, I sighed. I understood his point, but it didn't mean I agreed. I had a strange feeling inside me, my chest feeling impossibly tight at the thought of these men protecting me.

It was almost like they didn't care about their own lives. It was always about…me. My safety. My needs.

It saddened me to think they might care less about themselves.

Phoenix must have noticed my change of emotion because he sent me a kind smile. "You are carrying our future, Ayla. I don't know if you understand this, but this baby will continue the Ivanshov's legacy. Your protection and her protection are our first priority. We don't protect you only under Boss's order. We protect you because we want to."

Everything he said made sense. "I understand," I murmured, my eyes going to the staircase.

I felt him before I even saw him. His presence

already made my heart beat faster. My stomach fluttered, and I felt giddy. Was that what they called butterflies? I felt it every time I thought of Alessio or saw him. Even at the mention of his name.

When I finally saw him, my lips stretched in a smile. Like my body wasn't my own anymore, I glided toward him. He opened his arms for me, and I curled into his embrace. Alessio had this effect on me.

The pull I felt toward him was too strong to fight. And I didn't want to fight it. Instead, I wanted to bask in his presence and live in him.

"You can leave," Alessio said, his voice hard and grating to my ears. My eyes snapped open, my arms tightening around his waist.

"Boss." Phoenix acknowledged his Boss's order with a nod and walked away, but not before slightly bowing in our direction.

I stared up at Alessio to see his face emotionless. That was when I noticed the dark aura around us, the air feeling chilled. His face was hard, his eyes gleaming dangerously. There was a sense of viciousness around him.

When he looked down at me, his eyes meeting my own, his expression didn't change. His head descended until our lips were inches apart. Our lips met in a breathy kiss. It started slowly before he pressed his lips harder to mine, demanding access.

My lips parted, his tongue sliding against the seams of my lips before meeting my own. I moaned into his kiss, standing on my toes, wanting to be closer to him.

When he finally pulled away, I felt breathless

and was left wanting more. I felt flushed as I looked up at him.

My heart sank when I saw his eyes. They held no emotions.

My gentle lover was still missing. The realization pierced my heart.

I missed him, and I wanted him back.

But I knew he wouldn't be back until Alberto was dead. This was a side of him that I had to grow accustomed to. He was, after all, a killer. The *Pakhan*. A ruthless and heartless one at that.

I sighed and grabbed his hand, entwining our fingers together. His gaze stayed on my face. This was something that would never change.

His attention. When he was with me, I had all this attention. When we were in the same room, his eyes were on me. Always.

"C'mon. I want to play for you," I said, pulling him into the piano room.

Alessio took his place on the couch while I made my way to the piano.

Princess moved around, almost eagerly, as I placed my hand over the piano keys. When I started to play, the melody came through, a soft wave cocooning us. The little one almost instantly settled down.

My eyes went to Alessio, and I saw him relaxed in his seat too. His eyes never left mine, and I reveled in the fact that I had all his attention.

He was mine…and I was his. We were one.

After the first song, I paused. The baby kicked, and a small laugh bubbled out from me. "You like hearing me play?" I whispered, my hand caressing over the bump.

Another kick. A hard one at that.

I played another song, and her movements paused again.

Just like her papa, I thought as I played a third song.

When I was done, I made my way to Alessio. He pulled me into his lap, his arms going around me.

Placing my head over his shoulders, I relaxed in his embrace, letting him hold me. He buried his face in my neck, and I felt him breathe in my scent. His lips pressed against my neck, a soft kiss that made me shiver.

"I missed you," I whispered. Alessio didn't reply.

I looked up and palmed his cheeks. That was when I noticed that his hair was wet. I didn't pay attention before, but he was only wearing a black dress shirt and black slacks.

There was no blood on them.

In fact, he smelled clean.

Did he shower before he came to meet me?

I caressed my thumb over his cheek, feeling the rough stubble under the pad of my fingers. Of course he showered. Not for himself. But for me.

After some time, Alessio stood up, still holding me in his arms.

"Will you sleep?" Before I could stop myself, the question was already asked. I knew the answer, but I still hoped.

His steps paused for a second before he continued to our room. Alessio placed me under the comforter before crawling in bed behind me.

Pulling me into his arms, he laid out a simple command.

"Sleep, Angel."

My eyes closed, and safe in Alessio's arms, I felt asleep. Our baby eventually settled down too.

I felt him shift beside me. With my mind hazy with sleep, I felt Alessio getting out of bed.

I wanted to call out to him, tell him to stay, but sleep was dragging me under. My eyes stayed closed, and my mind drifted off.

The last thought that registered was that Alessio never answered my question.

But now I had his answer.

***

I dried my hair with the towel, making sure my dress didn't get wet in the process. I woke up to Maddie beside me. Alessio was long gone. He had left just after I fell asleep, and he never returned.

I didn't catch a glimpse of him at breakfast, either. With a heavy heart, I came back upstairs and spent some time in the tub, letting my mind think of something happy.

A knock on the door pulled me out of my thoughts. My back straightened, my heart pumping faster.

Even though I knew I was safe, the fear was always there. It was instilled in me.

I wondered how long it was going to be like this. Would I always be this scared? Would my nightmares ever end?

My past kept haunting me—every single

memory kept playing in my head. I had a feeling that it wasn't something I could escape easily.

"Ayla?" I heard Viktor call.

My shoulders sagged in relief, my breath leaving my lungs too fast. "Coming!" I called back. So it was Viktor's time.

Quickly combing my hair, I let it fall against my back. With a sigh, I opened the door to meet Viktor's worried gaze.

"You were taking too long," he said, his eyes raking over me protectively, like he was looking for some sort of injury.

I shook my head and closed the door. "I was just taking a bath. It's relaxing, especially for my aching back and feet."

Viktor nodded before stepping back, quickly realizing he was crowding my space. He rubbed his head nervously before clearing his throat.

"What are your plans for today?" he asked, waiting for me to move. How was it possible for them to talk so casually when I knew exactly what he was doing just an hour ago in the basement?

They changed so fast. One moment, a ruthless killer while the next, they looked like a typical man. Someone gentle.

"Nothing really. I think I will just spend it with Maddie."

And wait for Alessio to come back to me.

My steps faltered when I noticed Lyov coming up the stairs, looking too pale. My eyes widened in surprise, and I quickly lurched forward.

Viktor followed suit, grabbing Lyov by the arms and helping him over the last few stairs. My arm was wrapped around his waist, supporting his other side.

"What are you doing? You should be in bed," I reprimanded.

Lyov tried to shrug us off. "I'm fine. I was just shot…I'm not an invalid."

My eyebrows furrowed. "That's not good, Lyov. Sam said you should be resting. You will tear your stitches if you keep walking around."

"Am I being scolded?" He chuckled dryly, peeking up at me with a hard stare.

I swallowed hard and grew nervous under his unyielding stare. For a moment, I had forgotten who he actually was.

"No…I didn't mean—" I stuttered.

"Only my wife scolded me," he whispered. It wasn't something he meant for us to hear. But we did. Viktor's eyes met mine, and we both hid our smiles. He wasn't angry at me.

Viktor and I helped Lyov to his room. When he was finally settled in his bed, I pulled the bedsheet over him. His breathing was labored, showing sign of pain.

"Should I get you a painkiller?" I asked quietly.

Lyov shook his head. Stubborn man. At least now I knew where Alessio got his traits. They were exactly the same.

"Thank you," he breathed out.

I froze in shock, and I blinked. And blinked again. Finally, I smiled, patting his hand. "Don't thank me. Just get well soon."

I took a step back and saw him wince in pain. He shifted around, looking for a position that was comfortable.

Seeing him in pain brought another thought to mind. My gaze shifted to Lyov, and I finally asked the question that was burning in my head.

"How did you know Alberto was there?" I asked, moving closer. Looking back at Viktor, I waited for their replies.

"I was...watching you and Alessio. My window faces the path to the creek," Lyov mumbled, breathing harshly through his pain. My eyes went to his windows and saw that he was right.

"After you disappeared into the woods...I saw another shadow. Didn't see the face. I didn't...know who it was. I just ran. I just knew I had to get to you both. Isaak and the others saw me running out of the house. They followed, not really knowing why I was running to the creek."

Lyov paused and looked out of the window. "I didn't know it was Alberto until it was too late. I didn't have time to pull out my gun or anything."

"We're just glad we got there in time," Viktor continued when Lyov fell silent. "If something had happened to either of you—the three of you—"

He didn't finish his sentence, leaving his thoughts hanging. But I knew what he meant.

"Thank you. I don't know how to properly thank you for this. I will forever be grateful. You saved our lives. If something had happened to Alessio or my baby, I don't think I would have survived it."

I knew my words affected both men, because they both looked away. I saw Viktor pinching his eyes closed, his fingers tightening in fists.

I smiled, placing a hand on his arm. "Let's go.

175

Lyov needs to rest."

Viktor and I left Lyov to sleep, closing the door behind us. Placing my forehead against the door, I released a sigh. We could have lost so many lives. The thought sat heavy in my heart.

"Alessio is a lucky man to have you."

My eyes snapped open, and I turned around to face Viktor. "Why do you say that?"

He regarded me for a moment, his eyes turning soft. "You have a kind heart. You see the good in people, even when there isn't really anything to see. You disregard all the bad and focus on the good."

My heart fluttered, and I could feel my cheeks heating under his praise. "Maybe it's because nobody ever cared about me. I don't want others to feel the same pain I have felt. It slowly eats you alive."

Viktor stepped forward, moving closer. His hand came up, and I stood frozen, forcing myself not to flinch at this man's unfamiliar touch.

His fingers caressed my cheek softly. "You've been through so much, yet you hold so much strength. He tried to taint you. He tried to break you, but instead you came out stronger."

"Alessio is my strength," I whispered back, thinking of him. "If it wasn't for him, then maybe I wouldn't have made it out alive. He kept me alive, Viktor. Alessio kept me going."

Viktor paused at my words, and I saw him swallowing hard. He looked like he was in pain.

Confusion clouded my mind as I stared up at him. "How much to do you love him?" he asked quietly.

"More than I can love myself," I replied, the truth so easy to speak. "He is everything. You've got it wrong. It's me who is lucky to have Alessio."

"Maybe." He chuckled, but the look in his eyes... Why did he look so heartbroken?

"Tell me how much you love him again," he said, moving even closer.

A shiver ran down my spine, and I licked my lips nervously. Viktor wasn't acting like himself.

"I love him. He is my reason for living," I replied, trying to move away from his touch. I knew he wouldn't hurt me, but that didn't mean his touch was welcomed. Not like this. There was something too intimate in our position.

"Viktor...what are—" I started but quickly broke off in a gasp when he placed his forehead against mine. He pinched his eyes closed, his chest moving against mine as he tried to control his breathing.

"Say it again," he demanded. His eyes were still closed, but his fingers continued to caress my cheek, his touch feather-light. I barely even felt it.

"I...love him."

Viktor opened his eyes, and I saw his gaze drifting toward my lips. My eyes widened, and my heart leaped to my throat.

No. Not this. Please...not this.

"Good," he muttered.

I stayed frozen against the door, not daring to move a muscle. Was this really happening? Did Viktor have...?

No. He couldn't.

"Good," he said again. And then he smiled. "Keep loving him."

I almost flinched when he moved his head up. When I felt his lips on my forehead, I swallowed hard, waiting for this to be over.

His next words made my heart flutter. "Don't ever stop loving him. Because no other man is worthy of your love."

My shoulders sagged, and I let out a harsh breath. Viktor pulled away, his heat leaving me. I stayed against the door, watching him.

"You both deserve each other," he continued. "I'm just really happy that Alessio found you—"

He paused, his eyes twinkling mischievously. "Or should I say, it was you who found him."

Viktor winked, reminding me of the time when I first met Alessio. He was right. It was me who found him. Everything started when I got into his car.

"I'll never let Alessio live that one down. Poor bastard. His woman had to come looking for him while he was wallowing in self-pity."

His laughter made me feel better, all the tension leaving me. "Hey. That's not nice." I swatted his arm. "I don't think you want to get killed, Viktor."

He chuckled low. "No. He loves me too much to kill me. Seriously speaking, I'm like his first love."

Shaking my head, I rubbed my baby bump. When our laughter finally died down, Viktor nodded toward the stairs.

"After you, baby girl." He smirked with a wink.

This...this was the Viktor I knew. The other one from before...he had confused me. It wasn't him.

Mumbling a thank you, I walked away, Viktor following closely behind.

"Lucky bastard," I heard him whisper.

I shook my head but continued moving. There was no use thinking too much into this.

Viktor cared for me. I knew that.

But I also knew he would never betray Alessio.

And he would never betray me, either.

Viktor was Alessio's brother. The trust they had between them was something that couldn't be broken. I also trusted Viktor wholeheartedly.

When Maddie pulled me in her arms and Viktor kissed Lena on her cheeks, I smiled.

We were a family.

Sitting on the stool, I watched Maddie and Viktor bicker over small things.

My mind drifted to Alessio. I felt a pang in my chest. *I'm waiting, Alessio. I miss you, but I will wait for you.*

I just had to wait for my gentle lover to come back.

While I waited for him, I knew he was avenging me in the most horrific way. His thirst for revenge had clouded his mind.

But I didn't mind.

I loved him either way.

Because just like Alessio said; he was my Monster. Just like I was his Angel.

Chapter 21

Alessio

I felt his bone crunch under the force of my punch. It was so loud that it vibrated through my ears.

I heard his scream, but it only fueled my anger. It only pushed me for more.

Grabbing his hair, I pummeled his face over and over again.

Two days. Two days since the fucking bastard was captured and tortured mercilessly under our hands.

But still my thirst for his blood has not been sated. The fury I felt was still boiling inside of me, threatening to break him.

I was not done. I was not close to being done.

In fact, I was just starting.

I was going to make him bleed. He would pay in the most horrific way.

We had a long way to go until I would be satisfied.

What Alberto didn't realize was that I was just as deranged as him.

Pushing his head back, I felt it snap against the back of the chair. I released my hold on Alberto, his head falling forward. He groaned in pain, his blood dripping all over him.

Twisting my fingers in his hair, I pulled his head back sharply until he was looking at me. His eyes were so swollen he could barely keep them open. There was a long cut on his forehead. It was deep, the skin peeled back until I could see his bones.

I took my knife and pressed the handle against the deep cut. Alberto thrashed in my arms as I twisted the handle into the wound. He screamed, but his voice was almost gone from the hours of screaming.

He could only whimper in pain, his voice sounding like a baby.

When I saw he was bleeding too much, I pulled back. Nikolay came forward and pushed the towel against the cut, stopping the bleeding.

I couldn't have him bleed to death.

Not yet.

I still needed him alive.

"How does that feel?" I sneered at him, pouring all my hatred in my words. "Feels good, doesn't it? It's refreshing to be on the other end, isn't it?"

He coughed, heaving forward. I pushed him back, holding my knife against his chest. I didn't press the blade into this skin.

No, I played with him.

Just like he played with my Angel.

Dragging the knife over his chest, I let him feel

the blade. It whispered over his skin but never broke it.

Alberto shuddered in pain, his eyes rolling into the back of his head. He was about to lose consciousness. My palm met his face in a hard slap. "Don't you fucking dare. I'll cut your dick off if you do."

His eyes snapped open, and he regarded me with pure distaste. I laughed at his audacity. He could barely open his eyes, and yet here he was, thinking he stood a chance.

Pressing the blade harder into his chest, I felt him suck in a harsh breath. I still didn't cut his skin. There were already several cuts over his chest and body. But right now, I had other plans.

The blade traveled up his shoulder, leaving a cold trail. Then down his right arm. Alberto stilled as my knife started to press harder and harder against his skin.

When I reached the back of his hand, I paused. The whole time, my eyes were on his, and I reveled when I saw fear in them.

"Do…n't…don't…" he begged.

"Was that how Ayla begged you? She begged you to stop, didn't she?" I roared, holding his throat in my other hand.

I pressed against his windpipe, feeling his trachea under my fingers. My fingers pressed against his set of bones. I could have easily crushed him.

When his face started to turn red, then purple from suffocation, I released his fragile neck.

"You didn't stop. Then why should I?" I hissed

in his face, holding the knife to his hand. Nikolay came to stand behind him and held Alberto's arm still.

I held the tip of my spiral knife to the back of his hand. My eyes watched him stare at the knife. I watched him shuddering in fear. I watched him bleed, and I laughed.

I laughed at his agony as I pulled my knife back and drove it down. Hard.

He screamed and screamed, his wails filling the room. It was a song to my ears.

Alberto tried to move his arm away, but I twisted the knife, holding his hand still. I stared down at my handy job, my eyes following the length of my knife. Half of the blade was lodged in Alberto's hand.

Blood poured around us, but I didn't care. That was the least of my concerns.

"Do you know why I love this knife?" I asked. "Because it's the most painful. It hurts like a son of a bitch. Your hand probably feels like it's going to fall off, right?"

Alberto cried out when I twisted the knife again. I could hear the sound of his flesh mashing together, his bones crunching—breaking. The sound of skin and flesh against blood.

"Don't worry, though. It's not going to fall off," I tried to soothed him. "Not yet anyways."

"Pl…ea…se…"

Tsking at his weak attempt, I pulled back and stared at him. "Aww, poor baby. Are you begging? It's music to my ears, Alberto. Go ahead. Beg me. Maybe if I like the way you beg, I'll spare you."

Watching him writhe under my assault made everything worth it.

"Pl…ea…se…no…more…pl…ease…"

His begging twisted my heart because all I could hear was Ayla begging Alberto to stop. She begged and begged, yet he never stopped. He kept hurting her…over and over again.

"You beg so well. I feel almost bad." I pulled the knife out of his hand before driving it into his flesh again. "But unfortunately, I don't like the way you beg."

"Get me the cutters," I growled. Phoenix did as I commanded and handed me the red cutters I had sharpened just the night before. A gift for Alberto.

"Those fingers, you hurt my Ayla with them, right? Those disgusting fingers…"

Alberto tried to shake his head, his eyes going impossibly wide. As wide as they could with how swollen they were.

Nikolay held his right arm while I held the cutter to his pinky. "Maybe you should count this one. It might help," I suggested with a mocked smile.

I didn't give Alberto time to think.

Pressing the cutter to his pinky, I cut.

I didn't stop there. No, I sliced off all his fingers. In only one cut. From pinky to his thumb.

In mere seconds, he lost all his fingers on his right hand.

I watched the blood drip as I watched his fingers fall to my feet.

Alberto stared at his hand in shock. And when the pain finally registered, he roared.

Nikolay released his arm, and I stepped back,

letting him bask in his newfound agony.

I took the towel and wiped away his blood from my blade and cutter.

The door opened behind me, and Nikolay left. Viktor took his position behind Alberto.

I looked up at Viktor, our eyes meeting. He nodded.

Ayla was okay.

At the thought of Ayla, my mind drifted back to the scene when she shot Alberto.

I was so fucking proud of her. She was my equal.

In that moment, she looked like a true avenging Angel.

If she had done more damage, I would have been there to support her. Fuck, I would have held her hands and let her cut him open.

But this wasn't for her.

I knew Ayla. Shooting Alberto took everything in her, all her strength, and hatred. But killing someone...that was not my Angel.

Let me be your monster. Let me kill for you, Angel.

I didn't think I could speak any truer words than that. I meant every single word. I was hers. I would kill for her. I had done it before, I would do it now, and I would fucking kill for her in the future too.

Do your worst.

I smiled as I remembered her words.

Yes, Ayla...I was about to do my worst.

After all, my Queen has spoken, and her wish was my command.

Snapping out of my thoughts, I saw Viktor taking his turn on Alberto. Punching, kicking,

185

slicing, and cutting. Alberto had already been a mess, but now he was unrecognizable.

The smell of blood was heavy in the air, but I had gotten used to it.

I raised my hand, and Viktor halted his assault. He was breathing hard, his glares burning into Alessio.

"Phoenix, bring in Enzo and Artur. It's time for a family reunion," I ordered calmly. Sometimes, the calm was just as deadly.

I saw Phoenix's face twisting in pure hatred at the mention of Artur.

Alberto sagged against his chair, almost falling off. We had a long way to go.

My eyes moved to the door as I watched Phoenix drag in a beaten-up Enzo and Artur. He pushed them in front of Alberto. I walked closer, and they fell to their knees, kneeling in front of me.

Their fear was so heavy it saturated the air. I could almost taste it. It just fed the monster inside of me.

Taking the latex gloves from my pocket, I put them on. I did it slowly, taking my time. They watched me with terror, so much terror.

The cutter was held tightly in my hands, and I squatted down in front of Artur. He was my man. One of my most trusted man.

I took him into my house. Gave him my name. But in the end, he showed no respect. He had no loyalty.

Viktor grabbed his hair and pulled his head back. He whimpered in pain as I pried his jaw open. He shuddered and twisted, trying to get away.

He knew what was coming. But there was no escape. Not this time.

Viktor pushed him back until Artur laid flat on the floor, thrashing for his life. I held his jaw firm in my hand, my fingers biting into his cheeks.

He pounded his fists against the floor, tried to dislodge my hold, but it was no use.

I showed him the cutter, moving it in front of his face. Viktor held Artur's jaw, forcing his mouth open for me.

He screamed, but it only came out as a gurgling sound. My fingers latched onto his tongue, my fingers pressing hard. I held the piece of flesh firmly in my fingers.

His eyes widened with horror when I brought the cutter closer to his tongue. I smiled as he tried to shake his head.

He begged me with his eyes.

But it was too late.

My Angel suffered because of him. And now it was his turn.

Holding the cutter to his tongue, I cocked my head to the side. I waited, counting the seconds in my head.

When he saw me not taking action, Artur eyed me suspiciously.

I waited and waited.

And then he stopped thrashing, falling silent.

His muscles started to relax; his guard fell down.

I cut.

One single cut and I was holding his tongue in my hand. It was no longer attached to his body. Standing up, I watched him writhe on the ground, his agony too much to bear.

Artur screamed. He wailed. He cried. He sobbed. And I smiled.

"You chose to talk too much. And I choose to end your talking. I think it's a fair decision, isn't it?" I asked casually, holding his tongue for everyone to see.

Enzo stared at me in horror, his face turning white. Alberto looked like he was about to pass out. I chuckled at the weakness they showed.

Phoenix brought me a plastic bag, and I dropped the tongue in it. Making a knot, I closed the bag and threw it at Artur. "There you go. Your tongue. Who knows? You might need it."

He grabbed the bag and brought it to his chest. Blood pooled from his mouth. Such a pathetic sight.

I turned to face Enzo, and he shook his head. He tried to scramble away, but Phoenix held him down.

"You're not going anywhere," I hissed, stopping in front of him.

I kicked his stomach, feeling his rib breaking under the force. He howled in pain.

But it was only the beginning.

Nodding at Viktor, he came to Enzo and pulled down his pants. Enzo screamed, trying to break free.

"No…no…please…no," he begged, but his words fell on deaf ears. They meant nothing to me.

I grabbed his dick in my hand and chuckled when he screamed again. I pressed the cutter to his flesh, moving the blade up and down. I didn't cut him. I was only letting him feel the blade.

"Please…" he begged again.

"Every time you beg, it reminds me of Ayla. How she begged you. It just makes me angrier. So really, I think it'll be better if you *don't* beg," I hissed, pressing the cutter a little harder.

Enzo nodded his head. "I...won't...beg...don't do this..." He hiccupped back a sob, his whole body shaking violently.

"I didn't tell you to speak, though. Now I'm more pissed."

I didn't give him a chance to react or beg me again.

My cutter sliced through his dick, severing it from his body.

I stood up and watched him scream in pain. His whole body spasmed in agony, his screams continuing to fill the room.

After watching him thrash around, I threw his limp dick at him. Artur was no longer screaming, but he was still sobbing and moaning in pain.

"Make sure they don't bleed to death," I instructed in a deadly voice. It sounded harsh even to my own ears.

Turning toward Alberto, I stared at his pale face. He looked too white, like a ghost. His head hung limply against the back of the chair, like he had no strength to hold it up.

"That was only a warning. To you. Just to give you a little glimpse of your future. I would say be prepared, but no matter how much you prepare yourself, it won't be enough."

With those as my final words, I walked out of the basement.

I would be back. Soon.

But right now, it was time to see my Angel.

My heart felt light at the thought of her. The pain inside of me, the fury…it all soothed to a calming wave.

Climbing up the stairs, I made my way to my office. After showering and changing into another clean shirt and slacks, I went to the piano room.

My steps faltered, my heart hammering in my chest when I saw the lights were off.

My chest grew tight as I walked to our bedroom. I opened the door, my eyes falling into the darkness. There was only a lamp on, casting a soft glow into the room.

My eyes scanned the room, looking for her.

There she was. On the bed. Sleeping.

Relief coursed through me as I closed the door behind me. Walking closer to the bed, I stared down at my sleeping Angel. She looked so beautiful.

Her eyebrows were pinched together, and I knew her sleep wasn't peaceful. I gently rubbed my finger over the stressed lines, smoothing it out.

I climbed into the bed and pulled her against me. Holding her close, I molded my body around her. My hands rubbed soothing circles around the baby bump.

Ayla moaned in her sleep and turned around in my arms. She must have been really tired if she didn't wait for me in the piano room.

"Alessio," she said sleepily, rubbing her eyes.

My lips pressed against her forehead in a soft kiss. "I'm right here. Go back to sleep."

"Hmm…"

She snuggled into my embrace and was asleep in

no time.

I stayed awake, my mind refusing to shut down. After a few hours of holding Ayla, I pulled away from her. I gave her a kiss on the lips before slipping out of the room again.

I was back in the basement in seconds. Artur and Enzo were both propped against the wall, while Alberto still sat on the chair.

His eyes met mine as I walked into the room. I didn't walk any closer.

Instead, I waited. There was someone who needed to join us.

Phoenix and Viktor were leaning against the wall. Nikolay paced. We waited.

Then the door opened.

The sound of heels clicking against the floor sounded in the silent basement.

I chuckled when I felt her standing by my side. She wore the same outfit she always did. Black leather pants. Black leather jacket. Her heels were always different, though.

This time she was wearing dark pink heels.

I turned to see her pulling her hood down. Nina smiled at Alberto. "Hey, love. Miss me?"

Alberto stared at her in shock, and he glowered. That was something not even Artur knew. Nobody did. It was only between Nina and me.

I placed her as an undercover at one of the clubs. She got closer to Alberto, playing the perfect whore for him.

It took everything in her to submit to a man like Alberto, but she did. Her loyalty to me came first.

Nina took a step forward, and I watched the

scene unfold. I felt someone else at my back. Swiveling around, I faced the unknown man.

He was young. Probably twenty. There was a long scar on his face, one very similar to Nikolay's. There was another scar on his neck.

His dark eyes were only trained on Nina, and I lifted an eyebrow.

"He's with me," Nina said without me even asking the question.

"Come here, boy." She snapped her finger. He quickly moved to her side, like an obedient dog. He was taller than she was, her head only coming to his shoulders even with her heels on.

Nina patted his hair, and I saw her give him a small smile. In that moment, I knew that smile was only reserved for him.

"He's under my wings. Under my protection. I'm training him," Nina explained. "When he's ready, I'll send him to you. He will be perfect. I'm sure of it."

Viktor, Phoenix, and Nikolay stared at her in surprise, but no one uttered a word.

Turning to face Alberto, Nina walked forward. "Do you remember him? Three years ago. You slaughtered his family. You scarred him. He wasn't supposed to survive."

Alberto's eyes widened, watching the boy.

"But he did. He survived your cruel joke," she hissed, punching the hand that I had made a hole in.

Alberto howled in pain.

Nina turned to face the boy again. She placed her hand out, waiting for him to take it. He took it almost immediately.

She palmed his cheek. "Go ahead. I'll let you have a little fun. But don't kill him, okay?"

He nodded, looking at Alberto eagerly. Nina stepped back and let her protégé have his fun. She came to stand beside me.

And we watched.

I had to admit, the boy was good. After all, he was trained by Nina. I wouldn't have expected anything less.

"What's his name?" I asked, watching him hold a cigarette in his hand. I knew what was coming next.

"Xavier," she replied, her eyes never leaving the boy.

He lit the cigarette, and Nikolay went to hold Alberto down. No matter how much he screamed, it had no effect on anyone.

The boy pressed the cigarette to Alberto's skin, watching it sizzle. All over his chest, he left burn marks.

He twisted the cigarette into Alberto's flesh, making a hole in his stomach. I could almost smell the burning flesh.

Over and over again, he did it. Lighting more cigarettes, pressing them into Alberto's skin, watching it burn.

When Alberto started to lose consciousness, Nina stepped forward. "Stop."

The boy stopped and returned to Nina's side. She patted his cheek. "There you go. I'm proud of you. Are you satisfied? Is that enough for your revenge?" The boy paused. "Be honest with me," Nina demanded.

The boy shook his head. "I know you aren't satisfied. But he is not yours to kill. This is your lesson. You need to know when to stop and when to continue. If you continued, he would have died. You need to learn patience and control. Learn to play with your prey."

He nodded his head, looking eager to please Nina.

I slowly shook my head at them. Glancing at Alberto, I saw his head hanging low. I pierced Nikolay with a look, and he nodded. Filling a bucket with cold, chilling water, he dumped it over Alberto.

He sputtered and grimaced in pain, but his eyes opened.

I put on another pair of latex gloves. Walking to the table, I got the one thing I'd wanted to use for a very long time. Holding the cow whip in my hand, I walked back to Alberto.

My fingers wrapped around his hair, fisting it and dragging him out of the chair. My knees came up hard into this side, cracking his ribs. When I heard the satisfying sound of bones breaking, I released him.

Alberto fell to the floor at my feet.

Viktor and Nikolay came to hold him down. Phoenix held his legs. I squatted down next to him.

I held the whip in my hand, but it was no use to me. I didn't want the whip. I wanted the handle, the splintered handle. It was made of wood, perfect for what I had in mind.

I pulled his pants down and laughed as he tried to thrash, but he was completely trapped. Nowhere to go. Just like he had trapped my Angel.

"You're going to enjoy this," I whispered in his ear. "Take it like a good boy, okay?"

Watching him struggle under me, I chuckled darkly. Slowly I pushed the handle into his ass. His screams rang in my ears, but I savored them. I savored his pain.

The handle was just a few inches inside his rectum. I paused, waiting, letting his agony drive him insane, pushing him further into the darkness.

He sobbed against the floor. With an angry growl, I shoved the handle fully up his ass. Alberto bellowed out, but I just kept going, pulling out slightly before pushing it back in. Again and again, I tortured him.

His hole was bleeding severely. The splintered handle was covered with his blood, but I kept going. "You took her. Again and again. When she didn't want you, you still took her. How does it feel to have something up your ass when you don't want it? Huh?" I roared.

Alberto whimpered and cried out. I patted his back. "Shh...didn't I tell you? Take it like a good boy. You like this, don't you?"

Blood continued to seep out as I shoved the handle back in, lodging it deep inside of him. His head came off the floor as his body spasmed in absolute agony.

I left the handle there and turned to face him. His face was wet not only with his blood, but his tears too.

"She cried too. But you kept assaulting her. Your tears just remind me of Ayla being in pain," I sneered, grabbing his head and slamming it into the floor.

I pulled the handle out, painfully twisting it as I did. Standing up, I turned away from Alberto.

I walked to Nina and handed her the whip. "Have some fun," I said, raising an eyebrow. She took the whip from my hand and walked toward Alberto.

"Oh, I will definitely have fun," she replied, her lips widening in a sadistic smile.

I watched as she pressed her heel into the back of Alberto's knee. The heel sank into his flesh, and he screamed, trying to escape the cruel assault.

"You know how disgusting it was, letting you touch me every time? You make me sick," she hissed, straddling Alberto's back. Without warning, she shoved the handle into his hole again.

I nodded at Viktor, and he quickly came to my side. His eyes were just as deranged. I knew I looked the same.

The very monsters everyone knew us to be.

"Do what you want with him. I don't care. I will come for him in the morning," I said and then paused when Alberto let out another loud scream.

"I want to spend tonight with Ayla."

Viktor nodded in understanding. "She misses you."

I sigh, already knowing that. I fucking missed her too. Every minute away from her felt like a stabbing pain in my chest.

"Just keep them alive," I said, nodding towards the Alberto, Enzo, and Artur.

"Tomorrow they will meet their end. I will finish

what the fucking Italians started," I snarled, my fingers tightening in fists.

Viktor nodded again. "I've got your back, Alessio."

I knew he did. He always did have my back.

After clasping his shoulder in a show of gratitude, I left the basement and made my way to my Angel.

Chapter 22

I opened the door quietly and walked inside. I stopped next to the bed, staring down at my Angel. She was sleeping peacefully, a tiny smile on her lips. She must be having a good dream.

Making sure I didn't wake her up, I took a few steps back. I didn't want her to see me like this. This was the last thing she needed.

I knew she wasn't scared of me...of who I truly was. But I didn't think she was ready to know the things I had done. And would keep doing.

In the end, I was truly a monster.

That was never going to change, and I didn't want to change. It was who I was.

I stared at Ayla, and for a brief moment, I let myself think of a different possibility. What if I was different man? Someone Ayla could proudly say was her man?

Not a deranged monster. Not Alessio Ivanshov.

With a sigh and a heavy heart, I walked away. Closing the door of the washroom, I shrugged off my shirt.

I got into the shower, letting the cold water rain down on me, washing the blood away. Washing any evidence of what I had done in the past hours away.

With my hands pressed against the wall, I tried to breathe through my constricting chest.

I stayed there, not moving until I heard the door open. My eyes squeezed shut, knowing who it was.

There was some shuffling and then the shower doors opened. I felt a soft hand on my shoulder and heard her sweet voice.

The water went from cold to hot, and I knew she switched it.

"Alessio?"

I didn't turn around. "Alessio, look at me."

Not moving, I leaned against the wall.

"Please, Alessio." As soon as the word *please* was out of her mouth, I swiveled around, facing my Angel.

She palmed my cheeks and stood on her toes. Ayla placed a soft, gentle kiss on my lips. It was a sweet kiss.

I couldn't move. Her lips moved to my cheeks, kissing each side. She nipped playfully at my nose before kissing it.

And then her lips moved to my forehead. They lingered there for a second before she placed another soft kiss too.

My Angel wrapped her arms around my waist, her pregnant belly pressing against my stomach. She held me to her, her head over my racing heart.

She laid a kiss there and then hummed almost lovingly. "I missed you, Alessio."

My throat closed up. The love in her voice made

my heart leap. Wrapping my arms around her, I pulled Ayla against me.

We held each other like this, our arms firm around each other. We didn't let go as the water cascaded around us.

She held me in her embrace, and I held her in mine.

"I love you, Angel," I whispered in her ears. "I love you so fucking much."

Chapter 23

Ayla

The sound of the door opening brought me out of my slumber.

I saw Alessio coming to the side of the bed. He blended almost fully into the darkness, but I saw him. I felt him.

He didn't touch me. I thought he would take me in his arms, but I never felt his warmth. Alessio was silent while I kept my eyes closed, waiting for him.

When I felt him move, I looked to find him walking away. My heart drummed, feeling his loss.

The air felt heavy around us. Alessio's shoulders were hunched together, like he was in pain. I didn't like that. Alessio's pain was my pain.

I watched him go into the bathroom, closing the door behind him. I waited for a few seconds, my fingers itching to touch him, to feel him, to hold him.

When I couldn't bear it any longer, I threw the covers away and struggled out of bed. It came to a point where it was harder to get up from lying down.

I padded to the bathroom quietly. My fingers stayed on the door knob, debating if I should give Alessio privacy. My mind told me yes, but my heart refused. It pulled me inside, telling me to hold Alessio. To give him comfort.

I didn't know what was eating him from the inside, but I had to take it away.

His back was to me when I walked inside. Alessio heard me, but he stayed still. His hands were against the walls, his head hung low. Alessio had his shirt removed, but he still wore his pants.

I watched the water cascade around him as I removed my dress. Dropping it the floor, my eyes moved to his discarded shirt. It was black, the same color he always wore.

I licked my lips nervously when I saw the wet patches. I couldn't see the color, but I knew it was blood.

My heart stuttered at the sight, and my eyes moved back to the man in front of me. I should be disgusted, but I wasn't.

Alessio Ivanshov was the man I loved. Whether he was a monster, a heartless killer, or my sweet lover, I loved all sides of him.

Every side of him was what made him Alessio. He wouldn't be the man I loved if he wasn't the killer.

Taking a deep breath, I stepped inside the shower. Alessio's shoulders tightened, but he didn't move. The water was freezing cold, so I quickly turned the tap to the warm side.

My hand came in contact with his cold skin, my body moving closer to his. "Alessio?"

He didn't face me. "Alessio, look at me."

Alessio leaned heavily against the wall, and I moved even closer. "Please, Alessio," I begged.

As soon as the word please was out of my mouth, he swiveled around, facing me. His expression was pained, like he was battling something in his mind.

Without a word, I palmed his cheeks and peppered his face with kisses. With each kiss, I showed him my love. No words were needed. I just held him. I loved him with my touch.

Standing on my toes, I kissed his closed lids and then his forehead. Alessio released a shaky breath, his shoulder slumping in what looked like defeat.

I hugged him to me. My pregnant belly was in the way, but I was still able to lay my head on his chest. His steady heartbeat drummed in my ears, and I placed a kiss on his chest, right over his beating heart.

"I missed you, Alessio," I whispered the truth. My fingers rubbed over his skin lovingly as he hugged me back, his arms wrapping around me tightly.

His breath left his chest in a loud whoosh as he crushed my body to his. I felt his lips on my ear. "I love you, Angel," he whispered harshly. "I love you so fucking much."

I felt giddy at his declaration of love. A small serene smile touched my lips as I pulled away from his embrace. I held his face in my hands and moved closer until our lips were inches apart.

When our lips met, it felt like fireworks. We created magic as our lips moved against each other. I kissed him with everything I had. Slow and deep at first, our tongues moved together in a mating dance.

Alessio groaned against my lips as he deepened the kiss even further. He angled my head to the side before nipping at my lips. My fingers gripped his hair, pulling him more into me.

I was going to show Alessio how much I loved him.

Our harsh breathing filled the shower as we pulled away. Alessio bent his head for another kiss, but I stepped back. His eyebrows pulled up in a frown when my hands went to his belt.

"Let me take care of you," I said, pulling his pants down. He lifted his feet without a word and allowed me to remove his pants and boxer briefs. I pushed them away and stood up again.

Alessio stared at me curiously, his eyes darker than usual. "What are you doing?" he asked, wrapping his arms around me.

"You never give me a chance to take care of you. Let me do this," I murmured before squeezing some soap in my palm.

Alessio opened his mouth to argue, but I shut him down with a quick kiss. He stared at me, dumbfounded, and I smiled, almost cheekily. I knew how to render him speechless.

I lathered up his body with soap, even going down to my knees to wash his legs. Alessio tried to stop me again, but I leveled him with a look before continuing with my task.

I pushed him under the shower head, letting the water cascade around us. Alessio stayed still for me while I washed him, rubbing my hands over his skin softly and with care. I entwined our fingers together and brought our hands up to my lips. After placing a kiss on the back of his hand, I washed myself.

Alessio stared at me with his intense blue eyes, his gaze never wavering. His whole attention was on me, and I reveled under his loving eyes.

When I was done, I stepped out and took the towel in my hand. Alessio followed closely behind me, and I dried him with the large towel. He was strangely silent as I took care of him.

He took the other towel and did the same thing for me. When I tried to stop him, he silenced me with a kiss. His bruising kiss left me hot and wanting.

My hands held his as I pulled us out of the bathroom. I pushed Alessio on the bed. His eyes widened slightly as he regarded me curiously. An eyebrow was raised in question, but he stayed silent.

No words. Only silence. Only us.

I climbed in bed beside him. When I laid down, he turned toward me, pulling me close.

His lips descended on mine, and we kissed. He licked along my lips, demanding access. I moaned, opening my mouth for his kiss. I shivered in anticipation, my body burning hotter as the seconds ticked by.

He pushed his tongue between my lips, seeking mine. My hands lifted to his head, my fingers wrapping his hair, pulling him closer.

We didn't break the kiss as his hand whispered

across my thigh, pushing my legs slightly apart. I gasped into his mouth, but Alessio just kissed me deeper.

My nails dug into his shoulders, a small moan escaping me. He groaned into the kiss, nipping softly at my tender lips.

When I felt his hand between my legs, caressing my inner thigh, his finger moving closer to my core, I broke the kiss. My heart hammered hard against my ribcage. My chest moved up and down faster with my harsh breathing.

Alessio's lips moved to my neck as he continued kissing a downward path. He licked the skin, nipping and biting softly, leaving his mark. A deep rumble echoed from his chest when my nails bit into his back.

Alessio's thigh nudged my legs apart, and I licked my lips. He rolled on top of me, and my eyes fluttered shut. Alessio lowered his body over mine, his lower torso settling between my parted thighs.

I felt his hard length resting against my dripping core, and my eyes snapped open. His lips continued to trail wet kisses to my breast.

My hands went to his shoulders, and I pushed. "No."

Alessio's eyes immediately snapped open in shock. I pushed again, my voice coming out husky as I repeated my word. "No."

His eyes flared in shock, disappointed and then disgusted. With himself.

Alessio swore, quickly moving his body off mine. "Fuck! Shit. I'm so sorry, Ayla. Fuck! I didn't think. I shouldn't have pushed you for more."

Watching him beat himself up over a mistake that wasn't even made, I felt my heart constrict. I shook my head and palmed his cheeks, bringing his attention back to me.

"No, that's not what I meant. Stop beating yourself up when you did nothing wrong," I soothed gently, moving my fingers over his rough stubble.

He opened his mouth to say something, but I pushed him flat on his back. Alessio snapped his mouth shut, swallowing hard several times. "What are you doing, Ayla?"

"Taking care of you," I simply replied.

When I moved my body over his, his eyes widened in understanding. "You don't…"

I kissed his lips soundly. My hands traveled down his stomach toward his hard cock. It laid hard and firm against his lower belly.

My fingers wrapped around his length. Alessio sucked in a hard breath, breaking the kiss in the process.

His eyes flared dangerously when my fingers tightened around him. "Ayla," he groaned, and I smiled. I loved how I affected him so easily.

I stroked his hard length, watching Alessio, this heartless killer, coming undone with my touch.

His jaw was clenched, his breathing coming out harder and faster. I grew wet between my thighs, but I ignored the ache there.

A deep grunt escaped past his parted lips when my thumb moved over his tip. He was rigid as I continued to move my hands up and down, faster now. Alessio dragged in a strangled breath as I stroked his length.

I glanced down, watching my hand move over his swelling cock. I clenched my thighs together and licked my lips.

I worked him faster as his hips started to move with my hand. Alessio grabbed his fingers around my own, tightening my grip on his hardness. My eyes snapped to his, and I sucked in a harsh breath at the primal look he was giving me.

My breasts ached, my body vibrating with need under the intensity of his gaze.

"Like this," he ordered roughly, moving our hands faster and harder. He released my hand and let me do the rest.

His hips jerked as he fucked my hand. My thumb swirled over the tip, coating it with Alessio's pre-cum.

He groaned, becoming taut. I knew he was close. Leaning over him, I took his lips in a kiss. Alessio gripped my neck, biting on my lower lip before kissing me hard.

He stiffened beneath me and broke the kiss. Holding my gaze with his fiery blue eyes, Alessio came all over my hand and his stomach.

Feeling breathless, I looked down at the result, my eyes moving to my hand. Alessio bent down over the bed to retrieve the discarded towel.

He cleaned my hand, his cock, and his stomach before dropping the towel to the floor again. My heart was wild in my chest, my inner thighs wet from my excitement as I stared at my man.

I couldn't stop looking at him. Alessio grabbed my knees and pulled me over him so I was straddling him. Smiling down at him, I leaned my forehead against his.

When I felt his hand slowly moving to my inner thigh, I jerked in surprise. He pushed a finger against my wet core, and I let out an unashamed moan.

Quickly giving myself a mental shake, I gripped his hand, stopping his movement. I removed his hand from my leg. Alessio looked at me in surprise, but I just kissed him.

"Only you tonight, Alessio," I whispered against his lips. "Only you."

I wanted to love him and take care of him. Tonight, Alessio needed me more than I needed him.

He needed my love, so I gave it to him freely.

Alessio's eyes darkened possessively, and a low growl vibrated from his chest. When his lips made contact with mine, he showed me exactly who I belonged to.

I nipped at his lower lips, demanding control, and he gave it to me without question. He let me take and give whatever I wanted.

In return, I gave him everything.

With my kiss, I showed him how much I loved him. I made it so that he never questioned my love for him.

Chapter 24

My eyes fluttered open the next morning when I felt Alessio getting out of bed. He placed a quick kiss on my forehead before getting up. My eyes followed him quietly.

I usually woke up later in the day. But today, I wanted to spend the morning with Alessio.

My little princess kicked me hard in the side, almost like she was disapproving that we woke up so early. I rubbed my hand over my rounded belly, waiting for her to calm down.

My precious little princess.

I smiled at the thought. I couldn't wait to meet her and spoil her. Love her the way she deserved. Give her all the love Alessio and I never had.

My baby would never live the life I did. I would fight tooth and nail if anyone opposed me.

But I knew no one would. As much as I loved her, I knew Alessio and everyone else loved her the same. She was everyone's princess…the miracle everyone was waiting for but never realized they wanted.

She finally settled down when I walked to the bathroom. Opening the door, I walked in to see Alessio brushing his teeth. I stood beside him and did the same.

He was done before me. Alessio came to stand behind me. His arms wrapped around my hips in a hug, and he kissed my neck before leaving the bathroom. After washing my face and brushing my hair, I walked out to see Alessio putting his clothes on.

He already had his shirt and slacks on. I could see his back muscles bunching beneath his fitted dress shirt as he shrugged on his suit jacket.

I took the opportunity to look at him. When he turned around, Alessio gave me a crooked, sexy smile. His eyes were dark and fierce with power. I almost shivered at his intense stare.

Alessio was in his element. He exuded power and total control. His expression was hard. He almost looked terrifying as he walked toward me. His eyes, his steps, the way he held himself...everything spoke of dominance.

Alessio looked like the ruthless mafia Boss that he was.

Under his scrutinizing gaze, I grew bolder. More powerful. This man...he was mine.

When he came to a stop in front of me, his arm snaked out quickly. I gasped when he pulled me close. "Good morning," he whispered roughly in my ear.

"Good morning," I replied. He chuckled low, and my arms tightened around him. "Do you want to have breakfast with me?" I asked.

Alessio paused and pulled away. "I have things to take care of, Ayla," he replied curtly. A look of pure fury appeared on his face, and I knew exactly what he meant.

Placing a hand over his chest, I rubbed softly. "Please."

Alessio sighed, his shoulder dropping slightly. Just then, a knock came on the door. I smiled sheepishly. "That's our breakfast."

He shook his head, a small smile ghosting his lips. "Fine."

I let out a squeal and gave him a quick peck before running to the door. Opening it wide, I smiled at the maid and took the tray from her hand. "Thank you," I said before closing the door.

I placed the tray on the coffee table and waited for Alessio to take his seat. He pulled me to his lap, and I settled sideways against his chest.

Alessio picked up a piece of toast and held it to my lips, waiting for me to take the first bite. I did, and then I fed him.

We fed each other like we had done before. When the tray was empty, Alessio placed a kiss on my temple. "I need to go."

I nodded reluctantly. "What are you going to do?" I asked quietly.

Without answering, Alessio picked me up and walked to the bed. He placed me under the cover and pulled the comforter to my neck. After tucking me in, he kissed my forehead and then lips.

"I'm going to end it today. I am going to fucking end everything," he said roughly against my lips.

His words left goosebumps across my skin. I

almost trembled at his tone. With those words, he gave me a final glance before walking away.

I closed my eyes, releasing the long breath I didn't realize I was holding.

This was it. The ending Alessio had been waiting for. The ending I was desperate for.

Closing my eyes, I waited for my man to come back.

After he was done slaughtering his enemies. *Our enemies.*

***

Alessio

I walked downstairs to see Viktor and Nikolay waiting for me at the landing. Their faces were pensive, but I knew they were waiting for the same thing as me.

Nodding in their direction, I made my way to the basement. They followed closely behind.

"They lost too much blood," Viktor said, coming beside me.

"It doesn't matter," I snapped. My mind raged at the thought of them dying. I wanted to torture them more. I wanted them to bleed and hurt more.

"It's not like they will be alive by the end of the day," I finished with a dark laugh. Viktor shook his head, but I didn't miss the sinister smile that appeared on his face.

Nikolay was stoic as always, but I could feel his edginess. We all couldn't wait for those bastards to stop breathing.

I would make sure to end their lives as painfully as I could, because they didn't deserve anything less.

My steps echoed around the silent walls as I walked into the basement. Phoenix and Nina were there, standing over the limp bodies.

"Stop," I growled. Nina immediately stopped her cruel ministration, but it took Phoenix longer to snap out of his killing haze. Viktor had to pull him away.

"You have to learn control," I hissed at Phoenix, leveling him with a hard glare.

He swallowed, his vengeful eyes still on Artur. "I'm sorry, Boss. The sight of his face makes me sick. He needs to pay."

For what he has done to Maddie. Silent words but they still rang loud in our ears.

Clasping his shoulder, I gave him a firm squeeze. "He will pay," I said, looking at the bloodied body in front of me.

I walked closer to Alberto. He was on the floor, his arm twisted in an impossible angle. I almost laughed at the pathetic sight in front of me. Actually, I did laugh.

I kicked his side, and he groaned before lifting his head up. Alberto stared at me with swollen eyes. I could see the hatred there, but it didn't faze me.

His hate for me didn't even come close to how much I loathed him.

I gripped his hair, matted with blood, and smacked his head into the hard floor. He yowled in pain, but even that sounded weak, like a newborn lamb.

"How does your ass feel?" I hissed in his ears. "Feels good, right? To have a taste of your own medicine?"

Alberto whimpered, and I chuckled darkly. "The only difference is that Ayla is safe and alive. She is loved and still breathing. My baby is safe. But you—you. Are. Dead. Meat."

"I gave it to him plenty last night," Nina drawled, coming to stand beside him. "I think I even heard him say he enjoyed it." She laughed, kicking the bloodied man. "Can I have another go?" she asked innocently. I shook my head. Without looking, I knew she was pouting. Only Nina would pout about not getting a chance to torture and kill someone.

"Move out. We need to go," I said with loud authority. My voice went low with dominance. No one questioned me.

"I think it's time we pay the Abandonatos a visit," I continued.

Alberto's head snapped up in surprise, and I smiled. "It's time for your men to see your downfall."

They would watch him take his last breath while I rose as King. As the motherfucking Boss.

He tried to say something, but only gurgling sound came out. Shaking my head, I stood up. "Let's go."

Viktor went to grab Alberto by the hair as he dragged him out of the basement. Phoenix had Artur by the hair, while Nikolay had Enzo.

It was going to be a parade. Let everyone watch these men as they fought for their lives. It was a lesson to never cross me.

I walked first, Nina behind me, while the others followed. The air smelled of death, and I reveled in it. I fed on it, drawing my power from their hopelessness.

It was too sad for them. They angered the wrong man.

I heard my maid gasping as they watched the scene in front of them. Some of my men smiled as they watched the limp bodies go by.

Some hollered almost victoriously. Then they bowed as I passed them.

From the corner of my eyes I saw Maddie standing near the stairs. Tears streamed down her face as she choked back her sobs.

Her whole body shook. Lena stood beside her, trying to console her daughter.

Maddie's eyes followed Artur's body. My steps faltered, and I swiveled around. Nina gave me a curious look but didn't utter a single word. My eyes moved to Artur to see him glancing at Maddie too.

His face was pained, and I knew it wasn't because of his wounds. He looked like a heartbroken man as he stared at Maddie.

I looked at Phoenix, but he was already shaking his head. "He is not even going a foot near her. I'll snap, Boss."

I sighed, pinching the bridge of my nose. Before I could make a decision, I saw Maddie come closer.

"Stay away, Maddie," Phoenix snapped loudly.

She ignored him, approaching even closer. "Maddie, I'm warning you," he growled, his eyes glowing furiously.

"Don't order me around, Phoenix. You will regret it," she hissed at him.

"Maddie…"

"You don't get to make any decisions for me," she snapped back.

I felt my eyebrows reach my hairline. It looked like things were still messed up between them. Maddie was hard to crack. Phoenix was going to have a hard time with this spitfire.

Maddie stopped about two feet away from Phoenix and Artur.

"Release him," I ordered.

Phoenix swallowed hard. His first instinct was to refuse, but his grip eventually loosened. He stepped away, his chest heaving with fury.

Artur went to his knees, his swollen eyes staring at Maddie. I saw his gaze moving to her stomach. He crawled closer until he was only inches away from Maddie.

I saw her flinch, but she stood her ground, her chin lifted in defiance. With the strength of a baby lamb, he buried his face in Maddie's stomach.

He was shaking, a strangled cry coming from his chest.

I saw Maddie's chin wobble, but she didn't cry. Everyone stayed frozen, watching the scene in front of them. I almost felt bad for the bastard. The loss of his child…knowing he was the cause of his baby's death…it could break anyone.

Right then, Artur was a broken man.

He continued to cry, and Maddie just remained still. Slowly, she lifted her hand and placed it on top his head, caressing his hair. It was a brief touch before she pulled her hand away. His face was still buried in her flat stomach, and I nodded at Phoenix. He came forward and pulled Artur away.

I knew in that moment, if Artur was able to speak...his words would have been *I am sorry.*

But I took that chance away. I hoped that Maddie saw the words in his eyes. She needed it.

When a single tear streamed down her cheek, I knew she saw it. Maddie nodded and walked away without a second glance.

I felt my skin prickle under an intense stare. Immediately, I knew who it was. It was almost as if I was drawn to her.

My head snapped up to the top of the stairs to see Ayla standing there. She stood still, and my heart hammered in my chest.

The monster side of me wanted her to see this. The bloody mess. I wanted her to see what I did for her.

But the other side, the gentle side I never knew I had...that side wanted to shield her from all of this.

"Let's go," I growled. Breaking our gaze, I turned around.

"Wait."

The soft voice was firm yet gentle. I paused. My men paused. Everyone fucking froze at the soft command.

I almost smiled. She really was the queen.

Turning around, I saw her walking down the stairs. All eyes were on her as she made her descent, but her eyes were only on me.

Ayla continued walking until she was only a few feet away from us. I saw her swallow hard, and then she took a deep breath. Her shoulders straightened back firmly, and her chin was held high.

Her eyes moved to Alberto. I felt mine widen, and I took a protective step forward, a small growl escaping past my lips.

I could see Phoenix raising an eyebrow at me, mocking me.

I moved forward until I was standing at her side. Ayla smiled up at me sweetly, and she stood on her toes. "Let me do this," she whispered before kissing my lips quickly.

I went to refuse, but she was already bending down to Alberto's level. I moved behind her, my stance protective. A possessive surge went through me at the sight of her being this close to the bastard.

She grabbed Alberto's face and lifted it up so they were staring at each other. He grimaced in pain but didn't make any move.

Ayla leaned forward until her lips were next to his ear.

"I forgive you," she murmured loud enough for me to hear too.

Alberto stiffened, and when she pulled away, his eyes were wide. I saw him swallow hard, almost like Ayla's action was unbelievable.

I wasn't shocked, though. Instead, all I felt was pride. I was in awe of her strength.

"I don't know why you hurt me, but if it wasn't for you, I wouldn't have found Alessio. I forgive you...I don't know if that will give you peace, but I thought those words needed to be said. For both our sakes. Especially mine."

Her voice was soft, almost angelic. Alberto

looked at her in shock, and he shook his head. He opened his mouth to say something, but no words came out.

I wrapped my arm around Ayla's waist and pulled her up. She turned in my arms and smiled. "I needed this to move on. Do what you have to do, Alessio. I will be right here waiting for you."

Ayla stepped out of my embrace and took a step back. Lena and a few of the maids came to stand behind her. Some of my men followed suit, flanking her sides protectively.

Giving her a nod, I walked away. Time to end this fucking war and get back to my woman.

I moved to the car and leveled Nina a look. She nodded. "I'll stay here."

She sneered at Alberto as Viktor pushed him into the car. I got into the front seat and waited for everyone else.

When the cars were full and ready, we pulled out of the driveway.

My back was stiff as we rode to the Abandonato estate. When the car finally stopped, I stepped out and took a deep breath.

Alberto's men came running out, guns in their hands. I chuckled and shook my head.

"If you value your lives, I suggest you put your guns away," I said lightly, moving forward.

My men were surrounded by Alberto's men, but it didn't scare us. In fact, his men should be cowering in fear. After all, I had their boss.

I could already see the fear in their eyes, but they weren't cowering yet. No problem, though. They would be kneeling in front of me in no time.

"Bring him out," I ordered Viktor. He nodded and opened the car, pulling Alberto out.

They cocked their guns at me, and I tsked at them in return. "You don't want to do this."

Their eyes widened at the sight of their boss. There were gasps. Some paled. Some stood back, and others froze in shock.

I loved the look of fear in their faces. But I would love the look of surrender more.

Nikolay pushed Enzo down in front of me. I controlled their lives. There was no escape. I just won this bloody game.

"Viktor, I think these men are deaf," I drawled. "Can you do something about it?"

A shot rang out in the courtyard. A man fell down...dead.

Before they could retaliate, Nikolay, Phoenix, and Viktor already had ten men shot down. I stood back, watching the scene in front of me.

"Stand down and no more lives will be lost," Viktor growled. "Not that I mind killing all of you. But it's for your own good."

They slowly put their guns away, and I raised an eyebrow. That was easy.

All of them were a bunch of pussies. Weak. Cowards.

Shaking my head in disgust, I stepped forward. I gripped Alberto's hair and snapped his head up. "There is no point if you shoot at me. The war is over. Alberto is in my hands, practically dead."

I raised my head and leveled each and every one of his men with a hard glare. "So I suggest you stand back and enjoy the show."

I kept my unwavering eyes on them as I continued. "Whether you like it or not, I am taking over as your boss. It doesn't matter if you agree with me. If you disagree, you will take your last breath. It's simple. You shut up and watch what I am about to do."

More of my men spilled out of the cars, flanking my sides. Viktor and Nikolay stood in front of me.

"Phoenix, bring Artur out," I demanded.

Releasing Alberto, I walked over to Enzo. I saw a few of Alberto's men taking protective steps forward. But with my men's guns pointed in their direction, they stopped.

I took my gun out and pointed it at Enzo's forehead. "I'm about to show you what happens when you side with the wrong people. You should learn from this."

Nikolay handed me a clear bag. I raised it up for everyone to see. Several men took a step back. Enzo's severed dick was in it. I threw the bag on the ground next to their feet.

Their shocked gaze moved to it before staring at me again. "This is what happens when you choose the wrong side."

My finger pressed against the trigger. A shot rang out, and I smiled. Enzo fell at my feet, his eyes open, staring at me lifelessly. One man down.

The driveway was silent as I kicked Enzo's body away.

Keeping my eyes on Alberto's men, I walked to Artur. Phoenix handed me the bag with Artur's tongue in it. For everyone to see, I threw that on the ground too.

This time, I pointed the muzzle of my gun to Artur's neck. He swallowed. After giving me a final look, he closed his eyes. He didn't have any fight left.

My gaze moved to the crowd. "And that's what happens when you betray me."

Another shot. Artur's limp body fell to the ground. Blood splattered on my suit as I stepped away.

"Lesson number one. Never betray me. You won't like the consequences," I growled loudly for everyone to hear.

I made my way to Alberto. His whole body was shaking. He tried to fight me, but he was too weak.

Gripping Alberto by the hair, I pulled him up. He stood on trembling legs. "How does it feel? Having your men watch your demise? You have no honor. No power. You have nothing left."

My words were low for only him to hear. His choked on his own blood, his body falling limply forward. "And in a few minutes, you will be nothing but a corpse," I finished, spitting in his face. Alberto flinched, and I could hear the angry rumble from his men.

But nobody made a move to come save their boss.

I pulled away slightly before lurching forward again. My foot hit his knee, a loud crack resonating through the courtyard. Alberto buckled forward, his legs giving out as he roared in pain.

I released him, and he fell to his knees in front of me. Just where he needed to be. Beneath my feet. He fell to his side, rolling in agony.

I squatted down beside him, my mouth next to his ear. "I know how to break two hundred and six bones in a thousand ways. You are just lucky that I didn't use all one thousand methods on you." Although I found the idea very tempting.

"I'll give you an easier death, just because I want to return to my woman quicker. You heard her. She's waiting for me. And it's very rude to keep a lady waiting," I said lightly, playing with his mind.

"I want everyone to watch!" I bellowed, snapping my head up.

Letting my rage take over, I pulled out my spiral knife. I had made my first kill with that knife. It was only fair that I avenged my woman with the same knife.

I pressed my blade to Alberto's neck.

My blade made the cut, slicing his neck. He gurgled and struggled out of my hold. The cut wasn't deep enough to cut any major arteries.

I had other plans for him. That cut was just the start.

The blade of my spiral knife trailed down toward his chest. His eyes widened, recognition flashing there. I didn't give him a chance to think, though. He screamed when the knife stabbed into his chest.

Blood was everywhere. On the ground. My clothes. My hands. My face.

But I kept going.

I thrust the blade repeatedly into his chest. Alberto had long stopped struggling.

Of course he did. He wasn't breathing anymore.

The sound of the blade cutting into his flesh filled my ears. Blood and flesh meshed together, his blood pooled around us.

He deserved everything and more. I was just pissed that I couldn't torture him more. His death was too easy. Too easy.

"This is what happens when you take something that doesn't belong to you!" I roared out, twisting the knife deeper into Alberto's chest.

When the hole was big enough, I dropped my spiral knife on the ground. I pushed my bare hand into his lifeless body. Then my fingers made contact with what I wanted.

I ripped his fucking heart out.

I stood up, covered in blood. Throwing the heart on the ground, I stared at everyone. "I am your motherfucking King!"

My voice boomed loud and clear. Everyone understood the meaning.

"Bow down," Viktor growled.

That was the worst. Kneeling in front of your enemy. Serving your enemy. Bowing in front of him.

But they had no choice. I owned them now.

When nobody bowed, I smiled. "Anyone want to challenge me?"

I opened my arms wide, inviting any opponent. Without a second thought, a large man charged toward me. He never even made it a foot near me. Viktor got him halfway.

Throwing him on the ground, he lay there...dead.

More men rushed toward me, trying to end my life.

But none of them made it to me.

225

I stood back, watching my soldiers…my men fight for me. Blood was spilled. Men lay on the ground, dying. Some were already dead. I watched the chaos around me, laughing.

They really thought they stood a chance. No fucking way. Not this time.

This time it was my turn to rule. With my queen…my Angel by my side.

When the willing opponents stopped moving, I walked forward. From the corner of my eyes, I saw one coming my way. Taking the knife from my back, I made the throw.

Straight in the left eye.

The man fell to the ground lifelessly.

Turning toward the crowd, I raised an eyebrow in question. "Anyone else?"

Silence.

My words were met with silence.

And then one by one, they knelt down in front of me, surrendering.

The one thing my father couldn't do, I accomplished it today. Two decades of pain and enmity, I ended it today.

The Italians belonged to us.

"I have rules. But I will go over them next time. For today just remember, do not betray me. Ever. What you saw today was only a show. Don't test me. You won't like the consequences."

I paused, wiping my hands with my handkerchief. "Viktor, pull the bodies together."

Alberto, Enzo, and Artur were pushed together in a pile of dead bodies. Nikolay handed me the lighter. I clicked the lighter open, watching the flame dance around.

Keeping my eyes on Alberto's men...now my men...I threw the lighter on the bodies. Nikolay threw another lighter on the bodies too. They instantly inflamed. The fire danced around the corpses, the smell of burning flesh filling my nostrils.

I watched the bodies burn, my Angel's tormentor one of them. Her nightmare was finally over. Ayla was finally safe. Our daughter would be safe.

I had avenged my Angel in the only way I knew how.

"Respect. I demand respect from all of you. Not just me but for your Queen, Ayla Abandonato. If I ever hear someone disrespect her, you will take your last breath. You are beneath her. She commands you, and you fucking do whatever she says, like a fucking loyal dog," I growled low, making sure everyone understood the rule.

They bowed their heads.

A smile whispered across my lips.

I was done here. Turning around, I got into the car.

I'm coming for you, Angel.

Chapter 25

Ayla

Maddie sat beside me, painting her toenails deep red as I tried to focus on my book. But I just couldn't.

My mind kept going back to Alessio.

"Ayla, relax," Maddie mumbled. "I can feel the tension from here. It's not good for the baby."

"I just worry," I said, turning to face her.

Her forehead furrowed. "Worry? About who? Alessio?"

I nodded sheepishly. "Girl, you should be worried about the men he captured. Definitely not Alessio." She laughed.

"But he's taking so long," I argued back.

"Because he is prolonging their death," she shot back with a wink.

That shut me up. Because it was probably true.

I stayed silent until Maddie released a loud breath. She got off the bed and walked to my dressing table. "You know, I can't believe this is

Alessio's room. I never thought I would see the day. A dressing table. Closet filled with women's clothes and shoes. A little feminine touch to the room," Maddie said, looking around the room. "You got him wrapped around your little finger, babe," Maddie gushed, coming back to the bed with a different nail polish.

She settled in front of me, sitting cross-legged. Maddie took hold of my feet and gently pulled them to her lap.

"Wait. What are you doing?" I asked, trying to pull away.

"Stop moving. Let me do your nails. It's not like you can reach your feet now," she mumbled, taking the cap off the nail polish bottle.

It was partly the truth. Because of my large belly, it had become harder to reach my feet. I could only imagine how it would be further into my pregnancy. Would I even see my feet? Probably not.

"Is this color okay?" she asked, showing me the light pink bottle.

I nodded. The color was pretty and one of my favorites. Silently, I watched Maddie apply the color to my nails.

Nowadays, Maddie had been quiet. Quieter than usual. There was a dark shadow in her eyes. Sometimes I would notice the sad expression, the tears in her eyes.

No matter how much she tried to hide it from me, I saw past her fake exterior.

Artur betrayed all of us. But Maddie was feeling most of the pain. My chest tightened at the thought, and I grabbed her hand.

"Maddie," I started. "Talk to me."

She stared at me questioningly and then laughed. "Talk about what, silly?"

I shook my head. There she was again. Laughing when it was probably the last thing she wanted to do.

"Stop lying and stop hiding from me, Maddie. I know you. I know what Artur did hurt you more than you're letting me know, but please don't keep it inside. It will only hurt you more," I tried to soothe.

Her chin wobbled, and she blinked her tears away. "You don't know anything," she whispered.

"Because you won't tell me. I could ask anyone, but I want you to talk to me," I replied, moving closer to her.

A tear fell down her rosy cheek, and I quickly swiped it away. I would be there to wipe her tears away, only if she'd let me.

Maddie opened her mouth to say something but quickly snapped it shut when a knock sounded on the door. She closed her eyes and took a deep breath.

"It's nothing, Ayla. Please let it go," she muttered.

I could feel the back of my throat closing, the emotions suffocating me. "It's not nothing," I whispered back when another knock came.

"Let it go, Ayla. Please."

When a third knock came, I closed my eyes. "Come in."

My eyes fluttered open to see Nina standing in the doorway. My mouth fell open in shock, and

Maddie turned around to face the door too. I saw her eyes glistened with anger.

"What are you doing here?" she hissed, getting to her feet.

Nina stepped into the room. "I'm not here to argue. I want to talk to Ayla."

Her voice was calm, her eyes never wavering from mine. She stared me down, and I stared back.

"Well, she doesn't want you here. Actually, nobody wants you here. Get. Out," Maddie growled defensively.

"Can you stop speaking for her? She has a mouth," Nina snapped back.

"Ayla," Maddie said, turning to me.

I shrugged, facing Nina again. "What is it?" I asked.

Nina scoffed and crossed her arms. "I'll make it quick and only say it once."

I raised an eyebrow, waiting for her to continue. She flipped her blonde hair over her shoulder and walked closer to the bed, her heels clicking hard against the floor.

Nina paused and took a deep breath. "I'm here to make amends."

"You little bitch," Maddie swore.

"Can you stop talking for a minute so I can speak? Did your on-off button break or what?" Nina sneered.

Maddie stared at Nina, gaping. "Thank you," Nina joked, turning her attention back to me.

"As I said, I'm not here to fight. Actually, I'm here for the opposite. It's due time that I do this now. What I said way before, it was out of line. I shouldn't have insulted you like that," Nina started, her voice firm.

Her eyes were cold, her face expressionless. In that moment, she reminded me so much of the Ivanshov men.

Her words brought back the scene in the kitchen. I looked down, remembering all the things she said and how the words had pierced my heart.

"I know it's hard to believe when I tell you that I didn't mean them," she continued.

My head snapped up, and Maddie scoffed, rolling her eyes. Nina glared holes into Maddie's head. "Fine," she growled. "Maybe I meant it a little. But I was bitter and angry. It's no excuse, but please know I had no intention to cause you serious pain."

I rubbed my stomach, seeking comfort from my princess as I tried to take in Nina's words.

"It was mostly a test. To see your strength. If you really were strong enough for Alessio. To lead with him."

"Well, she is way stronger than you," Maddie spat.

This time, a tiny smile appeared on Nina's lip. It was a ghost smile. It was there for a second and gone in the next. "I have no doubt in that."

Her words went straight to my heart. I knew she wasn't talking physically. Her words held a deeper meaning, and in that moment, I was thankful she said them.

"This is why I'm here to apologize. I am sorry for what I said. You'll be seeing more of me, so I thought it would best if we're on good grounds,"

Nina explained. "I don't want Alessio. Yes, I fucked him before. Not going to lie, and I sure as hell am not going to sugar-coat it for you. But Alessio and I are over. We were over the moment he fell for you, and I respect that decision," Nina continued in the same monotone voice.

Taking a deep breath, Nina moved to my side. Maddie took a protective step toward me.

"I'm not going to hurt her. God, who the hell do you think I am?" Nina said, clearly looking offended that Maddie wanted to protect me from her.

"Someone who needs to get lost very soon," Maddie replied, glaring at Nina.

"Well, that's not going to happen," Nina shot back.

They both glared at each other, and I rolled my eyes. Why did I get a feeling that I was going to be stuck with two Maddies? Or was it two Ninas?

Oh my God.

I cleared my throat, and both of their attentions snapped to me. "I understand what you mean. And I think I forgave you a long time ago, Nina."

Shrugging, I gave her a small smile. She didn't smile back. I wondered if she knew how to properly smile?

"I guess we can start over," Nina said after a few silent seconds. She gave me her hand, waiting for me to shake it.

"Nina Ivanshov," she introduced.

I took her hand, my heart beating wildly. "Ayla," I introduced back. Swallowing hard past the sudden lump in my throat, I continued. "Ayla Abandonato."

Nina's hand tightened around mine, and this time she smiled. It didn't reach her eyes, though. They stayed cold.

"Not for long," she replied with a raised eyebrow. "You will be Ayla Ivanshov in no time."

My eyebrows furrowed in question, and when understanding finally dawned to me, I looked down, feeling my cheeks flushing red.

Maddie suddenly squealed as I released Nina's hand. "Oh my God. Yes! She's right! Oh my God. Ayla Ivanshov. That sounds perfect, right? Right? We have so much planning to do."

My cheeks heated under her words, and I bit on my lips shyly.

Ayla Ivanshov.

I liked the sound of that. Actually, I loved it.

"You will be Ayla Ivanshov in no time," Maddie said. "I'm sure of it."

"That's what I just said," Nina said, rolling her eyes.

Maddie placed her hands on her hips. "Whatever, bitch."

"Yeah whatever, stupid cow," Nina mumbled under her breath.

"Did you just call me a stupid cow?"

"Yeah. So?"

"Fuck you!"

"Nope. Not interested," Nina snapped drily.

I watched them bicker back and forth, my eyes wide. What universe did I just get transported in?

Maddie paused and then busted out laughing. "I never thought I would say this. I think I like you, bitch."

Nina shook her head and turned back to me. Giving me a nod, she turned to walk away.

"Wait," I called down. A question was burning in my mind.

"You said your name was Nina Ivanshov. How is your name Ivanshov?" I asked curiously.

Nina faced me and crossed her arms. "Only a small set of people have the privilege to take the Ivanshov name. Only the most loyal. I am one of them. Alessio trusts me with his life. And yours. My loyalty to this family comes first...before anything else. And now my loyalty is extended to you."

Maddie nodded. "I forgot to tell you. My name is Maddie Ivanshov too. Same as Mum. Viktor. Nikolay and Phoenix. We all carry the Ivanshov name. It's kind of a tradition for the most fiercely loyal people to the Boss."

"Although I never thought Nina would take the name," Maddie continued, staring at Nina curiously.

"You know nothing about me. But it's not like I have to hide my identity any longer. You will know my truth soon enough, so it would be best that you don't anger me. I hate annoying pests," Nina replied lazily.

The threat was there, but Maddie just chuckled.

"I think we'll be good friends." She winked while laughing.

Nina's back straightened, and her expression changed to a hard look. "I'm not here to make friends."

That sentence did something to me. It reminded me so much of Alessio. The one who tried so hard to push me away.

I wanted to rebuke Nina, tell her that everyone needed friends, but I stayed quiet.

She stared at us for a second. Maddie's arms were wrapped around me, and I was leaning into her. Nina shook her head and took out her cellphone.

"They're coming," Nina simply said.

With that, she walked out of the door. Maddie and I stared at each other.

Alessio was back. My heart suddenly felt a hundred times lighter.

Maddie helped me out of the bed, and we walked down the stairs together. As I reached the last landing, I saw Alessio coming through the main doors.

He came in first, looking big and fierce. His stance exuded dominance. Behind him, to his left, Viktor and Phoenix walked closely. Nikolay was to his right.

His most trusted men flanked his sides as they walked inside the house. They all had the same dark aura surrounding them. Their expensive suits did nothing to make them look less dangerous.

My feet took me forward, moving me toward Alessio before I could stop myself. We met in the middle, our bodies molding together.

Alessio held the back of my neck, pulling me closer. His fingers wrapped around my hair, pulling my head back. His breathing was ragged as he stared down at me with intense blue eyes.

His fingers tightened around my hair, and he brought my head closer. His lips descended toward me, and my heart hitched when his mouth met mine.

Alessio kissed me roughly, demanding access. I opened my lips, surrendering to him. His tongue swirled around mine in a fierce battle. He gripped my hair at the nape of my neck, giving it a sharp tug.

He kissed me desperately, almost savagely. I returned his kiss with the same fervor, my hands going to his shoulders to hold on.

His lips moved over mine, never once breaking our kiss. His kiss turned deeper, more aggressive. I was drunk on his kisses while he seemed lost in me.

Alessio claimed me in front of everyone.

I heard a loud roar. From the driveway, the courtyard, the whole mansion exploded. The men roared out their victory. The women clapped, joining this joyous moment.

Alessio and I kissed as our people celebrated.

The proud screaming continued, and I knew it wouldn't end soon.

After all, the war just ended.

The Italians had lost.

And the Russians had won.

Chapter 26

My heart drummed in my chest as the realization settled around my shoulders.

Alessio's kisses didn't slow down. No, he continued to claim my lips in a possessive kiss, making my heart flutter with so much love.

I returned his kisses with the same fervor, as if we were starving for each other. Maybe it was the adrenaline of winning.

His fingers tightened in my hair as he bit on my lower lip. "I'm home," he muttered roughly.

I pulled away, my fingers still holding the back of his neck. Smiling up at Alessio, I leaned up for another kiss.

"Welcome home, my love," I whispered against his lips.

He groaned, his arm growing tighter around my waist. If it wasn't for my rounded belly, our bodies would have been molded together.

"Say that again," he demanded.

"Welcome home, my love."

"The last part. Say it again," he ordered, kissing

my lips.

I let out a small laugh, feeling my cheeks heating up. I was blushing. How was that even possible after everything we had done together?

My fingers caressed the back of his neck as I gazed into his bluish steel-colored eyes lovingly. "My love," I whispered again, just loud enough for only his ears.

Alessio smirked and pulled his head back, roaring with happiness. "We have won!"

I laughed, holding him to me.

Yes. We have won.

I swallowed past the lump around my throat. My father was gone. Alberto was gone. The Italians were under the Ivanshov family.

I didn't think this day would come, but here I was, seeing it with my own eyes. Experiencing it.

I should have been shattered that my family, the Abandonatos, had lost.

But I wasn't. Simply because the Abandonatos weren't my family. They never were.

My *real* family had won, and I was going to celebrate with them.

The guys came and clapped Alessio on the back. Then they hugged me. There were many hugs and kisses. Laughter and huge smiles.

They treated me and pulled me in as their own.

When the roars of victory finally settled down, Alessio bent his head to my ear. "I have to take care of some things. I'll see you tonight."

My eyes found his, and I pouted. "Do you have to go? You only just came back."

Alessio's intense blue eyes glowed fiercely at my

words. Almost possessively. "I have to, Angel. It's important. Now that *he* is gone, I have to clean up his fucking mess. Get everything straightened out under new rules."

The way he sneered the words out, I almost shuddered.

It was on the tip of my tongue to ask Alessio how he killed Alberto. How he ended it. But I refrained myself in the last second.

Maybe it was better I didn't have the details.

Alessio placed another quick kiss on my lips before pulling away. I couldn't help myself. My lips pursed in another pout.

He sighed before kissing my pout. Hard. A bruising kiss that had his dominance all over it.

"No pouting. You're making it harder to leave," he growled low.

That was the plan. Not that I was going to say it out loud.

Alessio sent me a wink before walking upstairs, the guys following behind him.

A sigh escaped past my lips when Maddie came to stand beside me.

"A little less PDA next time, babe. It would be highly appreciated. Thank you very much," she teased with a raised eyebrow.

I closed my eyes tightly, feeling my cheeks burn under her gaze. "Oh. Now you're blushing! Look at you all red. What about when Alessio was practically mauling you in front of twenty other people?"

I heard a smack, and my eyes opened to see Lena glaring at Maddie. "Behave."

Maddie laughed and winked at me. She grabbed my arm and pulled me to the kitchen. "Let's go, babe."

I took my seat at the stool, watching Maddie get us some lunch. "Do you need any help?"

She shook her head. "Nope. Just sit down. You shouldn't even be out of bed. Remember what Ivy said? She wants you on bed rest most of the time. I'm surprised Alessio didn't haul your ass back to bed."

Maddie paused, shaking her head. "Never mind. He was *busy* doing something else."

Her teasing tone just made her words funnier. My shoulders shook with silent laughter.

Maddie brought two plates to the counter. Before she could take a seat, my hands lashed out, my fingers gripping her wrist.

"We're not eating until you talk to me, Maddie."

My voice was firm yet gentle. She needed to talk to me. Maddie was holding everything inside. I knew it was slowly eating her alive.

Her haunted eyes found mine, and she shook her head. "Ayla."

I ignored her warning tone and pressed on. "What are you hiding? Why don't you want to tell me? I know that Artur hurt you, and I know that it's hard to imagine. I couldn't believe it at first either. He betrayed Alessio. But he betrayed you too. I know it hurts, but you're hiding something else."

Maddie snatched her wrist from my hand. "Stop it, Ayla!"

I stood up so I could hug her. My arms wrapped around her shoulders. "You know you can tell me

241

anything, Maddie. I'll be there for you. I can't see you like this. You remind me of myself. How I used to be before. It's not easy to see you like this."

She struggled out of my arms, her glare intense. I had seen her angry before but never angry at me. This time her glare was directed at me.

"You don't know anything!" she screamed.

"Because you won't tell me," I replied softly.

Her chest was heaving with each breath she took. I saw tears filling her eyes, and she sniffled, taking another step away from me.

It broke my heart, seeing her like this.

"I lost him!" she hissed.

My shoulders sagged. "I know. I'm sorry, Maddie. I'm so sorry he turned out to be the traitor," I replied, my voice broken too.

Maddie shook her head, her tears freely running down her cheeks. "No. I lost *him*. I lost…my baby."

Her words were choked out, but they rung so clear. Her words seemed loud even though they were whispered.

Maddie's knees gave out, and she sunk to the floor soundlessly. She hunched over as she held her stomach in a fetal position. Her sobs were loud and heart wrenching.

I lost…my baby.

I stared at Maddie, speechless. My heart stuttered, and I felt suddenly weak in my knees. My hand instinctively went to my stomach, holding my baby bump.

Maddie was pregnant?

Tears blinded my vision as her sobs made their way straight to my heart. Her words kept ringing through my ears.

I looked at Maddie so heartbroken, and my heart ached for her. I couldn't imagine losing my little princess. It would break me beyond repair.

Just then, she gave a little kick, and my hand rubbed over the bump.

"He shot me...he freaking shot me...and killed my baby. How could he do that, Ayla? Why?" Maddie wailed.

I stepped closer, trying to kneel down beside Maddie. It was hard, but I eventually settled down beside her. My arms went around her shoulders, pulling her shaking body to mine.

Maddie buried her face in my neck, her tears an endless flow. "He killed...my...baby."

I knew what Artur had done, but I didn't know the extent of the damage. He killed his own baby. Their baby.

My arms tightened around Maddie as we cried. She cried for her loss while I held her. Her pain seeped into my pores as if I was feeling it for myself.

"I'm sorry, Maddie. I'm so sorry," I whispered.

They were the only words I had for her. What could I say? Her loss wasn't something that could be fixed with mere words.

"I didn't know," I continued. Princess continued to kick, rolling around in my stomach, and suddenly I felt sick.

Maddie had to watch me every day. She had to look at my baby bump and be reminded of her loss. How did she survive?

How did she not hate me?

I was the living reminder of what she could have had.

Maddie's hand moved to my stomach, her touch feather-light.

"Right now, he would have still been too small for me to feel him move."

I squeezed my eyes shut. "I'm sorry."

There was another small kick from Princess as Maddie caressed the bump. "Now, I will never feel my baby kick," she whispered through her tears. "I will never get a chance to hold him." Maddie continued to cry. She kept cradling the baby bump, almost protectively.

I always wondered why Maddie loved holding my stomach so much. Sometimes she laid down beside me and left her hand over my baby bump for hours until I fell asleep.

She always found a chance to touch my stomach and feel the baby move.

Now I understood why she did it.

I laid my hand over hers, both of us holding Princess. "They would have grown up together," I whispered.

Maddie nodded. "They would have. In a perfect world, I can see them playing together. Fighting. Laughing. But always loving each other. Maybe even a wedding later on."

My chin wobbled with the effort to hold my tears in. I had to be strong…for Maddie.

"They would have been inseparable," she continued.

"Maddie," I soothed.

We stayed silent for a few minutes, both of us

lost in the perfect world we imagined.

"I can't have kids anymore."

My eyes snapped open at her words. My heart may have stopped beating for a second, and then it drummed against my ribcage harder than before.

"What?" I sputtered.

"From my cancer, it was almost impossible for me have kids. I gave up hope a long time ago. But then it happened. I was pregnant, and I was so happy, Ayla. So damn happy. It was a miracle. I was going to have a baby," she broke off at the end.

A loud sob wracked her body. "Then he was taken away from me. Ripped away from me. And then I found out I can't have kids anymore. The bullet damaged my womb. I can't ever...carry...a baby again."

"No," I said, completely horrified.

Maddie nodded. "My ability to have a baby was taken away from me before. I was given one chance, and that too was ripped away from me."

Her tears soaked my neck and dress. My own tears left a wet trail down my cheeks.

How did Maddie hold all of that in for so long?

My heart was hurting for her.

"You know, Ayla, since I lost him, I've wondered...why me? Why did I have to lose my baby?"

I stayed silent, but my hands never stopped caressing her back, soothing her with my touch when my words failed me.

Maddie pulled her face away from my neck and stared at me. I swiped her tears away and she squeezed her eyes shut. "It was meant to be. I see it as a sacrifice. It's the only way I can get over this. It sounds weird when I say it out loud." She chuckled drily. "In losing my baby, we gained you back."

The words slammed right into me, and I stared at her with wide eyes. "So it was meant to be. I want to believe that I had a hand in saving you. If I didn't catch Artur that day, then maybe we would have never found you. If it all hadn't taken place, maybe you wouldn't be here with us right now. That's how I see it," she continued when I stayed silent. "It was a sacrifice to get you back, and I will *never* regret it."

I shook my head, refusing to believe what I was hearing. "Maddie, you can't mean that."

She gave me a small broken smile. "Yes, I lost my baby. I will never get that chance again, but I got you back. I gave Alessio his Angel. It's not something I will ever regret."

Her fingers caressed my rounded belly. "And I saved Princess too. I couldn't save my baby, but I saved her. We lost one but we gained another."

"Maddie…"

"You wanted the truth. This is the truth, Ayla."

My shoulders sagged in defeat, and I stared at her hand, the one that was resting on my stomach. "I'm sorry."

Maddie shook her head and wrapped her arms around me for a hug. "It's not your fault, and I don't want you to be sorry for me. It's hard. It hurts so much sometimes, Ayla. Sometimes, I can't sleep. All I do is cry. It's hard to close my eyes. It's hard to continue moving on, but I have to do it. My heart will always hurt with my loss, but I know...eventually the pain will be less."

She pulled away and sent me a wink. "I have a princess too. She will make the pain less." Maddie paused and then smiled. "What am I saying? She *already* makes my heart overflow with love."

Maddie bent down and placed a sweet kiss over my belly. "I will never regret this."

I was in awe with this woman. How she managed to be this strong...I didn't know.

"Maddie," I started saying, but she shushed me.

"Promise me we won't ever speak of this again. You wanted to know so I told you, but I don't want to talk about it anymore. I want to bury it behind me and move on. Please, Ayla. Promise me."

I couldn't do anything but nod. We hugged, our hold tight on each other.

"I love you," I whispered.

"Love you too, babe. We got this."

I nodded. "Yeah. Just promise me though. Don't hurt yourself by keeping it inside. When it gets too much, talk to me. I will be there for you. Sometimes just talking makes everything easier."

"I promise," she said, pulling away.

We gave each other a tearful smile, our hands holding my baby bump.

"What's going on here?"

A loud, angry growl caused my head to snap up in surprise. I met Alessio's eyes as he stalked toward us.

"Why are you on the floor?" he demanded, coming to stand beside me. He towered over us, his face angry but worried.

His eyes raked over me protectively. "Are you

hurt? Shit. Are you in pain?" He started to panic.

Alessio bent down and grabbed my arm. Maddie went to stand up, holding my other arm. They both helped me up, and Alessio pulled me into his embrace.

His hands whispered over my body, looking for any type of injury. "Ayla, are you hurt? Answer me!" he snapped.

I shook my head. "No. I'm not hurt. Calm down, Alessio."

"Then what were you doing on the floor?" he questioned, his accusing eyes going to Maddie.

"We were talking," she retorted, crossing her arms.

"On the floor?" Viktor jumped in. He was leaning against the doorway, watching all of us. "Your eyes are red. You were both crying."

Great. He just added fuel to the fire.

Alessio's eyes turned to slits. Placing my hand over his chest, I tried to calm him down. "I'm fine. Really. We were talking. It got emotional, that's it. Now stop growling."

He sighed, his shoulders sagging in relief. "You are not hurt."

Alessio didn't pose the sentence as a question. It was mostly a relieved statement.

Giving him a sweet smile, I placed a kiss on his lips. It was instinct...I couldn't stop myself.

He kissed me back. More than what I had planned. When I heard a groan behind me, I pulled back, feeling a deep red blush make its way to my cheeks.

"You need to be in bed. Promise me you'll rest

while I'm gone," Alessio said in my ear, his arms a band of steel around my waist.

"Okay. I promise," I readily agreed. I knew there was no point arguing with Alessio. He would just carry me upstairs himself and put several guards at my door to stop me from leaving.

Alessio gave me a fierce stare. "Have you eaten yet?"

I nodded toward the food. "I was going to."

His lips were feather-light on my forehead. Placing a kiss there, he pulled away. "Good. I'm leaving now, but I'll be back tonight."

I hummed into his chest before stepping out of his embrace. He nodded at Maddie before turning around to leave. Viktor gave me a smile before following Alessio.

From the corner of the doorway, I saw Isaak. His hands were in his pockets as he stood there watching me. He had a strange look on his face. It wasn't the first time I noticed him watching me from afar.

When he caught my stare, I saw him swallowing hard before quickly leaving. A strange feeling went through me at the encounter, but I didn't have a chance to think about it before Maddie was breaking into my thoughts.

"Let's eat, babe."

I nodded, turning to the stool.

Chapter 27

Two weeks later

My gaze followed Alessio around the room. I couldn't take my eyes off him. He moved fluidly, his steps filled with purpose.

Alessio moved around like he owned the room...like he owned everything. And it was reality.

I liked his strength and the dominance he exuded. The pull I felt toward him made my body hum with pleasure.

Alessio shrugged on his dress shirt, quickly buttoning it up. His form was the most perfect I had ever seen. Not that I had seen a lot.

But he was absolutely perfect in my eyes. Inside and out.

I got off the bed and took his suit jacket in my hand. He gave me a warm look as I helped him. My hands made their way to his chest.

I laid my palms there, over his chiseled stomach. I could feel every muscle definition through his shirt. Alessio's hands held my hips, moving me closer.

"How are you feeling?" he asked, running his fingers over my hips.

"Perfect." I smiled up at him.

He nodded, and a sudden shadow crossed his face. Alessio looked thoughtful for a moment, and then he swallowed hard, like he ate something big.

I could feel that he was suddenly nervous. "What's wrong?"

"This is going to be huge, Ayla. But we thought it's time for you to know," he started.

"Know what? What's wrong?" My eyes went wide as panic started to course through my system.

Alessio placed a gentle finger over my lips. "Shh…calm down, Angel. Everything is fine. But Isaak wants to talk to you."

My eyebrows furrowed in confusion. "Isaak? But why?" I questioned.

Isaak had barely said any words to me. He never talked. But I caught his stare every now and then. It felt like he wanted to speak, but he just didn't know what to say.

If I wasn't mistaken, he was avoiding me. Just watching from behind the shadows sometimes. It was strange, but I never thought much of it.

"He has a lot to say, Angel, but he means well. Okay? Just keep that in mind. He's not the bad guy," Alessio explained, staring at me expectantly.

I nodded but then jumped in fright when a sudden knock sounded on the door. I was too tensed, my muscles locked tight.

"That's him," Alessio muttered before calling

out. "Come in!"

I stood, staring at Alessio as the door opened. He gave me a small smile and turned me around so I was facing Isaak.

"Hey," Isaak started with a tight smile. He looked *really* nervous. His hands were fisted by his sides, and he fiddled around on his feet.

It was a once-in-a-lifetime type sight. To see a man like him nervous.

"Hi," I replied almost timidly.

Alessio walked us to the couch and sat down before pulling me on his lap. He settled me sideways, his hands drawing circles over my rounded belly.

I breathed out a sigh of relief and stared at Isaak expectantly.

He swallowed again and looked around before moving his gaze back to me.

"This is going to sound crazy, and you might even hate me after this, but I think you need to know. I *need* to tell you. It's driving me fucking insane keeping it inside for so long," he started.

"Whatever it is, I'm sure it's going to be okay," I replied, trying to make him as comfortable as I could.

After my years of torture, I had learned that it was easier to see the positive in things.

Let the wave of negativity flow around you but never let it affect you. I guessed I was my own medicine to the virus.

My eyes caught Alessio. His attention was already on me.

Or maybe he was my medicine?

I smiled internally at the thought. My savior. I had the sudden urge to kiss him again but quickly bit on my lips and tried to concentrate on Isaak again.

When Isaak started talking, I didn't have to force my attention anymore. He had my full attention.

My breath hitched as he continued his story. My heart ached with each word, and tears slid down my cheeks.

Alessio caught them for me. He soothed me with his touch.

But every word Isaak uttered, it broke my heart further.

When he was done speaking, he let out a loud breath and stared at me, watching my reaction. I sat still and stared back in shock.

My throat closed as I tried to speak. "You knew my mom?"

He nodded.

"You loved her?" He nodded again, a wave of pain crossing his face.

My eyes blurred with tears. "I can't remember you."

"Of course, you can't. You were only a year old," he replied gently.

My heart stuttered at his fatherly voice.

"But I wish I could remember you," I whispered. "You were more a father to me than my own ever was. You cared for me when he didn't."

"I always cared for you, Ayla. Since the very first time I laid eyes on you. Even when I thought you were dead, I still loved you. You were *my daughter*."

I sniffled and choked back a sob. How long had I craved to hear words like these? To have a father who loved and protected me?

For years, I dreamed of my father looking at me with soft eyes...if only just once. But he never did. He treated me as if I didn't even exist.

But this man standing in front of me, he was looking at me with the love my father should have had for me.

I stood up from Alessio's lap and went to Isaak. He straightened up instantly, standing to his full height.

"I never had a father," I said, stopping in front of him. "I prayed and wished that I did, but that never happened. I didn't have anyone."

Before he could move a muscle, I wrapped my arms around him in a hug. He was startled, freezing in shock. "What I didn't realize was that I had a father, loving me from afar."

Isaak sighed, sagging with relief. I felt every tense muscle in his body relax, and he slowly brought his arms up, hugging me tight.

"I'm sorry I couldn't save your mom. I'm sorry I couldn't save you. All these years—" he broke off.

My emotions clogged up my heart and throat. "I don't hate you. It's not your fault. It's not mine. We can't blame ourselves for something that wasn't in our hands."

"You sound so much like your mother, Ayla," he said softly.

"Am I like her?" I asked curiously, my heart beating just a little faster.

"You look so much like her. The first time I saw

you, I thought it was a dream. I thought I was being haunted," Isaak replied, slightly pulling away so he could look at my face.

"And you have her wisdom too. So gentle. Just like my Leila. I don't think I will ever forgive myself for not being able to keep my promise to her. But having you here, safe and loved now, I think I can live and breathe a little better," he finished, his eyes holding unshed tears.

My chin wobbled, and I nodded. Taking a deep breath, I uttered the most important question.

"Can I still be your daughter?"

I felt like a child, hoping and looking for a scrape of love.

My mind went back to when I was just a few years old. I always waited for my father to come see me. I wanted him to play with me, put me to bed, read me stories.

Anything…I just wanted a small bit of his time and attention. Maybe just a few minutes. One soft and loving look.

But I got none of that.

In this moment, I got all of that. In just mere seconds, Isaak Ivanshov gave me years of love that I was yearning for from a father.

"You were my daughter and still are. Always will be, Ayla."

I sniffled and closed my eyes. Isaak pulled me into his arms again. "Thank you," I murmured through my tears.

"You were always meant to be an Ivanshov. From the very beginning," he replied as we pulled away.

I felt Alessio standing behind me, his heat warming my back, and I moved slightly back. Our bodies molded together, and his arms went around me. I felt his face in my neck as he placed a kiss there.

Isaak smiled and shook his head, muttering something under his breath. "I will see you both downstairs for lunch."

He gave me a final look and smiled, a huge warm smile that lit up his whole face. I smiled back, feeling my heart flutter with absolute happiness.

Isaak walked away, and I turned around in Alessio's arms, facing him. "Thank you for giving me this. It was meant to be, you know. Me finding my way into your car."

He chuckled. His lips turned up in a small sexy smirk. "Thank God I parked my car there."

We laughed, and then he kissed me, our laughter falling silent.

We broke apart when we felt a kick. A hard kick.

"Already a cockblocker." He huffed, sending my stomach a mock glare.

I sighed, pulling at his arm. "Time for lunch. She's hungry, which makes me double hungry."

***

We settled at the table, Alessio and I taking the head. I no longer worked as a maid. That was out of the question.

Alessio would probably blow a fuse if I ever brought that up.

I sat to his right as the others started to take their

seats. Including Maddie.

She no longer worked as a maid either. We both found it very weird that she would serve me, so that was out of question too. Anyway, she was more a sister than a maid. Maddie only worked as a maid because she didn't have anything else to do.

Not that she did much anyway as a maid. She only helped Lena cook.

Alessio made sure I had my food first before himself. He always did that.

The guys talked while eating. I just ate, content that my stomach had food. I was starving. Maddie was strangely silent, but she kept looking at Alessio every now and then.

Alessio listened to Viktor, but his left hand was over my bare thigh. Like always. He ate with his right hand while holding my thigh possessively under the table.

I didn't know why he did that, and I didn't question him.

Only because I loved it.

His thumb drew circles over my skin, and I shivered as his fingers hitched my dress higher, his thumb moving closer to my crotch.

My eyes widened, and I gripped his wrist, stopping his movement. I caught his smirk.

He was impossible.

Alessio continued his torturous touching, leaving my skin warm and burning. He left me wanting more.

He leaned closer. "Are you wet for me right now?"

The words were only for me, yet I almost choked

on my chicken.

I coughed, holding my chest. Everyone stopped eating, looking at me, worried. Alessio held my glass to my lips, waiting for me to sip.

After my coughing fit ended, I nodded at everyone and sent Alessio a glare.

"No," I hissed under my breath.

He smirked. He freaking smirked at me!

His gaze grew fierce, his blue eyes turning molten with desire. I bit on my lips and looked down at my plate.

His hot breath touched my ear, and goosebumps raised over my skin. "Hmm. Shall I check, kitten?"

My breath hitched when his wrist moved upward, closer and closer toward my crotch. He pushed my thighs apart under the table, his hand moving between my spread legs.

I tried to stop him, but my grip on his wrist was nothing compared to his strength.

"Alessio, stop it," I begged under my breath.

"I just want to check if you're lying or not, kitten."

He continued to tease me and turned his attention back to Viktor. His hand paused but stayed between my thighs.

When he didn't make any move, I breathed out a relieved sigh. My spoon made its way to my mouth but stopped in mid-air.

Without warning, Alessio pressed this thumb right over my core.

The thin barrier of my lingerie didn't stop the electrifying shock I felt course through me.

I jumped slightly at the sudden contact and bit on

my lips, placing my spoon down again. Alessio continued talking like he didn't do anything.

I sat there, trying to keep a straight face.

And then his thumb started moving, light touches, drawing circles over my wet core.

No. No. No. Damn him!

I pressed my thighs together, but his hand stopped me. I gritted my teeth, pinching his wrist hard.

Nothing fazed him.

He talked and laughed while he masterfully played me under the table.

I brought my glass to my lips with a shaky hand and tried to sip. Alessio being the devil himself, pressed his thumb harder against my clit.

Clenching my eyes shut, I breathed through this torture.

My lingerie was already soaked, my legs shaking. My heart fluttered and drummed like the wings of a bird.

And then he paused.

Alessio's eyes met mine, and he winked before taking his hand away.

He brought his hand up…the finger that was soaked with my juices…and licked it clean. Right there at the table.

Yup. I was about to have a heart attack.

"That was good." He nodded.

"Huh?" Viktor asked.

"The sauce. It tastes *really* good. I should try more later," Alessio explained, that devilish smirk present on his face.

Maddie was staring at me, and she looked like

she was about to choke.

Oh God. How mortifying.

Everyone else was eating, completely oblivious to what just happened. I just sat there, looking at my plate, contemplating what I was going to do with the impossible, annoying man sitting beside me.

"I was right. You *are* dripping for me, kitten. I had your juices all over my finger. Do you want me inside you right now? My finger or my cock?" he whispered in my ears.

I was going to kill him.

"Stop it!" I hissed, pinching his thigh hard.

He finally flinched and then smiled. "Okay. I'll stop."

And he did. Surprisingly.

I knew what he wanted. We both wanted it, yet we resisted.

I didn't know if I was ready, and Alessio never pushed. We made out, kissed a lot, but never went further than that.

That was the first time he took such a step. And at the dining table. I shook my head.

Alessio was just being Alessio.

I looked at him, and my heart overflowed with love. Could I give him what he wanted? What we both wanted?

Alessio's eyes moved back to me as if he sensed my stressful thoughts. He brought his lips to my ear and whispered so softly that it made my heart ache with his gentleness.

"Don't push yourself. I will wait for you. Whenever *you* are ready."

My heart settled as his hand came back to my

thigh. He didn't try anything mischievous. No, he just held my thigh firmly. Showing me that I belonged to him.

I liked that. Actually, I loved that.

"Sooo…"

Maddie's voice snapped me out of my thoughts, and I turned my attention to her. She had an eyebrow raised, regarding Alessio curiously.

"Have you proposed yet?"

Thank God, I wasn't eating or I would have choked. My heart stuttered to a stop and then started again. Faster and harder against my ribcage.

What was she doing?

I sent her a warning glare before my gaze moved to Alessio.

His spoon was paused in mid-air.

He was frozen in his seat. My throat went dry, and I wanted to smack my head on the table.

Maddie! This girl!

Alessio placed his spoon down slowly and cleared his throat. "What?"

"I was just wondering if you've proposed yet?" Maddie asked again.

"Why do I have to propose?" Alessio asked, his eyebrows furrowed.

Viktor and Phoenix looked like they were hiding their laughter behind their fists. Even Nikolay looked like he was smiling.

Lyov and Isaak just shook their heads and carried on eating.

"You said so yourself a few days ago. Ayla was an Ivanshov. But did you propose?"

Alessio spared me a glance before looking at

Maddie again. "Was I supposed to propose?"

Maddie's face turned red, her eyes bulging out. She held her fork and knife tighter and speared Alessio with a glare.

I had a feeling she was plotting his murder.

"Did you even ask her if she wanted to marry you?" Maddie hissed.

Alessio looked completely confused and oblivious.

I could feel my cheeks heating up, and I looked down at my plate.

"Ayla, do you want to get married?"

What? WHAT?

Alessio's questioned was imprinted in my brain. Did he really just ask that? In front of everyone?

I looked at Maddie again. She was about to have a heart attack. But she was going to kill Alessio first.

I turned to Alessio. "Emm…"

He looked at me expectantly, waiting for my answer. Actually, everyone was waiting for my answer.

Feeling flustered, I played with the hem of my dress nervously.

"Yes?" I answered hesitantly.

No wasn't an option. It was never an option.

Alessio nodded, looking proud of himself. "Okay. We're getting married then."

If it wasn't for Phoenix holding her down, Maddie would have leaped over the table. "That was hardly a proposal," she hissed with a tight smile.

Alessio looked confused again. "I asked, and she

said yes. We're getting married."

My shoulders sagged. That was it?

Alessio went back to eating. Viktor chuckled and coughed, hiding his amusement. Phoenix did the same before they continued eating too.

A few seconds later, I picked up my fork too. Maddie was still glaring holes in Alessio's forehead, but her shoulders went down in defeat.

When our plates were almost cleared, Alessio leaned closer. "I love you, Angel. I don't care about getting married. It doesn't change anything. But I will give you my name. You *will* be Ayla Ivanshov. That's my promise to you."

His words were low enough for only me to hear, and they made their way straight to my heart. I turned to him, my lips stretched in a smile. It was impossible not to smile.

Alessio smiled back, his eyes filled with so much love for me.

"Okay," I agreed.

I guessed I didn't need a proposal after all. Just being with Alessio…it was enough to make me the happiest woman alive.

Later that night, after playing the piano, I settled on Alessio's lap. We stayed like that for some time, both of us refusing to move.

He played with my hair, my head laid against his shoulder. I placed a kiss there, and he held me tighter.

"What do you need, Ayla? What do you need from me? I want to be the man you deserve," he said, breaking the silence.

I brought my head up and looked at him. He

looked a little lost.

Holding his face in my hands, I brought our lips together. I kissed him softly, pouring all my love into the kiss.

"Only you. I just need you," I whispered against his lips.

Alessio's eyes held mine. Blue to green.

He kissed the tip of my nose and hugged me to him.

Chapter 28

1 week later

Maddie held my arms as we descended the stairs. "I can't wait for you to meet her!" she said excitedly.

I laughed. She was so cute. "I can't wait to meet her either."

Maddie's friend was coming over. More than a friend, actually. They'd been best friends since they were kids. It was almost like they were sisters. She used to live here too, in the estate, until she moved away four years ago.

Maddie didn't have a chance to tell me a lot. She only got a call an hour ago and came banging at my door.

When we reached the bottom, Maddie was practically bouncing on her toes. She was glowing. "I have missed her so much," she pouted. "That little bitch. I hate that she moved away."

We walked toward the door, getting ready to meet her friend. I was excited too.

"Is she like you?" I teased with a wink.

Maddie laughed. "Ha. She's worse!"

My eyes widened. "You mean crazier than you?"

She nodded. "She is insane! But you're going to love her, Ayla."

Oh dear. I looked at the door both impatiently and excitedly, Maddie doing the same.

I heard a loud squeal.

"Maddie!"

Then a flash of blonde hair.

Next thing I knew, Maddie was on the floor.

I gasped, moving away, my eyes wide in shock.

She tackled her. She freaking tackled Maddie to the floor.

I stood, agape and staring at Maddie and the new woman. They were laughing, getting up and hugging each other tightly.

"I missed you!" Maddie exclaimed.

"Missed you too. Damn it! I'm going to cry," she replied.

They pulled apart, and their eyes went to me.

"Hi?" I gave her a tiny wave.

She smiled a breathtaking smile. She glided over to me, and before I could move, I was in her arms.

"I have finally met you," she murmured in my ears. Pulling away, she held on to my hands. "Do you know how desperate I have been? I couldn't wait to see you. Maddie and Viktor have told me so much about you."

"Thank you. I was pretty excited to meet you too," I replied. Her smile was infectious. My cheeks were hurting from smiling too hard.

She was such a bubble of joy. A breathtaking

beauty too. Her blonde hair stopped in the middle of her back. She was smaller than Maddie but taller than me. Her hazel eyes practically glowed with happiness.

"I'm Evaline." She gave me her hand to shake.

"Ayla," I replied, shaking her hand. I already knew her name, but I guessed introductions were a must.

"I know." She winked. Her eyes moved to my rounded belly. "May I?"

Without answering, I brought her hand to my stomach. We waited for Princess to make her presence known. And being herself, the attention seeker, she immediately kicked.

Evaline laughed. "Oh my. That was a hard kick. Finally, Alessio did something right."

But when her eyes moved back to Maddie, they sombered. A wave of pain passed across her face, and she moved away from me.

Maddie shook her head. "Don't."

"I can't believe no one told me, Maddie. Do you realize how pissed I am? I only found out two days ago. It's been weeks!" Evaline hissed, angrily. "Nobody called and thought I needed to know? Not even Viktor. He didn't say anything."

"Because I told them not to say anything. I didn't want you to worry. We've been over this, Evaline," Maddie shot back.

"You were hurt and you—" Evaline broke off, her eyes moving to Maddie's stomach. My heart fell too.

"I should have been there for you, but nobody said anything. I would have been there for you,

Maddie. If only…"

Maddie wrapped her arms around Evaline. "I wanted to do this on my own, babe. It's over and done with. Can we not talk about this now, please?"

Evaline nodded, swiping her tears away. "Phoenix—"

Maddie's face turned furious. "Don't even."

Evaline's shoulders sagged in defeat, but she didn't say anything else.

I knew something was going on between Phoenix and Maddie, but I stayed silent. Only because of Maddie's reaction.

We were silent for a few seconds, and then Evaline jumped in. "Why are we just standing here looking like lost puppies? I need a drink, and I need to get laid. Tonight."

I busted out laughing at that. So did Maddie. "I need to get laid too."

Evaline turned to me. "You?"

Wh-at?

"I know we can have sex while pregnant. Have you tried it yet?" she continued.

Did she just ask that?

I caught Maddie's eyes. *Told you*, she mouthed.

She didn't have a filter. "Like, does it feel better? I heard that we get hornier and want sex all the time. And our sensations are heightened during pregnancy."

"I don't know."

Both of them paused. Maddie looked at me, confused. "Are you saying…?"

I just shrugged.

Evaline and Maddie looked at each other and

268

nodded. Like they just mentally made a plan together. I didn't like the look they were giving me.

"She needs to get laid," Evaline announced.

"She does," Maddie agreed. "We'll figure it out."

"Yeah."

I was standing right there, yet they spoke like I wasn't. They were discussing *my* sex life.

They were crazy...insane. Both of them!

Evaline winked and started to pull me toward the kitchen. Maddie was on my right side, her arm linked with mine.

When we got to the kitchen, Evaline was on Lena in seconds. "Mama Lena!"

"Oh, dear. Look at you! I have missed you, my little girl," Lena gushed, hugging her tight.

"I missed you too," she pouted, pulling away.

"Then why did you move?" Lena sent her a mock glare.

"Exactly. Tell her, Mom," Maddie added. I smiled, watching the interaction between the three. Maddie was right. They really were close.

"I had to. It was the only way," Evaline replied softly.

Lena looked confused. "What do you mean?"

Maddie looked pissed and mumbled something under her breath.

"Don't worry, Mama Lena. I love it up north. Canada is like my home now. But I do miss you guys. Everyone. Sometimes I wish I was back here." Evaline gave us a sad smile. "Just like before."

She took the champagne out of the fridge, her

back turned to us. There was a hint of sadness and pain in her words. I knew Maddie heard it too.

Maddie shook her head and looked down at her lap.

"Forget about it. Do you know where the guys are?" she asked, quickly changing the topic.

"Like they ever tell me where they go," Lena replied, with a hint of amusement. She smiled and kissed Evaline on the cheek.

"I'll see you girls later. I'm sure you have lots of catching up to do."

Lena walked away, and we settled around the table. Evaline was a chatterbox. She talked a lot. Maddie and her were so much alike.

But I was already in love. Evaline wasn't the type of person who made you feel awkward. No, she pulled you in like you were a long-lost family member.

We talked for what felt like hours until we got interrupted by Viktor.

He walked in, and Evaline jumped up, going straight in his arms. They hugged and muttered something quietly to each other.

I sat back and smiled, watching the two. When they pulled away, Viktor ruffled her hair and turned his gaze to mine.

"I see you have already met my little hedgehog."

Evaline growled, patting her hair down. "Don't do that."

"We are half brother and sister." Evaline repeated what she said earlier.

I already knew that. Maddie had filled me in. I just stared at the two siblings. They were so similar, and I could see how much Viktor loved her sister.

They talked and joked, both of them fighting each other. When Viktor left, Evaline took her seat beside me again.

"Same father, different mother. Actually, our moms were sisters," she said. "It appeared that dad had no control. He was the true definition of a playboy when he was younger."

Isaak a playboy?

In that moment, I realized that Evaline was my *sister*. My eyes widened, and I stared at her. This was my chance. To know more about Isaak. Did she know who I was?

"Was he always like that?" I asked curiously, trying hard to act nonchalant.

Evaline shrugged. "Pretty mu—" Her words caught in her throat.

I saw her eyes widen, and then her expression changed. Her eyes held so much pain.

It looked like her heart had shattered in that moment.

"Yeah. Okay."

Another voice pulled my head the other way.

Nikolay walked into the kitchen.

"I will let Boss kn—"

He stopped mid-sentence too.

Actually, he froze, standing still in the doorway. His eyes widened, and I looked back toward Evaline.

Both of them stared at each other, their eyes drawn to each other, like they were the only two people there.

I looked back at Nikolay. He looked like he was

in pain too. He swallowed hard several times, his eyes moving over Evaline's face.

"Nikolay," I heard Evaline say. Her voice was soft. So soft and gentle. She said his name like she was whispering a prayer.

And then anger. So much anger. Nikolay's face turned thunderous. He sent Evaline a piercing glare before stalking away.

I sat still.

Nikolay and Evaline?

She choked back a sob. "I'm sorry. Excuse me."

Before I could say anything, Evaline got up and ran toward the back. The door to the back garden banged closed as she ran outside.

"That fucking asshole," Maddie hissed. "I swear to God, I am so done with his bullshit."

"What just happened?" I asked.

"Long story, babe. Long story. Let me get the drink—juice for you, though—and I'll tell you."

Chapter 29

One week later

"Are you done?" Maddie knocked at the door loudly.

I quickly wrapped the towel around me and opened the door. "Yes, I'm done."

"Did you shave?" Evaline asked.

"Yes."

"Everywhere?" Maddie added.

I glared at her. "Yes. I'm only going to the creek anyway. Why do I have to shave?"

Without answering, Maddie shoved a dress in my hand. "Here. Go change."

I stared at the dress, confused. "That's not the dress I picked."

I looked over her shoulder, searching for my purple dress, but it was nowhere to be found.

"We thought this would look nicer," Evaline said. "Hurry, go change. Alessio is waiting."

"But—" I started to refuse. Maddie glared, and I shut up immediately.

273

With a sigh, I walked back into the bathroom and shrugged on the dress.

It was a long flowy white dress, coming down below my ankle. It was backless and sleeveless but very simple and elegant. It fit perfectly over my baby bump.

I stared at my reflection and smiled. I felt…beautiful.

I fixed the strings of the dress properly over my shoulders and then quickly combed my hair. It fell in waves down my back, and when I was satisfied with my appearance, I walked out.

Maddie and Evaline attacked me before I could say anything. After a little make-up, they finally let me breathe.

"Why?" I simply asked, looking at my glossy pink lips and coated eyelashes. I even had a light eyeshadow on.

"We just felt like dolling you up," Evaline answered. I shook my head, feeling quite suspicious.

But then again, they were crazy. I stopped guessing a long time ago. It was best to just go with the flow.

Maddie placed a single peony above my ear. She made sure it was attached to my hair without having it fall out or hurting me.

"There. You look breathtaking, babe. You're ready to go now," Maddie announced. I smiled up at her.

"Alessio hates waiting," I replied, standing up. Evaline handed me a pretty pair of black sandals, and I quickly put them on.

Maddie muttered something under her breath that I couldn't quite catch, but I didn't care. My whole attention was on getting to Alessio.

I hadn't seen him since the morning, and I was a little disappointed that he didn't even wake me up before he left. He wasn't at breakfast either.

"Okay. You can go now, pretty girl!" Evaline said. I sighed and rolled my eyes.

"Thank you."

Before leaving the room, I turned around. "Really. I mean it. Thank you."

They both smiled. "You'll thank us more later. Go, go, go!" Evaline said with a laugh.

Shaking my head, I left the room. Maddie was still beside me, helping me down the stairs.

Alessio would get really angry if he saw me walking down the stairs alone. I always had someone accompany me.

When we reached the bottom, Maddie let go of me and winked before running back upstairs again. She seemed a little too excited today.

I walked out through the doors to see Viktor waiting for me at the entrance. He wasn't alone. Nikolay and Phoenix were there too.

"We are to escort you to the creek," Phoenix explained.

My mouth formed an *O*, and I nodded. Smiling kindly at them, I replied, "Okay. Thank you."

Viktor stood to my left while Nikolay took my right. I walked forward, but they stayed where they were. I glanced back, confused.

Viktor sighed and came back to my side. Nikolay followed. I stood there, waiting.

And then both of them presented me their elbows. I stared at them, my mouth falling open. What?

They waited, and I stood still. Nikolay coughed. It was fake, but it was probably to bring me out of my sudden daze.

"You want me...to take your arms?" I asked slowly.

"Yes," Viktor simply replied.

"Oh." I bit on my lips and took their elbows. It felt weird but strangely comfortable.

Phoenix took the front, leading us. We walked slowly, making sure I didn't trip on anything. The walk was silent but comfortable.

I couldn't wait to see Alessio.

When we reached the clearing, my steps faltered.

Alessio was standing there. His back was to me; one of his legs was placed on a rock as he leaned against it.

I instinctively moved toward him, but Viktor and Nikolay held me back. I gave them an impatient look.

Viktor was the first to move. He leaned forward and surprised me with a kiss on my forehead. I stilled, my heart fluttered.

"You both deserve each other," he whispered before pulling away.

And then Nikolay took his place. Another kiss on my forehead.

He too whispered in my ears. "Be happy."

When he stepped back, Phoenix moved forward. Placing a kiss on my forehead, he smiled. "Make him a happy man."

And then they were walking away, leaving me in shock. I blinked several times, trying to wrap my mind around what just happened.

But I was just drawing blanks.

I turned back toward Alessio to see him staring at me. He had a small smile on his face. And in his hands, he held a large bouquet of white peonies.

I could feel my lips moving, spreading in a loving smile. Slowly, I made my way to him. Alessio held out his hand for me, and I immediately took it.

His hand was warm and gentle as he wrapped his fingers around mine. Pulling me closer, he held me against him.

"Angel," he whispered softly before claiming my lips.

His kiss was tentative at first, but then he kissed me harder, kissing me like he owned me. I loved it when he did that.

He kissed me like he'd never have enough. When we pulled apart, we were both breathless. I didn't mind though. I wanted him to kiss me more.

His hand found its way to my neck, his fingers softly caressing my veins there. His soft touch sent shivers through me.

The way he stroked my skin, his touch, everything about him...it warmed me. My heart fluttered like crazy. My stomach flipped with nervous butterflies.

"Ayla," he rasped, his voice suddenly rougher.

"Alessio," I whispered in response, moving even closer. As close as I could get.

"You look so beautiful right now. Like a true

Angel," he said, his eyes smiling down at me. "I love you in white. It's the best color on you."

I felt my cheeks flush under his compliment and looked shyly at his chest. "And this," Alessio continued, placing a finger under my chin and tipping my head back. "I find it so endearing that you are still shy around me."

That made me blush even more. I couldn't help the smile. I felt so at peace. So loved and treasured. Alessio did this to me.

He pulled away slightly and presented me the flowers. "These are for you."

I took the flowers with a soft thank you. "I love these flowers. They're my favorite."

"I know," he replied ever so arrogantly.

I looked around the creek. Next to the tree, I found some pillows, a basket, and a large blanket laid down. My eyes moved back to Alessio's, and I pointed at the tree.

"What is this?"

He shrugged and cleared his throat.

Alessio swore under his breath, and he avoided my eyes for a few seconds. He took a deep breath before meeting my gaze again.

I waited for him to speak.

He opened his mouth but then snapped it shut again.

He hissed, running his fingers through his hair agitatedly.

"I had this planned. I even fucking practiced," he growled under his breath.

"O-kay?"

I held the flowers closer to my chest, waiting for

him to continue.

"Right," he said, clearing his throat again. "You deserve everything, you know that, right? Even a romantic proposal. I want to do this right."

Oh. Oh. OH!

I gaped at him. He was proposing?

Was it possible for my heart to beat faster? I didn't know, but it sure felt like it.

"Flowers..." he said suddenly. Alessio pointed at the flowers, and I nodded slowly.

Okay. Flowers.

"It's you...I mean, flowers represent beauty. That's you. The most beautiful."

That was really sweet. Like really, really sweet. So I told him. "Thank you. That's really thoughtful and sweet."

"The pink peonies are supposed to be romantic," he continued.

I looked down to see two light pink peonies in the middle of the white bouquet. *Awww.*

"But I'm giving you the white because that's the first flower I ever gave you. It was the start of us," Alessio broke off at the end and paused. "Why the fuck am I talking about flowers?" he asked suddenly.

"I think it's sweet. The meaning behind why you gave me the flowers. I love it," I replied honestly. He really did think this through, even if he was being a little funny at the moment.

He looked so lost and bashful, confused but really determined.

"Okay." He nodded. Alessio took a deep breath again.

I saw him jerk at his tie in frustration. Unable to see him like this, I moved closer and laid a hand over his wildly racing heart.

"It's okay, Alessio. Stop trying so hard," I soothed gently. "Just be yourself. I need only you."

"I ruined the proposal, didn't I?" he asked, a frown on his face.

I leaned up and gave him a quick peck on the lips. "Nope. So far it's perfect. Just say what you want to say. From your heart. That's all I want."

He nodded and took a step away from me.

Only to kneel on one knee.

I brought a shaking hand to my mouth and held back the tears.

Alessio took my hand in his. He placed a soft kiss at the back of my hand, letting his lips linger there. "I love you, Angel."

With his lips still against my skin, he continued. "I was such an asshole when we first met."

He paused and let out a low chuckle. "Okay. Maybe sometimes I still am. But you changed me, Ayla. You made me feel when I didn't want to. When I didn't think I was capable of feeling."

A tear slid down my cheek. He brought his head up and kept holding my hand.

"You taught me how to love when I didn't even believe in love. I thought no Angel existed. I had lost hope a long time ago, but then you came into my life and proved me wrong," Alessio said, his voice a little scratchy with emotions.

"I know I'm not the perfect man. But I know I can be the perfect man for you. I will be the one who holds you at night, wipes your tears away.

Makes you smile and laugh. I will be the man that makes your heart flutter. I will make sweet love to you." He paused, and his gaze moved over my face.

I saw a small smirk. I should have guessed what was coming next, but I didn't because I was so lost in his sweet words and captivating blue eyes.

"I will be the man who fucks you too. Slow. Fast. Deep. Rough."

I shook my head, a small laugh bubbling from my chest. "You are impossible."

He shrugged before swallowing hard. Alessio was silent for a few seconds before speaking again.

"Give me a chance to love you, Angel. Let me love you the way you deserve. Let me be the man for you. Will you marry me, Angel?"

I couldn't do anything except nod. My voice...my words were robbed from me.

My throat was closed up with emotion, and I swallowed back my sob. Alessio continued to break and mend my heart with his words.

He reached behind him, removing something from his pocket. And then he was presenting me with a box. A small red box. He opened the lid, and a small gasp escaped past my lips.

The ring that lay in the middle was beautiful. It was simple, small, but oh so beautiful. So elegant. There was a round diamond in the middle. On either side of the bigger diamond were several smaller ones.

"Will you do me the honor of being my wife? Will you be Ayla Ivanshov? Will you lead with me...rule with me...by my side as my queen?"

"Yes," I whispered, my voice barely audible.

Alessio smiled and took the ring out of the box. He placed it on my ring finger. It shone in the sunlight.

He stood up, towering over my smaller height. "Alessio, you make me the happiest woman. I don't think I can ever be happier than this."

"I know neither of us wants a big wedding. We have already made vows to each other before. So I wanted this to be our small wedding. Just us. We don't need anyone else," Alessio explained.

And it was absolutely perfect. I loved it.

He was right. We didn't need a big wedding. This was much better. Just us. Only us.

I looked down at Alessio's hand. "But you don't have a ring."

He gave me a sheepish look. "I got everything planned. Well, I did get a little help from the others."

"The dress. It's white. Like a wedding dress. The bouquet," I said thoughtfully, finally understanding what went on.

Alessio nodded.

A sudden realization dawned on me, and my eyes widened. "The guys," I exclaimed.

He smiled and pulled me closer. "They were walking me down the aisle?"

"They wanted to. We thought it was fitting. They are your champions. They gave you away...to me."

That was really sweet. Tears slid down my cheeks, and I sniffled. Alessio wiped away my tears.

"Do you want to finish this ceremony?" he teased in my ear.

I nodded. Alessio pulled back and kissed me on the forehead. "I take you to be my wife. I promise to honor you, support you. I will be your savior. I promise to love and cherish you until I take my last breath."

He took a deep breath before continuing. "And I promise to protect you and our kids."

His voice got lower, for only my ears. "I will kill for you...I love you, Angel."

My breath hitched and caught in my throat. "So do you take me as your husband? Do you accept me?"

"Yes. I do."

"Fuck yeah!" He crushed me to him and took my lips passionately.

"Wait," I mumbled. "My turn."

I placed the flowers down as he nodded and handed me another box. I opened it and there lay his ring. It was a simple wedding band, but it held so much power. Placing it on his ring finger, I said my vows.

"I take you to be my husband. I accept you, Alessio. Every part of you. You are mine just like I am yours. I may be your Angel, but you are *my* guardian Angel. My savior. I chose you to be my love, my husband, and the father of my babies. I promise to hold and love you forever, until I take my last breath. You are in my heart, Alessio Ivanshov."

Alessio pressed his lips together, his blue eyes shining. "Do you take me as your wife? Will you let me love you the way you deserve?"

"Yeah. I do."

I smiled while Alessio bent his head. "You are my wife, Ayla Ivanshov."

And then he kissed me.

Slowly at first. He took his sweet time.

Until he got impatient. Which was *so* Alessio.

Alessio's hand cupped my cheeks and angled my head to the side, pushing his tongue into my mouth. We kissed, taking each other in. Our tongues mated together, just like our hearts did.

His fingers whispered over the length of my neck, and I shivered. I heard him groan, the sound going straight between my legs.

I clenched my thighs together as Alessio continued to explore my mouth. His kiss became more aggressive. More demanding. More possessive.

And I let him in. I let him take whatever he wanted...needed.

I needed him too.

Alessio nipped at my lower lip, pulling it between his teeth. And then he kissed it better.

Hot and cold. Soft and hard. That was how he kissed me.

My hands tightened around his shoulders, pulling him closer. My fingers went to his hair, holding on. I kissed him back with the same passion.

His fingers continued to trail a warm path down my neck, resting just in the middle of chest, between my breasts.

I pulled back, breathless but needing more.

Alessio's lips trailed kisses down my jaw, reaching my neck. He nipped at the skin before sucking it between his lips, leaving his mark there.

I moaned, my fingers tightening in his hair. He continued to lay kisses on my neck, leaving a wet trail. My head fell back, giving him better access.

He groaned in appreciation, and my eyes pinched closed when his fingers moved over my breast, feeling my nipple through my dress.

Alessio pulled the strap of my dress down, lower and lower, until my breasts were freed from my dress.

"Alessio," I whimpered as he thumbed my hard points. "Here?"

"Here," he said.

"Now?"

"I want you, Ayla. I want you so fucking much."

My breath hitched as he unclasped my bra and threw it away. My breasts were bared to him, and he lowered his head, his lips hovering over my left nipple.

I shivered in anticipation, and when he licked a hardened point, an unashamed moan left my lips. His fingers played with my other nipple, circling, pinching and pulling…driving me crazy.

His tongue continued to masterfully play me. He was careful not to hurt me. His touches ignited sparks between my legs.

I trembled against him, pulling him closer. "Alessio."

I was lost in his touches…lost in the fire he created in me. My skin felt warm and flushed. I felt out of breath.

His lips explored my breasts. Kissing, sucking, not letting an inch of the skin go untouched and unloved.

Alessio palmed my breasts together, and I moaned. He hissed when I pulled at his hair urgently.

"I love seeing you like this, losing control," he whispered against my skin.

"Alessio…please…"

He stood to his full height and pulled my dress over my head in a swift movement. I bit on my lips as his fingers played with the string of my lingerie.

"I want you naked to my eyes. I want to feast on your body, Ayla. I'm going to eat your pussy, then I am going to make love to you," he said roughly in my ear. "Maybe I'll fuck you later too."

He pressed his finger to my burning core. Even though he wasn't touching my skin—the thin barrier of my lingerie stopped him—I felt him.

He pressed against my clit, circling his thumb over it. Alessio slowly pushed the lacy cloth aside, his finger pushing against my wetness.

"You are already so wet for me, kitten."

He pushed a single finger inside of me, and my head snapped back. "Oh…"

Alessio pumped his finger inside of me. In and out. Slowly. Teasing me. I whimpered, wanting more.

When he pressed another finger in, I clenched around him. He hissed, moving his fingers inside of me. He pulled me over the edge, so close. But he stopped me from falling.

His thumb circled over my clit faster and faster. I grew dizzy with need, but still…he didn't let me fall.

I dug my fingers into his back, but Alessio was relentless. He continued his torturous assault, and then he stopped, pulling his fingers out of me. Leaving me empty.

A small growl of frustration escaped past my lips, surprising me.

Alessio pushed a finger deep inside of me. I bit on my lips hard, suppressing my moan. He stopped again and pulled his finger out. My eyes snapped open to see him smirking, licking his fingers clean.

His lips met mine in a hard kiss. I could taste myself on his lips. His words drove me close to the edge, my body flushing red. "You taste so fucking good, baby."

Alessio pulled me in his arms, cradling me to his chest. He walked us to the blankets and pillows. Laying me down on the softness, he knelt between my spread legs.

Without warning, he had my underwear removed until I was completely bared to his eyes. With my legs open, he saw everything.

I tried to close my legs, but he spread his thighs more, stopping my movement. His eyes feasted over me with hunger and so much desire.

Alessio quickly removed his suit jacket and shirt. He almost ripped it off him in his haste. Before I could move, he was bending his head to my dripping core.

There was no warning before I felt his tongue licking at my wetness, lapping at the juices gathered there.

I let out a small scream as he pressed his tongue to my opening. His fingers gripped my thighs tighter, spreading me open. He pushed my knees up and bent outwards.

I could hear how wet I was as he continued to lick and suck. His tongue circled over my nub as my legs quivered with the need for release.

"Play with your nipples," he demanded. "Pretend it's my hand."

I shyly brought my hand to my breast, doing as I was told. I imagined it was his fingers circling and pulling at my hardened points.

"Alessio…I need…"

I broke up with a moan when he pressed a finger inside of me again. His tongue never stopped working its magic on my core.

When his finger curved inside of me at the same time he softly bit my clit, my back bowed off the ground. A small scream escaped me, my eyes closing as I came.

I surrendered to Alessio. Wave after wave of ecstasy coursed through me.

When he pulled away, my eyes dreamily opened to meet his heated ones. I blinked down at him. He wiped his chin off with the back of his hand and quickly removed his pants.

When he was finally naked, he settled between my spread thighs again. "I'm going to make love to you, Angel."

"Please, Alessio. I need you."

His eyes were filled with love as his lips descended to mine. He kissed me for a long time.

"Put me inside of you," he ordered huskily against my lips.

My heart stuttered as my hand went between our

bodies. I wrapped my fingers around his hard length, and Alessio groaned, thrusting against me.

He pulsed in my hand as I rubbed my thumb over the head, feeling a bit of wetness there. "I need to be inside of you. Right now."

Alessio pushed his hips closer, thrusting in my hand. Our mouths fused together, tongues licking and sucking.

I was hyperaware of his warm skin against mine. The way he felt above me made me quiver in anticipation and need.

I ran my other hand over his back, feeling his tensed muscles. A low groan came from him as I continued to stroke his cock.

Alessio knelt in front of me. He was cautious of my stomach. His hips nestled between my legs as I brought him closer to me. He lifted my hips up slightly, aligning us.

When the tip of his cock pressed against my entrance, I bit on my lips and closed my eyes.

"No," Alessio hissed. "I need your eyes on me. I need you to see me. Only me."

Realizing what he was doing, my eyes snapped open. "Only you," I whispered.

My heart lurched, and my mouth parted in a silent gasp when he gently pushed inside. Our bodies trembled, and I knew he was holding himself back.

He thrust inside. Deep and slow. His cock rested inside my heated core, and I moaned. I wrapped my legs around his hips, urging him for more.

And he gave me more.

His length filled me completely until I was

impossibly full. His hard cock stretched me. My hips raised against my own will, moving with Alessio.

Alessio's breathing was uneven as sweat formed across his forehead and neck. His taut arms held him above me, and I kissed his lips.

"Take me, Alessio."

Alessio's hips bucked against mine. He moved inside me, pulling almost all the way out before pushing in again.

A small relieved cry left my lips.

Alessio moved again, his cock spilling out before thrusting deep inside. Again and again, he moved against me.

Thrusting deeper and faster. Our moans melted together.

Alessio buried his head into my neck, his tempo increasing. When he moved, resting deep inside my core, I moved against him, wanting more friction.

He pulled out, and I gasped. Instead, he turned me on my right side so he was behind me. Alessio gathered me in his arms like I was a precious jewel.

I panted softly, my breath squeezing out of my lungs when I felt Alessio's between my legs again. I couldn't see his face in my position.

We laid on our sides. Alessio pulled my thigh over his, opening me to him. His length nudged my opening again.

Without warning, he thrust hard inside. A gasp of surprise caught my throat as he started moving. From this position, this angle, I felt him deeper inside of me.

I fisted the blankets as he continued pounding

inside of me, harder each time. A shudder rolled through me, and I felt him rigid behind me.

His harsh breath was next to my ears. "You are so tight and wet."

"Turn your head. I want your lips."

I turned my head, and his lips took me. He devoured me with his kiss. His lips took mine hungrily and desperately as his thrust become jerky.

He was close. I was too.

I kissed him back with as much hunger as he moved inside me.

His finger circled over my wet nub, and my screams were heard across the creek. My body quivered with my release.

My mind went blank for a few minutes. When I came back, Alessio was still thrusting inside of me.

One final thrust and he settled deep inside of me. It took my breath away.

I felt his warmth, coating my insides as he came. His hips trembled against mine as he groaned his release.

We stayed locked together like this, my back to his front. My leg over his, his cock still pulsing inside of me.

I closed my eyes dreamily as Alessio placed wet kisses along my neck.

"Thank you for loving me, Ayla Ivanshov."

Ayla Ivanshov.

That sounded so beautiful.

"And thank you for loving me, Alessio Ivanshov."

Ayla and Alessio Ivanshov.

So beautiful.

My mind went drowsy. Alessio wrapped his arms around me, holding me close.

That was how I felt asleep.

Wrapped in his arms. Loved by him.

Chapter 30

My body was limp and relaxed as my eyes fluttered open. I could hear the birds singing from far away. A sense of serenity went through me as I woke up.

I was warm. Really warm. Like I was wrapped in a safe cocoon.

Alessio's arm was wrapped protectively—almost possessively around my waist. My back was to his front as we spooned. My hand went over his as I smiled.

His fingers caressed my bare stomach under the soft blanket. He must have covered us up when I fell asleep. That made me smile wider.

I shifted around in his embrace and turned to face him. His eyes were already on me, his face peaceful.

"Hey," he muttered, pulling me as close as I could get with my stomach.

"How long was I sleeping?" I asked, my hand going to his face. I touched his rough stubble, my fingers slightly scratching his chin.

"About an hour and half. I see I have worn you out. And here I thought we could go for hours," Alessio teased with a mischievous glint in his blue eyes.

I poked his cheek. "I'm hungry, though."

He sighed and got up. I shivered from the cold air when the blanket was pulled away from my chest. I quickly wrapped it tightly around myself again.

Alessio winked before handing me my dress. I noticed that he already had his pants and shirt on.

Now that was a sorrowful sight. Or not. He looked really delicious in a suit.

Alessio pulled the blanket away. He palmed my rounded stomach and bent down, placing a kiss right above my belly button. As soon as his lips made contact with my bare skin, Princess kicked.

Alessio chuckled. "You are a fighter," he whispered against my belly.

After another kiss, he pulled back and helped me with my dress. When I was comfortable against the pillows, Alessio brought the basket to me.

"Lena prepared some sandwiches for us. I think they might be a little cold by now," Alessio explained.

I shrugged and practically dove into the basket. I had a bite in five seconds flat. "I'm really starving," I mumbled around a mouthful of sandwich.

Alessio raised an eyebrow and then shrugged. "Okay then."

We cuddled close as we ate in silence. When the basket was empty and all the food was gone, I closed my eyes. "I think I ate too much."

"You did," Alessio agreed with a laugh. "I guess Princess was really hungry."

I nodded before pulling away. "Let's go. I'm sure everyone is waiting for us."

Alessio helped me stand up. His arms instinctively went around my hips. His lips found mine in a hard, bruising kiss.

"You make me lose control, Ayla," he said against my lips. "I see you and all I want to do is kiss you. Make love to you. Fuck you so hard that all you can see, think, and remember is me."

I melted into his embrace, his words making my heart flutter. "I can't decide if that's really sweet."

He kissed me again. And again. Alessio kissed me until we were both breathless.

He looked down at me lovingly. "I want to be your first thought when you wake up and your last thought before you sleep. Hell, I want to be in your thoughts all the time."

I placed my hand over his heart. The heart he had given me so trustingly and with so much love. "You have nothing to worry about. Because you are always in my thoughts, Alessio. Even in my dreams. You are with me all the time," I replied.

"Good."

And then he smiled a breathtaking smile. It stole my breath away.

In that moment, I realized that I always wanted to see that smile. I would do anything to see that beautiful, joyous smile over and over again.

Alessio entwined our fingers together, and we walked back to the house as a married couple.

It may have not been official, but we didn't need

to be official. The vows were made, and we accepted each other. We were married. No one could deny us that.

When we reached the front door, Alessio paused and smiled. "Well, I have to do this. Don't want Maddie to kill me in my sleep," he said with a small laugh.

My eyes widened, and I let out a giggle as he cradled me in his arms. My hands went around his neck, holding him tight.

With me in his arms, he walked us into the house. There was a loud cheer as we stepped inside. Alessio didn't let me down until we were in the living room.

Everyone was standing there, surrounding us with laughter, smiles, and so much love.

I needed this. I needed this family. My daughter needed them.

I didn't know what I would have done without all of these people.

As soon as Alessio placed me on my feet, Maddie was on me. She hugged me tight before pulling away. Her eyes held tears, but they didn't fall. "Congratulations, babe."

Lena and Evaline hugged me next. Their happiness made my heart overflow with love. "Thank you," I whispered when they pulled away too.

From the corner of my eyes, I saw the guys hugging Alessio. There were a few punches and then laughter.

Alessio came back to my side. We stood together watching everyone celebrating our love. I even saw

Isaak and Lyov standing in a corner watching us from afar. I waved, and they smiled back.

When calm finally settled around us, I saw Viktor, Phoenix, and Nikolay walking toward me.

They stopped just a few feet away, facing me as they stood in a line. Behind them, I saw several of Alessio's men crowding closer.

I hadn't noticed Nina before. She was standing far away, hidden in the shadows. But now she walked forward.

She came to stand beside Nikolay, taking the front with Alessio's most trusted men.

The atmosphere suddenly shifted, the air feeling somewhat deadly and cold. The look of determination on their faces confused me.

A shiver ran down my spine when I saw them take out a small knife. Each held one in their hands.

I looked up at Alessio, but he only looked proud. His eyes held mine for a moment before he leaned down for a kiss.

"You are their Queen," he whispered in my ear before pulling away.

"What's going on?" I asked curiously.

The four of them took a step forward without a word.

I licked my lips nervously, waiting. My heart hammered in my chest when they took their next step.

And then they knelt down on one knee.

The men behind followed suit, bowing the heads. In respect.

"Oh no! What are you doing? Please stand up," I quickly said. I looked at Alessio for help, but he shook his head.

"Let them do this, Ayla. It's a ritual they all hold very close," he explained, nodding toward the kneeling men.

Even Nina was kneeling down, her head bowed in respect.

I saw Maddie smiling. Lena had tears in her eyes.

Viktor held the dagger to his right palm. I could see it wasn't a normal dagger. There were red crystals around the handle. An emblem was on the blade.

His head came up, his darkened eyes meeting mine.

And then he spoke.

His voice was deep and strong as he recited what seemed like a vow. But my eyebrows furrowed at the different language.

He was speaking Russian.

I saw him press the blade into his palm. My eyes followed the trace of blood, my heart hammering faster and harder in my chest.

I felt Alessio at my back. He wrapped his arms around me. His warm breath tickled my ear as he translated Viktor's words.

"I vow to protect you. As your warrior, my life is yours. I bleed for you. Your life before mine. In every sense, you are my Queen. With this blood, I make this vow."

When Viktor was done, Phoenix made a similar cut in his palm as he recited the same words.

Nikolay took his turn. And then Nina.

I stood speechless and completely immobile as

they made their vows to me.

When they were done, the men behind them made their blood oath together. Their voices were loud and rang clear through the house.

As silence fell upon us again, Viktor, Phoenix, Nikolay and Nina placed their daggers at my feet and bowed their head again.

"They are waiting for you to speak," Alessio muttered, giving the small push I needed.

What could I say? Never in my dreams did I ever think that a scene like this would have been possible.

To have such strong men kneeling for me, vowing as if their lives didn't matter.

I was shocked and rendered completely speechless. But they patiently waited for me to speak.

No, they waited for my command.

When I finally found my voice, I held onto Alessio's hand tightly. With his unwavering support and strength, I spoke.

"Please, stand up. All of you," I said softly.

My eyes blurred when they all stood up.

"I don't need this," I said. "I don't need your lives. I don't want you to bleed for me. That's not how it works. We are a family. Just because I am Alessio's wife, it doesn't mean that you are less than me."

Alessio's arm tightened around my hips. "It's our tradition, Ayla. It's a ritual that has been taken seriously for centuries. For every Queen that has been brought into this family, our men vow their lives for hers. It was like this for my mother. Now it's your turn. One day, it will be our son's wife. Or our daughter."

Viktor came to stand in front of me. "This is a tradition we all hold very dearly, Ayla. Grant us this wish. Let us serve you the way you deserve."

"The love that all of you give me is enough. I don't need warriors; I just need friends. A family," I replied tearfully. "I never had a family. But this family is all I need. Nothing else. Nothing more."

Viktor smiled. I saw him looking at Alessio, as if asking his permission.

When his eyes came back to mine, I knew that whatever he wanted to do, Alessio had given him his permission.

He leaned forward and placed a kiss on my forehead. "You already have all of us."

He pulled away and showed me his bloodied palm. "You will never be alone again. This blood means we are a family. We are one. If you want to take it like this, then you could say this is our vow to you."

My heart squeezed and Princess kicked against her father's hand. A single tear slid down my cheek as I regarded Viktor. I felt choked with emotion. My throat closed as I tried to speak.

I looked over his shoulders at the others. They were all looking at me expectantly. I took a deep breath and then nodded. "Okay."

Their shoulders sagged in what seemed like relief. As if my acceptance was everything they needed.

"I love you, Angel," Alessio said in my ear. His words were only for me. I closed my eyes and sank into his arms, letting him support my weight. "I'm so proud of you. You leave me in awe every single time."

"These types of rituals always make me cry," I heard Evaline say. There were some chuckles and laughter.

I opened my eyes to see Maddie holding her hand over her mouth. It looked like she was holding her tears in too.

"I guess the only thing left is the wedding ceremony!" she announced loudly.

"We are already married," Alessio snapped back.

Maddie's tears were suddenly gone. Instead, she glowered at my man.

Oh no. This was about to turn ugly.

"I mean an actual wedding," Maddie hissed.

"Are you saying Ayla and I aren't married?"

"I didn't say that."

"Actually, it's not official. Your marriage isn't legal," Viktor piped in.

"Excuse me?" Alessio growled.

"You need to sign the papers to make it legal. You had no witness either," Lyov explained.

"Well, actually, about that…" Maddie started.

My eyes widened when I saw her biting on her lips nervously. Alessio must have noticed it too because he stiffened.

Viktor, Phoenix, Nikolay, and Evaline looked suddenly guilty.

Oh no. No. No. Nope.

"You did not!" I gasped out loud.

"We were only there for half of it! I swear!" Evaline quickly tried to plead innocence.

Maddie nodded. "As soon as the rings were exchanged we left."

"I'm about to shoot someone," Alessio snapped.

Everyone took several steps back.

"We just wanted to make sure you stuck to the plan and didn't mess it up," Phoenix tried to reason. "You were having a hard time memorizing the lines the night before."

"Not that you said anything remotely close to what you practiced anyway," Viktor continued.

"But it was so sweet. If I wasn't already in love, I swear I would have fallen for you, Alessio," Evaline swooned.

Viktor's head snapped toward Evaline. "What did you say?"

Nikolay paled and looked like he ate something huge and it was stuck in his throat.

Not good. Not good at all.

"About that," I jumped it. "Alessio, you said you practiced. Who did you practice with?"

"Don't, Ayla," Alessio started, but it was too late.

"Me!" Viktor announced, his attention back on us. He puffed his chest and smiled a Cheshire smile. "I was his bride."

I raised an eyebrow and looked at Alessio over my shoulders. He swore under his breath.

"Oh really?" I questioned, hiding my giggle behind my hand.

Viktor came to stand beside Alessio and threw an arm around his shoulders. "We practiced everything."

"And by everything, I mean…everything. If you

know what I mean."

"What the fuck!" Alessio bellowed.

Alessio let go of me. When I heard Viktor scream in pain, I didn't have to turn around to know what happened.

"You broke my nose. What the fuck?"

"You deserved that one," Evaline sighed.

I couldn't hold myself any longer. My laughter bubbled from my chest, and I let it out, laughing uncontrollably at all of them.

They were crazy. Insane.

But I loved them. They really did make me the happiest woman.

"You guys are crazy," I wheezed between my laughter.

Alessio was back to my side. He wrapped me in his embrace as I smiled, looking at everyone.

My gaze found Maddie, and I sent her a small smile. "Maddie, it doesn't matter if we have the wedding. It won't be official anyway. I'm supposed to be dead, remember? I have no identity."

Her expression turned sorrowful at the reminder of my previous life. "Okay, no papers then. But can we still have a big-ass wedding? Please? I have been planning this for months! Years even! Please, Alessio. Ayla," she begged.

It was impossible to say no to her puppy eyes. She pouted, and I saw Evaline doing the same.

"No," Alessio simply stated.

I sighed and shrugged. "How big?"

"About a thousand people? Only the close ones," Evaline suggested.

Woah.

"Will I get to wear a wedding dress?" I asked, feeling suddenly excited.

"Yes!" Maddie squealed.

I knew Alessio and I were already married. I didn't really want another wedding.

But the thought of walking down the aisle toward Alessio, confessing my love to him, making my vows to him in front of everyone...it made me feel slightly giddy.

On top of that, I didn't think it was possible to say *no* to Maddie and Evaline.

I turned in Alessio's embrace and faced him. "I already consider us married. We don't need another wedding. The vows we made to each other are already enough." I paused.

"You want the wedding?" Alessio asked.

"Do you?" I shot back. "If you don't, then we won't have one."

"I don't care either way, Angel. You are already my wife. No one else can say otherwise." He shot everyone a glare.

"I want to wear a wedding dress," I whispered shyly, feeling suddenly nervous. "And walk down the aisle for you. Again."

I sucked in a quick breath when Alessio kissed me hard. "We'll have a wedding then," he announced loudly.

Evaline and Maddie squealed behind me.

I only smiled at my husband.

My heart was overflowing with love for this man.

How could he be a killer and so sweet at the same time...I didn't understand. But I didn't have to understand. I just needed him the way he was.

Dangerous, ruthless, yet sweet and loving.

He winked, and my stomach fluttered in response. My heart drummed faster at his smile and blue eyes.

"But bring down the guest numbers, and after Princess is born," I said when I turned to face the others.

"Deal," Maddie quickly agreed.

It looked like we were having a wedding after all.

Alessio placed a kiss on my temple. "You are so sweet, husband."

He teasingly nipped at my ear. "Only for you, wife."

I giggled…feeling so free…so loved…so treasured.

In Alessio's arms, I was whole.

Chapter 31

Two weeks later

"Where are we going?" I asked for probably the tenth time.

"You'll see," Alessio simply replied.

Our hands were entwined together, and he was pulling me somewhere. Although I had no idea where that somewhere was...because he wouldn't tell me.

We walked down the hall toward his office. "We're going to your office?"

"No."

I was about to ask again when we stopped two doors before his office. I glanced up at Alessio, waiting for him to explain.

"You have never been in here, right?" he asked, gazing down at me intensely.

I shook my head. "No. It's always locked."

"Today is an important day. I guess you can say this is another tradition," Alessio explained.

Confused, I stared at the door as he unlocked it.

He pulled me inside, closing the door behind us.

The room was dark, the curtains drawn down, hiding the sun. Alessio walked to the window and dragged the curtains away, letting the sunlight infiltrate the room. It cast a golden glow around us.

I had to blink several times, trying to adjust my eyes to the sudden light.

Alessio had made sure to position me toward the wall. Because of this, the first thing I saw were the large portraits.

My eyes widened, and I let out a barely audible gasp. There were two portraits that I realized were of Lyov and Maria. They looked young in the photos.

The first portrait had Maria sitting on a chair while Lyov stood beside her, his hand on her shoulder. They were both looking at the camera. Maria had a small smile on her face while Lyov looked intense and serious. Almost vicious.

The second portrait, there was only one addition. A small boy sitting on Maria's lap. When I saw her rounded pregnant belly, I instantly knew the little boy was Alessio.

That portrait was taken when Maria was pregnant with her princess. Tears blurred my eyes at the thought. A princess they never got to meet.

Lyov had the same expression as the first. I wasn't surprised that he looked like the very killer he was.

I stared at the second portrait for a long time, my eyes on Maria and Alessio. He was a chubby kid. Such a cutie.

He looked so serious in that picture, like he knew

this was something important.

My heart ached at the thought. Alessio had to grow up so fast. He never had a chance to enjoy his childhood. His mother's death had caused him to spiral down so fast toward the dark side.

I felt his warmth behind my back before he even pulled me into his embrace. Alessio wrapped his arms around my waist, his lips placing wet kisses down my neck.

He was always touching me, holding me, showering me with love. I was the happiest when I was in his arms.

"You were so cute," I muttered, still staring at the portrait.

"Yeah?" he questioned curiously.

"Yeah. I hope Princess has your eyes," I replied.

"Hmm...I'm hoping that she has yours."

I cuddled closer into his arms. "Want to place a bet?"

Alessio paused. "You need to stop hanging out with the guys."

I laughed at that one. "You're cute."

"No. I'm hot. Sinfully deliciously sexy. Remember?"

I shook my head. "I should have never said that. You're always going to remind me of it, aren't you?" I said with a sigh.

This man. He had such a huge ego and was so damn arrogant. I shouldn't feed into this arrogance.

But then again, whatever I said was the truth. And he knew it.

"Say it again," he demanded.

"No." I chuckled at the demand.

He nipped at my neck playfully. I felt his hips moving against my back, and my mouth fell open. Alessio thrust against my back, letting me feel his hard length.

"Oh my God," I hissed when he laughed.

"Say it," Alessio ordered teasingly. His hand made its way to my breast, and I froze when his fingers made contact with my nipple.

He softly dragged his finger tip over it through my dress.

"You are impossible, Alessio."

I couldn't stop the moan when he played with my hard nipple, pinching and tugging at the pebbled point.

"Not exactly what I want to hear, kitten," he returned huskily.

"Your body is made for sinning. You are deliciously sexy," I quickly said as he continued to tease me.

His slow ministration stopped. "Do you want to sin then? Right now? Right here?"

I took a deep breath. The invitation was quite inviting. I loved the idea, but I shook my head. "No. Because that's not why you brought me here. After you explain, then maybe we can go back to our room, and I will let you have your way with me."

"Hmm…I think that's a good deal. You won't be able to walk tomorrow, though. Is that good with you?"

He was making it more impossible to resist him. Turning around in his arms, I smiled at the goofy smile on his face. I kissed his lips slowly before pulling away. "You can just carry me around.

That's what you do most of the time anyway."

"You make a good deal, Ayla Ivanshov," he said proudly. He loved calling me by my full name. Maybe it was a way to remind himself that I was truly *his*.

After all the heartbreak, I was finally *his* in every sense of word.

"You taught me well, Alessio Ivanshov," I replied.

We stared at each other, both wearing silly smiles. His loving gaze finally moved from mine to the portrait behind me.

His expression changed, and a wave of pain took over. I hugged him to me, trying to take some of his pain as my own.

"I'm sorry, Alessio," I whispered in his chest.

His arms went tight around me. "Don't apologize, Ayla. You have nothing to be sorry for."

I hiccupped back a sob. His unwavering love for me always made me speechless. I cried softly in his chest, trying to find my words.

"It still haunts me, Alessio. To know that it was my family who destroyed yours. I still wonder how you can look at me and not hate the mere sight of me. How can you love me when I am the offspring of the man who killed your mother?"

His hand caressed my back soothingly. When he spoke, his words held power and strength. "It's not your fault. I'm not going to blame you for this. You ask me how can I love you? Well, I don't know. I really don't know, Ayla. I don't need a reason to love you. All I know is that I can't live without you. When I look at you, when I see your smile or hear your laughter…it's enough to make me feel at peace. You calm me. I can't be without you. It's simple…there is no me without you."

I stayed silent, letting his love cocoon me in a safe embrace.

"You wanted to know why I brought you here?" he asked.

I nodded and waited for him to continue.

Alessio sighed and slightly pulled away. He brushed my tears away. "It's because it's our turn to be on that wall."

"It's your turn to take that seat as Queen. It's another tradition for the Ivanshov family. Something we have been practicing for decades. For some families, their women hold no power. But for us, our wives are our queens. Our Angels." Alessio paused, looking slightly chocked by emotions.

"The photographer will be here in a few hours. By tomorrow morning, our portrait will be on that wall," Alessio continued before he kissed forehead sweetly.

"I'm really your wife…in every way," I stated tearfully.

"Yes, you are, Angel," he replied with a small smile.

He turned me around so my back was to him. Holding me close, we stared at the two portraits. "And you are not only the Queen of the Ivanshov family, but you have thousands of men under you. Four Russian families. They all belong to you."

His lips were so close to my ear as he whispered his next words. "And the Italians are yours too. They are at your feet. You are above them, Angel. I made sure of that."

A shiver ran through me. His voice was rough and held a hint of hard dominance. I swallowed nervously. "This is a bit overwhelming, Alessio. Months ago, I had nothing. And now I have more than I want."

"You have everything you deserve, Ayla."

Alessio palmed my pregnant belly. "I will never let our daughter go through what we went through."

My heart soared, and I closed my eyes with a relieved and happy sigh. "You are amazing; you know that? Sometimes I feel like it's all a dream. Like you aren't real. You can't be real."

He stiffened behind me, and my eyes snapped open at the sudden change. "I'm not amazing, Ayla. I'm far from amazing. If you knew what I had done...then you wouldn't say that."

I turned in his arms, looking at his cold face. "What are you talking about?"

"I'm a killer, Ayla," he stated, staring at my face intently. He was looking for my reaction.

"I know that," I replied softly.

"I have killed for years, and I will keep doing it—for this family. To protect my empire. And to protect you and our kids. It's who I am," he explained quietly.

"I know."

"No. You don't. You don't know, Ayla. You have no idea of the things I have done. I'm not an amazing man. I'm a monster," he continued, looking slightly heartbroken. "I don't deserve you."

My hands went to his chest. "Stop saying that. Just stop, Alessio. I get to decide if you deserve me or not. And I say you deserve me. Just like I deserve you."

Alessio let out a dry laugh. "So innocent, Angel. I'm tempted to keep you that way. I don't want to drag you into the dark side with me, but I can't let you go either."

"Alessio—" I started, but he shook his head, cutting me off.

"If I were a good man, I would have let you go to have a good life. Not trapped you here with me."

"But it's my choice. I decided to stay here with you. I chose *you*," I quickly fought back. He was just being plain ridiculous now.

Alessio brought his hand to my face. His thumb caressed the underside of my eye, slowly dragging his finger to my cheek. "I'm not any better than your father or Alberto. You ended up falling in love with the Devil."

My eyes widened, my lips parting in shock. "You don't mean that. Stop it!" I screamed. "Don't ever compare yourself with them. Do you understand?"

Holding his collar, I glared at the man I desperately loved. How dare he lower himself to their level?

"Tell me something, Alessio. Have you ever taken a woman against her will? Have you ever hit a woman? Rape her until she was unconscious and couldn't move? Rape her while she was pregnant with another man's baby? Have you ever chained a woman to a wall and beat her up…whipped her until she puked from crying too much?" I questioned fiercely.

Before he could answer, I continued. "Alberto did all of that to me and more. I know the difference between a good man and the Devil. You might be a killer, but you are a good man."

My tears ran freely down my cheeks. I wanted Alessio to believe me. I was desperate for him to believe me.

Grabbing his cheeks, I stood on my toes until our faces were closer. Our lips were mere inches apart. "You said you have trapped me here. But tell me, if I ever want to leave...if I ever want to take our daughter and leave this place, will you let me go? What if I can't bear to stay on this estate any longer...or stay with you? What if I chose to leave, would you let me go?"

He sucked in a shocked breath and looked pained. Like I had shot him, took his heart, and trampled over it.

"Even if it fucking killed me and I would be so tempted to tie you to our bed, I would let you go. Only if that's what you wanted and made you happy. But not after fighting for us," he choked out, like the words were hard to say.

I nodded, already knowing that would be his answer. I took his lips, and he let me lead the kiss. I kissed my husband slowly and softly, pouring all my love in that one kiss.

"And that's exactly why you are different from Alberto. You two can't even be compared in the slightest bit, my love," I breathed against his lips.

His arms wrapped around me so tightly that it was almost impossible to breathe. "You won't leave me?"

I shook my head. "No. I won't. It was used just for an example," I muttered. His heart drummed faster against mine, and I rubbed his chest, trying to soothe him.

"Don't ever compare yourself with them. I know you have killed, and I know you will kill again. It doesn't scare me. Because I know in the end, when you come back home, you will hold me in your arms and make sweet love to me...showing me exactly how much you love me," I continued softly, this time my lips on his chest, right over his beating heart.

"Always," he vowed.

I smiled. "Exactly."

"I have done horrible things, Ayla, but my love for you is true," he confessed.

"How horrible? Tell me," I demanded.

"I almost killed a man in front of his wife and daughter. I made them watch as I tortured him. I have killed more men than I could ever count. I cut Artur's tongue out." He paused when I flinched at the visual.

"I made him bleed for hours. I cut off Enzo's dick. I tortured them until they were unconscious and could barely breathe." Alessio bent his head down.

"And I ripped Alberto's fucking heart out of his chest with my bare hands," he hissed in my ear. "Is that what you want to hear, Angel?"

"They were all bad men. They deserved it, Alessio," I pushed out.

"Not all of them were bad," he said drily.

My breath was stolen from me and I froze.

"What?"

Alessio stayed silent, and I looked at him in shock. "Have you...ever...killed an innocent?"

He stared at me with hard blue eyes. "I don't know. Maybe. Maybe not. I do what I have to do for my family. For my empire. When I have a purpose, a goal...I go for it. I take what I have to take. I take what I want. It doesn't matter who is in front of me. Everyone who is in my path ends up soulless. I go for my target, not caring what disaster I leave behind."

My hands shook, and I took several deep breaths. "So, no. I don't know who is innocent or who isn't. I don't care. It's what I want and what I have to do to get it. Does that make me a bad person? Maybe. Do I care? No, I don't. But do I care what you think of me? Then yes, I do."

I brought a shaky hand to my lips and shook my head, trying to find the proper words. He chuckled low and looked hurt when I didn't say anything.

"Go ahead. Say it, Ayla. I'm a monster. Your husband is a killer," he goaded.

I shook my head again.

"I know exactly who you are. I married you knowing what you do and how you do it. I'm not surprised. Just a little overwhelmed with the information. You're right. You are a killer. You are a monster." I paused.

His eyes widened, and he took a step back, like I had burned him.

Taking a step forward, I crowded his personal space again. "But you are *my* monster."

Alessio sucked in a surprised breath, his

shoulders sagging. "Do you understand what I'm saying? I accept you for who you are. You are *mine*. All of you. So I would really appreciate it if you stop lowering yourself. I decide what I deserve, and I say we deserve each other."

Alessio was silent for a moment, his expression deadly.

And then he threw his head back and laughed. Pulling me into his arms, he buried his head in my neck. "You are crazy for loving me. You can't back out now. It's too late. I'm never letting you go, Angel."

"I don't want you to let me go," I murmured, burying deeper into his chest.

"Good," he replied arrogantly.

We hugged, both of us refusing to let each other go. I felt so warm and loved in his embrace that if someone tried to pull us apart, I would fight them.

Chapter 32

Almost three months later

I woke up with an uncomfortable feeling in my lower region. My stomach tightened for a moment, and I moved around, trying to get rid of the stiffness.

My stomach and back muscles contracted, and my eyes snapped open when I felt a gush between my legs.

Oh. *Oh.*

Not again.

I pinched my eyes closed in embarrassment.

This would be the second time I peed the bed this week.

How mortifying.

My cheeks heated, and I struggled in a sitting position. Thank God Alessio was downstairs. Last time, he was unlucky.

We were both sleeping, and in the middle of the night, I had the urge to pee badly. I was too late, though. By the time I was able to get up, I had already peed. Right there on the bed.

I cried in embarrassment, and Alessio woke up. The tears just kept flowing at how shameful it was.

But being the gentleman he was, Alessio never complained.

He kissed me softly on my forehead and got up from the bed. After helping me stand up, he walked us to the bathroom and pulled me into the shower.

While I stood there crying, he took care of me, showering me with care and then drying me with a soft towel. Alessio had dressed me again in a clean nightgown. He had even removed the wet sheet and had a clean blanket on.

And then he held me in his arms until I had fallen asleep again.

This time I was on my own. I was slightly grateful for that.

I got off the bed and looked down at the wet blanket. My eyebrows furrowed when the fluid kept leaking out.

I was still peeing!

Wasn't that too much?

I stomped my foot in frustration but then paused.

The fluid trickled down my legs as I stared at bed. This wasn't normal. The fluid was clear...colorless.

I touched the wet spot with two fingers and brought it to my nose.

It didn't smell.

When realization dawned, my mouth fell open.

OH!

Ignoring the wet trail I was leaving behind, I waddled to the bathroom as quickly as I could…which wasn't too quickly.

My belly was huge. Even Ivy said I was really big for my body size.

Alessio loved it, though. He showered my pregnant belly with so much love. He mentioned a couple of times that he loved me pregnant.

Because it showed everyone that I was *his*.

I could never understand men and their possessive tendencies.

My back was aching as I stripped off and took a quick shower. After changing into a clean dress, I tied my hair in a bun and walked out.

I glanced at the bed one final time and left the room. The maid would have to clean it.

Slowly, I walked down the stairs. Alessio was going to throw a fit, but I had a perfect way to shut him up.

I came to a stop on the final step when I noticed the men in the living room. Maddie and Lena were there too. They were both sewing baby booties for Princess.

Perfect. I had everyone in one place.

When Alessio noticed me, he immediately stood up.

"Ayla! Why are you walking down the stairs alone?" he bellowed, making his way to me. He looked really mad, and I almost flinched at his loud tone.

Alessio held me by the waist and half-carried me to the sofa. I planted my feet on the floor before he could push me in a sitting position.

"Wait," I muttered.

He paused.

I swallowed hard and felt suddenly nervous.

He took my silence in a bad way and started panicking. "What is it, Ayla? Is something wrong? Is it the baby? Are you hurt? Are you in pain?"

"No. I'm okay. Everyone, stay calm. It's all good and okay."

He raised an eyebrow and waited for me to continue.

My gaze went to everyone before meeting Alessio's again.

"My water broke." I could hear the excitement in my voice as I waited for their reaction.

There was about five seconds of shock and silence before everyone exploded together.

"What?"

"Shit!"

"We're not fucking ready!"

"Oh dear."

"Oh my God!"

"You're not due for another two days!"

That last one was Alessio. For the first time, he appeared almost speechless.

He looked at me like I had grown two heads. Actually, all the men had the same expression on their faces.

Viktor looked like he was about to faint. Nikolay was practically ready for make a run for it. Phoenix was already taking a few steps back.

"You're not ready. We're not ready. The baby isn't supposed to come out now. Ivy said so! Another two days. We have another two days, Ayla!" Alessio rambled.

His eyes were filled with fear when he palmed

my very pregnant belly. There was a hard kick, one that I felt in my lower stomach, and my back contracted painfully.

"Ouch," I muttered, rubbing the sore spot.

"What's wrong?" Alessio's eyes went even wider with panic. He pulled me closer and pointedly looked at Viktor.

"Get the car," he demanded.

Viktor stared at me, not moving an inch.

"I think he's in shock," I whispered to Alessio.

"Viktor!" Alessio bellowed this time. I winced and sighed at the catastrophe in front of me.

Viktor snapped back to the present, tripped over his own feet, broke Lena's favorite vase, and went down in a heap.

He laid there for a second before quickly getting back up and running out of the door.

"Phoenix, go get Ayla's bag. Princess's bag is in the piano room," Maddie ordered as she came to stand by my side.

"Nikolay, can you make sure Viktor doesn't crash into something with the car? I don't think he can drive at the moment," I told him.

He looked the calmest. Well, as calm as he could be in this situation. If it was his choice, he would have been out of the door by now.

At my suggestion, he nodded and quickly ran out to check on Viktor.

"Are you having any contractions?" Lena asked, pushing Alessio away.

Alessio glowered before coming to stand in front of me.

"No. Nothing yet. My water broke about twenty

minutes ago. Or a little less," I explained.

"Hmm…you'll probably start your contractions before you reach the hospital," she continued.

I nodded in understanding. "How bad will it be?" While speaking, my gaze stayed on Alessio.

"It's different for everyone, dear. I can't say for sure."

I hummed in response, watching my man silently freak out at the thought of his wife giving birth. He was already sweating heavily, and I noticed his hands shaking at his side.

Placing a hand out, I waited for Alessio to take it. When he did, I pulled him to me. My rounded belly was cradled against Alessio's lower abdomen as I hugged him.

"I'm going to be fine. You need to breathe or you're going to pass out, and I can't have you passing out on me, Alessio," I said softly against his chest.

I could feel Lena and Maddie at my side. They were practically plastered against me, not that I was complaining. I was glad for their support. I needed it more than I would admit.

Alessio's arms went around me, hugging me tight. I felt him relax as he breathed out. With my ear over his chest, I could hear and feel his pounding heart.

It matched my own.

I was a nervous wreck inside—panicking but trying to act as calm as I could. If everyone else was freaking out, they needed someone to be calm.

It appeared that the pregnant lady herself was going to be the peacemaker.

"Are you hurting?" he asked quietly. I could hear the tint of fear in his voice.

I shook my head before pulling away. "I'm okay. For now. We just need to get to the hospital."

"I got the bag!" Phoenix practically screamed from the top of the stairs.

"The car is here. It's parked." Nikolay came rushing in, screaming too.

"Where the fuck is the baby's bag?" Alessio snapped.

"Huh?" Phoenix looked at the bag he was holding stupidly. "I got Ayla's bag."

"You are useless." With a growl, Alessio was taking off himself. I watched him run up the stairs as I felt another pain shoot up my spine.

I winced, my hand going to rub at my back.

"What's wrong?" Maddie asked nervously.

"My back is hurting," I finally admitted.

Just then I felt my stomach cramp. It wasn't too painful, but it was enough to make me gasp in shock. It felt like my skin was stretching, and my lower belly felt heavy. It was an uncomfortable feeling.

"The contractions have started, haven't they?" Lena said with a knowing look.

I nodded.

"Will you be coming with us?" I asked Lena, with a pout.

She shook her head. "Maddie will be there for you. I'll stay home and get everything ready for the big homecoming."

Lena pressed her palm dramatically to her forehead and sighed. I rolled my eyes because it was such a Maddie move.

"There is so much to do," Lena sighed but with a happy, serene look on her face.

"While Mom is busy, we'll pop the baby out. It's a fair plan," Maddie added.

More like I would be doing the popping.

I shuddered at the thought just as another intense ache went through my back and lower belly. That hurt!

And it was only the beginning.

I felt a slight tremor of fear, and the panic continued to rise. "Maddie, you can't leave my side, okay?"

She soothingly patted my arm. "I'm not gonna leave. Even when you threaten to kill me."

"Okay, good."

When I was finally reassured, Maddie and I made our way out of the kitchen. I was slow, much slower as each step felt too uncomfortable. It felt like my stomach would drop any second now.

I heard a shout. I furrowed my forehead in confusion.

Alessio?

"I got the bag," he bellowed.

Maddie and I were just walking into the living room when we saw him practically beeline toward the door without even a glance our way.

Huh?

I waddled to the entrance with Maddie at my side. Just when we reached outside, we saw the two cars rushing out of the driveway as if some kind of demon was chasing them.

Wait, what? WHAT?

"Did they just drive off without us?" Maddie growled at the empty parking spot. "Who's going to pop out the baby? Alessio? Or Viktor? Freaking stupid assholes."

I rubbed my temple tiredly. This was a mess...a total mess.

When another pain coursed through my lower belly and I doubled over, the cars rushed back in.

Alessio and Viktor jumped out, almost falling in their haste. "What the fuck? Why aren't you in the car?" Viktor snapped.

Alessio silently made his way to me, and I glared. There was a sheepish look on his face, and he mouthed a quick *sorry.*

From the corner of my eyes, I saw Lyov and Isaak coming from the courtyard. They looked at everyone gathered, and their steps hastened to me.

"What's wrong?" Lyov asked quickly.

"It's time. The baby is coming. But she's two days early. That's not good. Not normal, right?" Alessio rattled back, his hand molding over my stomach protectively.

Isaak's and Lyov's eyes widened, and they paused with their mouth hanging open.

Great. Just what I needed. Two more panicking Mafia men.

"Alessio, two days early is nothing. I'm sure everything is good," I tried to reason.

Isaak's and Lyov's mouths snapped shut.

"It's time," Isaak muttered. "Fuck."

"It's okay. We got this. It's cool. Everyone stay calm. Stay calm. Isaak, we have done this before. We're good," Lyov muttered back.

He was surprisingly calm. Huh?

Isaak nodded. "Yeah."

"Where the fuck is the car?" Lyov suddenly bellowed.

Or not. He was definitely not calm.

"The car is right behind you," Maddie returned, a look of exasperation on her face.

"Right. Right. Let's get her in the car. Get going, boys," Lyov ordered harshly. He sounded out of breath.

Alessio swept me off my feet and cradled me to this chest. "I got you, Angel."

I locked my arms behind his neck and held on. He carried us to the car. After placing me on the seat, he climbed in beside me. He wrapped his arm around my shoulder and held me to him before barking out his order. "Let's go."

Maddie was half-sitting, her legs still out when the car tore out of the driveway. "Fucker!"

"Pull your fucking legs inside," Viktor snapped.

"If you can give me the time, asshole," she snapped back fiercely.

I pressed my forehead in the crook of Alessio's neck and breathed in his manly smell. Alessio's smell. The scent of his expensive cologne touched my nose, and I sighed as my shoulders slowly relaxed.

He was tensed underneath me; his legs felt like a rock. One of his hands was fisted at my hip while the other was gently rubbing my pregnant belly.

From my position, I could feel his wild heart and the throbbing vein in his neck. Placing a kiss there, I closed my eyes. "It's going to be okay." My voice was quiet, only for him to hear.

His hand paused on my stomach. I felt him take several deep breaths, but he didn't say anything.

The rest of the ride went quickly and silently. Nobody spoke a word, and the tense air was suffocating.

When Alessio helped me out of the car, it felt like I could finally breathe normally. He cradled me yet again in his arms and carried us into the hospital.

"Where is Dr. Cooper?" he shouted inside the entrance.

There were doctors, nurses, and patients all around, and everyone paused at his shout.

"You aren't supposed to shout," I muttered. My cheeks heated under everyone's scrutinizing stares. Alessio was completely oblivious to the attention he brought upon ourselves.

"Are you Alessio Ivanshov?" an elderly nurse asked.

"Yes," he growled, giving the woman a mean look, though she didn't look at all scared. She just looked pissed that Alessio was causing a commotion.

"Dr. Cooper has already prepared a room for your wife. I'll lead the way," she continued before turning around without a second glance.

We followed her to the elevator. Getting inside, Alessio didn't relinquish his hold on me. Not even when I tried to wiggle free.

"You can let me down now," I said softly. "I'm too heavy."

He glared at me, and I stared back, waiting for

him to calm down. "No," he snapped.

Okay, now he sounded like a caveman.

"I can carry you," he continued, sounding much calmer now.

With a sigh, I shut up. There was no point arguing. He would win in the end.

When we stepped out of the elevator, the nurse steered us to a room at the corner. "You will be the only one on this floor. Your husband has it reserved for you."

My eyes widened when I realized she was speaking to me. Reserved? The whole floor?

I stared at Alessio, but he was concentrating in front of him as he led us to my room. The room looked nothing like I expected.

It was a huge room. Couches in the corner with a coffee table. The bed wasn't small, either. It was most likely a double bed. Even the pillows looked too soft. The machines looked dainty next to the bed in the large room.

I guess Alessio really prepared for this.

He settled me on the bed and pushed me back against the pillow. "Where is Ivy?" Alessio asked again.

His blue eyes stayed on mine, though.

"She's doing a surgery right now," the nurse calmly replied as she fussed over me.

"What? She's supposed to be here. With Ayla. Who's going to deliver the baby?" Alessio shouted.

I rubbed my forehead as I watched him lose control yet again.

From the corner of my eye, I saw her checking the machines, and then she came back to my side with a syringe.

"This won't hurt," she murmured, pushing the needle into my arm. I closed my eyes, refusing to watch what she was doing. I winced, but she was right. It didn't hurt. Just a tiny prickling sensation.

But Alessio being Alessio saw my wince and went crazy on the nurse.

"What did you do to her? What are you doing?"

If Viktor didn't pull him back, Alessio wouldn't have probably leap over the nurse.

Oh God. *Someone do something.* This was about to turn ugly.

"Sir, please would you calm down. I am just doing my job. With that said, your wife has just started her contractions. She won't give birth for many hours. But then again, that just depends on her body and the baby. I have had a few women whose labour went as long as eighteen hours," the nurse explained as kindly as she could.

But it was obvious she was losing patience. And quickly.

"Your wife is not the first woman to give birth. She'll be fine," she muttered before walking out of the room.

"Well, she is *my* woman. And she's giving birth for the first time," Alessio retorted back. "There is a big difference!"

I closed my eyes, my head sinking into the pillow.

This was going to be a long ride.

A long, tiring ride with six overbearing, gun-carrying, ruthless mafia men.

Who promptly panicked at the idea of a woman

giving birth.

Chapter 33

When the contractions hit me again, it was impossible to hold my scream. Letting out a bellowed shout, I tightened my fingers around Alessio's hand.

Maybe I was crushing them impossibly tight. Too tight.

I even caught him wincing a few times.

I didn't have the time to care when I felt another pain in my lower belly. It felt like my stomach was going to burst open any second now.

"Ouch. Ahhhh…" I cried out as another contraction hit. This time, I was full-on sobbing. "It hurts…" I moaned, trying to find Alessio's face through my blurry vision.

When something cold touched my forehead, I sighed. So soothing. Maddie had been doing this for a while now.

I was sweating, it was too warm, and it hurt. After wrapping some ice in a towel, she pressed it over my forehead and dragged it softly over my face.

Only Alessio and Maddie were with me in the delivery room. Not that it stopped the others from bursting into the room whenever I screamed.

Like now.

"Shit. Is it time?" Viktor practically broke the door in his haste.

"No. She still isn't fully dilated," Maddie replied, sounding tired.

"Oh, okay," he muttered, closing the door again.

"Alessio, it hurts…too much…" I huffed as I felt another contraction coming.

"It's okay. Breathe. Breathe. Ivy said breathe," he said stiffly. I could hear the fear and panic in his voice. His voice was too low…too soft for my liking.

The pain hit me harder than before, and I screamed yet again, bearing down at the pain.

His voice was next to my ear. "Breathe, Ayla. Breathe."

"I am breathing!" I screamed at him. Anger suddenly swelled inside of me, and I gripped his hand harder.

He hissed painfully.

That hurt? Huh? Huh?

I was pushing his baby out of my vagina, and he was complaining about his hand?

I tightened my fingers even more, maybe too much.

"Alessio!" I hissed angrily.

Weren't my contractions coming too hard and too fast?

Alessio was saying something incorrigible, and I heard Maddie arguing with him. My ears couldn't make out the words. The pain was too much.

When Alessio let go of my hand, I wanted to cry.

Why did he let my hand go? Was I too mean?

No. Come back!

Opening my eyes, I saw Alessio pacing the length of the room. He gripped his hair tight in frustration, and I suddenly felt bad for taking my anger out on him.

For the first time, I noticed that his suit jacket was no longer on. His tie hung loosely around his neck, and the first two buttons of his shirt were open. His hair lay on his forehead, and sweat masked his skin.

He looked as tired as I felt. Like he was feeling *my* pain.

"Where is Ivy?" he growled for the hundredth time.

Ivy came and went a few times. But because I wasn't ready and Princess wasn't ready to make her appearance yet, she went to check up on her other patients.

"Alessio, can you help me up?" I croaked out. My throat felt dry from hours of screaming out my pain.

His head snapped to me, and his eyes met mine. Those intense blue eyes never failed to get all my attention, even when I was in impossible pain.

He hurried to my side again and pushed a hand behind my back, helping me in a sitting position. Ivy said I could walk around; it might make the labor go faster.

And that was exactly what I was going to do.

The little smart princess was coming out of me

soon, whether she liked it or not.

"Are you sure?" Alessio asked quietly. He appeared almost scared to talk to me.

I nodded silently as he helped me off the bed, with Maddie always at my side.

They helped me around the room toward the huge blue bouncy ball. With Alessio in front of me, he helped me sit on it. He knelt between my legs, his hands on either side of my hips, holding me securely.

I could see the lines of stress on his forehead. He looked like he'd aged by five years in just hours.

I held Alessio's cheeks while softly bouncing on the ball. "I'm going to be okay. Princess is going to be okay too. Have a little faith in me, would you? I can do this. *We* can do this."

"I can't see you in pain like this, Angel," he muttered hoarsely.

Just then, another pain ripped through me. My nails bit into his cheeks before I quickly moved my hand away.

It felt like I was being ripped apart from down there. My breathing was labored, my chest heaving with exertion.

"Oh...oh..." I breathed through the pain as another contraction hit right after the other. Again and again, my stomach rippled in pain. It traveled all the way to my back. It felt like the whole lower half of my body was being contracted in pain.

Alessio's hand went to my stomach, and I saw a flash of pain on his face. "I'm...fine!"

It was meant to be soothing, but it ended with a shout as another contraction ripped through my lower belly.

My princess wasn't happy in there any longer. It looked like she was ready to come out even if it meant ripping through my belly and vagina.

"Help...me...up." I huffed through my harsh breathing. "It hurts..."

Alessio sprang into action, and in mere seconds I found myself reclined in the soft bed. My fingers found their way around his wrist, refusing to let him go.

I had a killer grip on Alessio as the contractions kept coming, right after the other. I had no break or chance to breathe through the agony.

A sudden urge to push ripped through me. My legs fell open, and with Alessio helping me sitting up halfway, I bore down on the pain.

Finally, Ivy made her entrance.

I sighed and then shouted. Her eyes widened, and she hurried to me, peeking under my gown.

"Oh. I see the head. A full head of black hair," she sang happily.

"At least she isn't bald," Maddie mused with a wink.

"My daughter isn't bald," Alessio replied, looking quite affronted that Maddie would even think such a thing.

I was pretty affronted too.

But there was no time to think through it when I was hit with another agonized contraction. "Ahh..."

My scream was probably heard all over the floor. I panted, but still my princess didn't make her way out into the world.

Stubborn. She was going to be stubborn like her

father.

Just what I needed…another Alessio.

I felt Alessio's warm breath next to my ear as he whispered soothing and supportive words. He was gentle, kind, and so loving.

I fell more in love with him in that moment.

But then hated him the next.

When another pain came, he tried to encouraged me with "Breathe, Angel. Push. Just breathe. It's okay."

Breathe? Just breathe?

I crushed his hand in mine just when Maddie yelled, "Shut up!"

"Okay. Sorry. Don't breathe. It's not okay. Don't breathe."

WHAT? *WHAT?*

That earned him another hand crushing.

Maybe I also bellowed that I hated him and never wanted him to touch me again.

"Alessio, just shut up," Maddie growled when I started crying through the pain.

Ivy, from her position between my legs, threw supportive words at me, telling me to push on every contraction.

She had been repeating this for too long now. I had been pushing! But no baby yet.

I sobbed with each push. I even pushed Alessio away.

I saw the look of panic on his face. He looked hurt. And the fear…it was all over his expression. He was slightly shaking with it too.

My emotions were a mess. One minute I hated Alessio and couldn't bear for him to touch me, while the next minute I cried because he was a few steps away.

"I'm sorry," I screamed with another contraction. "I am such…a bad…wife. I'm…sorry…come back here."

Alessio was at my side in a second flat. He gripped my hand again, but this time his lips were on my forehead.

He placed kisses over my sweaty face, gentle sweet kisses as I pushed and screamed through each contraction.

Alessio whispered against my skin. How much he loved me. How strong I was. He was in awe with me and loved me more every minute.

It made my heart soar, and I even smiled once.

"I love you, Angel," he whispered against my lips. Such a sweet kiss. Sweet words. Everything I needed.

"You amaze me every day. Every time. You are my strong Angel. I know you can do this. I know you can bring our daughter into this world like a true warrior Angel. Push. Just one more push," he said against my forehead.

His arm held me up as I screamed with a push. I felt something wiggle out but not enough for my baby to slip out.

"Arggg," I gasped and then bellowed.

I was dying. Was it possible to die?

Nope. I couldn't die. I still had to meet Princess. I still had to walk down the aisle in a wedding dress to my husband.

"What are you doing? Can't you see she's in pain? Do something!" Alessio finally screamed, losing his patience.

He poured his fear and anger on Ivy, who just shook her head.

"Alessio, stop screaming! They're going to kick you out!" Maddie snapped, her hands holding mine firmly.

"They can't kick me out! I own the fucking hospital!"

Huh? That was news. Since when?

I looked at him, confused, as another pain crashed through me. This time I bit my lips and tried the hardest to breathe through my nose.

"Alessio bought the hospital a few weeks ago. To make sure it was safe and all for you and Princess. He was quite obsessive about it," Maddie explained in my ear.

Wow. Just wow.

But I didn't have a chance to be thoroughly wowed because Alessio was still screaming at Ivy. He looked like he wanted to shoot the woman. Or maybe he was plotting her murder in many different ways.

Oh dear. Not good.

"Natural birth is like this, Mr. Ivanshov. Please be patient. One more push and your daughter will be here," she said calmly.

His gaze turned to mine. "You should have accepted the drugs for the pain, Angel."

His eyes were begging me. Just like they did when a nurse came and asked if I wanted the drugs. I screamed a *no*, and they scurried out of the room.

Alessio was hot on their tails, trying to bring them back to put the drugs in me. He almost forced them and dragged one of the women inside.

I refused yet again.

I regretted my decisions some hours later, but it was too late by then.

Another contraction was making its way to my belly. At the same time, Ivy yelled for me to push.

With Alessio's lips next to my temple, the words *I love you* ringing through my ears, I pushed with a shout.

We kept going back and forth like this. An urge to push, a wail of agony, another push. Finally, I felt a hard pressure in my lower region, then something—*someone*—slid out. It felt weird, but I didn't have a chance to think through the pain.

The pressure finally alleviated and then…silence. For about two seconds.

Because when my screaming ended, my daughter's wails were heard.

"It's a girl!" Ivy announced proudly, holding my baby girl in her arms.

A daughter. A princess. A tiny little baby girl to call our own. Someone who we would shower with so much love and care.

"Mr. Ivanshov, do you want to cut the cord?" Ivy asked.

She moved closer and brought our daughter next to Alessio. He looked completely in shock and lost as he followed Ivy's instruction and cut our baby's cord, while still holding my hand in one of his.

Ivy placed Princess on my bare stomach while she continued to wail.

A mighty loud wail. One that everyone heard because I heard a shout of victory coming from outside my room.

My baby girl was still wet and gooey with blood, but I didn't mind. Having her against my skin, actually holding her, it made my eyes blur with tears as I cried.

I was holding my daughter.

Months ago, I thought I would never get a chance. But now, she was here.

I pressed my palm against her bloody rump as her cries slowly started to calm.

Faintly, I noticed Alessio kissing my face. Peppering my face with kisses, his lips never left my skin. He trembled against me as I cried softly.

"I love you," he whispered over and over again. With each kiss, those words were whispered against my skin. "Angel."

My daughter was taken out of my grasp. I watched them clean her as she started crying again. So grumpy. So loud. So lovely.

"Alessio…" I whispered, my voice hoarse and soft.

"You were so strong," he said against my forehead.

"Thank you, my love."

"I love you."

"I know."

I heard quiet sniffling beside me and saw Maddie crying softly. "She's here." I nodded toward the baby.

Maddie nodded. "I'm so proud of you, babe."

"Thank you for being here with me. I needed you," I replied, holding her hand tight.

When my baby girl was cleaned and her crying

had stopped again, I smiled at Maddie. "Why don't you go see her?"

She scurried from my side and made her way to my daughter. The little princess was placed in her crib.

Maddie peeked at the princess and be beamed happily. "Aww…she is the cutest!"

Did my heart just accelerate a little bit?

Of course, she was the cutest! After all, she was mine and Alessio's baby.

I turned my head to the side and faced Alessio. "You have to go see her, Alessio," I muttered against his lips.

He kissed me soundly, breaking my words. He kissed me until I was breathless.

Alessio still hadn't seen our daughter yet. What was he waiting for?

"I'm scared, Angel," he murmured.

"Of what? The man I know is not scared of anything."

"I don't know. It's just that my chest feels a little weird and too tight," he replied. His gaze was still on mine.

Blue eyes bored into my green ones. Both stared intently, showing the same love.

"She needs you."

Alessio swallowed hard and nodded. He stood up straight just in time for Ivy to bring our daughter to him.

One second his hands were empty, and the next he was holding our princess.

Well, kind of holding.

He panicked and held the baby out, away from

him.

"I don't…know…what…you…" he stuttered.

"Here," Ivy explained patiently. She helped him wrap his arms securely around our baby girl, showing him how to hold her properly.

Alessio instinctively brought Princess closer to his chest, and he cradled her there. His eyes were no longer on mine.

No, his eyes were on our precious daughter.

He didn't blink. He didn't utter a single word.

Ivy cleaned me up and finished the last stage of delivery. When I was washed and cleaned, I sunk against the pillow and watched my husband hold our daughter.

I watched him watch our princess.

He was completely lost in her. Mesmerized by the tiny baby in his arms.

I saw his arms tighten the slightest bit. Was it a protective hold? Or a possessive one?

Such a sweet sight. My eyes drooped a little as tiredness took over.

Alessio's chin trembled, and I blinked.

A tear slid down his cheek.

I blinked again.

Another tear.

He was crying.

"My princess," he whispered gruffly.

His gaze came back on mine. "Our princess. She is so beautiful, Ayla. So, so beautiful."

He paused and then frowned. "And too small. Is that normal? Why is she so small?"

Maddie snorted. Ivy laughed.

I smiled…my heart full with so much love.

Alessio was right. Princess was a small baby. She was dainty in her father's arms. Was Alessio's arm bigger than her tiny body? Yes, probably. She was practically hidden against his chest.

I placed my hands out. "I want to hold her."

Ivy left the room quietly. Maddie placed a kiss on my forehead and quietly left the room too.

Alessio came to my side and settled on the bed beside me. He placed Princess into the crook of my arm. I cradled her lovingly to my chest.

She shifted around and mewled softly. Her forehead was scrunched up, like she was about to cry.

Her eyes were closed. I wondered what color they would be?

My baby girl was wrapped tightly in a soft blanket. She barely had any place to move. Her head was covered with a pink hat, just as soft as the blanket. I moved the hat, and my eyes found black hair.

"She has black hair," I muttered. Leaning down, I placed a sweet kiss on her head.

With the help of Alessio, we moved the blanket around. Ten tiny fingers and ten tiny toes. Perfect. Absolutely perfect.

She was so small, it made my heart ache. I imagined her in pain, and my heart broke.

No, my daughter would never be in pain. Not like me.

She had an army to protect her. A vicious army at that.

Her father had made sure of it.

Her tiny arms flailed a little, her leg kicked out.

Her little cute pink lips burst in a pout. So adorable.

And then she started crying.

"Aww...no crying, Princess," I said softly. "What do you want? Are you hungry? Shhh...Mommy is here," I soothed when she continued to cry.

Alessio quickly wrapped the blanket around her again. "I think she's hungry."

I nodded. "Can you help?" My head pointed at my laced bodice.

My husband shifted around and unlaced my gown from the front. When my breast was freed from the fabric, I brought Princess closer to my chest.

Her head moved around slowly, looking for something. Her lips made a suckling sound. She was definitely hungry.

With my hand under her small head, I brought her mouth to my left breast. She instantly latched onto my nipple and sucked. Hard.

I winced and let out a yelp.

"That's my girl," Alessio said. Proudly, I should add.

"Seriously?" I huffed as my baby started to suckle, taking in her fill.

Alessio's arm wrapped me as he buried his nose into my neck. He placed a kiss there, letting his head lay on my shoulder. "I love you, Angel."

His other hand came up and rested against our baby's fat rump.

We held our daughter, cradling her in our embrace as she fed.

While still suckling, she made a small

noise…maybe it was of contentment. But it sounded sleepy too.

And then she slowly blinked her eyes open.

Oh.

A tiny gasp escaped past my lips.

Then I smiled. So beautiful.

Our gazes locked. And I fell in love for a second time.

Blue to green.

Tears blurred my vision. "She has your eyes, Alessio."

The same exact eyes as her father.

Her crying and moving halted.

Giant bluish steel-colored eyes blinked up at me, framed with thick long lashes.

Her little rosebud mouth pursed around my nipple, and I thought she sighed.

Wait…did she smile? Was that a smile?

"She smiled," Alessio said, completely enamored at the sight of our daughter.

I knew someone would argue and tell us it was caused by gas or that newborn babies didn't smile…but she smiled. At me.

And then at her father when her eyes met his.

My heart constricted as father and daughter watched each other. My breath caught, and I sniffled back tears.

Her suckling had stopped, and she blinked.

"She really is your daughter," I muttered, holding her even tightly.

"She is…she is ours," Alessio replied, rubbing a finger gently over Princess's plump rosy cheek. "She is so perfect," he continued.

I agreed. Perfect. That she was.

When it was clear she'd had her fill and was almost asleep, Alessio helped me tie my bodice again.

Princess blinked her eyes sleepily, and then they closed. She was asleep in mere seconds.

I pulled her up and buried my nose in her tiny neck. Breathing in her sweet baby smell, I smiled and then whispered ever so gently, "I love you, my sweet baby."

I held her for as long as I could. But sleep and tiredness took over me. There was no helping it. I was going under faster than I wanted.

Alessio quietly took her out of my arms, and I dreamily saw him carrying her to her crib. After placing her down, he came back to my side.

"Go to sleep, Angel. I will be watching over both of you," he muttered softly to my ear.

He kissed me on my lips. I savored his taste before closing my eyes and succumbing to my sleep.

I had no fear. No panic.

Only love. I felt fulfilled.

I felt safe under my husband's watchful gaze.

I knew he would protect me and Princess. We were both safe and loved by this ruthless man.

Chapter 34

My head was drowsy when I woke up. Blinking my eyes open several times, I tried to stare around the dark room.

Only a lamp was on.

I turned my face to the side to see Alessio sitting on the couch next to my bed. He wasn't alone, though.

In his arms, Princess laid there. Actually, she was laid on his chest. Alessio had a hand supporting her head and the other over her butt.

Her cute round cheek was pressed against Alessio's chest, her eyes closed as she slept soundly.

"You're awake," Alessio murmured quietly.

"Was she crying?" I wondered out loud.

Alessio shook his head. "No. I just felt like holding her."

It appeared like this would be an everyday occurrence.

"How long was I asleep for?" I questioned, trying to sit up.

He stood up with our baby girl still held tightly in his arms. "About an hour. Everyone is waiting to meet you and Princess."

My eyes widened, and I smacked my forehead. "Oh no. I fell asleep. I'm so sorry. Why didn't they come in? They could have met Princess while I was sleeping."

Alessio placed Princess back into her crib and came to my side. Placing a kiss on my forehead, he smiled. "I forbid them from coming in. They would have disturbed both your and our daughter's sleep."

"That's not nice. They have been waiting so long to meet her," I fought back with a hard look.

Alessio shrugged. "Don't care. You were tired, and that's more important."

"Call them in now. It's time they meet the little one," I replied with a sigh. I couldn't help but smile though.

With a sigh, he went and did as he was told.

The door opened, and a few minutes later, everyone started to pile in.

Lyov and Isaak practically pushed everyone aside and came inside excitedly. Poor Viktor was crushed against the side of the door.

Then in came Viktor and Phoenix. Nikolay and Maddie were last.

"How are you feeling?" Lyov asked, coming to stand in front of my bed.

"Tired but happy. I can't wait to go back home," I replied.

He nodded. "Of course."

I saw his eyes seeking the crib. When his gaze found it, he looked at me, as if asking for permission. With my nod, he walked over there.

Alessio was already standing beside the crib protectively.

Isaak came to my side and placed a kiss on my forehead. "Thank you for giving everyone this gift. I haven't seen Lyov this excited and happy in years. Decades."

My eyes blurred with unshed tears as I watched Lyov stare at Princess. He was speechless and held a fist to his mouth. I knew he was trying to hold in his tears.

Isaak walked over to the crib too, standing beside Lyov.

"She is a beauty," Isaak announced proudly.

"Why is everyone calling her beautiful? Newborns look like a bunch of old potatoes," Viktor drawled with a laugh.

Did he just call my daughter ugly? That earned him a fierce glare from me.

"Move. Let me see the potato," Viktor said. He sauntered to the crib and stood beside Alessio.

And then silence.

"Potato, my ass," Maddie chuckled in my ear.

Viktor's eyes widened, and he froze. He looked completely mesmerized, just like the other three men standing around her crib.

I noticed that Phoenix had made his way there too. Only one person was missing.

When my eyes met his, I found him leaning against the wall in the far corner. Always alone. Always reclusive.

"Why are you there?" I asked softly.

Nikolay shrugged, his eyes going to the crib. He

looked like he wanted to be there, but he stayed still.

"Don't want to scare her," he finally replied, pointing at his scars.

My heart stuttered at his words. Did he really think that?

I had the urge to go to him and wrap him in a tight hug.

Shaking my head, I looked back at the five gathering men. Nikolay belonged there. With them, watching over my daughter.

Phoenix stepped away. He made this way to his cousin. "Stop being a pussy," he said lightly.

I smiled when Phoenix dragged Nikolay to the crib. The poor guy appeared frightened.

And then they were all standing around the crib.

It was an impressive sight. Six big muscled men standing around a crib that held only a tiny baby.

From my bed, I couldn't even see the crib...let alone her.

Viktor had his head practically shoved inside the crib. Alessio puffed his chest out, looking very proud.

"Fuck. This is not good. Not good," Viktor muttered quietly. I saw all the men nodding in agreement.

Huh?

"Definitely not good," Lyov added just as quietly. My eyebrows furrowed in confusion.

"She has them wrapped around her tiny fingers already," Maddie muttered, sitting beside me.

I simply nodded. It was true. Was it possible to say that I was the happiest mother alive at that moment?

My princess had all the love she needed. All the love I never had.

"You did good," Maddie continued.

I held her hands in mine as we watched the men watching the princess.

A knock sounded on the door, and I called out a soft, "Come in."

Evaline walked in with a large bouquet of flowers. "Hey, babe!" she said cheerfully, coming to my side.

"How did you get here?" I asked, astonished as she hugged me.

"Viktor sent me the private jet. I came as soon as I got the news," she mumbled back quietly.

Her eyes went to the boys, and she raised her eyebrows in question. Maddie chuckled. "You don't even want to know, girl."

"Looks like she'll be leading them with just a flick of her finger. I can imagine them wagging their tails and following behind her," she replied with a humorous laugh.

"Have you thought of a name yet?" Evaline continued.

"Uh huh. Alessio and I will announce it when we get home."

We had the perfect name for our princess. And we couldn't wait to share it with everyone.

"I'll just wait for the boys to finish with their admiring so I can see the princess," she said with a sigh.

"You'll be waiting for hours. I don't see them moving anytime soon," Maddie laughed.

I laughed because Maddie was absolutely right.

"Well, never mind then. My turn to hold the princess." Evaline winked before walking to the crib. She pushed her way between the men and bent down.

Holding my baby girl in the crook of her arms, she smiled. "Look at the little cutie. She is so adorable and so small."

"You're supposed to hold her neck," Alessio said urgently. He moved and tried to hold Princess with his hand.

"Emm…I know how to hold a baby, Alessio. And I am holding her neck."

"Make sure the blanket is wrapped tightly around her. Ivy said it keeps her warm. Like she's still in her mother's womb. Don't move her too much. She's sleeping…"

Oh well.

I leaned back and watched the drama unfold.

Chapter 35

When the car came to a stop, I stepped out. Alessio helped Princess out of her infant car seat. Placing her in my arms, he gave me a quick kiss.

My heart fluttered like it always did whenever Alessio was close or touching me. His arm went around my waist as we walked into the house with the guys, Maddie, and Evaline following closely behind.

As soon as I was inside, my baby was no longer in my arms.

Nope. One second she was there and then Lena stole her from me. I didn't have a chance to blink, either.

Everyone was gathered, trying to take a peek at the little princess.

"Awww, just look at her. Such an innocent and adorable face. It's hard to believe she's Alessio's daughter. But it's definitely obvious she is Ayla's," Lena joked, her eyes practically twinkling with happiness.

"Oh, just wait until she opens her eyes. She is

Alessio's all right," I replied.

Alessio had his hands on either side of my hips, and I leaned back against him, my back to his front as I laid my head on his chest.

"Oh yes. Maddie said she has Alessio's eyes."

"Maria's eyes," Lyov added. He went to stand beside Lena, looking down at the small bundle of joy.

At the mention of Alessio's mother, my heart ached for Lyov. But I knew he was going to be okay. He had smiled more than I could count in the last twenty-four hours than I had ever seen him.

Isaak said he was the happiest he'd been since Maria's death.

We didn't have to go far to see how much Lyov admired his granddaughter. His gaze was filled with tenderness and warmth, not something I was used to seeing on Lyov.

But there he was, completely wrapped around her little finger.

With Lena still holding the baby, we walked into the living room. Alessio made me sat down on the couch as Lena settled beside me. Alessio stayed standing as Maddie sat on my other side.

Lena softly moved her fingertips on Princess's lip. And then her cute button nose. She made a small adorable quacking sound and moved impatiently in her tight blanket.

For a newborn, she moved a lot. No wonder she was always playing practice in my belly.

"What's her name?" Lena asked.

I looked up at Alessio, and his smile widened. The indent in his cheek made my stomach squeeze.

I could feel my own smile.

"Maila Lena Ivanshov."

The name slipped past my lips effortlessly. It felt so right. Alessio had instantly agreed on the name when I asked him about it a few months ago.

I still remember clearly how affected he looked when I explained the meaning behind the name. He had kissed me soundly, hard and bruising. And then he had proceeded to make love to me for the whole night.

"It's for all three mothers," Alessio explained, his voice warm and deep.

"Maila is after mine and Alessio's mother. Maria and Leila. We put both names together to get Maila. And it's sounds really beautiful too. Lena...well, Lena is for our second mother," I continued.

My gaze found Lena's, and she was silently crying. "She is also named after you. For being our mother and for giving us the love that our mothers never had a chance to give us."

"Maila Lena Ivanshov," Lyov said slowly. He looked down at *Maila*, our little princess.

Lyov smiled and took her in his arms. He held her out, a palm under her neck while her tiny feet rested against his chest. "Such a beautiful name. A strong name too. After three strong women. Fit for a true warrior princess."

"It's beautiful," Isaak agreed. His voice sounded a little weird too, like he was trying not to cry.

"Your mothers would be proud of both of you," Lena said. "Look at you both. After everything, you have come out stronger."

I didn't say anything, only because I didn't know

what to say. My throat felt tight with emotions, and Alessio looked like he was having the same problem.

"Okay...gift time!" Maddie announced when everyone fell silent.

I smiled. I guessed it was gift time.

Everyone presented their gifts, and my heart leaped with happiness. *My family.* Finally, it was the boys' turn.

"Her gift is upstairs," Nikolay announced. "In the piano room."

Oh. Feeling giddy at the thought, I got off the couch.

I finally noticed that Alessio had disappeared. Looking around me, I stopped and searched for him.

"He's upstairs, waiting for you," Maddie said gently. With a push, I made my way to the piano room...with everyone following behind.

I got inside to find Alessio standing in the middle. He winked and smiled before opening his arms for me. My feet took me right into his open arms.

Curling into his embrace, I sighed in utter contentment.

"Ready for their gift?" he muttered in my ear. I nodded against his chest before pulling away.

He stepped back and moved away from me. That was when my eyes noticed something new next to the piano. It was covered with a blanket, so I couldn't see it.

"What is this?" I asked, already making my way to it.

"It's for Princess. Our gift to her," Viktor said,

his time his voice serious.

I pulled the blanket away, and a small gasp escaped past my lips.

Oh, how beautiful.

"This is…I'm speechless…" I said, running my hand over the soft silk material.

It was a cute baby bassinet. Small but so beautiful.

To my surprise, it was a rocking bassinet. The bedding was soft and a pale pink color. The curtains were made of lace, and it fell on either side of the bassinet.

The rest of it was made of wood, but everything was practically covered with the curtains and silk sheet.

I rubbed my hand over the wood and smiled. Now Maila had a beautiful place to lay in when I was playing the piano.

It was simply perfect.

I moved to its front, and my smile widened. On top from where the curtains came together and were attached, there was a small piece of wood.

On it, **PRINCESS** was written in cursive letters.

I felt Alessio at my back, and I leaned into his warm body.

"This is so beautiful and thoughtful. I will keep the bassinet in here, so that Maila can listen to me play while resting," I said softly.

"That's the plan," Phoenix replied. I could hear the cheeky smile in his voice.

"They spent two months building it," Alessio muttered against my temple.

My mouth fell open. "You guys built it?" I asked

358

in shock.

Swiveling around, I faced all three of them. They looked suddenly shy.

"It took us some time and many tries. But we got it right in the end. Maila deserves a gift made from our own hands," Nikolay said.

I blinked back unshed tears. My nose was prickling, and my eyes were burning. Happy tears. I remembered Alessio promising me only happy tears. He kept his vow.

Lena handed me Princess, and I placed a kiss on her tiny forehead. Alessio did the same. A sweet soft kiss.

Her lips pursed in a cute pout, and I smiled. Completely and utterly happy. I was finally whole.

I gently placed her in the bassinet. Alessio wrapped his arm around my hips, his head buried in my neck.

This was what I needed. What I had dreamed of since I was a child.

While every day I was living a nightmare, I had dreamed of this. Hoped for this.

And now it was my reality.

Love, happiness, and peace.

I had all of it.

And my daughter had all of it too.

Thank God Alessio parked his car there on that fateful day.

It was meant to be from the very beginning.

We were meant to be.

Chapter 36

Alessio

5 weeks later

A quiet but sudden cry woke me up. I groaned sleepily and pulled Ayla closer into my body. My face was buried in her neck, my arm wrapped tightly around her waist. I heard her moan, and she shifted around.

The cries continued.

Opening my eyes, darkness welcomed me. Except for the tiny lamp shining behind my back.

Princess continued to cry softly. She seemed annoyed and agitated. Definitely not hungry. Ayla just fed her a few hours ago.

Ayla sighed, her naked body moving against mine. "It's my turn. I'll get her," she whispered sleepily.

She started to sit up, but I pushed her back on the bed. "Go back to sleep. I got her."

Ayla stared at me sleepily, a small smile curving

360

her lips. So fucking beautiful.

She mumbled a quick thank you as I got up. She curled around my pillow, her eyes closing with a sigh. I knew she was asleep within seconds.

Giving her a final glance, I walked over to the crib. Ayla and I decided to keep Maila with us until she was a few months old. We weren't ready for Princess to sleep on her own.

Though with her sleeping in the same room, it was harder for us to make out. But we found our ways. Creativity at its best.

Stopping next to the crib, I saw Maila moving around agitatedly, her legs kicking out in anger, her tiny fists moving in frustration. It appeared I took too long to get to her. Demanding little Princess.

I smiled at the thought. Maila might love the attention, but she was good baby. Barely cried and slept most of the nights. Ayla and I were both thankful for that.

Princess noticed me standing there, and her movements stopped. She lay there, making small mewling sounds. She was the cutest little thing ever.

I bent at the waist and picked up the Princess. My arms went around her safely, and I brought her closer to my chest. She instantly stopped crying.

Her tiny fist rested against my chest as she blinked up at me. Her blue eyes were blurry with tears, making my heart ache a little.

I hated the tears in her eyes. It did things to my heart, watching my baby cry.

My daughter would never experience pain. Not like her mother has. Not like I had. She would be loved and fiercely protected.

The thought of someone hurting my princess made me want to rage. I would kill anyone who would hurt a single hair on her. Anyone who made her cry a single painful tear. They would die. Plain and simple.

I swiped her tears away and let my thumb linger over her soft cheeks. "Settle down now, little one," I crooned next to her ear.

She hiccupped back a small cry, and her lips pursed in a pout. A dry chuckle was heard from me. Maila had us all wrapped around her finger.

Turning my head to the side, I looked at Ayla. She was sleeping soundly. With a smile, I gave her a final glance before walking out of the room.

The door to Maila's nursery was partially open, so I pushed my way inside. Princess continued to stare at me, blinking sleepily. I knew she would be asleep in no time too.

Her legs kicked out, and she made another hiccup sound. "Yeah. Yeah. I know. You need a diaper change."

I could feel how full her diaper was. Most probably, that was why she woke up. Shaking my head, I placed her on changing table. She cooed, and her lips twitched in the smallest smile.

Damn it, she was the cutest.

And she had fucked with my mind too. Just like her mother had done so many months ago.

If a year ago you had asked me if I would be cooing and changing the diapers of a baby, I would have laughed and kicked you in the guts for asking the stupidest question.

But now, I couldn't imagine my world without

Maila.

She had wrapped herself around my heart and was there to stay. Just like my Angel.

They both belonged to me, making my heart whole again.

It was a laughable thought…hard to imagine. Everything felt surreal. Like a dream.

But then I would wake up beside Ayla, her body wrapped around mine like a vise. She would open her eyes, regarding me with such a loving look. From a distance, Maila would either be crying or cooing.

And I would remember that none of this was a dream.

I found my Angel…and she gave me a princess.

I snapped out of my thoughts when I felt Maila's leg kicking impatiently against my chest. She was lying down, moving agitatedly.

"You are an impatient one," I said as I removed her onesie.

I reached over the changing table and grabbed a diaper. Taking a deep breath, I set to do the impossible task.

"Okay. Let's do this, Princess."

With that, I quickly removed the diaper and cleaned Maila. While counting the seconds in my head, I slapped a clean diaper on her and fixed it properly.

Thirty seconds!

And she didn't pee on me. Fuck yeah.

Last time, Viktor wasn't so lucky.

But seriously, who the fuck plays with a naked baby?

I laughed silently to myself. His horrified screams still rang through my ears.

Moral of that day? Never play with naked baby. Or better yet, never take too long to change their diapers. You would get peed on.

After dressing Maila up again, I had her cradled in the crook of my arm. She settled against my chest, and I thought she sighed.

Her eyes closed instinctively, causing me to smile. I had Ayla's love, but a few weeks ago I realized that I also had my daughter's love.

I settled on the rocking chair and watched my princess sleeping. Her small body went limp in my arms as I rocked us back and forth.

My eyes grew heavier as sleep started to take over. I rested my neck against the back of the chair, closing my eyes in the process.

My last thought was how lucky I was. I remembered my days before Ayla...and then after meeting her. How much I have changed, but also how much I was still the same.

My Angel might have made me more human, but she also accepted the monster's side. She loved me despite of everything.

She gave me a family, a princess I could love and dote upon. Ayla has completed this broken family. She made me a better man. For her and our princess.

My lips twitched in a smile as I brought Maila closer to my chest.

With my daughter sleeping safely in my arms, I also fell asleep.

***

Ayla

I woke up to an empty bed. Surprised, I sat up quickly. My eyes adjusted to the morning light with great effort as I blinked away the sleepiness.

Getting off the bed, I made my way to the crib to find it empty too. I remembered Alessio waking up to take care of Maila. Did they not come back to bed?

I shrugged my robe on while walking into the bathroom. I quickly brushed my teeth and washed my face. After tying my hair in a fast messy bun, I made my way to Maila's nursery, the room next door.

The door was already open. When I peeked inside, the first thing I saw was Alessio's back.

He was bent over the changing table and murmuring soft words to our daughter. I smiled at the sight. He really was a doting father.

Leaning against the door, I admired my husband as he showered our baby with love. Alessio picked her up, and I saw her head over his shoulders. She had a small pink flowered headband on.

Alessio turned, and I noticed that Maila was wearing a pinkish dress. It appeared that her father already had her dressed this morning.

"Good morning," I said, walking into the nursery.

Alessio shifted around, facing me as he bounced Princess in his arms.

"Morning," he replied, his voice deep. "I thought

I'd dress her up before you woke up."

Smiling, I walked forward. "I can see that."

When I placed my arms out, Alessio gave Maila to me. I brought her closer to my chest and bent my head down, smelling her sweet baby scent.

"I should feed her before bringing her downstairs," I said, turning my head to Alessio. I moved closer to him and hooked an arm around his neck.

Our daughter was cradled between our bodies as I placed a sweet kiss on his lips. He smirked before taking my lips in a more demanding kiss, obviously not caring that Maila was plastered between us.

When she cooed, I pulled away, feeling breathless as I stared at Alessio. He winked before placing a kiss on my forehead and pulling us to the rocking chair.

I settled on his lap, holding Maila to my chest. After Alessio had untied my robe, I brought Princess closer to my breast. She latched on immediately and took her fill. My head rested on Alessio's shoulder as Maila fed.

"Maddie and I will be discussing the wedding today. We have put it off for too long. The wedding is in three weeks, and I still haven't made any preparations," I said quietly.

"You haven't, but Maddie has. I'm sure she has everything prepared," Alessio replied, his arms tightening around my waist.

Smiling at the thought, I shook my head. "I'm not surprised. Do you want to be there when we discuss the decorations? It's not just my wedding. It's ours. Shouldn't you have a say in it?"

Alessio's chest vibrated with a quiet chuckle as he placed a kiss on my forehead. "Do whatever you want, Angel. It doesn't matter to me. All I care about is that I will be waiting for you at the end of the aisle. As long as the day ends with us saying our vows and with me making love to you, I'm all good."

That earned another smile from me. He really had a way with words. "Hmm...making love to me? I like the sound of that," I replied before shifting Maila to my other breast.

Alessio groaned, resting his head against mine. "This is torture. Why didn't anyone tell me we had to wait?"

A laugh escaped past my lips as I pulled my head away. "Patience, Alessio."

He huffed, giving me a hard stare. "Do you find this amusing?"

"A little," I replied with a shrug.

We stared at each other for a second before busting out laughing. Maila jumped in my arms, her mouth opening with a loud cry. My eyes widened, and I quickly soothed my frightened baby.

Alessio's laughter died down to a quiet chuckling. "We scared her," I muttered when she continued suckling hungrily.

Alessio and I were quiet as we watched Maila feed. Her eyes were closed, her tiny fist resting against my other breast.

My eyes moved around the nursery, admiring the room that Maddie had helped me put together. Alessio had his hands in it too.

The room was big, too big for a baby. But it was

the closest to our bedroom, so that was our first choice.

The walls were painted a soft beige. Maila's crib was against the wall in the middle of the two large panel windows.

The crib was fit for a princess. Soft pinkish curtains came down on either side. Next to the crib, there was a couch and an ottoman. The rocking chair was on the other side of the crib.

My gaze went to the wall behind the crib, where the curtains weren't covering it. My heart fluttered at the quote there.

Your first breath took ours away.

Oh, how truthful these words were. She was our miracle, our light.

There were two more quotes around the nursery. My gaze flitted to the second one. It was on the wall next to the window, where the dresser was.

We loved you before you were born. And now, our love for you shines brighter.

When my eyes went to the last quote, I had to suppress my laugh.

There is no Prince Charming for me. My Daddy is my only King.

Actually, that wasn't the original quote. The

original said,

> *Someday I may find my Prince Charming but my Dad will always be my King.*

But Alessio being Alessio, when he came into the room to find that quote painted on the wall, he went straight downstairs and came back with the paint.

No amount of arguing had stopped him from repainting that wall and writing down his own quote.

And now we had the new version.

To say that Alessio was protective and possessive was an understatement. I wondered what would happen to Maila's first boyfriend. The thought left a shiver down my spine.

It wasn't just Alessio's possessiveness. That boy would also have to deal with three overbearing uncles and two grandfathers.

Not good. Not good at all. It appeared that there would be no Prince Charming for a very long time.

I was snapped out of my thoughts when Maila stopped suckling.

I stood up, noticing that she was finished. Rocking her in my arms, I glanced up at Alessio. "Can you bring her downstairs while I get dressed?"

Alessio stood up too. He gave me a quick kiss on the tip of my nose before pulling away.

I handed Maila to him and he held her gently in his arms. "I have to take care of some things, so I won't see you for breakfast."

I simply nodded. With the Italians under the Ivanshov reign, Alessio had been busy. Alberto had left a mess behind. A mess that Alessio had to clean now.

I saw the shadows behind his eyes. He wanted to keep me away from all of this, but it was impossible. I lived and breathed this life with him.

As much as this life was a part of him, it was a part of me too. I was born into the Mafia life. I was just unfortunate that I had to experience the darkest side. But I have also found love in this life.

After all, my husband was The Boss. He was King. And I was His Queen.

I smiled up at him, trying to ease the tension in his eyes. His shoulders were stiff, but at my smile, his muscles loosened.

"I'll see you later then," I murmured. He nodded as I walked to the door.

My legs froze in the entrance. Looking over my shoulders, I sent him a teasing smile. "Only three more weeks, Mr. Alessio Ivanshov. And then I'm all yours...to do whatever you want with."

His eyes flared dangerously, the look of desire and pure unadulterated lust had me biting on my lips.

Alessio growled low in his chest, and I quickly stepped out of the room.

But not before I heard his warning voice. "You will regret those words, kitten."

I laughed, my heart thumping wildly with excitement. My cheeks heated as I impatiently waited for those three weeks to be over.

Chapter 37

I came downstairs to find Maddie, Nina, and Evaline in the living room. Nina was bouncing her knees with Princess sitting on her lap, trying to keep her entertained.

A smile crept its way to my face at the sight. Who would have thought?

Aunt Nina.

It was hard to believe, but Nina was a doting aunt. She didn't always show it, but it was clear as day that she cared for Maila.

She wasn't sweet and gentle like Evaline or Maddie. No, her face was always cold. Her stares emotionless. Her smiles empty and dark.

But there were a few times when I noticed a slip in her hard character. A small genuine smile on her face when she played with Maila. A soft look in her eyes. It wasn't always there…but I noticed. I saw, and I knew Maila was loved by Nina too.

To top it off, Nina spoiled her rotten.

Evaline enveloped me in a hug as I stopped beside her. "Welcome back home. When did you get here?" I asked, after pulling away.

"A few minutes ago. We've got the wedding to plan. I'm here just for a few days though. My boss is being an asshole. We have a project to sign with another company, so I have to go. But I'll be back a day before the wedding," she explained with a sad pout.

Smiling, I hugged her again. "Okay. That's good enough. As long as you're here for the wedding. After all, you are my bridesmaid."

Maila's cooing snapped me away from Evaline. When I saw her chin covered with spit, I took a step forward. But Nina already got it.

Taking a small baby towel in her hand, she wiped Maila's chin clean. "I got her," she muttered.

"Who dressed her up this morning? The dress is so cute!" Evaline crooned, waving her finger in front of Maila.

"Alessio did," I replied, trying to hide my own laughter.

Maddie laughed. "Oh Lord. She has them all wrapped around her fingers. It's too cute!"

I nodded because of how true it was. Viktor, Nikolay, and Phoenix were her godfathers. It was hard to choose between them. And they threatened each other too. A big fight broke out on who was the godfather. In the end, I decided on all three. The more the better, right?

After all, they all loved her the same.

My eyes went to Maddie. I saw her gazing at Maila, smiling at her. My own smile widened. From the very beginning, there was no second thought that she would be the godmother.

My heart still ached for her loss. But every time she smiled at Maila, her love pure, I would slowly forget about the past. I knew she was still hurting, her loss still fresh, but her wounds were healing, slowly but surely.

We sat down and discussed the wedding. It must have been hours when we finally came to a decision. Maddie and Evaline eventually left to call the designers and take care of everything else.

My gaze went to Nina. She was strangely quiet. Over the months, we became close. Not as close as I was with Maddie or Evaline, but I could say we were friends.

Nina wasn't who I thought she was.

Yes, she was rude, mean, and sometimes outright cold.

But after putting our differences away, we got along. Against her wishes, Maddie and Evaline pulled her into the group. She had no choice but to accept us.

"I can hold her, if you want," I said, pointing at the sleeping Maila in her arms.

Nina shook her head. "It's okay. I got her."

We were silent for a few seconds before I cleared my throat. I moved beside Nina and softly rubbed my fingers over Maila's head. She loved it when I did that.

"I want you to be my bridesmaid, with Evaline."

Nina froze beside me, and then there was utter silence. I licked my lips nervously before finally facing her.

"You want me to be your bridesmaid?" she asked incredulously.

"Yes, we're friends. I want you to be part of this wedding," I replied quietly.

Nina gave me a dry laugh. She was careful not to jolt Maila. "Ayla, I fucked your husband and you want me to be your bridesmaid. You know that makes no sense, right? We might be *friends,* but we aren't that close."

I steeled my features against her words.

Shrugging, I gave her a smile. "You're right, but I care for you. Don't try to act cold with me, Nina. I can see past that fake excuse. You care, and you want to be friends, although you try to hide it. We all need friends, Nina. You mean a lot to me. Like Maddie and Evaline. So you need to accept this and stop fighting it."

The words were true, and for weeks, I had been desperate to say them.

Nina looked at me silently before taking a deep breath. She smiled, and for the first time, her genuine smile was directed toward me. "I remember a time when you used to hate me."

I smiled too. "You hated me too," I replied drily.

Nina shook her head, looking down at Maila on her lap. "Hate is a strong word, Ayla. I didn't hate you. Maybe the word you're looking for is jealous."

My eyes widened at her choice of word. "Jealous? Of me? Why?"

Nina lost her smile and shrugged. "You came and everything changed. I didn't like it. I didn't like how all of a sudden Alessio went from being this cold person to loving you, while I had been with him for ten years."

Before I could say anything, she continued in the

same monotone voice. "I was fifteen when I met Alessio. Fifteen when he found me in that dark alley, beaten up and bleeding. He saved me. I looked up to him. You know what happened two weeks later? He brought me to the basement, pushed me forward, and handed me a knife. I realized the man strapped to the chair in front of me was the same man who tortured me. I didn't ask Alessio any questions. It didn't matter. All that mattered was the man in front of me. I was fifteen when I was introduced to this life and realized this was what I needed. What I wanted."

Her cold stare pierced mine, and I almost shivered. "I took my revenge that night. I killed him in cold blood while Alessio stood behind me. He was proud of me. For killing a man. Alessio is the devil in disguise, Ayla. He is heartless and ruthless. You have absolutely no idea. And I was his equal."

My heart stuttered, and I looked down. My mind tried to wrap about the story she was telling me. I knew who Alessio was…but Nina, that was a whole other story.

"I still am and always will be," she continued. I looked up to see a small smirk on her face.

"But only on the field." Her words were left hanging as she brought her hand up and touched a finger to my chest.

"Because you have his heart. I won't ever have that. Thing is, I don't want it either. I don't feel. I don't care about anything. I like it this way. Heartless and cold. But then you came along and boom, everyone started feeling. Alessio cared. Maybe I was jealous. I was with him for so long and he never cared, but you…you came and wrapped yourself around him."

I swallowed hard against the ball of emotion. "He cares. You are part of this family. He cares for everyone, Nina. Including you."

Nina nodded and gave me another smile. "I know. So no, I didn't hate you. I just didn't understand why everything was changing so fast. But now I do. We don't know the definition of love, Ayla. We were not bred to love and be loved. You changed that."

"You don't hold any hard feelings against me?" I asked quietly.

Nina chuckled. "No. You were right. Alessio and I only had sex. That's it. We don't have any feelings for each other. Never did."

I didn't say anything. My mind was still reeling from everything Nina had told me. Was I jealous that Nina had him before me? Yes, I was, but it didn't matter anymore.

Alessio chose me.

"I'll be your bridesmaid." Nina's voice snapped me out of my thoughts.

"You will?" I asked, my eyebrows shooting up in surprise.

She nodded, her gaze going to Maila, who was slowly waking up. Nina handed my daughter to me, and I curled her small body against my chest.

"I don't really have a choice now, do I? You already decided we were friends," she muttered.

Small steps. Baby steps. But we were all slowly finally coming together.

Chapter 38

Three weeks later

Alessio dragged me close to him until I was practically lying on top of him. My arms went around his waist as I buried my face into his neck. One leg was thrown over his hips as his hand burned on my thigh with its possessive hold.

I lay there, just breathing him in, listening to his heartbeat. Alessio drew random patterns on my back, and my eyes slowly closed at the calmness.

"Where do you want to go for the honeymoon?" he asked in my ear.

I moved closer into him, trying to get as close as possible. With my head over his chest, I replied quietly. "To the beach house."

Alessio stiffened underneath me, his whole body freezing at my words. I knew he would react this way, but my decision was final.

I had to do this. I had to move on.

"No," he snapped loudly, his fingers going impossibly tight around my hips. I winced and wiggled in his embrace.

"Alessio—" I started, but he cut me off with an angry growl.

"We aren't going back there again," he hissed in my ear. His tone was angry, his body tight with tension.

I knew he was trying to control himself but quickly losing it.

"But—"

He cut me off again. "I said no!"

Alessio pulled away and rolled us over until I was under his firm body. His fingers went around my wrists, pulling them over my head. "Ayla, I won't repeat myself. We are not going back there. Ever again. Understood? It's not even up for discussion."

I could see the tension lines around his eyes and forehead. My heart squeezed when I saw the pain in the depth of his bluish eyes.

"Alessio," I started again. He was already shaking his head, but I continued. "Please, let me do this. I need to do this. It's important for me to move on. You bought the beach house for me, right?"

He didn't answer, his jaw grinding with the effort to keep his anger in check.

"Yes," he finally hissed.

I twisted my hands from his grip. With great reluctance, he let me go. Instead of moving away, I pulled him even closer.

My hand caressed his rough stubble as I spoke. "Well, then I want to go to my beach house. You can't stop me. I want to do this, Alessio. I have to move on, and we can't let what happened stop us from living. If I'm always going to cower in fear and hide behind you, how will I face my past? It hurts to think about it…our happy moments were cut short because of *him*. We never got a chance to enjoy it."

I cut off as tears started to build up in eyes. My throat felt tight as I talked. "But I want to go back. I want to face it and move on, with you by my side. I know you'll be there for me, holding me when I need you to. We have to move on, Alessio."

My fingers danced over his cheeks as I leaned up and kissed him. "I have to fight it…my past. He's gone, but he's still living inside of me. Sometimes the nightmares come back. Sometimes, I fall back into the deep end. You always pull me back. But *I* have to fight *him*. This is me fighting him. I won't let him stop me from living and enjoying my life with my husband…my family."

Alessio's throat moved. He looked like he wanted to speak, but his voice was stolen from him. His jaw ticked, his eyes flaring with anger and hurt.

"Please let me do this. I want to go back to the beach house. This time, it will be different. We will be happy," I murmured against his lips.

He groaned, his forehead touching mine as he closed his eyes. I wrapped my arms around his back, holding him to me. I could almost feel his pain bleeding out to me.

Going back there…it was going to be hard for both of us.

"Angel," he whispered so softly.

My hand caressed his back soothingly, waiting for him to agree with me. Finally, he opened his eyes, but his forehead continued to rest against mine.

His lips curled in distaste when he replied. "Fine. We will go. But I don't want you out of my sight for even a minute. It's going to be crazy. I will drive you insane. But for my own sanity, Ayla…for God's sake, you can't leave my sight."

I knew he didn't want to agree with me. But he didn't have a choice. We were going to spend our honeymoon at the beach house.

"Thank you," I replied, my heart soaring and full of love for this man. "I won't leave your sight. You will just have to follow me to the bathroom too."

His lips twitched, and I fought the urge to laugh too. "You are fucking impossible, Ayla."

"You love me," I shot back, this time a smile curving my lips.

Alessio's lips brushed against mine as he spoke. "So fucking much."

Then he took my lips in a deep, breathless, and senseless kiss.

***

I woke up to find the bed empty. Alessio must have left some time ago, because his spot was already cold beside me.

After freshening up, I went to find Maila. In the end, I found her in Maddie's bedroom.

They were both sleeping on her bed, with Maddie cuddling and holding Princess close to her chest.

Such a sweet sight. One that also made my heart

ache.

Maddie would have been holding her baby too. Just like this. But now…she could only hold Maila.

Tears stung my eyes as I continued to watch them. With a heavy heart, I closed the door softly, letting them have their moment.

Next stop was Lyov's office. I knocked at the door and heard him call me in. Walking inside, I found Isaak there too.

They both looked deep in discussion, but everything stopped when I stepped in. Smiles were sent my way as I moved closer.

"Ayla," Lyov acknowledged me.

Smiling, I nodded his way before Isaak took me in his arms. He hugged me and then stepped back, Lyov taking his place.

It was a surprise seeing Lyov change from someone harsh and hateful to loving me as a daughter.

The last few months, he had transformed into someone totally different. He and Isaak were the perfect grandfathers. I couldn't have asked for better grandparents to lead Maila and support her.

It further proved that even ruthless killers had a heart. I would have never thought that I would find solace and a loving family with my enemies. Yet here I was, living with them. Loved by them.

"What are you doing here?" Isaak asked.

"I wanted to ask Lyov something. I was hoping you wouldn't mind," I started gently, watching Lyov's reaction.

"Of course. What is it?" he asked, taking his seat behind the desk.

I opened my mouth to reply but quickly snapped it shut again. My voice couldn't seem to come out. I had wanted to say this for such a long time, but now that I was here, I didn't know how to start.

My throat bobbed as I swallowed several times. Nervousness coursed through me as they waited for me to speak. Their eyes were on me, watching me intensely.

After a few seconds of silence, I tried again.

"Isaak is supposed to walk me down the aisle tomorrow," I said softly, glancing toward Isaak for a brief moment. He smiled, his chest puffing out proudly.

There was no question that Isaak would walk me down the aisle. It was his right, something I had dreamed of. A fairy tale coming true.

But there was someone else who deserved this moment too.

He would never get this chance, but I wanted him to experience this. Something that was robbed away from him so many years ago, I wanted to return him this happiness.

My eyes went back to Lyov. "But I want you to walk me down the aisle too. Both of you."

His mouth fell open. There was silence, only the sound of us breathing could be heard in the room.

"You want me to walk you down the aisle?" he questioned, his eyes wide in shock. "But—"

I cut him off before he could continue. "It's something that I want and I hope you would be part of, Lyov. I might not be your real daughter. I might not be your princess, but just this once, I want to give you this moment. Both Isaak and you deserve this."

Isaak rubbed his chest, like it was hurting him. He looked down at his feet but not before I saw the raw emotion on his face. Lyov had a very similar look.

"So, will you? Walk me down the aisle with Isaak?" I asked again.

Lyov stared at me and then shook his head. My heart dropped, and my hands grew clammy. I twisted the end of my dress, trying to calm my breathing.

"Where the hell did you come from?" he asked, his lips twitching in a small smile.

Lyov stood up, pushing his chair back. He walked around the desk and wrapped me in a hug. "It would be my honor," he whispered.

My eyes widened, and my breath was stuck in my throat. Tears blinded my vision as I hugged him back. "Thank you," I whispered back.

As we pulled away, I went to give Isaak a hug. "And thank *you* for being my father and for choosing to walk me down the aisle. It is something I will forever be grateful for."

Isaak patted my back and cleared his throat. Both men stared at me with a small smile on their faces.

I felt mine widen, and then I giggled. "Alessio would be laughing at you all if he saw you now."

They lost their smiles, their face turning dark and serious. "Fuck no," Lyov muttered. "If you say anything to him…"

I snapped my mouth shut, trying to keep my laughter in.

"Go. Go. Go…" Isaak shooed me away.

My feet took me out of the door as my laughter bubbled out. I heard both of them curse when the door closed behind me.

***

"Okay, close your eyes, babe. I'm going to turn you toward the mirror," Evaline murmured.

I could hear the smile in her voice. My own smile made its appearance. I closed my eyes, and with shaky legs, I turned to face the mirror.

"Ready?" Maddie asked.

"You guys didn't turn me into a clown, right?" I joked.

There was laughter. I giggled and then finally opened my eyes. I blinked and then gasped.

"You look gorgeous, babe," Maddie said. From the mirror, I saw Evaline and Nina nodding.

They really did work their magic. Perfectly, I should say.

The first thing I noticed was my hair. Maddie didn't overdo it. It was simple yet so beautiful. My hair was still down, but instead it was designed into a messy braid but with curls.

White flowers were pinned along the length, with a simple and elegant crystal tiara on top of my head.

My gaze moved down, and I was thankful to see that Nina kept my make-up light. My eyelashes were coated with mascara, and they appeared really long. My lips were painted and glossed with a light shade of red. Even my eyeshadow was a light brown, although it appeared a little sparkly. The eyeliner looked like a deep maroon. My green eyes sparkled with the colors that were chosen.

My neck held a single diamond pendant, the chain made with white pearls. My earrings were similar.

And then my dress. When I chose it, I was nervous, scared that Alessio wouldn't like it. But now as I stared at myself in the mirror, I knew he was going to love it.

I looked beautiful. I felt beautiful.

The wedding gown was almost sleeveless. There was only a thin lace strap that went over my shoulders. My bodice was a V-cut, and the color was a light beige. White lace covered it with beads scattered all over. The dress was tight over my chest, but it became flowy around the middle of my stomach. It flared down on either side. The end of the dress was covered with the same lace design as my bodice.

I turned to my side, watching the dress trail behind me. It was long from behind, the train dragging. The dress wasn't exactly white. The cloth underneath was a light beige, but it had white lace covering the whole dress.

My back was half covered with the lace, while the top part was backless. The dress flared at my back too, looking very flowy.

"I absolutely love this gown. It's simple yet so elegant and beautiful," Evaline said, her eyes on my dress.

"Thank you," I whispered, staring at myself in the mirror.

"Here, let me get your veil on," Maddie said. I

bent down slightly so she could pin my long veil behind my tiara. It trailed behind my back, even longer than the train of my dress. The veil was made with the same lace material, covered with beads and flower designs.

Lena had it designed and made for me. It was my *something new* from her, representing her blessings for my happy future.

Just when I was about to whisper another thank you, there was a knock at the door. Maddie went to open it. She moved to the side as Isaak and Lyov walked inside.

They both halted in their steps at the sight of me, and I felt a smile stretching my lips.

"Look at you," Isaak said, coming forward. "You look beautiful, Ayla."

He hugged me, and my arms went around him, hugging him back just as tight. "You remind me so much of your mother. She would be so proud of you, Ayla," he whispered in my ear before pulling away.

My eyes stung, but I quickly blinked the tears away. As Lyov hugged me, I tried my hardest not to cry.

"Are you ready?" he asked, pulling away. I nodded and looked down at myself.

"As ready as I can be," I muttered. "Is Alessio ready?"

They both chuckled and raised an eyebrow. "What do you think? He has been ready for hours and getting very impatient. The guys had to lock him in the room to stop him from seeing you," Lyov explained with a laugh.

A giggle escaped at the thought. I could only imagine. Alessio was impossible. Well, that was an understatement.

"It's time, Ayla," Isaak said.

Taking a deep breath, I nodded. On shaky legs, I took a step forward only to be stopped with Lyov's hand on my arm.

"We got something for you," he said. My eyebrows furrowed in confusion as I stared at him, waiting.

That was when I noticed they each held a small give box in their hands. Oh.

Isaak came forward first and opened the box for me. Inside, I found a pair of teardrop crystal earrings. "These were your mother's. They are the only thing I have of hers. I believe they should be yours now."

I stared at the earrings with my mouth open. "This could be your *something old*. If you don't have one already."

I shook my head, speechless. "No, I don't have one," I muttered, looking back up at Isaak. "Are you sure you want me to have this?"

He nodded and handed me the earrings. "Thank you," I whispered, feeling so overwhelmed with emotion that I could barely speak.

I removed my earrings and wore the ones that Isaak gave me, my mother's earrings. When they were in place, my heart felt heavy, and my stomach rolled with butterflies.

They were the only thing I had of my mother's, and for the first time, I felt close to her. It felt like she was here, watching me. Closing my eyes, I imagined just that.

I imagined her in a white dress, standing behind Isaak, smiling at me, her eyes filled with so much love.

I saw her blowing me a kiss and then waving at me. I saw her glancing at Isaak, her eyes holding the same deep love. In my vision, she placed her hand over his back and kissed his lips ever so lightly.

And then she disappeared. Like she was never here. But I could still feel her presence.

Opening my eyes, I stared at Isaak with tear-filled eyes. "I wish she was here. I wish I knew her, Isaak. I wish she was here right now, holding me," I said, my fingers whispering over the earrings.

He took a deep breath, like he was controlling his own emotions. Isaak rubbed my arms soothingly before replying. "I know. I wish she was here right now too. But Ayla, you might not see her, but she is here. I'm sure she's watching over you. Your mother loved you so deeply. You were her everything. The light in her fucked-up world. Never forget that."

I nodded, pressing a hand over my heart. My breathing calmed, and I sniffled, blinking away the unshed tears. Evaline silently handed me a tissue, and I mouthed a quick thank you.

When Isaak moved again, Lyov opened his box. Inside was a hair pin. "This was Alessio's mother's. If you don't have a *something borrowed*, you can use this. I thought it was fitting for you to use Maria's hair pin. She is my Angel, and you are Alessio's. I would be honored if you include her in this wedding."

I took the hair pin, feeling grateful for this. "Of course, Lyov. I'm the one who is honored. Thank you," I replied, handing the hair pin to Maddie. She placed it in my hair and fixed my curls around it.

"She would have loved you," Lyov continued when Maddie was done fixing my hair.

"I have no doubt that I would have loved her too. Because of her, I have Alessio. For that I am forever thankful," I whispered, kissing his cheek in appreciation.

After pulling away, I looked down at my wrist. The bracelet that Evaline gave me sparkled in the light. "Looks like I have two *something borrowed*."

Everyone smiled, the previous emotional moment breaking away.

"You have your *something blue*?" Isaak asked.

I nodded, smiling in the process. "Alessio's eyes."

My cheeks heated when both Isaak and Lyov raised an eyebrow, amusement dancing in their eyes.

"It's time, babe," Maddie said.

My eyes went to hers as she quickly fixed her hair. All my girls were ready. Both Evaline and Nina were wearing a beige ankle-length dress. They were simple and sleeveless. The dresses weren't tight but instead flowy around their hips and down.

Maddie's dress was a little different. Same design and color but there were golden beads over her bodice. She was my maid of honor.

Taking a deep breath, I looked at Isaak and Lyov. Their faces were serious, their backs straightened, and their chests puffed out proudly.

Maddie handed me my cascading bouquet, made with white and pink peonies. As both men presented me with their elbows, I swallowed nervously, sucked in another deep breath, and then took their arms.

I tightened my hold on their arms as we took a step forward. My heels wobbled with my first steps, but with Isaak's and Lyov's help, I finally steadied myself and was able to walk with no problem.

We walked out of the room and then down the stairs, which was decorated with flowers. So many flowers covered each step and the banister. We could barely see the woods. Only pink and white flowers were visible. On each step, there were two candles on either side.

We walked down the stairs effortlessly and then continued out of the house, to the back garden where the ceremony was being held.

The door opened, and we stopped. I could hear the piano playing, a melody I didn't recognize, but it sounded just as beautiful.

"Ready?" Isaak patted my hand. I nodded, and the three of us took a step forward. Together, we walked out.

I was blasted with sunlight, warmth spreading through me. I blinked, my heart accelerating.

It beat faster at the sight in front of me. Nothing else mattered. I didn't see anything...no one except the man standing at the end of the aisle.

My breath was stolen from me as I walked to Alessio. I couldn't remember the walk. All I could see and feel were his eyes on me.

His bluish steel-colored eyes stared at me

intensely, following my every step, my every movement.

His black suit was similar to what he always wore, except for the golden tie. His hair was sleek on his head, but he didn't shave. I told him not to. He looked so much better with a few days of stubble.

His eyes stayed on me as I made my way to him…my husband.

My heart drummed in my chest, so loudly I was sure everyone could hear it. My hands grew clammy, and I held my bouquet tighter.

I breathed through my nose, trying to act normal when all I wanted to do was run to him and jump in his arms.

I quickened my pace just a little. I heard Isaak's low chuckle in my ear, but they matched my pace, not once complaining.

When we finally reached the end of the flowery aisle, we stopped. Lyov placed a kiss on my cheek, over my veil.

When he whispered in my ear, his voice was low, only for me to hear. "Keep smiling just like this. And keep making my son happy. He deserves it. Both of you do."

Lyov stepped away, leaving me a tearful mess. Isaak kissed me on the other cheek before whispering in my ear too. "It is my honor to get a chance to be your father, Ayla. You were my sweet little girl and always will be. Be happy, my sweet girl. You deserve everything…all the love and happiness."

I grabbed onto his arm, refusing to let go when

he went to step away. "Thank you...Dad."

His eyes filled with tears at the words, and he nodded, kissing my forehead. This time, I let him go.

After I handed my bouquet to Maddie, Isaak took my hand. Alessio was already reaching forward, and Isaak placed my hand in his.

When my palm made contact with Alessio's, he instinctively wrapped his fingers around mine, holding my hand firmly and tightly in his.

Isaak held our hands together. "I'm giving my daughter away to you, Alessio Ivanshov. You make her cry, just once, and I will come after your heart. This is not a joke. I have more than a decade of experience on you. You are nothing compared to me."

Alessio raised his eyebrow. "The arrogance doesn't suit you, old man. But know that Ayla will never cry a tear of pain as long as she is mine. As long as I am breathing, she will only know happiness."

Isaak nodded. "Good. I wish you both many years of happiness."

With that, he stepped away, letting our hands go.

It was only Alessio and me. Just us, standing, staring at each other. Holding each other's hand.

His grip tightened, and he pulled me closer. Someone cleared their throat, but Alessio didn't care. I didn't either. I was lost in his eyes.

Alessio brought my other hand up too, holding both close to his chest. He stepped forward until our bodies were touching. So deliciously close.

I could feel his breath close to my lips, my veil

the only barrier between us. Alessio let go of my hands and pulled my veil over my head.

A smile stretched my lips as he leaned closer, as if to kiss me.

"You look so beautiful, Angel. Took my breath away when you walked out of those doors," he murmured, moving even closer. "But you will look more beautiful with the dress off."

"Boss, you can't..." Mark, one of Alessio's man and our minister for today, said.

"Fuck off, Mark. You don't want to die," Alessio growled.

A second later, his lips touched mine in the sweetest kiss. It was only for a moment, though, because he pressed harder, more demanding. My lips parted, giving him access. His tongue slipped inside, dancing with me.

We kissed, both lost in each other when Alessio was suddenly pulled away from me. I gasped, my eyes going wide.

"Okay, I think one kiss is enough. You can do the dirty in private. Damn it!" Viktor snapped, holding Alessio back.

I could feel my cheeks burning under everyone's stares. There was laughter, and I looked down, suddenly shy and nervous. *Way to go, Ayla.*

Alessio glared and shrugged off Viktor's hold before moving closer again. This time, he didn't make a move to kiss me. Thank God.

Instead, he pulled me closer, holding my hands to his chest. "Do you stuff, Mark. And hurry the fuck up."

Pinching his nipple, I hissed quietly. "Stop it."

He snapped his mouth shut but looked restless. I knew how much he didn't want to be here right now, doing this. But well…he had to stick with it.

At the thought, I smiled. He was going to love it in the end. It was going to be a day he would remember forever. I was going to make sure of it.

"Friends and family of the bride and groom, welcome and thank you for being here on this important day. Today, we are gathered together to celebrate the very special love between Ayla Abandonato—"

"Ivanshov," Alessio growled, breaking Mark off.

"—and Alessio Ivanshov by joining them in marriage," he continued over Alessio.

I smiled, feeling the happiest in that moment. My heart overflowed with love for the man standing in front of me.

As Mark continued with his speech, I tuned him out. I thought of everything, from the very beginning and to this moment.

The time when I was scared and running away from home. The moment when I hid in Alessio's car and under his bed. And then when he found me.

The first look, the first touch, the first word, when blue met green…the beginning of our love story.

How *he* changed *me*…and helped me with my past. His undeniable love made me alive.

How *I* changed *him*. From someone heartless, from someone who only wanted me as a plaything to someone loving me unconditionally.

We were both broken. Two broken halves making a whole.

We learned to love together, taking baby steps. Such small steps that it would have looked impossible for us to be standing right here in this moment. But here we were, getting married in front of our friends and family.

In front of our daughter.

My mind traveled back and then to this moment. I stared in his blue eyes as his fingers rubbed back and forth over the back of my hands.

He stared back at me, his eyes holding the same amount of love, if not more.

Mark's voice broke through my thoughts, and my heart drummed. "You fell in love by chance, but you're here today because you're making a choice. You both are choosing each other. You've chosen to be with someone who makes you smile and laugh. Someone who lifts you up and makes you into a better someone. You're about to make promises to each other that you intend to keep. Your vows are sacred, something you'll hold till your last breath."

He paused, taking a deep breath before continuing. "So, Alessio Lyov Ivanshov, do you take Ayla Abandonato as your wife, to love, honor, comfort, and cherish her from this day forth? Do you vow to hold her, be her strength, and wipe her tears, cherishing every single moment with her? Do you vow to share all that you are and all that you have with her, and promise to continue loving her and supporting her through sickness and health? Pain and happiness?"

Alessio opened his mouth, his grip tightening around my hands.

"I do," he said. His voice rang loud and clear, holding every ounce of seriousness.

In that moment, I realized that this meant as much to him as it meant to me.

My heart tripped, and my stomach cramped with too many butterflies at his words. Two simple words, uttered in front of hundreds of people. His love for me…it was my undoing.

Mark turned to me. "Do you Ayla Abandonato…"

"No," I quickly said.

Alessio's eyes widened, and he sucked in a harsh breath. There was utter silence.

Realizing that I just messed this up, I cleared my throat. "I mean wait."

I glanced at Mark, and he too was staring at me with wide eyes. Smiling convincingly at him, I quickly finished. "I want to say my own vows, if that's okay."

I felt Alessio's tensed muscles relax under my palm, and I rolled my eyes internally. Silly man. Did he really think I would stop our wedding?

"Of course, you can," Mark replied, smiling kindly.

When he gave me a nod, I looked back at Alessio. He stared at me intensely, his blue eyes growing darker with need.

Feeling suddenly nervous, I swallowed and licked my lips. "Well, I had this memorized, but now I'm a little nervous. I hope I don't mess this up," I started.

People chuckled in the crowd, and I saw Alessio's lip twitching. I closed my eyes and took a deep breath.

Opening them again, I stared at Alessio and finally found the courage to speak. "When we first met, I didn't think we would be standing right here in this moment. It seemed impossible back then. You were mean and rude. And I was scared of everything. We were both scared of taking this step. But when we did, we found out how beautiful love really is."

He smiled then. A breathtaking smile that stole my breath away. His hands released mine and wrapped around my hips, anchoring me to him.

"You taught me how to love, Alessio. You taught me how to live. How to be myself. You gave me a chance at seeing this world. When everything seemed impossible, you made it possible. You made the sun shine brighter for me. You were the little light in my darkness, pulling me forward, telling me that it was okay to leave the darkness behind and embrace the light, our love."

I heard sniffling behind me, and I knew it was Maddie. Or even Evaline. From behind Alessio, I saw his men…his most trusted men, looking just as deeply affected.

My eyes went back to my husband. My voice rang clear for everyone to hear as I continued. "When I gave up on everything…on us, you still didn't give up. You fought and told me to fight for us. You saved me and brought me back. Alessio, you held me closer every day, and every moment, your love made me forget the pain. I don't think I can ever thank you enough for loving me and for fighting for us. But all I know is that I will never leave you. I will forever be at your side, just like we were meant to be. From the very beginning, we were fated."

Looking up at him, my fingers whispered over his chest, his wildly beating heart. "So this is my vow to you. Alessio Ivanshov, your love is my anchor. You are my strength. I promise to give you all my love from now until eternity ends. I vow to care for you, trust your love, be what you need, to make sure your feelings are always considered. I vow to show my love and respect. I want to live out the days of my life with you. I, Ayla Abandonato, vows to take you as my husband, to love, honor, comfort, and cherish you from this day forth. We are one and always will be."

Licking my lips, I said my final words. "I make this vow because my heart is yours."

"Can we have the rings, please?" Mark said.

I turned around to see Lena walking down the aisle, holding Maila in her arms. My sweet baby was wearing the cutest white tutu dress, with a flower headband on her head.

Our rings were exchanged, and I couldn't help the way my heart fluttered.

Finally, I palmed Alessio's cheeks, holding him to me. "I love you, Alessio Ivanshov. I love you so much."

The tears slid down my cheeks unashamedly. Those words...I have longed to say them, and I knew this day was perfect.

I felt Alessio sucking a harsh breath, and then he was kissing me, devouring me in front of all our friends and families.

He had no care in the world as his lips met mine in a hard, bruising kiss. Alessio nipped at my lips, and I kissed him back with the same passion.

My hands went to his neck, pulling me closer to me. "I love you, Angel. I fucking love you so damn much."

His breath mingled with mine, his tongue sliding along mine. My lips felt swollen, but I still didn't let him go.

Mark cleared his throat, but Alessio still didn't let me go. He tried again and again, but there was no success. Alessio and I were lost in each other.

"Boss," he said, trying to get Alessio's attention.

Another clearing of a throat. "Well…emm…by the power vested in me, I now pronounce you husband and wife. You may *continue* kissing the bride."

Laughter could be heard, and I felt my own smile. Alessio was smirking against my lips.

"You are *mine* now," he whispered against my lips.

"Always have been and always will be. Only *yours*, Alessio," I whispered back.

We finally pulled away, both of us breathless. My cheeks felt warm, my lips swollen….and my heart…well, it was wild.

Alessio grabbed my hand, and we turned to face the audience. Mark stood behind us, and I could hear the smile in his voice as he spoke again.

"It is with great honor I present to you Mr. and Mrs. Alessio Ivanshov."

Everyone stood up and clapped. There were shouts and roars of happiness.

Alessio bent down and swept me off my feet, cradling me to his chest as he stepped off the platform. My hands went around his neck, and he walked us back.

"I love you, Alessio," I said to him. Placing a kiss on his cheek, I let my lips linger there. "I promise to continue loving you until I take my last breath."

His hold tightened around me, and I smiled.

My husband. My king. My love. My savior. My monster. My made man.

And I, his Angel.

Chapter 39

Alessio

As I carried Ayla off the platform, all I wished was that we were in private. But no, we had more than five hundred people watching us.

Ayla was so beautiful in this moment that all I wanted to do was steal her away, hide her from everyone's eyes…so only I could feast on her.

When she walked out of those doors, it felt like my heart had stopped. I found it hard to breathe as she walked down the aisle to me.

And then she said her vows, taking me by surprise but messing with my head at the same time. I didn't think I could love her any more than I did, but the moment I heard those words from her lips, it felt like my heart would burst.

Ayla's arms tightened around my neck, her lips pressing against my skin in the sweetest kiss.

I pulled her even closer. "Can we leave now?" I muttered in her ear.

She laughed and shook her head. "No. Maddie

will hunt us down."

Fucking Maddie.

When I reached the middle of the garden, where all the tables and chairs were, I let Ayla down. She grabbed my arm to steady herself.

Pulling her closer to me, I gripped her hips possessively. The guests started our way, excited to finally meet Ayla.

With Ayla at my side, I introduced her to the rest of the *Bratva*.

"Alessio," Dmitry said, coming closer with his wife and kids at his side.

Slapping me on my back, he said his congratulations. "Ayla, this is Dmitry Agron. Boss of the Agron Family. He is part of the *Bratva*."

She smiled kindly and shook his hand. "And this is his wife, Lidiya. The little girl in her arms is Anastasia," I continued to introduce.

Lidiya came forward and hugged Ayla. "It is so very nice to finally meet you, Ayla."

"I would like to say the same. I have heard so much about the Agron family," Ayla replied, placing a kiss on Lidiya's cheek.

"And this is my son," Dmitry said, pulling Grigory forward. He was fourteen years old, the next in line as Boss after his father.

"It is my pleasure to make your acquaintance, Ma'am," he said with a slight bow.

Grigory nodded at Ayla, his face stern and hard. Emotionless. Well trained. I nodded at Dmitry in approval.

Behind Dmitry, I saw Valentin making his way to us. Fucking Solonik. I pulled Ayla closer to me, and she looked up at me, confused.

"Alessio, son...I am hurt that I had to hear of the wedding from someone else," he said, coming to stand beside Dmitry.

His eyes went to Ayla, his stare burning into her. A small smirk appeared on his lips, and all I wanted to do was punch it in.

I felt a hand on my back. "Control, Alessio," Viktor said quietly, coming to stand beside me.

"A lovely wife you have there," Valentin continued, his voice thick with his Russian accent.

He moved forward, taking Ayla's hand before she could even react. My fingers bit in her hips, trying to control myself at the sight of him touching my wife.

Valentin bent his head, placing a kiss on the back of her hand. "It is my pleasure, Ayla Abandonato," he said, his eyes darkening.

"Ivanshov. Ayla Ivanshov. That's my wife you are speaking to," I growled, pulling Ayla away from him.

"Of course. My apologies," he quickly said, his eyebrows raised in amusement.

"Valentin, how nice to see you after so many years," Lyov said in Russian, standing beside Ayla. Isaak took his side, both of them glaring daggers into Solonik.

Ayla looked up at me, demanding answers. "It's Valentin Solonik," was my only reply.

Her eyes widened and stepped closer to me. Solonik might be part of the *Bratva*. He might have been a boss, but I was still the Godfather. He hated it. He loathed that the Ivanshov led the other families.

Valentin had always tried to find a way to take over, but he never got a chance. Not now and not ever.

Valentin and Lyov continued to converse in Russian.

"Where is your wife?" Isaak asked.

"She is at home," Valentin answered drily.

He might have been old enough to be my father—his reign started around the same time as Lyov, but his wife was years younger than me.

"Are they speaking Russian?" Ayla whispered.

I nodded and slightly bent my head down so I could whisper in her ear. "Yes, Valentin's estate is in Russia. He takes care of the business there. Barely comes over to the US or Canada."

We stepped away from the crowd, Dmitry nodding at me in understanding. He took his wife by the hips, kissing her on the lips before leading them away.

"Can you speak Russian?" she asked quietly, her arms going around my waist.

I chuckled at the questions. "Of course, I can, Ayla."

"Say something in Russian," she demanded. "Emm...it sounded...nice when the others were speaking it."

Pulling my wife against me, my fingers grazed her neck. She shivered at my touch, her eyes half closing as I trailed my finger down.

"*Kotyonok*," I whispered roughly before nipping at her earlobe.

She jumped in response, her arms tightening

around me. "What does that mean?" she whispered back, breathless.

"Kitten," I replied, my teeth grazing her neck, biting down softly.

"Oh." Her lips parted, and other ideas jumped in my mind.

"Alessio, man, do you need a room?"

I groaned and pulled away from Ayla. Erik Gavrikov smirked as he stared at us.

"Ayla, this is—"

"I can introduce myself," he said, pushing me away.

"Fuck off, Erik," I snapped back.

He laughed and pulled Ayla in a hug. He winked over her shoulders before stepping back. "I'm Erik Gavrikov. I'm sure you've heard of the name. The better-looking Boss," he teased.

Ayla's cheeks turned red, and I watched her flustered over Erik.

"Emm, yes…Alessio has told me about you," she replied.

"I can't fucking believe that you're hitched, Alessio. Am I the only single one left?" he said, running his fingers through his hair.

"Pretty much. If you don't count my men," I replied, rolling my eyes.

"Well, I like my pussies varied. Can't stick with just one." He shrugged. His eyes went to a woman as she passed by us.

"I'll tap that one anytime," he said, smacking her on the ass. "Tonight, *kotik*. What say?"

Too bad for him the woman turned out to be Nina.

She swiveled around; her glare could kill anyone on the spot. "Touch me again and I will rip your arms off and beat you with them," she growled.

Erik raised his hands up. "Damn, Nina. I thought we were good. You liked it last night."

Ayla coughed, hiding her laugh behind her hand.

Without answering, Nina started to walk away, only to stop again. "Oh, and call me a pussycat again and you won't be able to speak. Got it?"

Erik stared at her speechless. "What crawled in her ass? She need the stick removed or what?"

He smirked then. "I'll remove it...and then replace it with something else."

He thrust his hips forward and winked. I could see Ayla blushing, and she looked down.

"Where is Viktor?" Erik asked. "Can't see the best man anywhere."

"He must be somewhere," Ayla asked. "He was right beside us a few minutes ago."

Erik nodded and started to back away. "I'll see you both later."

Ayla waved and then sagged against me. "Is he always like this?"

"Yes," I replied drily.

"It looks like I have met all of the Families," she said, watching the guests mingling around. "They seem...very enthusiastic. I can't explain it. It's strange."

"Most of us here are killers, Ayla. Of course, it's strange. We don't mingle and party."

Ayla nodded in understanding as other guests made their way to us. She talked, smiled, and laughed at everyone.

406

I watched her getting along, and pride filled my chest. She has come a long way. We both have.

Ayla deserved this more than anyone.

I snapped out of my thoughts when Ayla made her way to me. Leaning on her toes, she placed a quick kiss on my lips, catching me by surprise.

I love you, she mouthed.

I heard people laughing and clapping as I pulled her onto my lap. Yeah. I fucking loved this woman.

And she was getting deliciously fucked tonight.

***

Ayla

My heart drummed as Alessio pulled me onto his lap.

I bit on my lips, feeling my cheeks heating under his eyes. His eyes followed my movement, and if possible, his gaze was growing more lustful. He looked so sexy in this moment.

From the corner of my eyes, I saw Maddie motioning me over. "I guess it's time for our first dance," I said softly.

Alessio cradled me to his chest and stood up. He carried me to the platform before placing me on my feet. Wrapping my arms around his neck, I moved closer.

Alessio held my hips as we started to move to the song. It was slow and perfect. He twirled me around and then pulled me back.

We moved together as the others started to join us. Placing my head over Alessio's shoulder, I let him lead the dance.

The moment felt so surreal, so perfect that tears blinded my vision. We danced for a long time, neither of us wanting to let go.

When my feet were tired and aching, I finally pulled away. The sun was setting, casting a beautiful soft orange glow in the sky.

From the corner of my eye, I saw Evaline dancing with someone I didn't recognize.

Maddie tsked beside me. "What is this girl doing?"

I didn't reply. My gaze stayed on Evaline, who was dancing way too close. Oh.

Her arms went around his neck as they laughed, the man enjoying her closeness.

Maddie laughed. "She's crazy."

I glanced Nikolay's way.

Not good. Not good at all.

He looked like he was ready to commit murder.

I looked at Evaline again. This time, her eyes were on Nikolay as she continued dancing. She moved closer as she rolled her hips against the man's groin.

"Emm..." I started.

"She's playing with fire," Maddie replied before I could say anything. "But God, I'm loving this!"

Nikolay finally snapped, and I winced.

He prowled toward the dancing couple and grabbed the guy by his collar, practically pulling him off his feet. He pushed him away, the man tumbling over.

Oh dear.

Nikolay grabbed Evaline's hips, pulling her

against him. He bent his head down and whispered something in her ear. His face looked harsh and angry.

He thrust his hips against her before twirling her around. It wasn't a slow, romantic dance. No, it was angry and sensual.

Even I blushed at the scene.

Evaline was laughing, clearly not affected by Nikolay's anger. She pulled away from him but not before I saw her palming him between his legs.

She winked and then sashayed away.

Nikolay stood there for a second before following after her.

"Is she going to be okay?" I asked, worried.

Maddie chuckled. "Babe, she is definitely going to be okay. She just won't be able to walk for days."

When realization finally dawned to me, my eyes widened, and I had to hide my smile behind my hand.

Could this day get any better? I didn't think so.

Chapter 40

As I seated myself on the plane, I looked at Alessio curiously. It was his private jet, although I wondered why we were taking it.

"Last time we went by car," I said.

He nodded. "I needed to make a few stops on the way. But tonight, we don't. The jet is faster. We'll be there in about three hours."

I nodded in understanding and settled against the plush couch. Alessio took the seat in front of me, surprisingly. He spread his legs, pushing them forward and caging mine between his.

We were both quiet as the jet took off. My gaze moved to the small window, staring outside. I could feel Alessio's stare burning into my skin.

After a few minutes of silence, I swallowed nervously and looked back at Alessio.

His eyes were intense and dark with needs. My skin felt warm, my heart accelerating under his gaze.

Anxious and waiting for a reaction, I played with the hem of my dress, but Alessio was completely in his element.

The air around him crackled with dominance as he sat back, a small smirk on his lips.

He watched me lick my lips and swallow against the ball of nervousness. His eyes tracked my every movement, like a predator hunting his prey.

I hated to admit that I grew wet, his stare alone making me excited. I squeezed my legs together trying to stop the tingling between them.

He smirked like he knew the affect he had on me.

"Lift your dress up," he finally demanded.

My mouth dropped open before snapping closed. I shook my head in denial.

"Alessio," I hissed, glancing toward the door that separated us from the cabin crew. "They will…"

He cocked his head to the side, waiting for me to finish. When I didn't, he lifted the phone up, the one beside him.

He punched in something and then brought the phone to his ear. With his gaze still on mine, Alessio spoke. His voice low and deep, husky even.

"I don't want anyone coming into the cabin until I call them specifically."

He listened to the other person talk and then smiled, dangerously I should say. "Oh, I will definitely be enjoying my flight."

My eyes widened as he hung up. He did not just say that!

"Now, will you lift your dress up and bare your pussy to me, Ayla?" he asked again, raising an eyebrow.

I gasped, my heart stammering.

"Or should I do it for you, kitten?" he continued.

Shaking my head, I held onto the hem of my lace dress. He waited, yet I still couldn't move.

"Kitten," he warned, leaning forward.

With shaky hands, I slowly hitched my dress up over my thighs and then my hips.

My breathing increased, my heart running wild.

"Does it make you wet, knowing what I am about to do with you?" he asked, his eyes still on my face.

I swallowed and made a soft noise at the back of my throat. It was somewhere between a moan and a whimper.

Finally, his gaze traveled down to my neck, my chest, and then between my legs. I still had my lace underwear hiding me from his view.

He tsked with a shake of his head. "Remove your panties, Ayla. I want to see your wet pussy," he murmured roughly.

I was unable to say no. His words were enough to drive me over the edge. Slowly, I pushed my panties down my legs.

Alessio placed his hand out, and I handed them to him. He stuffed them into his pocket, and I could only stare with wide eyes.

"Spread your legs, kitten."

I spread them without any complaints. "Look at you...you are weeping for me. I can see how wet you are from here."

"Alessio," I moaned, trying to squeeze my legs together.

He stopped me, pushing his legs between mine, forcing my thighs open.

"Look at yourself," he demanded.

My head snapped down, and I licked my lips, trying to calm my breathing.

"Beautiful," he said gruffly. "So fucking beautiful."

"I want you to place one foot over the armrest," he ordered.

I straightened, glancing toward the door. "I won't repeat myself, kitten. They won't come out. Not until I ask them to."

I nodded slowly, my cheeks heating. There was denying that I was bright red.

Alessio was dominant in bed but never like this.

Clenching my eyes closed, I felt myself dripping between my thighs. My chest tightened as I lifted my leg up and placed a foot on the armrest.

I was completely open to his lustful eyes.

"Open your eyes. Look at me, kitten."

My eyes snapped opened to see him staring at me. He crossed his arms, watching me.

I glanced down at his lap to see his hard length pressing against his zipper, looking ready to spill out. It appeared uncomfortable.

Alessio waited for my eyes to meet his again before he lowered his gaze between my legs. He groaned at the sight, the sound traveling straight to my wet core.

"I'm not going to touch you, kitten. You are going to fuck your pussy with your fingers while I watch."

My heart stuttered at his words, my mouth falling open in shock.

"Surprised, kitten?" he asked, raising an

413

eyebrow.

I was panting now, and I was sure my face was a mask of pure unadulterated lust. Alessio was driving me crazy with need.

"C'mon, kitten. Play with yourself. Pretend it's my fingers fucking you."

With a word, I pushed my hand between my thighs. Alessio's eyes flared, and I swallowed. Licking my lips, I pressed a finger against my center.

My back bowed, and I moaned, massaging my clit. Alessio adjusted himself between his legs, his gaze unwavering.

A jolt of electrifying pleasure coursed through me as I pushed a finger in. My chest heaved with each breath as the pressure inside of me intensified.

I pressed my thumb over the nub, circling as I pushed another finger inside of me.

"Fuck...just like that," Alessio groaned, his hands fisting at his sides.

My wet walls pulsed, clenching around my fingers as I pulled out and pushed back in. My hips thrust forward with the movement. I circled my clit harder, quicker, striving to drive me over the edge.

My lips trembled, my eyes closing. I could hear how wet I was. Each time as I pushed my fingers in, my pussy clenched around them greedily.

I felt embarrassed, shy even...but I was too far gone to care.

I needed the relief but couldn't find it.

"Open your eyes, Ayla!" Alessio growled.

They snapped open at his order. His head tilted to the side while his eyes burned holes into my skin.

414

Butterflies erupted in my stomach, and I throbbed between my legs.

Again and again, I thrust my fingers in and out, harder and faster, trying to relieve the ache building inside of me.

"You can't come, kitten?" he asked knowingly.

Alessio smirked, looking pleased with himself. Confused, I shook my head.

When I saw him move, I moaned, desperate for him to come closer.

He rewarded me with just that.

Alessio knelt down between my spread thighs, his head moving closer to my dripping core. Before I could say anything, his warm mouth covered my clit.

His tongue darted out, and he flicked the tip of it over my nub.

A muffled scream echoed from my throat. My body shook and pulsed. I screamed again as my orgasm hit me.

I removed my fingers as Alessio swirled my clit with his tongue, licking my juices.

Closing my eyes, I sagged against the couch. My legs were still shaking.

When Alessio pulled away, I opened my eyes to see him wiping his mouth with the back of his hand. He pulled my wet fingers into his mouth and sucked my cream away. He grunted low in his chest.

"You can't come without me, kitten," he said, smirking. "Your greedy cunt needs my touch."

In a daze, I could only stare at him. He sat back in his seat, not looking the least bit affected with what just happened.

"Come here, Ayla."

He placed his hand out, waiting for me to take it. Silently, I took his hand, and he pulled me roughly onto his lap until I was straddling him.

I gasped when my still-sensitive core pressed down onto his hard length. His slacks moved roughly against my bare skin, and I moaned at the new sensation.

I was hypersensitive to his every touch.

He thrust his hips upward, and my eyes widened, my mouth opening in a silent cry.

"Alessio," I whimpered, holding onto his shoulder. My fingers bit into his skin as I tried to grasp my surroundings.

He rocked his hips against mine, his hands palming my bare ass cheeks. Alessio dragged me back and forth over his still-covered cock.

The action was so dirty, yet it turned me on more. I grew wetter, my moans coming louder.

"Ride me as if you have my cock inside of you right now," he ordered.

"Oh…" I whimpered, pulling myself up and then pushing down, circling my hips over his lap.

He groaned, his hold growing tighter around me. "Alessio…I can't…"

"Yes, you can…you will come for me again," he growled roughly in my ear before biting down on my neck.

I felt overheated. I was tingling all over, close to falling over the edge again. When Alessio pressed a hand between us, his hand cupping my sex, my head snapped back, my back arching with pleasure.

His palm pressed against my clit at the same

416

time as he thrust his cock between my thighs, sending thousands of electrifying jolts into me.

I screamed again, pressing my mouth into his shoulders. My screams were muffled, but it was obvious that I had just come again.

Everyone must have heard it.

My eyes closed, my body going limp over Alessio's. I felt him placing a sweet kiss on my neck, and I hummed softly.

We stayed like this for a long time. I couldn't bring myself to move, and Alessio was in no hurry to move either.

When I could finally grasp my surroundings, I opened my eyes and pulled back. Alessio stared at me intimately, his gaze just as dark and lustful as before.

"I..." I started but then stopped.

I had nothing to say. Couldn't find any words.

"I know, kitten," he said gently, kissing my lips.

"They heard me," I murmured, feeling my whole body go red in embarrassment.

"Of course they did. And I know for a fact that it turned you on more knowing that they could hear you and knew exactly what we were doing," he replied, biting down on my lips.

I gasped, pulling away. "No." I shook my head, feeling completely horrified at the thought.

Alessio laughed shamelessly. "Kitten, I know your body more than you do. You can't deny that it excited it more."

Hiding my face in his neck, I refused to answer. Only because I didn't know the answer myself.

Alessio chuckled low in his chest. That

infuriating man. I couldn't believe he made me come like that.

"I got you," he whispered, holding me to him. Alessio dragged my dress down again and moved me around so I was sitting on his lap, my side to his chest.

I could still feel his hardness against me. When I wiggled onto his lap, he hissed, his finger tightening on my hips.

"What about you?" I whispered, peeking up at him shyly.

"Later. What I have planned for you...we'll need more privacy."

My eyes widened and sucked in a harsh, surprised breath.

Oh dear Lord. What did I get myself into?

But even then, excitement coursed through me at the thought.

I smiled and kissed his lips. "Hmm...okay."

Closing my eyes, I rested my head on his shoulders. Fatigue took over, and even when I tried to stop it, sleep cocooned me.

***

Alessio woke up when the plane started to land. I blinked my eyes open several times. He stared down at me, his gaze loving.

"How long was I asleep?" I asked sleepily.

"About two hours," he replied, placing me on the seat beside him. He fastened my belt for me and then his own.

Alessio held my hand as the plane landed.

Minutes later, we were being ushered out and then going through all the other processes before finally getting in a car.

"The beach house," Alessio barked, pulling me onto his lap.

Without a word, the driver was pulling out of the parking lot. We were silent during the drive, both of us lost in our thoughts.

I knew being back here was hard for Alessio. My stomach was already cramping painfully, and I felt nausea.

We were both feeling the pain...the past still haunting us.

When the car finally stopped, Alessio stepped out with me still cradled to his chest. The door was open, and he walked us inside, carrying me over the threshold yet again.

I kissed his cheek, letting my lips linger there. "I love you, Alessio."

His hold grew tighter. I didn't realize how much those words meant to him.

Alessio turned his head to the side, his lips mere inches away from mine. He growled before kissing me. Hard and demanding. He took my lips, devouring me with hunger. I kissed him back with the same fervor.

For a moment, I knew he was taking his frustration out in the kiss, and I took the punishing kiss gladly.

Alessio let me down, and I wrapped my hands around his neck. He pushed me against the wall, gripping my hair tight as he continued kissing me.

I moaned against his lips, my hand now trying to

get his jacket off. He shrugged it off quickly, never once breaking the kiss.

When I tried to unbutton his shirt, he nipped at my lips. His grip on my hair tightened, and he gave a gentle tug back, showing me exactly who was in control.

I threw my head back as he trailed kisses down my jaw and then my neck, nipping and sucking at the skin, leaving his mark.

He growled a guttural groan that had my legs trembling in desire. He forced one of his legs in between mine, parting my thighs.

My eyes clenched shut as he pulled me forward harshly, my body throbbing with need. My bare pussy dragged over his thigh until I was practically straddling his leg.

His crotch skimmed across my stomach, and I felt his hard bulge pressing into me. His other leg forced itself between my thigh, spreading me open until I was only balancing with his hold.

A light moan escaped past my lips as I held on to him for dear life.

His hand glided up my thigh, leaving a burning sensation on my skin. I tingled everywhere, my mind cloudy with need.

"You like this, don't you? Being completely helpless to my touch?" His voice was deep and rough, filled with so much lust.

I moaned in response, my words failing me. His hand skimmed past my thigh and reached between my legs.

But he didn't touch me. Alessio teased me instead, his hand so near but never touching me where I needed him the most.

He left me hanging, precariously close to the edge but not letting me fall.

"I'm going to own every single inch of this delicate body, kitten," he whispered against my neck.

He bent down slightly, his mouth over my breasts. Alessio didn't even care that I still had my dress on. His mouth latched around an erect nipple through my dress, and he sucked hard.

My screams could be heard around the room. He hummed, his fingers playing with my other nipple.

"Sensitive?" he asked, although he already knew the answer.

"Yes," I murmured as he continued to masterfully play me.

"Even better," he groaned, continuing to suck my nipple through my dress. I didn't think something like this could be so sensual, so arousing.

When his hot mouth left my breast, my eyes snapped open. But it was too late. A ripping sound echoed through the room, and I looked down at my body.

Alessio had ripped my dress, leaving the top of my body bare. The mount of my breasts were currently held back only by transparent white lace.

I saw him licking his lips, his eyes heating with passion. Without breaking eye contact with me, he pulled the cups down, freeing them.

He bent down, taking a nipple in his mouth, biting softly on it before sucking. He played me like that, licking, sucking, and biting until I was dripping and begging him.

"What do you want?" he asked against my skin.

"Please…Alessio…"

"Hmmm…what?"

"Fuck me! Please!"

I rocked against his thighs, looking for relief, but he chuckled before pulling away.

"What a filthy mouth, kitten." He tsked, looking at me. "What am I going to do with it?"

"Alessio…I need you."

"No, kitten. It's my turn," he said, smirking down at me.

Alessio stepped back and removed his shirt, practically ripping it off him in his haste.

"Remove your dress," he ordered.

Doing as I was commanded, I removed my dress and threw it on the ground. He nodded at my bra that was hanging off my body. I removed that too until I was completely naked to his hungry eyes.

"You look so fucking beautiful, Ayla. Mesmerizing," he murmured, unbuckling his belt.

He unbuttoned his slacks and then pulled the zipper down. He was naked underneath, his hard cock pushing free through the slit.

I clenched my legs together, and he smiled at the sight.

"Come here, kitten."

Walking toward him as if I was under a spell, I moved against him. His thumb pressed against my lips, sliding back and forth sensually.

He tsked again. "Not an Angel anymore, are you? You know what I'm going to do with you?"

I shook my head, my heart drumming wildly. "I'm going to make you come until you beg me to stop. I'll rub my cock all over your wet slit until you are fucking begging me to fuck you. And then I'm going to fuck you so hard that you won't be able to do anything but submit to me."

His voice dropped to a low murmur. "I'm going to corrupt you, Angel."

His dirty words made my head spin. I should have been running away, those words a clear warning. But I couldn't.

Instead I moved closer, wanting him to touch me.

This was my Alessio. Even though his words should have been frightening, I knew he wouldn't hurt me. No, he would bring me pleasure until I wouldn't be able to take it any longer.

His hand wrapped around my waist, and he anchored me to him. I felt his hot breath next to my ear as he whispered his next words.

"Get on your knees, kitten."

My breath left me in shock, my eyes widening. Oh.

He pulled away, his fingers gripping my neck in a possessive hold. "I want those pretty green eyes looking up at me as I fuck your mouth."

I closed my eyes, but when his hold grew tighter, they snapped open.

His thumb moved over my lips. "And I want to see your lips swollen from sucking my cock."

My body vibrated with need, tingling all over. His hand pushed down on my shoulder, and my knees gave up. I knelt in front of him.

My mouth was in front of his cock as he pulled his slacks slightly down. He palmed his hard length as he coated the tip with his pre-cum.

"Open," he demanded gruffly.

My lips parted as he grabbed his other hand around my hair, tugging me closer. Slowly opening my lips, I allowed him to slip inside my mouth.

My lips closed around him, taking in as much as I could take. His head snapped back, the veins bulging in his arms and neck.

He groaned when his tip hit the back of my throat. For a small moment, I fought against the invasion as he slightly pulled back and then pushed back in.

I peered up at him, his face a mask of undeniable pleasure. My muscles started to relax as I let him take control, fucking my mouth like he wanted.

He thrust into my mouth over and over again, his breathing shallow as he stared down at me. I opened my mouth wide, sucking him when needed. I licked the tip, my tongue swirling, following the thick veins coursing the length of him.

I heard him hiss, his hips bucking forward. He thrust hard into my mouth, holding himself there for a second before pulling out and repeating the process again.

"Ahh...fuck, Ayla!" he groaned as my teeth slightly grazed him. "Just like that...fuck yes!"

His thighs bunched, his muscles cording, and I knew he was close. I doubled my effort as he continued to thrust.

But before Alessio could come, he pulled away. His breathing was ragged as he pulled me up, slamming me against the wall.

With an expert movement, he had one of my legs

wrapped around his hips, his cock resting against my wet slit.

My lips parted with a moan as he pressed slightly inside, just the tip of him in me.

My eyes widened when he came, coating my inside walls, his come running down my thighs.

I gasped for breath as he groaned, his hips bucking against mine. Alessio rested his head on my shoulder, his chest heaving with each breath.

When I felt his hand between us, I gripped his hair harder. I didn't think I could take anymore.

His fingers brushed against my thigh, pushing his cum back into me. I clenched around his fingers, my head thrashing to the side.

He removed his hand and brought it up, pushing two of his fingers past my parted lips.

"Suck it. Suck it like you sucked my cock."

My heart stammered at the order, and I closed my lips around his fingers, sucking tentatively.

I swirled my tongue over his fingers, sucking, cleaning him from our cum. He dragged his wet fingers down my neck before taking my lips into a deep kiss.

Alessio pulled my other leg around his hips and walked us into the bedroom. We fell on the bed together, with him on top of me.

My legs spread open to accommodate him. He leaned over me, taking my lips in a long, demanding kiss.

When I felt him pressing against me, I sucked in a hard breath. My whimpers filled the room as he ran his length up and down, coating himself with our cum.

I clenched and then he thrust inside slowly, filling me completely. My back arched off the bed, my hands going to his shoulders for support.

Alessio pressed me into the mattress, pulling out fully before thrusting back inside. He pushed my legs up, bending my knees so that I was fully open to him.

He slid in deeper, his pace going faster and harder with each thrust inside me.

I stretched painfully around him yet loved it so much.

"You feel so good," he said as he slammed inside. My walls clenched around him as he pulled out again.

I throbbed between my legs, pulsing with need. With each stroke, his pelvis brushed against my clit, and I had to bite on my lips, trying to stop my screams.

"Alessio…"

My breathing was shallow. He started to pump inside of me harder, each time his cock reaching so deep, stealing my breath away.

My hands slid to his back, my nails digging into his skin. I clawed at his back, my hips rising up to meet each of his thrusts with my own.

He groaned, slamming into me harder.

"Tell me what you need," he whispered roughly, kissing me senseless.

"Make love to me," I whispered back, my back lifting off the bed as he pounded inside of me again.

"I am," he said, his eyes shining with both love and desire.

Alessio pulled back slightly, only to bring my

legs over his shoulders, spreading me open to his hard, relentless thrusts.

It felt like I was going to break apart, and I gladly welcomed it.

My body tightened, and I was deliciously close. Alessio's muscles corded, his body tightening too.

He reached down and slid his finger over my nub, pressing down as he rammed inside of me at the same time.

My lips parted as a scream escaped past my lips. My body went tight and tingled as my orgasm hit me with a never-ending wave.

I floated, my eyes closing as Alessio continued to pump his cock in my clenching pussy.

He came with a roar, filling me to the brim. I was impossibly full as I came yet again.

Spent, he laid his forehead against mine. I breathed through my nose, trying to catch my breath. We were both left breathless, and I couldn't complain one bit.

Our love-making was explosive, something I needed and craved from Alessio. I knew he felt the same way.

I stared into his blue eyes as he remained sheathed inside of me. After a few seconds of silence, he pulled out, our mixed essence dripping out of me.

Alessio stared at me, his gaze lowering between my legs. "You look so fucking sexy right now. Your legs spread open with my cum dripping out. You look beautifully used, kitten."

I blinked, a slow smile appearing on my face. Alessio leaned down and kissed me softly, gently and oh so sweetly.

"I love you, Angel."

"I love you, Alessio."

Our words were soft and whispered just to each other. A beautiful moment, something I would remember till the end of my days.

"I'll let you sleep for now. But later..." His voice held a promise as my eyes closed sleepily.

I hummed as he turned us to our sides. With my back to his, he curled around me, holding me protectively and possessively in his embrace.

Epilogue

The next time I woke up, I was alone. The sunlight made its way into the bedroom, and I could hear the waves crashing from a distance.

Rolling around in bed, I looked for Alessio, but he was nowhere to be found. I shifted around, my muscles sore and refusing to move. I ached everywhere, but it was a good ache.

When I stood up, Alessio's voice could be heard from downstairs. There was some clanging of dishes, and I smiled when realization dawned on me that my husband was in the kitchen.

Quickly getting in the shower, I washed myself and took a bath. After freshening up, I stepped out and stared at myself in the mirror.

My body was covered with Alessio's marks. Whether it was from his kisses or his tight hold, I loved it. Loved the ownership he had of me. He made me feel that I belonged…and it was exactly that.

I was his.

And he was mine.

I wrapped a towel around myself and walked out

of the room. My legs took me to the window, and I watched the ocean, the waves crashing together.

Such a beautiful, peaceful sight.

My throat clogged up, and tears blinded my vision.

I was happy. I was finally happy.

I felt him before I even saw him. His presence caused a tingling over my body. His arms went around my waist, and he pulled me into his body.

Resting my head against Alessio's shoulder, I stared out.

"Thank you for bringing me here," I said quietly. "You erased all the bad memories, Alessio. Not once did I get a chance to think about what had happened. You made me feel alive last night. You made me feel loved, adored, and cherished," I continued, my hands going over his.

Alessio placed a soft kiss behind my ear. "You saved me, Alessio. You made me whole again."

"I'm the one who should be saying that, Angel."

"Thank you for loving me," I continued.

"Never thank me for loving you, Ayla," he replied.

Our hearts had chosen each other as their mates. There was no stopping it, and I was glad that Alessio and I hadn't fought it.

I was still not healed. Not completely.

Sometimes nightmares still plagued my sleep. A few times, I still got panic attacks.

My past wasn't something easily forgotten. It was etched deep inside of me. It was rooted to my core, no matter how much I tried to get rid of it.

But I was moving forward. I had learned how to

push it away and focus on the good. On the happiness and love around me.

I would never be completely normal. Alberto had changed me...he had ruined that for me. He left his scars on my mind and body.

But with Alessio...I was whole. I could live and love.

And in return, Alessio had handed me his heart.

We were one.

I could finally be happy, and because of that, I would live the rest of my days loving with all my heart.

Turning around in his arms, I faced him.

We stared at each other.

Blue to green.

Alessio smiled down at me, my own smile widening.

"You are my Angel," he whispered.

Yes, that I was.

I was his Angel just like he was my savior.

The start of it all...

The Mafia and His Angel.

THE END

Or is it?

You can turn the next page for an excerpt of the next book in the *Tainted Hearts Series*.

Sneak Peek

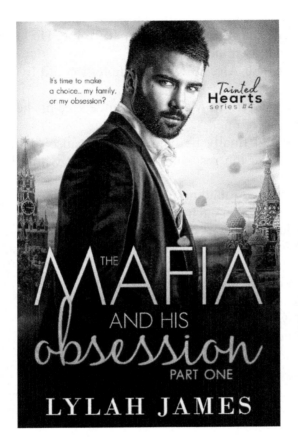

The Mafia and His Obsession: Part 1
(Tainted Hearts, #4)

Chapter One

HIM

Some say we were cruel. Disgusting human beings. Heartless. Ruthless.

I would agree.

But I liked the word barbaric better. Unsympathetic. Sadistic. Vicious.

After all, we were killers.

We were born into this life. Since the very beginning, we breathed it.

From first breath...till our last.

His whimpers snapped me out of my thoughts. Was that piss I smelled?

Most probably. They always turned into disgusting carcasses when their death flashed in front of their eyes. Too bad for them it was always too late.

He opened his mouth to speak, but I never gave him a chance. My fingers tightened around the knife before I drove it down, right in the middle of his throat.

The man gurgled his last breath as his blood poured around him…and on me. Shaking my head in disgust, I spat on him.

"Foolish. They know the consequences, but they still try and play us," I sneered at him.

His chest expanded as he took his last breath…and then silence. Nobody spoke a word as we stared at the dead man, his eyes still open. Still staring into mine.

The only difference was that his were empty, while mine were still very much alive, glowing with power.

I heard Phoenix talking over the phone while I stood up. My handkerchief was already out of my pocket, and I cleaned my hands, trying to remove the blood. My face was next. It felt sticky where the blood had splattered.

Disgusting filth. I need a fucking shower now.

Why didn't Alessio do it himself?

Oh, wait…because he didn't want to get his hands dirty this time. His Angel was waiting for him at home.

Like that made him the lesser evil.

He was just as fucked up.

We were all fucked.

But we had her to bring us some light. A little bit of happiness. Some smiles…some occasional laughter. Some scraps of love.

She gave it all to us without expecting anything in return. She loved so much and so hard that sometimes our hearts were not big enough to take it all.

Someone swore behind me. My eyebrows

furrowed in confusion as I was brought back to the present.

Annoyingly, I had been lost in my thoughts too much lately. Very bad.

I'm going to get killed if I don't get my shit together.

"Boss," I heard Phoenix warn.

What the fuck is he warning Alessio about? I turned around, facing the others.

Only to come face to face with Alessio pointing his gun at me.

"Seriously? We don't have time for this," I said, my eyes on the gun. He cocked his head to the side, his eyebrows lifted in amusement.

"Can we do this later? After we have disposed of the body? C'mon, man."

I rolled my eyes, knowing Alessio wasn't going to do something stupid. He wouldn't. Not after everything.

Turning my back to him again, I put my life...everything in his hands. I gave him my full trust.

That was my first mistake.

I heard the gunshot first. It rang so loud in the silent alley. My heart thumped in response.

Then I felt it. The indescribable pain and burn that came after the bullet pierced my body.

He shot me.

He actually shot me.

In the ass.

What the everloving fuck?

He did not just fucking shoot me.

I swiveled around to face him, ignoring the pain.

Trying so hard to ignore the fact that I had just been shot in the ass. I had a hole in my ass cheek!

This wasn't some *Deadpool* bullshit. And I sure as hell wasn't some super mutant who could pop bullets out of their asses.

Yeah…he's a dead man.

"Ayla's going to be pissed when we get back home and she finds both of us shot," I drawled, reaching behind me.

I never got a chance to get my gun. He was now aiming at my chest, right over my heart.

I froze. My muscles locked as I stared at Alessio in surprise. He wouldn't…

Raising my hands in surrender, I took a step back. "Alessio, we can talk about this."

At least not my heart. He could shoot anywhere but the heart. Or my dick.

"No. We can't," he simply replied. His eyes appeared darker than usual, anger glistening in them. Alessio was a madman when he turned angry.

He would blur the lines between right or wrong. Nothing mattered to him except his revenge. He would do anything and…everything.

In that moment, I was on the other side. Not beside him. But against him. For the first time since I had known him.

Instead of our guns pointing at some other bastards, his gun was pointed at me. And only one reason made sense.

"Did you think I wouldn't find out?" he hissed. I saw his fingers tightening around the gun. His index fingers laid on the trigger, waiting for the right moment, dragging out the suspense.

He loved the chase, the adrenaline in making others shake and whimper in fear. Except I wasn't shaking or whimpering.

That probably pissed him off more.

"I was going to tell you," I answered.

Lies. I wasn't.

Because there was nothing to tell. Nothing was what it seemed to be. Every action, every word had a meaning behind it.

Nothing in our world was the perfect image. Everything was in pieces and we had to put all of them together to find the truth. A piece in the puzzle to get the whole vision.

Everything was a lie.

Everyone was a lie.

Every fucking day was a game to play. A game we had mastered.

Believe nothing. Whatever you see or hear is a lie.

That was one of the lessons learned and a lesson to remember.

"Let me explain," I tried to convince him. Anything but another bullet in my body.

"You know damn well that I never give anyone a chance to explain," he snapped. Thrusting his gun toward my chest, his lips curled in disgust. "And you aren't any different."

"Boss," I heard someone say. There was a warning in his tone. Maybe he was trying to save me? We were a brotherhood, after all.

Alessio smirked, just the corner of his lips turning up, and I just knew. My death had just been signed, and I had no choice over it.

The veins in my neck throbbed. Blood rushed to my ears until the only thing I could hear was the pounding of my heart.

Their voices sounded like they were underwater as my dreadful life flashed in front of my eyes. This was it.

The end.

BANG!

I closed my eyes as the gun went off, sounding so loud, so evil to my ears. The connection of the metal and my skin was quick. So quick that I could have missed it.

But when the pain came later...there was no escaping it.

Sweat dripped down my forehead as my blood dripped down my body. The cold bullet penetrated my chest, and I prayed it didn't hit my heart.

A laughable thought that was.

Alessio had perfect aim. If he wanted me dead, shot in the heart, there was no escaping death.

He was death.

My eyes fluttered open as I regarded my boss for one final time. His hand dropped to his side, still holding the gun.

The anger in his eyes was gone, replaced with hurt and pain. His expression changed to one of regret. "I didn't want to do this, but you gave me no choice. You fucked up. And you fucked up bad."

I know that!

I wanted to scream, but my lips felt numb. My throat grew tighter as the pain spread across my body. It felt like I was burning from the inside as the ground turned darker with the red shade of blood.

Through blurry vision, I saw Alessio pointing the gun at me again. I closed my eyes, waiting for him to end this. Waiting for this indescribable pain to finally end.

The fired round seemed to float through fragile air, my ears barely registering the gunshot. It pierced my chest without consideration, without real meaning or relevance.

A sacrifice made from my part. A sacrifice I was willing to make. For my family. For her.

The small wounds leaked blood similar to how crying eyes leaked tears.

I sank to my knees, my body too weak to hold myself strong any longer. I gasped for breath, pleading for air.

Maybe I heard him whisper sorry. Maybe it was my mind playing tricks on me, but there was no mistaking the anguish in his voice.

I wanted to open my eyes, to give them a final look. A final goodbye. But my weakness won over.

"The only reason why I can regret this is because Ayla will be hurt. She is going to cry, and I won't be able to do anything," Alessio said. His voice sounded nearer but still so far away.

I was drifting. Falling deeper and deeper into the dark abyss.

Suddenly everything went completely silent. All movement around me slowed down to an excruciating pace. I could feel my pulse pounding through me as visions flashed behind my closed eyes.

The images swirled before me right until the end,

leaving that last scene of her imprinted upon my mind without the oxygen to sustain it.

Her smile. Her laughter. The look of love as she gazed up at him. Never me. Always him.

I bled out, losing consciousness faster…falling faster…until I hit hard ground.

I was jostled, and pain racked through me. It felt like my unbeating heart just started again, pumping blood through my body.

I died. I knew I died…then the voices…

What's happening?

I opened my mouth to speak, but no words found their way out. The burning sensation in my chest never ended. It hurt more and more every second.

"He's flat lining!"

The noises grew louder over the pounding of my heart.

"Don't let him die!"

New voices. They didn't belong to Alessio or any of our men.

"Fuck! I need him alive, damn it!"

No. I was dead.

"He needs to live," the voice hissed.

"You need to live. Do you hear me, son?" It sounded nearer now.

Is he talking to me?

My body was moved, pushed, pulled, and I bore down on the agony.

What the fuck is happening?

Leave me alone, I wanted to scream. I was with her…at least in my death moment, she loved me.

But now some stupid bastards were taking me away. I could see her fading…turning away from me.

I reached for her, but it was too late. She was gone, fading into the darkness. She left me alone again.

"This is what happens when you choose the wrong side."

Huh?

"Fucking Ivanshov. They will pay for this. All of them."

No.

"I told you to join us, but you didn't listen. Now bear the pain of being betrayed by your *brother*. Over whom? Some fucked up Italian *blyad*."

Don't fucking call her a whore.

Anger swirled inside of me, before realization finally dawned.

They were speaking Russian.

Ah, fuck my life.

"Don't worry. You will get your revenge. They all betrayed you. You will live and get your revenge."

His words penetrated through my mind, and I held them close, wrapping myself around the words.

They all betrayed you.

Other words were mumbled, but I ignored them.

You will live and get your revenge.

I smiled internally. *Oh, yes I will.*

I was going to live…fuck death. It was not my time yet.

"Get him to the estate. When he wakes up, we will put our plans into action. The time has come for my heir to join me."

The smile turned into a smirk. It was time.

441

Blood would be spilled, and only the strong would live. There could only be one conqueror. Everyone else was going to be ten feet under the cold, hard ground.

Deceit. Betrayal. Lies. Traitors. Hate. Revenge. Fraud.

We lived with them every day. We breathed them. We played them. And we welcomed them.

The game has begun.

Don't Forget to check out…

BLOOD AND ROSES

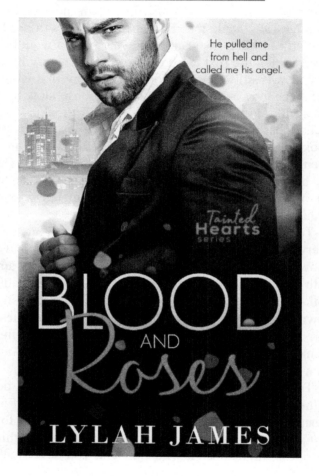

He pulled me from hell and called me his angel.

Tainted Hearts series

BLOOD AND Roses

LYLAH JAMES

A Short Novella in the
Tainted Hearts Series: Part 3.5

Acknowledgements

I remember in the last book, I thanked my parents first. They are the reason why I am here today, writing. They made me realize that I loved writing. If it wasn't for their constant push, years ago, I wouldn't have written the first word of a rough short story back when I was still in high school. I wrote my first word, and since then, writing has become my obsession. So I would like to thank my parents *again* for making me realize that writing is my passion. Since the release of book 1, they have stayed with me, supported me, opened my eyes to many things, and they have taught me better. I am so thankful for everything they stand for and for making me the person I am today. So, thank you Ma and Pa.

To Vivvi. My girl. My boobitoo. You are everything. I can't go a day without texting you, and I know you're pretty much as obsessed with me as I am with you. (; Thank you for being there for me. Thank you for always pushing me up when I am falling down. Thank you for loving my characters, my babies, just as much as I do, if not more. Actually, saying thank you is not enough. You are my soul sister. And I am so glad I found you.

To Jessica and Chelsea, my girls. What would I do without you? Seriously, I would be drowning if it wasn't for you two keeping me afloat. Thank you for being there and supporting me through all this craziness. It has been a wild ride, and you have stuck with me till now – thank you will never be enough.

The biggest thank you goes to my Publisher. Thank you for giving TMAHA a chance. I am holding my book right now, because you think it is worth it. So, thank you.

To my editor, Toni—you rock! I am so glad we worked together on this book. You truly did wonders. Thank you.

Thank you to everyone else who had a hand in making this book—my proofreader, formatter...you guys are stars.

To Deranged Doctor Design—Thank you for such a kickass cover. I couldn't stop staring at it! I had to hold my screech in when I first saw it because I was at work.

To the bloggers and everyone who took their time to promote TMAHA, you are awesome! My big thanks to you.

And I wanted to leave this for the end, because this is the important part. A huge thank you to every single one of my readers. My lovelies. If my parents are the reason why I started writing, then *you* are the reason why I am still here. In this moment, holding this book. Your never-ending support and love has taken us on this path. From the first word to the last, you have been here with me. I am proud we took this journey together. Together, we dreamed about holding TMAHA one day, thumbing through the pages. *We* did it, lovelies. Thank you for standing with me, even through my craziness. To all the fan accounts and groups out there, thank you! All the beautiful edits and posters you have made, they are my inspiration and motivation. I am going to say it loud and clear. "You freaking rock!"

About the Author

Lylah James uses all her spare time to write. If she is not catching up on sleep, working or writing—she can be found with her nose buried in a good romance book, preferably with a hot alpha male.

Writing is her passion. The voices in her head won't stop, and she believes they deserve to be heard and read. Lylah James writes about drool worthy and total alpha males, with strong and sweet heroines. She makes her readers cry—sob their eyes out, swoon, curse, rage, and fall in love. Mostly known as the Queen of cliffhanger and the #evilauthorwithablacksoul, she likes to break her readers' hearts and then mend them again.

FOLLOW LYLAH AT:

Facebook page:
https://www.facebook.com/AuthorLy.James/

Twitter page:
https://twitter.com/AuthorLy_James

Instagram page:
https://www.instagram.com/authorlylahjames/

Goodreads:
https://www.goodreads.com/author/show/16045951
.Lylah_James

Or you can drop me an email at:
AuthorLylah.James@Hotmail.com

Or check out my website:
http://authorlylahjames.com/

You can also join my newsletter list for updates,
teasers, major giveaways and so much more!
http://eepurl.com/c2EJ4z

Printed in Great Britain
by Amazon

84508863R00263